Edwin A. Abbott

The Anglican Career of Cardinal Newman

Vol. I

Edwin A. Abbott

The Anglican Career of Cardinal Newman
Vol. I

ISBN/EAN: 9783743336544

Manufactured in Europe, USA, Canada, Australia, Japa

Cover: Foto ©Raphael Reischuk / pixelio.de

Manufactured and distributed by brebook publishing software
(www.brebook.com)

Edwin A. Abbott

The Anglican Career of Cardinal Newman

THE ANGLICAN CAREER

OF

CARDINAL NEWMAN

THE ANGLICAN CAREER

OF

CARDINAL NEWMAN

BY

EDWIN A. ABBOTT

"'This goodly frame, the earth, seems to me a sterile promontory. . . . What a piece of work is a man! How noble in reason! how infinite in faculty, in form and moving how express and admirable! . . . the beauty of the world! the paragon of animals! And yet, to me, what is this quintessence of dust? man delights not me; no, nor woman neither. . . .'"

Hamlet.

"I look out of myself into the world of men, and there I see a sight which fills me with unspeakable distress. . . . The sight of the world is nothing else than the prophet's scroll, full of 'lamentations and mourning and woe.'"

NEWMAN'S *Apologia.*

VOL. I

London

MACMILLAN AND CO.

AND NEW YORK

1892

The Right of Translation and Reproduction is Reserved

RICHARD CLAY AND SONS, LIMITED,
LONDON AND BUNGAY.

PREFACE

I⊤ is not surprising if the Anglican career of John Henry Newman interests those who are outside the pale of the Church of Rome almost more than those who are within it. To the latter the truth of their own system cannot seem affected by the question whether Newman was converted to it in the right way; but the former may naturally ask, " If Newman was right, are not we wrong?"

There is a plain challenge silently conveyed by his Anglican works, and especially by his sermons. " Read us," they seem to say; "we represent, as it were, the weekly stages of slow but continuous development by which our author persuaded himself that he ought to leave the Anglican for the Roman Church*. All admit that he was an anxious seeker after truth. Many declare that his intellect was of the highest order. Some add that he had carefully and dispassionately studied the basis, nature, and growth of the Christian religion. If he had these three qualifications, and was led by them to become a Romanist, why ought not you to be led in the same direction?"

There are other reasons why Anglicans should take a special interest in Newman's Anglican career. The

Via Media and Tract 90 were experiments in Church Reform, described by their author himself as attempts to "infuse" into the formularies of the English Church meanings and truths that in his day seemed novel, and to ascertain how much in this way the Church would "bear." This experiment he called the "proving" of a "cannon." Elsewhere he speaks of it as resulting in a defeat, and of himself as "hoist with his own petard." But in truth it was not so utter a failure. Part of his work lives after him, not for one, but for all parties in the National Church. His "petard" (to take the latter of his two metaphors) made a breach ; and though he himself fell, or surrendered, in the heat of the conflict, others entered—and not his followers only—where he had opened a way. A school of thought in the English Church, widely differing from his, must admit a debt to the author of Tract 90 for an elastic interpretation of the Articles which has led to a lightening of their heavy yoke, and to a greater freedom enjoyed by all the clergy of every shade of opinion.

Where some have already entered, others may hereafter enter. We have not seen the last of these "experiments." Sixty years ago, Bishop Thirlwall pronounced the Tractarian controversy an old one, in new shape, and likely to recur in other shapes. It cannot therefore be useless—and assuredly it is intensely interesting—to deduce from the failure of the Tractarian leader, and the very considerable successes of those who followed him more than half way, auguries for similar attempts in time to come.

All these problems are so important, and the beginning of the Tractarian Movement puts them before us

in so definite a shape, that the author of this study
cannot feel it necessary to apologize for being interested himself, and for seeking to interest others, in
Newman's Anglican career, and in the following
attempt to trace his religious development step by step
up to the point where he joined the Church of Rome.

No one will maintain that this is done for us already
in the *Apologia*. Written though it is "in touching
good faith"—to quote Dean Church's happy criticism
—and very effectively indeed for its immediate purpose, it is nevertheless most bewildering as a record
of facts, following rather the lines of a drama than
of a history ; and of a drama, too, in which the plot
is not quite free from confusion.

Such sketches of the life of Newman as have already
appeared (to which the author's obligations will be
found duly expressed) fail, as a rule, to make a sufficient
use of the Anglican Sermons, which, when read (as the
author has read them) from first to last in *the order in
which they were written*, are almost as valuable as the
Letters for the light which they throw on the varying
phases of his religious thought. Further, the publication of his correspondence would, of itself, cause a
biographer to rewrite any biography written before
its publication.

The following work aims above all things at putting
Newman's most important actions and utterances in
chronological order, so as to help the reader to perceive
the sequence of cause and effect. The *Apologia* does
not do this. It uses—perhaps it sometimes abuses—
the dramatist's privilege of "jumping o'er times."
Post hoc, propter hoc is a fallacy : but to ascertain the

post is at least a necessary help to arriving at the *propter*. In doing this, some sacrifice has been made of brevity and of literary effect. But this seemed almost a matter of indifference in comparison with the attainment of something like a true narrative about one who is said to have drawn more Anglicans into the Roman Church than any other Romanist, and concerning whose future biography his brother has written, not without cause : " It must be expected that, the more *mythical* the narrative, the better it will sell."

The time has perhaps not yet come for writing a complete account of the whole of Cardinal Newman's life ; but when it is written, such a work as the present may be found to have saved a good deal of labour, and will almost certainly prevent some errors and exaggerations, for some future biographer who may add to other qualifications that of being in full intellectual sympathy with the subject of his task.

To such an intellectual sympathy the author of this work makes no pretension. On the contrary, he does not conceal his opinion that Newman's imagination dominated his reason, even more than his spiritual fears perverted his imagination ; that he was led to wrong conclusions by hasty judgment and insufficient study ; that the *Apologia* is by no means so accurate in its representation of facts as it is delightful in its literary style ; and that the Sermons, full though they are of varied and subtle beauties, and of a marvellous insight into the imperfections of human nature, and though they may well have exercised a magnetic power over those who have had actual experience of the living magnet, are nevertheless deficient in the Pauline spirit of hope and love, and inconsistent, as well as inadequate, in their exposition of the meanings and claims of faith and reason.   In a word, they are the utterances of one who, though he was anxious to love God, found it so hard to define what love meant, that (as we shall see hereafter) when he had used the word " love," he found himself obliged to correct himself, and to explain that " this means, not love precisely," but—something else that needs the Latin language to make it intelligible.

The rest of his writings lie, for the most part, outside the scope of this work.   On the *Essay on Ecclesiastical Miracles* the author has already commented with the severity which such a mixture of credulity and sophistry seemed to demand when viewed apart from the writer's life*.   But here such criticisms need not be repeated. Set in its biographical framework, both the *Essay on Ecclesiastical Miracles* and the *Essay on Doctrinal Development* are perceived to be the productions of a period " when doors are closed and curtains drawn, and when the sick man neither cares nor is able to record the stages of his malady."   And so they are treated here.

If psychological interest, and sympathy, and some sense of being fascinated, could be a substitute for indiscriminate admiration, the author might fairly hope to persuade even Newman's blindest admirers that he has been tolerably just ; but, by way of additional precaution, it has been thought best to let the course of events, as far as possible, reveal itself, not in the author's words, but in those of the principal actor and his associates. The *Apologia*, the Poems, the Sermons, the Letters ; the *Remains* of Hurrell Froude, the Reminiscences and Letters of E. T. Mozley and of James Mozley, the life of Ward, and Dean Church's *Oxford Movement*, have been so used as to put the reader in possession of Newman's thoughts from year to year, and, at critical points, almost from week to week. On the other side, contemporary critics, such as Connop Thirlwall, Hare, Whately, and Arnold have been occasionally introduced, repeating criticisms, some of which, though less popular, are no less true, than they were fifty years ago.

In the vast numbers of quotations, necessitated by the principle of the work, several errors were detected, while it was passing through the press, either by the author or by friends to whom he is greatly indebted for kind assistance and most valuable criticism. Some, he fears, remain; but he does not fear that they will reveal any such tendency as would seriously hinder the book from being useful to those who want to get at the facts.

CONTENTS OF THE FIRST VOLUME

CHAPTER I

THE MAN THAT WAS TO BE

CHAPTER II

EARLY MANHOOD

CHAPTER III

THE FORCES AT WORK

CHAPTER IV

AT THE PARTING OF THE WAYS

CHAPTER V

TRACES OF THE EVANGELICAL PATH

CHAPTER VI

TAKING NEW ALLIES

CHAPTER VII

RICHARD HURRELL FROUDE

CHAPTER VIII

THE NEW FORCE AT WORK

CHAPTER IX

PREPARING FOR THE CONFLICT

CHAPTER X

SEEKING A MIDDLE WAY

CHAPTER XI

SOUNDING AN ALARM

CHAPTER XII

"CRYING ALOUD AND SPARING NOT"

CHAPTER XIII

THE PAUSE

CHAPTER XIV

DECLARATION OF WAR

CHAPTER XV

THE DREAM OF THE CAMPAIGN

CHAPTER XVI

THE ADVANCE

CHAPTER XVII

WHO WAS TO LEAD? AND WHITHER?

CHAPTER XVIII

MARCHING AND COUNTERMARCHING

APPENDIX

CHAPTER I

§ 1. *Family life* [1]

NEWMAN'S autobiographical memoir describes him as "in no respect a precocious boy." Let the reader glance at the next paragraph and then decide for himself.

Born in the city of London (21 February, 1801), the eldest of six children, an omnivorous reader from his childhood, taught by his father from the age of five or six that he must learn something new every day or he would no longer be called clever, he felt, from a child—and was right in feeling—that he was not as other children, and not destined to be as other men. Other boys have got into Ovid and Greek at the age of nine; but very few at that age commit to paper dreams that a sister is dead, or poems on Nelson, or " Verses on the Death of a Beggar." Fewer still append to their productions criticisms expressing their dissatisfaction, and concluding, "I think I shall burn

---

[1] For references (and detailed dates), see the notes at the end of the volume. References are not given in the text; but an obelus † marks any doubtful quotation, *e.g.*, any variation between a letter as printed in the *Apologia*, and as printed in Newman's *Letters* or Hurrell Froude's *Remains*. Such variations are frequent. An asterisk calls attention to important notes.

it." On the whole, we hardly need the confirmation afforded by the composition of a "mock" drama at the age of eleven,* and a burlesque opera (music as well as words) at the age of fourteen, to convince us that Newman was not only precocious, but very precocious indeed.

In other and deeper respects he was not as other boys. He hated boyish sports and the noisy effervescence of boyhood, and, from a child, he lived on meditations. Pastured on books, and with no experience of nature beyond the shrubberies of his early home at Ham, or the enclosure of Bloomsbury Square, or the playground at Ealing, he dwelt in himself, and in a world of his own. This world was a world of dreams, in which everything was miraculous and paradoxical; angels as it were peeping round the corner, taking him by surprise, and laughing at him for supposing that visible substantial things had any reality in them. "I thought," he says, "life might be a dream, or I an angel, and all this world a deception, my fellow-angels, by a playful device, concealing themselves from me, and deceiving me with the semblance of a material world." There was a charm in this, a sense of superiority, to feel that he and these unseen beings were alone in a secret to which even his father and mother were not admitted.

London fostered the dreams of this, as of many another dreamer—not because the dreamers like their foster-mother, but because they hate her and flee from her into themselves. How many a child realises unconsciously that there is no such solitude as a large city! So it was with Newman. Bred among the lakes of Westmoreland he might have been a different being. He had a passionate love for the country, which appears again and again in his early and middle manhood, sometimes almost breaking down · his resolution to cling to his cloistered life in Oxford ; but as, in his later years, he fought against it, so in his childhood and youth, he does not seem to have learned from it. How different might things have been if Newman had had Wordsworth's rearing ! Basking or bathing with the Northern poet through a whole summer's day, or leaping through the little forests of yellow rag-wort within view of Skiddaw, Newman, at the age of five or six, might perhaps unconsciously have felt sinking into his heart something of that religious love with which Wordsworth approached Nature. But it was not so to be. There was nothing in the artificial delights of a London square or the shrubberies of Ham that could do the work of Skiddaw, and counteract the powerful dissolving influences exercised on a reserved, imaginative, and precocious boy by a too early introduction into the world of books, and especially religious books. The bustle of London or suburban existence, gossip about the Court, rumours about the doings of Napoleon, and the prospects of the British arms— these things did not carry away the boy ; they only confirmed him in the belief that the world was unreal. Not that he was unpractical, either ; far from it. This strong-willed dreamer mixed freely in the family life, talked, recited, played, composed music, discussed, argued, took pleasure in opposing ; but he was *in* these things, not *of* them. Family life, school life, social life, political life—all these were to him the mere surface of the stream of being ; or rather, not even the surface, but reflections from the surface, mere delusions and deceits beneath which there *was* something *to be* attained, not by means of them, but *in spite of them.*

At home he could laugh and jest as freely as any
in his work he never showed absence of mind or
melancholy.   An   impenetrable   reserve—seemingly
not broken till he came of age—concealed, even from
his parents, the fact that their son was living out
of their world in another sphere altogether, in which
he and the angels, or he and some invisible presence,
seemed the only luminously self-evident realities ; a
region in which parental guidance would be of little
direct use.   Yet his mother at least played some
part in her son's religious development.   From the
poems we learn that before his boyhood had passed
away, he had revolted from some of the doctrines
of Christianity.   He had read sceptical books ; and
he speaks of himself as "full of unlovely thoughts
and rebel aims and scorn of judgment flames."   From
this state of mind he describes himself (again in
the poems) as being " scared " back by " judgments."
Even after he had received the other truths of the
Gospel without difficulty,   he was startled by the
dogma of Eternal Punishment ; which he almost refused to credit till his mother showed him by textual
demonstration that the Lord Himself (so it seemed)
had not only enunciated it but, as it were, reserved it,
for His own lips :

> "The fount of Love His servants sends to tell
> Love's deeds ; Himself reserves the sinner's hell."

His father's part, if any, seems to have been quite
different.   Mr. Newman was a man of the world, and
manly, but of a coarser fibre than his son.   An admirer of Benjamin Franklin, and of plain, honest
common-sense, he had a passion for justice and a
burning hatred of oppression.   In almost all respects,

except in the love of music, he was at variance with John, who not only held his own against his father but even drew to his side his brother Francis. The latter thus describes the position of things :—

"My eldest brother, in my earliest youth, had more influence with me than my father, who was an admirer of Benjamin Franklin and Thomas Jefferson ; I had heard him say : 'I do not pretend to be a religious man,' also 'I am a man of the world'; nay once : 'I wonder that clever men do not see that it is *impossible* to get back to any certainty where they are so confident'—he meant in *religious history*. So I painfully whispered to myself : 'He is not a Christian.' But as I grew up, I began to honour a breadth, serenity, and truthfulness in my father's character. He was rather fond of a coarsely-worded maxim : *Give the devil his due.* After I had out-grown the shuddering at heresy and unbelief (a tedious process with me) I saw him in my memory, as an unpretending, firm-minded Englishman, who had learned his morality more from Shakespeare than from the Bible, and rejected base doctrine from whatever quarter."

Thus, the father representing the world and the son the Church, there could not but be conflict between them. They took different sides in other matters besides religion. The great quarrel which divided England into the partisans of George IV. and the partisans of Queen Caroline, did not spare the New-man family ; where there was sharp altercation between father and son, the latter, as usual, siding with authority, the former with what he considered the oppressed party. So completely had Mr. Newman misunderstood John's passion for the powers that be, that he attributed his advocacy of them to self-interest : "Well, John! I suppose I ought to praise you for knowing how to rise in this world. Go on! Persevere! Always stand up for men in power, and in time you will get promotion." After such an outbreak, we cannot be surprised at another and more serious quarrel. Francis had refused to copy a letter for his father on a Sunday. John, called in to the dispute, sided with his brother, and thus records the result: "A scene ensued more painful than any I have experienced. I have been sadly deficient in meekness, long-suffering, patience, and filial obedience. With God's assistance I will redeem my character." The incident just recorded (which occurred in Newman's twenty-first year) points to other similar scenes that had preceded, and leaves little reason for surprise that Mr. Newman's name is not mentioned in the narrative of his son's religious growth, except incidentally in a single passage, which shows how the boy took a delight in religious controversy from the first, and thought it a thing to be proud of: "When I was fourteen I read Paine's *Tracts against the Old Testament*, and found pleasure in thinking of the objections which were contained in them. Also I read some of Hume's essays, and perhaps that on miracles. So, at least, I gave my father to understand, but perhaps it was a brag."

Thus, for better or for worse, the boy had to work out his own salvation, without much aid of parental advice, and, so far as the father was concerned, without much aid (that he could appreciate) from parental example. Yet the same child who was so reserved and reticent to his parents about the subject that most interested him, was copious and unrestrained in his prayers to God. Most children are guided, consciously or unconsciously, from the types on earth to the Archetype in heaven. They may pray for fine weather, or toys, or holidays ; but they will hardly pray that God will mediate between them and their mother. A real, natural, wholesome child cannot realise—perhaps *ought not* to realise—that God "loves him better, and is nearer to him than his parents." That must come afterwards. But Newman expressly asserts that an "ordinary" child does this. We are led to the inference that it was so with him in his childhood. Afterwards, not having had children of his own, he does not even seem to have ever conceived that other children could be different. Hence in his old age he made this statement about "ordinary" children :—

"It is my wish to take an ordinary child, but still one who is safe from influences destructive of his religious instincts. Supposing he has offended his parents, he will all alone and without effort, as if it were the most natural of acts, place himself in the presence of God and beg of Him to set him right with them."

"Let us consider," he adds, "how much is contained in this simple act." How much indeed! Nothing less than a complete reversal of the ordinary sequence by which children should pass to the Unseen through the Seen.

§ 2. *School life*

When he was little more than seven years old, Newman was sent to a school of more than 200 boys at Ealing under a Dr. Nicholas, of some repute in those days. Though it was a private school, it had a great name. "It was conducted on the Eton lines," says a friend of Newman's ; "everybody sent his sons there ; they got on." "The Nicholas hit" was known in the athletic world. Yet the Ealing athletics did not make Newman sociable or fond of sports. A boy who went to the bathing pond but never swam, and about whom his schoolfellows have left on record that they never, or scarcely ever, saw him taking part in any game, can never have been popular, even though he worked his intellectual passage upwards from the bottom to the top with an ease and rapidity that elicited the praises of his masters.   In 1833, when journeying on the track of Ulysses in the Mediterranean, he was half disposed to attribute his want of interest in things to the many disappointments and the suffering that he had endured from " the rudeness and slights " of persons he had been cast with, and he detects in himself an involuntary shrinking from society, and a perception, almost morbid, of his own " deficiencies and absurdities."   Such as Newman was in manhood, such was he also as a child of seven and throughout his youth.   At no time could he say, with Wordsworth, that his heart was social and loved idleness and joy.   The strain and pressure of something ever to be done pursued him from his childhood onward.

We have an amusing account of some of his literary ventures at school.   In his fifteenth year he wrote two periodicals called the *Spy* and the *Anti-Spy*, and Francis Newman supplies some details about the former :—

" Many of the boys were made sore by the title, and told me that he *quizzed* everybody.   Gradually it leaked out that he had initiated a number of the boys into a special Order, with whom he was every week to read the *Spy*. . . . . Among these was my second brother, but I, no doubt, was too young.   Charles told me that there were degrees in the Order, marked by ribbons of different colours, with J. H. N. as Grand Master.   The Society met in one of the vacant rooms of this large school. . . . But indignation at the rumours of espionage soon culminated, and the *profanum vulgus* of the uninitiated forced the door open, swept away the faithful officer on guard, seized the papers, and tore off the badges.   Thus came the day of doom to the *Spy*."

Francis Newman's knowledge of the Cardinal's Anglican works is, on his own confession, too slight, and his memory of the details of the Oxford Movement appears to be too vague, to justify a critic in deducing important inferences from them; but this does not lessen the value of his evidence as to the early life and family relations of his elder brother. When, for instance, he describes the drama composed by John Henry as a boy, in which Frank, five years younger, played the part of "fisherman to the lord of a Welsh castle," and had to eulogize the great lord for "eminence in the four cardinal virtues, and, above all, for being so fond of fish "—does this throw no light on the mind of the precocious dramatist who could already throw himself so very thoroughly into a fisherman's views of "virtue"? And in the same way the rise and fall of the *Spy* is not unimportant as illustrating, at an early age, many of Newman's most striking peculiarities —his magnetic influence over a small circle of chosen friends; his shrewd judgment of the foibles, follies, and contemptible infirmities, of the world amid which he moved; his liking for quiet, unobtrusive, and almost surreptitious methods of action; and his deficiency in appreciating the limits of tolerance, and in anticipating those abrupt but effective methods by which a coarse, and commonplace, but not unnatural resentment can sometimes sweep to the winds the most neatly arranged organization.

§ 3. "*Conversion*"

From an early age Newman was superstitious; crossing himself in the dark—a habit which he possibly picked up from Scott's poems, as a thing that took his fancy and could do no harm while it might do good ; given to studying "signs" and "omens," making much of " coincidences," and apt to interpret events as special interventions of Providence in his own behalf. When young, he used to say that "our Lord ever answered" his prayers. Carried to an extreme, this habit of mind may tend to egotism. It is not good, for example, to pray to God for prizes in competitive examinations. It is better, perhaps, sometimes, to be sorrowful for the loss of friends without being able, at once, to think that their removal will be medicinal for our souls.* And a Providence that is too often regarded as intervening for us may perhaps seem too seldom to intervene for others.

To one of these interventions he traced his conversion. On 8 March, 1816, his father's bank failed. This led to his unexpectedly remaining at school for a month or two by himself ; and thus he fell under the special influence of one of the masters, Walter Mayer by name, a pious clergyman of the Evangelical school. By him he was converted. " On my conversion," he writes, a few months afterwards, " how the wisdom and goodness of God is discerned ! I was going from school half a year sooner than I did. My staying arose from the 8th of March."

Among the books which Mr. Mayer put into his hand was a work of Romaine's inculcating "the doctrine of Final Perseverance," concerning which he writes as follows in the *Apologia :*

" I received it at once, and believed that the inward conversion of which I was conscious (and of which I am still more certain than that I have hands and feet) would last into the next life, and that I was elected to eternal glory. I have no consciousness that this belief had any tendency whatever to lead me to be careless about pleasing God. I retained it till the age of twenty-one, when it gradually faded away; but I believe that it had some influence on my opinions, in the direction of those childish imaginations which I have already mentioned, viz., in isolating me from the objects which surrounded me, in confirming me in my mistrust of the reality of material phenomena, and making me rest in the thought of two and two only absolute and luminously self-evident beings, myself and my Creator; for while I considered myself predestined to salvation, my mind did not dwell upon others, as fancying them simply passed over, not predestined to eternal death. I only thought of the mercy to myself."

In later days, he found reason to doubt whether he had gone through those regular processes which are supposed to be essential to an Evangelical conversion. But that he experienced at the time a great and definite change, there can be no doubt at all. In his eighty-fifth year he found it "difficult to realise or imagine the identity of the boy before, and after, August 1816." For five years he firmly believed that he was "elected to eternal glory," and the belief appears not to have quite disappeared till after his ordination. Till his conversion, he had wished "to be virtuous but not religious." He adds—words difficult to reconcile with what he has told us above about an "ordinary child" recognizing "One who loves him better, and is nearer to him, than his parents," but they are his own words —that up to this time he had not seen "the meaning of loving God."

Now he saw it. Or shall we say, he thought he saw it? For it was that kind of love of God which did not include a thought of friends and parents. It looked in gratitude toward that mysterious Being, who by reason of His own sole will had predestined him, John Henry Newman, to eternal salvation; but it did not lead his mind to "dwell upon others." Is it not at least questionable whether this sort of "love" and this sort of Fatherhood are the love and the Fatherhood contemplated by the first two words (and especially by the first word) of the Lord's prayer ?

Be this as it may, his conversion was fertile in further changes. It led him already to speculate in an interesting manner, and to prepare the way for further speculations, on the sources and tests of certainty in religion. For the present, his test was inward conviction. He makes a note of it in a MS. book.

> "The reality of conversion as cutting at the root of doubt, providing a chain between God and the Soul that is with every link complete; I know I am right. How do you know it? I know I know."

Never perhaps (except during the irresistible temptations of Oxford class lists) was he ambitious or covetous with the common ambitions and covetings of youth or manhood ; but his conversion led him to despise more than ever the vulgar prizes of this world in comparison with the priceless treasure of communion with his Creator. Compared with such a gift, what was fame but a mere breath—a vibration of the air in words ? Nay, what else was man himself as conceived by man ? For who knew what was in man, save God alone ? "There is no such thing," writes this boy of sixteen, "as a *person* being famed. Let it not be thought a quibble when I say it is his *name* that is celebrated, and not himself."

A subtle and penetrating thought—calculated to pull down the proud aspirations and imaginings of those who look to Shakespeare and Milton, and the great poets and thinkers of all ages as dwelling in our souls, and fashioning our characters, through imperishable thoughts which we receive, and in turn pass on to others. Possibly Newman went wrong

here, as elsewhere, out of an excess of desire to make
out a case, as it were, for God, and to exalt Him by
disparaging His children. And this constant dwelling
on his own impotence and his own unimportance, and
even his own defects, leads him sometimes into an
egotism, which may be illustrated by another of his
youthful reflections. He is talking to himself on
paper about the stricter life that he hopes to lead
now that he is converted.

" Although it is far from pleasant to give my reasons, inasmuch as
I shall appear to set myself up, and to be censuring recreations and
those who indulge in them, yet when I am urged to give them, I
hope I shall never be ashamed of them ; presenting my scruples with
humility and a due obedience to my parents. . . . . I think these
things of importance to myself, but I hope I am not so enthusiastic
as to treat it as a concern of high religious importance. You may
think this contradicts what I said just now about the beginning
of sin, if so, I am sorry I cannot express myself with greater exactness and propriety."

Allowance must be made for a certain stiffness and
artificiality of style, natural perhaps for all young
composers, and especially for those who wrote at the
beginning of this century : still, it is refreshing to find
that Newman afterwards noted and condemned the
fault as arising from his habit as a boy *to compose*.
" I seldom wrote," he says, " without an eye to style,
and since my taste was bad, my style was bad. I
wrote in style, as another might write in verse, or sing
instead of speaking, or dance instead of walking.
Also my Evangelical tone contributed to its bad
taste." These words should be borne in mind when
we read many of Newman's earlier, and a few even
of his later, compositions. He had an excess of
rhetorical versatility, but he was aware of his danger.

In most of his later letters the fault appears, if at all, in the shape of a justifiable and interesting adaptability to his several correspondents ; but in his earlier years the consciousness of style is a fault. It is excusable that he should write English in the style of Cicero's letters to his old schoolmaster Mayer ; but Greek prose ought not to leave its traces in letters addressed to his sisters ; and a son on his twenty-first birthday ought not to write a letter to his own mother in the style of any author at all, least of all in one that seems to combine Gibbon and Johnson.

To return to Newman's conversion. " I fell," he says, "under the influences of a definite Creed, and received into my intellect impressions of dogma, which, through God's mercy, have never been effaced or obscured." This is an exact and carefully-weighed statement of the fact as it appeared to Newman in later years. It was not into his heart, but into his "intellect" that he received the new "impressions," and the "impressions" were of dogma. From his childhood he had received the Bible as inspired, and was familiar with its text. There was now placed before him a scheme of salvation logically deducible from Biblical texts, and leading him (in conjunction with his own feelings) to believe himself to be eternally predestined to salvation, whatever might become of others. This scheme commended itself to his "intellect," and into his "intellect" he received it. In later years the Protestant part of the dogma faded away ; but there still remained so much of the dogmatic basis as was common to the Protestant and Romish Churches. Dogma, to the last, was the basis of his religion.

The Letters at this time depict a youth meditating on mysteries, arguing on predestination, on efficacious grace, on baptism and especially infant-baptism, fond of Beveridge's *Private Thoughts*, and much disposed to set down his own religious thoughts on paper. Among authors to whom he was indebted he specially mentions Thomas Scott of Aston Sandford, admiring him, not only for his unworldliness but also for the minutely practical character of his writings. For years, he used, as proverbs, two sayings that expressed the essence of Scott's doctrine ; " Holiness rather than peace," and " Growth the only evidence of life." On these two maxims—excellent in themselves —we shall have occasion to dwell hereafter, but they demand a word or two of immediate comment.

What is holiness ? Things were called "holy" under the dispensation of the Old Testament when they were in a special manner set apart for the service of Jehovah. But the doctrine of the New Testament is, that all things, except sin, have been cleansed for Christians, so that henceforth, strictly speaking, the technical and ecclesiastical distinction has no existence for them. Although, therefore, the word is still used (and perhaps too often) because it lingers in the New Testament as a relic from the Old, it is always to be used with caution, for fear of a relapse from the freedom of Christ into the servitude of Law. Exactly defined, "holiness" means separation from, and antagonism to, sin. In the days of St. Paul, when "the Church" (like Hercules in his cradle) was fighting against a poisonous "world," it was natural to call the former " holy " and the latter unholy. But such an antithesis becomes unnatural, or at least exaggerated, if transferred to the relations between " the Church " of England and " the world " of England in 1816. However, Newman persisted in the transference, and throughout his Anglican life he was striving to act upon the antithesis with consistency. How little he knew, at this time, of " the world," and how little of " saints," may be inferred from his own words : " Reading in the spring of 1816 a sentence from Dr. Watts's *Remnants of Time* entitled ' The Saints unknown to the world,' to the effect that ' there is nothing in their figure or countenance to distinguish them,' &c., I supposed he spoke of angels who lived in the world as it were disguised."

" Holiness rather than peace " may have done something to prepare the way for Newman's rather controversial and militant attitude in later times. He had, indeed, by nature, an abnormally strong will. When, on one occasion in his childhood, he was laughingly told by his mother that he had not got " his own way," he replied, " No, but I tried very hard." This, of itself, might produce a tendency to argue, and to contradict, and to oppose majorities. If the world went one way, he instinctively desired to take another. But he would have suspected and suppressed this tendency if it had not been encouraged by the form of his religion. It was no spirit of restlessness or rebellion against authority that instigated him. On the contrary, to authority, once recognized as such, he was only too ready to defer. But against " the world " he was impelled by the fastidiousness of his own nature, by the letter of many texts in the New Testament, and (afterwards) by the desire of some definite sign to confirm his subjective assurances of salvation. "Peace" was, on many accounts, to be regarded with suspicion, but mainly because it suggested that the soldiers of Christ might have made unhallowed terms with the foe. How could he be *sure* that he was in "the Church"? Well, one test might be that he was fighting against "the World." How did he *know* that he was at peace with God? Well, at all events, he was not at peace with the enemies of God. As to the second maxim, "Growth the only evidence of life," the difficulty at once suggests itself of deciding between wheat and tares, between natural branches and grafted branches, between the growths of Nature and the accumulations or arrangements in which Nature plays no part at all—mere derangements, like the flowers which a child picks and places for a day or two in a sand garden that they may *appear* to be growing; or again, between healthy growths and unnatural ex-crescences; or lastly, between those changes by which Nature increases vigour, and those by which, in her ordinary course, she leads us to death and decay. Yet, whatever we may call this maxim, it is of the greatest importance to students of Newman's life, because it contains the germ of a thought that never left his mind after once entering it. It will find many expressions in his Anglican career; among the last of which will be the well-known *Essay on the Development of Christian Doctrine* by which he will prepare himself to join the Church of Rome.

With Romaine Newman combined another work of a character very opposite to Calvinism, Law's *Serious Call*. Besides impressing on his mind the doctrine of the warfare between the City of God and the Powers of Darkness, this book seems to have established in

him a " full inward assent and belief," from which he
never receded, in the doctrine of eternal punishment.
For some years to come, this belief might not greatly
affect him ; for he must be regarded as at present
resting safe in the doctrine of Final Perseverance.
But when that Calvinistic stronghold gradually crum-
bles away, it will leave him exposed to the fears which,
in his sensitive soul, must necessarily attend the recognition of an everlasting Hell.   Then we shall see this
belief—impotent in most minds by reason of an inconsistent and illogical human-heartedness which prevents
them from believing or realising its stupendous consequences—exercising its natural effect upon the whole
of his life and action ; largely shaping his theories of
the Church and his conceptions of the means of salvation ; and finally helping to drive him to seek refuge
in a new spiritual fortress, where, so far as it was
possible anywhere, he might find safety and shelter
from these intolerable terrors.   However, for the present, he felt no terror.   He himself was safe ; and his
mind did not dwell upon others.   He only thought
of the mercy to himself.   So he has told us in the
Apologia.

And now, being converted, and being in earnest,
Newman, in his sixteenth year, began to bethink himself of the new course of life and faith to which his
conversion committed him.   He had to believe in a
scheme or a system.   Then he would know what that
scheme or system was, and upon what it was to be
based.   He found that it was to rest upon a basis of
words.   Then he would know what those words were,
and how they ought to be arranged.   There should be
nothing vague or indefinite.   All should be as clear
and cogent as law and logic could make it.   In this

practical spirit he made a collection of Scripture texts in proof of the doctrine of the Trinity, with remarks of his own upon them. A few months later, he drew up a series of texts in support of each verse of the Athanasian Creed. We may think we discern a danger in such a precocious use of the vocabulary of religion ; but we cannot but admire the consistency of this theologian of sixteen, doing his best to ascertain to what he was committing himself, and to support it by what he thought demonstration. It was one of Newman's excellent characteristics that, until he had formed a " view" or " system," he was always ready to accept and combine truths that were commonly supposed to be incompatible. So it was now. Reading simultaneously Milner's *Church History* and *Newton on the Prophecies*, he was fascinated by the extracts in the former from the works of Augustine, Ambrose, and the other Fathers. In these there shone forth an ideal Church —primitive, definite, picturesque ; making war against the world and prevailing ; seeking holiness rather than peace ; and showing manifest signs of life in its vigorous expansion. If Milner charmed, Newton instructed him. From the latter he learned that the Antichrist predicted by Daniel, St. Paul, and St. John, was the Pope of Rome. Both these doctrines found access, not to his intellect merely, but to his heart. His " imagination," he tells us, was " stained " by the notion of a Papal or Roman Antichrist till his forty-second year.

This confession must not be forgotten. It helps us to understand many things that would be otherwise unintelligible. Newman was a poet, and he was imaginative ; but his was not a poet's imagination that shifts and ripples and varies in form and colour like

the surface of a lake.   Rather it was like the mortar of
those old builders of Rome, which was of such a substance that although in the process of building it would
furnish a soft and yielding surface, yet when the
structure was complete it became harder than the
stone itself, and impervious to the influence of time.
One other " deep imagination " took possession of him
at this critical time.   He conceived that it would be the
will of God that he should lead a single life.   This was
connected with the notion that his calling would require
such a sacrifice as celibacy involved, as, for instance,
misssionary work among the heathen, to which he had
a great drawing for some years.   Little or no reference
to this will be found in the autobiography or the letters,
and only a passing reference or two in the correspondence between him and his friend Hurrell Froude,
who joined and confirmed him in his resolution.   But
the very absence of mention ought to keep the unmentioned subject present in the mind of a student of
Newman's development.   Bacon calls a wife and
children a discipline of humanity ; but for some they
are also a discipline of theology.   Certainly, when the
time arrived for Keble to decide whether he and Newman should secede to Rome together or part company
for ever, the letters reveal that marriage had no slight
effect in severing the two friends.   In any case, if
Newman's thoughts were already prone to think only
of God's mercy to himself and "not to dwell upon
others," that isolation could hardly fail to be increased
by this "imagination" of his early manhood ; and such
was- the effect he himself ascribes to it, " It also
strengthened my feeling of separation from the visible
world."

CHAPTER II

§ 5. *Failure in the Schools*

In December, 1816, Newman entered at Trinity College, Oxford, going into residence in the following June. The term was nearly over; men were going down; and he found it hard to get information about his course of study. But the young undergraduate had an earnest determination to get on, and a profound belief that tutors were meant to teach and advise, and undergraduates to be taught and to take advice. Rather than miss his object, he was ready to waylay a tutor in top-boots on horseback making his way into the country for the vacation, or to call even upon so awful a personage as the President himself. There is a directness in this, and a straightforward contempt for conventionality, and a sense that a University ought to do what it professes to do—all very delightful and very creditable to the young freshman. Yet in these virtues there was nothing that would commend him to the other undergraduates unless he had some touch of the convivial, or at least of the social. Of these qualities the former was certainly absent, and the latter was not prominent. The following letter (dated Trinity Sunday, 1819) refers to the College

Gaudy or Feast Day, for which a wine subscription was usual among undergraduates. If, as appears to have been the case, there had been gross and repeated abuse in drinking, our sympathies ought to be with the recalcitrant against the college customs. We might have liked the protest to his old master Mayer all the better if it had been expressed somewhat less angelically; but it reveals a most commendable strength of will, by no means common among undergraduates:

"To-morrow is our Gaudy. If there be one time of the year in which the glory of our college is humbled, and all appearance of goodness fades away, it is on Trinity Monday. Oh, how the angels must lament over a whole society throwing off the allegiance and service of their Maker, which they have pledged the day before at His table,* and showing themselves the sons of Belial!

"It is sickening to see what I might call the apostasies of many. This year it was supposed there would have been no such merry-making. A quarrel existed among us; the college was divided into two sets, and no proposition for the usual subscription for wine was set on foot. Unhappily, a day or two before the time, a reconciliation takes place; the wine party is agreed upon, and this wicked union, to be sealed with drunkenness, is profanely joked upon with allusions to one of the expressions in the Athanasian Creed."

The next passage is worth adding, because it shows what a clear insight Newman already had into some of the weaknesses of human nature, and especially into that dread of ridicule against which he himself had to fight so hard a battle:—

"To see the secret eagerness with which many wished there would be no Gaudy; to see how they took hope, as time advanced and no mention was made of it; but they are all gone, there has been weakness and fear of ridicule. Those who resisted last year are going this. I fear even for myself, so great a delusion seems suddenly to have come over all.

"Oh that the purpose of some may be changed before the time!

I know not how to make myself of use. I am intimate with very few. The Gaudy has done more harm to the college than the whole year can compensate. An habitual negligence of the awfulness of the Holy Communion is introduced. How can we prosper?"

Clearly the writer of this letter was not destined to be a man clothed in soft raiment nor a reed shaken by the wind. If he succumbed to any evil influence it would be to something at least more subtle than luxury, or the love of comfort, or popular opinion. Already Newman had been elected a Scholar of his college (May 1818) with the possibility of being elected Fellow for five years without taking orders This last-mentioned absence of restriction was an important one for him; for at the present time he had no intention of being ordained. He was ambitious, he says, and hoped great things for himself. His father's intentions, and seemingly his own desires, pointed to the Bar. He attended Modern History lectures, " hearing that the names were reported to the Prime Minister;" and in 1819 he had entered at Lincoln's Inn. But an unexpected event was at hand which changed all his prospects and intentions. Although every one who knew him anticipated for him a brilliant success in the Schools, there were not wanting signs of possible failure. He worked hard. He had but one bosom friend, and wasted no time in sociability. But he was too discursive for exactness in anything, above all for exactness in examinations. "When I have taken my degree," he used to say, " I will do many things— compose a piece of music for instruments, experimentalise in chemistry, thirdly, get up the Persian language." Elated perhaps a little too much by his election to the Scholarship, he devoted the Long Vacation of his first year to Gibbon and Locke. He wrote a little poetry;

began (but ended in the month in which he began it) a periodical after the model of Addison's *Spectator*, and attended a few lectures on geology, besides the Modern History lectures before mentioned. Then, as young workers will do, he tried to make up for deficient work by overwork. During the Long Vacation of 1819, he used to work nearly nine hours a day. From thence to November 1820 it was a continuous mass of reading, and during twenty out of the twenty-four weeks immediately preceding his examination, he "fagged" at an average of more than twelve hours a day. He knew enough for a First Class, at least in Classics, but he aimed at two First Classes, one in Mathematics as well as one in Classics, and his mathematics were, even for those days, poor.

The result was that he broke down altogether when the crisis came. In the Mathematical list his name did not appear at all. In the Classical list it was found in the lower division of the second class of Honours, which, at that time, went by the contemptuous title of the "under-the-line," there being as yet no third or fourth classes.

§ 6. *Election to an Oriel Fellowship*

There was no ground for blaming any one, or anything but the exceptional temperament which we shall presently find causing him to break down again in the Schools as an examiner, and afterwards, on several other occasions, producing minor collapses, derangements, or failures. His youth was certainly against him ; for he was three months short of twenty when he failed. But Keble had gained two Firsts by the time he was eighteen ; and there were other instances

of men who had taken Firsts at the age of twenty.
If he had felt that he was attempting too much, the
obvious remedy was to attempt less and to try for a
First in Classics alone.   Newman himself sends an
eloquent protest to his father, asseverating that he
has done his utmost and that the examiners were as
kind as it was possible to be ; but his nerves quite
forsook him, and he failed.   He had done everything
he could, he says, to attain his object ; he had spared
no labour : " If a man falls in battle after a display of
bravery, he is honoured as a hero, ought not the same
glory to attend him who falls in the field of literary
conflict ? "

The fact was, he had made a mistake in judgment,
which he repeated many times in the course of his life
with far more serious results than missing a First.
He was always attempting to do more than could be
done in the time, and often with the result of not doing
it thoroughly.   Meanwhile, however explained, this
failure helped to change the course of his life.   Without
a Fellowship, the chance of which now seemed small,
how was he to remain at the Bar, waiting for practice
and burdening his father, who was not in a condition
to bear the burden ?   Thus, his collapse in the Schools,
combined with his own religious views, which became
more pronounced, to turn him towards clerical work,
and he decided in the course of 1821, with his father's
full acquiescence, on taking orders.   Two months after
his failure, he is not only resigned, he is joyful.   He
declines, he flees from, any kind of worldly success :
" I deprecate," he writes, " the day in which God gives
me any repute or any approach to wealth."

While preparing himself for ordination, he decided
to remain at Oxford, and to take pupils.   And now,

looking forward to his future work of converting others,
he sets down on paper, in a series of Scripture texts, a
detailed account of the stages of the regular Evangelical process of conversion ; but he is careful to note
that he speaks with great diffidence of this subject, his
own feelings, so far as he remembered them, being
very different from anything he has ever read. He
also notes his present opinion (against which he had
at one time contended) that the doctrines of Election
and Final Perseverance, however true in themselves,
were not fitted for the pulpit. This is perhaps a
natural prelude to the " fading away " of the latter.

His father's pecuniary anxieties, of which Newman
was always ready to bear his full share, stimulated the
young B.A. to the ambitious enterprise of standing for
an Oriel Fellowship. How lovingly and sympathetically he bore, and did his best to lighten, the parental
troubles, is indicated by a letter to his mother, consol-
ing her on the ground that " that distress which must
be, leaves unimpaired, or rather heightened, all domestic affection and love." But now the ambitious temper
—extinguished, as he thought, by his failure in the
Schools—burst out again, and he deplores the evil
passion of vain-glory within him. " Vain-glory " is
doubtless, a fault ; but there was nothing necessarily
vain-glorious in a vivid sense of the pleasure to be
derived from indicating his intellectual reputation and
gaining a Fellowship, especially since his success would
help him to relieve his father's pecuniary burdens.
But something worse than vain-glory is implied in the
following self-reproach :—

"Last 5th of January I wrote to my aunt : ' I deprecate the day
in which God gives me any repute, or any approach to wealth ! ' Alas,
how I am changed ! I am perpetually praying to get into Oriel, and

to obtain the prize for my essay. O Lord, dispose of me as will best promote Thy Glory, but give me resignation and contentment."

If he had prayed that he might do himself that full and ample justice which he had been unable to do himself in the Schools, there would have been nothing in such a prayer to be ashamed of. But to pray for success in a *competitive* examination is an altogether different thing. In some it would indicate a slight meanness ; in others egotism ; in others a somewhat low sense of the justice of God. In Newman's case it would probably be closest to the truth to say that he was misled by his conception of God as a Being who could do whatever He liked, and could make it right by doing it, and, in a less degree, by an unconscious feeling that he, more than others, was "luminously real" to God. But, after all, is not this saying in different words that Newman was egotistic and had no strong sense of justice ? The best extenuation of the fault is that he was ashamed of it. However, whatever we may think about the prayer, the result was achieved. On 12 April, 1822, Newman was elected Fellow of Oriel, a success which he always felt to be, in one sense, the greatest of his life, raising him from obscurity and need to competency and reputation. From this date what may be loosely called his University career may be said to terminate, and his career in the world begins.

§ 7. Solitude

"From 1822 to 1826," wrote Newman, in later life, " I used to be very much by myself, and in anxieties of various kinds which were very harassing. I then, on the whole, had no friend near me, no one to whom I opened my mind fully, or who could sympathise with

me.   .   .   Indeed, ever since that time, I have
learnt to throw myself on myself." So again : "God
intends me to be lonely. He has so framed my mind
that I am in a great measure beyond the sympathies
of other people, and thrown upon Himself."

The passage last quoted indicates that other causes
besides Calvinistic doctrine produced the sense of isolation which Newman felt during his early life at Oriel.
But his Calvinism and conversion may, in part,
account for it. Even before his election to the Fellowship, in answer to his mother's congratulations on
coming of age, he replied in language of such profound
melancholy that his parents were seriously alarmed.
" Not that I am sorry so great a part of life has gone
—would that all were over !—but I seem now more
left to myself, and when I reflect upon my own weakness I have cause to shudder." In answer to their
protests that he manifested want of self-confidence,
and an excessive dissatisfaction with himself, he
replied, " I assure you that they know very little of
me and judge very superficially of me who think I
do not put a value on myself *relatively* to others."
This indeed represents the exact truth. If he was
dissatisfied with, and despised, himself, much more did
he despise mankind in general. But to his mother he
imparts his secret. He " shuddered at himself." In
truth, he shuddered at everything. The whole world
seemed to him either profoundly unreal, or pitiably
abandoned to evil. It was true that he himself was
elected to eternal salvation, but not for any other
reason (apparently) except the arbitrary will of the
Elector. And what when his mind, now opening to
wider views, glanced at the fate of others ? What
about the great majority ? How could the world to

him be other than a ghastly riddle ? He did not "shudder" in society, nor in the family circle. There he seemed cheerful enough. But the mirth was merely on the surface. At bottom he was "shuddering," and had "shuddered" for the last five years, ever since his conversion. That this is no over-statement the following extract will show :—

"As to my opinions, and the sentiments I expressed in my last letter, they remain fixed in my mind, and are repeated deliberately and confidently. If it were any new set of opinions I had lately adopted, they might be said to arise from nervousness, or over-study, or ill-health ; but no, my opinion has been exactly the same for these five years. . . . The only thing is, opportunities have occurred of late for my mentioning it more than before ; but believe me, those sentiments are neither new nor slightly founded. If they made me melancholy, morose, austere, distant, reserved, sullen, then indeed with justice they might be the subject of anxiety ; but if, as I think is the case, I am always cheerful, if at home I am always ready and eager to join in any merriment, if I am not clouded with sadness, if my meditations make me neither absent in mind nor deficient in action, then my principles may be gazed at and puzzle the gazer, but they cannot be accused of bad practical effects. Take me when I am most foolish at home, and extend mirth into childishness ; stop me short and ask me then what I think of myself, whether my opinions are less gloomy ; no, I think I should seriously return the same answer, that 'I shuddered at myself.' "

On a first glance at this remarkable passage—written by a young man just of age, to a mother whom he dearly loved and whom he would not needlessly pain—we might suppose that the deep horror which it discloses proceeded from personal fears. " The doctrine of Final Perseverance," we might be disposed to say, " which gradually faded away soon after he came of age, is already beginning to droop ; and here we see the results." But this supposition is proved to be

false by the express statement that this opinion had
" been exactly the same for these five years," that is
to say, since his conversion at the age of sixteen. It
was therefore *his conversion that had made him
" shudder."* And why ? Because it had brought home
to his heart the presence of an ineffable Holiness, a
Hater of sin, a Being in Whose eyes he could scarce
conceive how (in spite of the Divine Promises) any
son of man could live, and before Whom, in spite of
those promises, he could not choose but "shudder."
And this "shuddering" constituted his true and inmost
life ; his real religious sense ; and this opinion entertained for the last five years of his youth, he, now a
man, " deliberately and confidently " repeated!

§ 8. *Whately*

In the autumn of 1821, Newman's youngest brother
Francis had come to read with him at Oxford. After
the Oriel election, the two brothers moved into a
lodging in Merton Lane where Blanco White had
rooms. This gave Newman a new companion. Blanco
White had been a priest in Spain, where he had
escaped from the Inquisition in 1810. Being now
nearly fifty years of age he was invited to join the
Fellows' table at Oriel, and he and Newman enjoyed
the violin together at their lodgings. Music was
sometimes exchanged for theological discussion, and
Francis records that these conversations often ended
with a warning from the older man : " Ah, Newman,
if you follow that clue, it will draw you into Catholic
error." Francis understood this to mean that his
brother would be led into self-flagellation, maceration of
the body, asceticism. If this was right, the " clue "

was probably "holiness," and, following this, the elder brother was working out the logical results of the antithesis between the Church and the World. Francis was too young, too different in nature, and too much indebted to his elder brother, to be of any substantial assistance to him in solving his religious problems. Blanco White, with all his advantages of age and diversified experience (and even an occasional flash of real genius), was too erratically impulsive and unstable to afford guidance to a keen, logical, restless, and exacting mind. But another guide now came forward whom none could call erratic.

Richard Whately, afterwards Archbishop of Dublin, was in many respects, the very opposite of Newman : a great eater and smoker, a loud talker, pronounced in dress, brimful of general and accurate information and not reticent of it, observant of the ways of animals and vegetables, fond of dogs and of fun, a little uncouth and not ashamed of it, absolutely hardened against all self-accusations for breaches of university etiquette, imbued with a profound sense of justice, detesting party spirit in all things, but especially party spirit in the Church, ready perhaps to give slight offence by brusqueness, but more ready to beg pardon when he had needlessly hurt any one's feelings, human-hearted, and forgiving—eager to forgive everything except what he deemed to be deliberate or malignant unfairness. He, too, had been reserved in his youth ; but he had cured himself by the same means by which he had cured others. "You are shy" he would say, "because you are thinking of the impression you are making. Think only of the pleasure you can give to others, not of yourself."

He was a great teacher, with a rich fund of pointed

illustrations.   He could teach his dogs how to climb
trees, and to take headers from them, and to consume
roast crow.   He could teach a young lady the need
of writing legibly by sending her a letter with
" My dear ——," and then a page of scribble
impossible to read, ending with the words, " Now
you see the evil of writing unintelligibly."   Lastly—
and these were lessons that he was specially fond of
giving—he could teach retiring young men who were
able to think for themselves but had never used their
ability, how to think, how to talk, and how (up to
certain limits) not to be shy.   Whately being what he
was, and Newman being what he was, the former
seemed to the Oriel Fellows the very man to rescue
the latter from solitary habits which at this critical time
seemed likely to prevent him from doing himself
justice and from growing to his full mental stature.
Though he was anxiously on his guard against temptation of every sort, and quite alive (theoretically) to
the unimportance of mere outside conventionalities,
still Newman was extraordinarily sensitive to his
own slight social slips, and spent days of acute suffering
from the recollection of solecisms.   Haunted by these
reminiscences, and (partly for his family's sake) over-
worked and worried as well, the freshly elected Fellow,
in his awe of his new associates, seemed at first to draw
more than ever into his shell ; and his bashful awkward-
ness made the Senior Fellows feel some " misgivings "
about their choice.   In this perplexity they put Newman into Whately's hands to " lick into shape."

This was Whately's own metaphor.   He liked to
have " cubs in hand," to do good to in this way ; if
they were worth anything, they would not mind being
knocked about in argument by such a trainer.   They

were like dogs of King Charles's breed, he said, and "could be held up by one leg without yelling." At other times, Whately called these young men his "anvils." If he had a piece of work to do, he would lay it on one of these youthful minds and then hammer it out. Just now, his piece of work was logic ; and it was logic mostly that he talked with Newman.   But he also taught him how to talk and think generally.   He took him out for rides and walks, and helped him "to pull his mind out," and rely upon himself.   To those who know what teaching means, this must always seem the highest praise—that a teacher at last leads his pupils to dispense with him.   What then did Newman mean when, in after days, he said to his old trainer that this was a "strange office for an instructor—to lead a man to rely upon himself" ?   Was it that he thought that men must *always* be in leading strings, *always* relying upon authority ?

For the present, however, no thought of "strangeness" or discord dimmed the relations between teacher and pupil.   Whately was like a June day with a north-east wind, and Newman rejoiced in the brightness and the bracing air.   His trainer was also kind to him in other ways ; spoke well of him to the Fellows of Oriel ; declared that he was "the clearest-headed man he knew ;" and got him work for the *Encyclopædia Metropolitana*.   The pupil responded to this appreciation and general kindness by what he himself calls an "affectionate abandonment" of himself.   So awkward, reticent, and uncouth among strangers, so unconventionally effusive among intimate friends, the Junior Fellow was in after days likened by the Provost to the lion's cub in Aeschylus, bred up like a kitten in a household, at first the plaything, presently the terror, of those who had fondled it.

Whately, having recently married, was only occasionally at Oxford, and could not therefore influence Newman as a resident Fellow might have done. He was also too much older,—the *Apologia* adds " superior "—to allow of Newman's being at ease with him ; and we find the latter afterwards writing thus about this period of his life : " I then, on the whole, had no friend near me, no one to whom I opened my mind fully, or who could sympathise with me." In truth, between the two men there was an impassable, though perhaps at that time imperceptible, barrier. Besides the difference of age—and the teacher was fourteen years older than the pupil—Whately could not understand Newman's profound sense of the unreality of material things and of the evil dominant in mankind ; and Newman, on his side, could feel no sympathy with Whately's enjoyment of life or with his belief in the human power to approximate to truth through natural faculties. There was a whole world of dark and creeping thoughts in Newman's melancholy soul which could not venture out to face the sunshine and north-easterly wind of Whately's presence. Further, Newman perhaps already recognized (though dimly and vaguely) that there are certain kinds of truth to which one is not led by logic alone, and which, even if grasped logically, cannot be permanently held by logic ; and this notion Whately may not have encouraged. It was sad that the two, when the time came, should part in anger ; but that they should part was necessary. On whose side there rested such blame as there was, we shall see hereafter. Meantime we must agree that the "affectionate abandonment" above-mentioned, though it implied gratitude, did not imply any "opening of the mind" in response to Whately's friendship.

§ 9. *Preparation for Ordination*

The days were now drawing on towards ordination, and Newman was busy trying to make his doctrines symmetrical. Contradictions, he writes in a letter to a young man, can be no more true in religion than in astronomy or chemistry. Adhering to his early opinion that Christian faith meant assent to a large body of dogmatic statements, he logically and consistently endeavours to ascertain what these statements are ; for we find, he says, in Scripture, that "he who holdeth not the faith" is incapable of true moral excellence, and so exposed to the displeasure of God.

In the same year he noted in his diary the great difference between his and other men's view of sin. Whereas others regard it as an infirmity or as an imperfection, he regards it as a disease or as a poison. This is the Christian belief. But when he goes on to say that sin therefore makes man "the foe of God," he seems to say what is inconsistent with his previous metaphor—if at least the phrase "foe of God " means "hated *by* God." Because men are " diseased " or " poisoned," does it follow that they should be " hated by God" ? Is it not rather true that the disease of sin makes man hate God just as insanity makes men hate and suspect their best friends ? Grant that the wrath of God visits sinners with just chastisements, just as the anger of parents punishes children for their good, yet that affords no reason for saying that God *hates* those whom he chastises. Admitting that men

may, by deliberate choice, so far identify themselves
with sin as to make it difficult for *us* to avoid hating
them, ought we to impute such hatred to God and to
say that He regards sinful man as His "foe"? Such
expressions as this, although they may be explained
so as to show that they are not destitute of truth, seem
so likely to cause misconception that they ought not
to be used without strong reason.

What reason had Newman for using them? In the
letter from which we have just quoted, he answers this
question: "The Scriptures," or his reading of the
Scriptures, told him so. Here we are confronted with
one of the most important influences that shaped
Newman's religious development—his belief in the,
we almost say, literal inspiration of the Bible. No
child in a family of Evangelical tendencies could very
well think otherwise in the first quarter of this century;
and in Newman the belief would be strengthened by
his love of definiteness, his desire to lean upon
authority, and his suspicion of the deceitfulness of the
voices of this world. Critical or historical study might
afterwards have modified this belief; but the historical
study came late, and the critical study, never.
Mr. E. T. Mozley in his *Reminiscences*, speaking of
his brother-in-law's attitude towards the Bible, says,
" He accepted, from very early years, every text, every
expression, every figure, every emblem and every
thought thereby suggested, as a solemn and abiding
reality which it was good to live in:" and again,
" Newman might be supposed to have really believed
the English translation inspired, for any critical comment he ever made on the Authorized Version."
Even to his latest days (though of course modified by
his belief in the interpreting power of the Church

of Rome) this belief in the letter of the Scriptures
appears to have influenced him.   On this point we
have interesting testimony from one who lived "for
more than seven years as a member of his community,
under the same roof and for the greater part of his
time in the closest communion with him."   Mr. A. W.
Hutton tells us that " In regard to the Bible, or
rather to Scripture, as he almost invariably styled it,
his position was pretty much that of the old Evangelical
school ; . . . Of recent criticism of the Greek Testament he knew nothing," and he adds that, "whereas
the Vatican Council declared that the whole Bible
"has God for its Author," Newman's belief was
practically that "God was its Editor," or in other
words, that the whole of the text of the Bible received the direct supervision of God, and was "inspired " in every detail.   Many people profess to
believe this, but Newman really believed it, possibly
because he saw no help for it.   He was ready, for
example, to believe that the world would actually *not
hold* all the books that might be written about the
miracles of Jesus upon earth.   Sooner than disbelieve
the astronomy of the Scripture, he was prepared to
suspend his judgment as to the assertions of the
Newtonian philosophy.   We have already seen, and
shall hereafter see more clearly, how this faith in the
exact accuracy of each statement in the English
Authorized Version of the Scripture influenced his
conception of the Church and his attitude towards the
world.   For the present we must simply take note of
this factor in his development and pass on.

Continuing, with scrupulous exactness, his preparation for ordination, Newman records, as one of
his faults, a tendency to become censorious of others

for persisting in practices—*e.g.* reading the newspapers
on Sunday—which he himself had but recently given
up.   There follows an important remark.   He reminds
himself that "humility is the root of charity."   Is it
not rather charity that is at the root of true humility ?
" Charity " helps us to see good in others and to love
it.   What magic is there in merely thinking meanly of
ourselves ?   Can we not, while doing this, think *yet
more meanly of others ?*   Is not this the key to many
of Newman's peculiarities—that he compensated, so to
speak, for thinking poorly of himself by thinking still
more poorly of human nature as a whole?   "*Relatively*
to others," he *did*, as we have seen, " put a value on "
himself.   This should prepare us for finding Newman,
before very long, interpreting " charity," or " love," in
a somewhat technical sense.

§ 10.   *Ordination*

A year after Newman's election at Oriel we find
him making entries in his diary about the election of
another Fellow who, with him, was destined to play a
leading part in the Tractarian Movement.   He begins
by recording his belief that Edward Pusey is favourably disposed towards religion, and goes on to pray
that he may be brought into the true Church.   A few
days afterwards we find him described as "a searching
man," and one who seems to delight in talking on
religious subjects.   Then follow entries growing in
appreciation.   (2 May),   "How   can   I   doubt   his
seriousness ? . . .   May I lead him forward, at the
same   time   gaining   good   from   him."   (17   May),
" That Pusey is Thine, O Lord, how can I doubt ?
. . . His high ideas of the spiritual rest of the Sabbath,

his devotional spirit, his love of the Scriptures . . .
yet I fear he is prejudiced against Thy children. Let
me never be eager to convert him to a *party* or to
a form of *opinion*. Lead us both in the way of Thy
commandments." In the following year respect ripened
into admiration. (February 1824), "Have just
walked with Pusey; he seems growing in the best
things—in humility and love of God and man. What
an active, devoted spirit!" The entries culminate in
the following description of a conversation (18 March)
to which Newman evidently attached the highest
importance, though he has not thought it right to give
us the substance of it: "Took a walk with Pusey,
discoursed on missionary subjects. I must bear every
circumstance in continual recollection. . . . At Magda-
lene Bridge he expressed himself to me (blank in
MS.). . . . Oh, what words shall I use? My heart
is full. How should I be humbled to the dust!
What importance I think myself of! . . . Bless him
with Thy fullest gifts, and grant me to imitate him."
How was it that Newman, with such a companion as
this, with whom he was brought into close contact
from 1823 onwards, describes this very period (1822–6)
as one during which he had no one to whom he opened
his mind fully—no one who could sympathise with
him! Pusey's absence in Germany, which appears not
to have begun till the summer of 1825, seems hardly
sufficient explanation.

Merely noting, for the present, this question as
one that must not be forgotten hereafter, we
pass to the mention of one who was rather a
lecturer than a friend, Dr. Charles Lloyd, the Regius
Professor of Divinity, whose lectures he attended in
the winter of 1823. Quaint, good-humoured under

an appearance of roughness, with more liking for exegetical criticism, historical research, and controversy, than for dogma or philosophy, he professed to regard Newman as a perverse Evangelical, sometimes making a stop before him in particular, as he paced up and down among his little class of eleven, and making a feint to box his ears, or kick his shins, for some quasi-heretical answer. Lloyd and Whately were diametrically opposed. The former represented what was called the High-and-Dry school, though with far larger views, says Newman, than were at that time common. The latter represented the intellectual or Noetic school of Oriel, looking down both on High and Low Church, and calling the two parties respectively Sadducees and Pharisees. Lloyd made much of books and reading, and authoritative and traditional teaching. When preaching at Lincoln's Inn, he used to say it was as much his office to expound to the lawyers the Christian religion and Protestant faith as it was the office of the Judges to lay down the law. Whately, on the other hand, called the Fathers "certain old divines," and avowed that *primâ facie* he was well inclined to a heretic, as being one who had at least thought for himself. Such is Newman's account of the differences between his rival instructors; and he adds that, although the former was the more Catholic in his tone of mind, he was not the man to exert the same intellectual influence, or leave the same impression upon his mind, as Whately had done.

After anxious consultation, Newman determined to take up parochial work without delay. A Fellow of a College, he thought, after years of residence in Oxford is unfitted for labouring among the poor. How

seriously he accepted his approaching responsibility
may be gathered from his memorandum on his twenty-
third birthday : " The days and months fly past me,
and I seem as if I would cling hold of them and
hinder them from escaping. There they lie, entombed
in the grave of Time, buried with faults and failings
and deeds of all sorts, never to appear till the sound-
ing of the last trump." On 13 June 1824, he was
ordained deacon. " It is over," he remarks on the
same day ; "at first, after the hands were laid on me,
my heart shuddered within me ; the words 'for ever'
are so terrible ;" and again, next day, "' For ever,'
words never to be recalled. I have the responsibility
of souls on me to the day of my death."

A few days afterwards, he preached his first sermon
at Warton, the parish of his old schoolmaster Mayer,
on behalf of the distressed weavers of Spitalfields.
Frank was present and has left it on record that both
he and Mayer felt a shock at a passage in the sermon
which implied that the weavers were entitled to
sympathy as being not only men, but also baptized
Christians. To them this seemed to imply such a
view of baptismal regeneration as was contrary to
Evangelical notions. On the other hand Newman
tells us that the sermon divided the Christian world
into two classes, the one all darkness, the other all
light, that its tone denied baptismal regeneration, and
that he was taken to task for this by Dr. Hawkins, then
Vice-Provost, but afterwards Provost, of Oriel. The
sermon is not extant, but Newman's account of it
seems decisive ; and it is confirmed by his mother's
commendation of it. Possibly the preacher may have
said that even nominal Christians, in virtue of their
formal admission through baptism into the pale of the

Church, had some claim upon the sympathy of their fellow Christians ; and this thought, expressed in subtle language by one who was feeling his way in the pulpit —a constant habit with Newman—may have given his old teacher and his brother a false impression. This is comparatively unimportant. The important fact is, that in this, the first of his sermons, Newman seems already, by his own account, to have laid stress upon that exaggerated antithesis which sets the Christian Church in opposition to the Christian World. In 1824, the basis of this antithesis was subjective and emotional ; in 1829, or before, it will become objective and sacramental. But the antithesis will remain, as strong as ever, preparing the way for development upon development of ecclesiasticism, and ultimately finding its legitimate goal in the Church of Rome.

CHAPTER III

§ II *" The Church "*

WE have followed Newman through youth and early manhood to the commencement of his campaign for the Church against the World. Here seems the point where, if we are to appreciate his subsequent life, we should pause for a brief review of those shaping causes around him and within him which were destined to press upon his mind and mould his action.

At the time of his ordination Newman was an Evangelical, and he remained one, at least in repute, for three or four years afterwards, though he must have felt—if others did not—that he was not of the ordinary type of his school. The Evangelicals had done indisputably good work both for religion and for the national life. They had kept alight some sparks of the spiritual flame when it seemed to have gone out in other sections of the Church ; they had forcibly reminded the middle classes in England that Christianity was not a mere affair of rites and ceremonies. Spite of some misinterpretations and distortions of fact and doctrine, they had leavened multitudes with a seriousness that might lead to something higher ; and here and there they had given to earnest souls some glimpse of the unutterable vision of love, mercy, and righteousness, revealed in the life and death of Christ.

Herein they had perhaps followed the Nonconformists, or at all events Nonconformist tradition. But, whatever might have been their originality or want of it, they had been at all events in earnest ; and having within them something of the essence of living Christian faith, they had shown signs of life. It was from them and from the Nonconformists that there had sprung—so far as they sprang from religious sources at all—most of the plans for the relief of the poor, the miserable, the ignorant, and the enslaved, which the end of the last century, or the beginning of this, had introduced. They had originated the great Missionary Societies ; their spirit had led Howard and Elizabeth Fry to attack the brutalities of our prison system ; from them came, first, the assault on the slave-trade, and ultimately the overthrow of slavery itself.

But their day was now passing. They had become popular, and had lost some of the vigour which rewards those who contend for an unpopular cause. In proportion as they found in themselves less truth to impart to the world, they had been forced by circumstances to profess, and endeavour to teach, not less but more. The Anti-Catholic feeling—as well as their traditions of earnestness—had thrust the Evangelicals into a position where they were compelled to speak much. Hence, an excessive proneness to words. They were great on platforms, and profuse of eloquence at tea-meetings. But their words were not always words of fire, and some of their old force evaporated in mists of verbosity. The prayers of passionate fervour, the songs of praise and psalms of thanksgiving, with which their fathers had made melody unto the

Lord, some now began to repeat with that incipient lifelessness which is not far off from cant.

One reason was, that their religion—though it had been well adapted for a special need—was not based upon human nature, or, at all events, not upon the whole of human nature, nor upon the facts of Christianity as a whole. They treated the soul as though it were always coming to Christ, not as though it were in Christ and to be kept there. To many of them the main and almost only duty of a Christian minister seemed to be to preach the Gospel as though their congregations had never heard it before. They could not derive help and sustenance for their faith from everything that is everywhere good, beautiful, and true; nor did they recognize in the opposites of these things a stimulus to religious action so as to find scope for Christian effort in every condition and circumstance of mankind. Inheriting a certain detachment from the continuity of the Christian Church, they held aloof from the past, and were afraid of reviving some of the old methods of representing the truth, the want of which weakened their hands when they strove to build up the permanent edifice of a Christian life. In a word, their religion was not broad enough to cover the whole of human experience.

Hence, by degrees, they were losing their hold upon some of the most active and religiously disposed minds, especially among the rising generation. To some Evangelicalism seemed to savour too much of the sick-bed; and, when applied to outdoor life, it appeared thin, weak, and unpractical. Others began to find fault with its narrow exclusiveness. Besides, it was inconsistent. Without definitely sanctioning joy, it was not definitely and logically austere. With high-flown

professions of spirituality, it seemed to combine conni-
vance at a selfish comfortableness or even luxury. To
the masses it was not so emotionally attractive as
Dissent, and its dulness was not compensated by any
of that solemn symbolism, which sometimes teaches
more forcibly than words. If, in spite of all these
disadvantages, the Evangelicals led many souls to
realize the Invisible, and here and there brought home
Christ Himself to some searcher after truth, it often
happened that the convert, afterwards, while keeping
what he had gained, passed into a wider field where he
could use it more freely.

The High Church party was commonly described
in those days as "High-and-Dry," and the epithets
fairly represented the facts. Taking little part in
philanthropic movements, which they left to the Evangelicals, they stood apart from, and above, the stir and
strain of the common-place needs of society. The
doctrine of some of them may fairly claim to be called
scholarlike, accurate, and careful ; but it could not be
called seasonably wise, and still less spiritual. There
was not wanting in some of them a sober, steadfast
piety, ready to ripen into some active development, if
occasion called ; but the call had not come. Its worse
members, says Dean Church, were jobbers and hunters
after preferment ; pluralists, who made fortunes out of
the Church ; or country gentlemen in orders, who rode
to hounds, and shot and danced and farmed, and often
did worse things. The average were kindly, helpful,
respectable routine-workers, but often dull and pom-
pous, and, when not dull, sometimes insufferably
dogmatic and quarrelsome.

Of High Churchmen, Oxford, at this time, counted
two or three men of learning. But of these the best

and most active was Lloyd, whose influence, as described above by Newman, was not likely to be powerful on the young Oxonians. Still less actively influential was the aged Routh, recently (1820) married at the age of sixty-five, but more venerable for age and learning than for force or depth of character. Cambridge had a scholar in Bishop Kaye : Connop Thirlwall and Julius Hare had begun to draw attention to the historical and critical aspects of the New Testament, and to the results of German thought ; and in H. J. Rose the Tractarians thought they had found a theologian ; but in that University Coleridge's philosophy was more potent than any theology. As a specimen of the Oxford divinity lecturing in those days, Mr. E. T. Mozley tells us that, in a certain learned college at Oxford, a certain learned tutor once gave a lecture on that chapter of the Gospel of St. John which describes the conversion of the water into wine. It consisted, he says, of the mere reading and translating of the text, unbroken by any comment save that, when the undergraduate translator came to the words "draw out now," the lecturer remarked, "Hence we may infer that the Jews in those days used spigots." In Cambridge, Herbert Marsh, afterwards Bishop of Peterborough, was giving (1807-39) Englishmen the results of German study on the formation of the Gospels. And things, as a whole, were better there. But still, looking at the ordinary run of the High Church professors and lecturers at this time in both Universities, young men of active minds and religious dispositions could hardly be reproached for using the language of the prophet Ezekiel concerning the vision of the valley of bones : "There were very many, and lo, they were very dry."

Such was the condition of the two great Church parties, at the time when Newman began ministerial work ; the one out of condition, tending to plethory, and, even at its best, deficient in the means for permanent and systematic action ; the other, scarcely living, keeping altogether out of the path of national progress. In Oriel indeed there were two thoughtful men who had begun to contemplate, if not actually to suggest, some middle course. The logical, or, as they were called, "Noetic" school, for which that college had begun to be famous, held aloof from both of the Church parties. Whately and Arnold, in particular, were forming ecclesiastical conceptions of their own. But at the time now under consideration, no middle course was in existence. The World, in England, if it looked to the Church for help, had to choose between two allies of various degrees of impotence, the Evangelical party, which seemed to some in danger of dying, and the High Church party, which was, to all appearance, already almost dead.

§ 12. "*The World*"

Meantime "the World" in England, having shaken off the incubus of the long and burdensome war during which it had fallen into all sorts of arrears, legislative, literary, scientific, and social, was determined to make them up, if not with the aid of the Church, then without it, or in despite of it. There was plenty to be done, and there were not wanting indications that it would be done in a combative spirit. Partly perhaps the energy that had found a vent in military enterprise was now to express itself polemically, though in civil reformation ; partly, there was so much to do, so many wrong things to be set right, so many galling, grinding, insolently oppressive, and inveterate abuses, that men were not disposed to wait indefinitely, or to go a long way round, when they could take a straight short path by over-riding—a little roughly perhaps—a few intervening obstacles.

Different classes and sections of the nation, the Romanists, for example, and the Nonconformists, had their special grievances; but almost the whole nation was complaining on the national account. The great mass of the people were not represented in Parliament, and the government was often out of harmony with the interests of the governed. High tariffs and protective legislation threatened to neutralize the effects of steam and chemistry and improved machinery; all who cared for justice chafed at the flagrant oppression of laws which punished debt with life-long confinement, and allowed no counsel to prisoners tried for their lives on a charge of treason. The game-laws, the laws of libel and conspiracy, the whole of our criminal code, required amendment. In our days, these abuses are undefended. To speak of them as abuses is to render oneself liable to the charge of uttering truisms. But in the days when Newman was a Junior Fellow at Oriel, it was far otherwise. Then, the people who ventured to raise a voice against them were called levellers or Jacobins by those whose sole idea of perfection was that things should remain as they were. Some reforms, too, were opposed, not by the Church, but in the name of the Church, by men who were quite ready to tolerate the slave trade; and if any one ventured to protest against a system which had converted the Lord's Supper into a political test, forced upon the unbelieving or the unwilling, he was liable to be reviled

as a Socinian or an atheist. Literature contributed
to the unrest. Some indeed of the younger poets
(Keats, Shelley, and Byron) had just passed away, as
though to leave the arena clear for political action ; but
already by its revolt from the formal spirit of the
eighteenth century, the new poetry had prepared the
way for more than literary changes. The revival of
the study of German was even now, directly and indirectly, influencing theology, modifying literary taste
and style, leading men on to a wider survey of history,
and rendering them more and more unwilling to ac-
quiesce in insular detachment from European thought
and movement. Scott's novels, beginning by recalling
their readers to *Sixty Years Ago*, gradually lured them
still further back, at the same time stimulating the
taste for warmth, colour, and picturesqueness in life
and manners, and infusing a sense of continuity and
kinship between widely distant ages and countries.

One more power remains unmentioned, a power too
long treated by Religion as a tributary foe, and now
tempted to inflict reprisals. Science had at last stepped
into such a position that every class and every individual had begun to recognize it as an influence in
their daily lives. Early in the century Cavendish had
passed away, before whom (it was said) were alchemists,
but after whom, chemists. Poor people might never
have heard of Cavendish ; but there were memorials
of Cavendish and his companions that could not be
misunderstood. Gas-lights in the streets, steam-boats
from New York to Liverpool, steam-engines already
in manufactories, and prospects of steam-carriages to
travel perhaps as much as twenty miles an hour, these
were changes—and most men were disposed to call
them blessings—that every one could appreciate : and

all these were so many credentials for the new Power
which was laying its finger everywhere on the earth
beneath and on the stars above, opening up the crust
of the globe; telling the secrets of its formation;
weighing the planets, determining their distances, and
predicting their motions. Not content with its secular
provinces, Science had even begun to glance at the
Bible, and to suggest how certain parts of it must be
interpreted; or rather to say what was fact, and to
leave the interpreters of Scripture to reconcile their interpretations, as best they could, with fact, or to confess
that they could not reconcile them, and to abide by
the consequences.

To have done so much for man was to have deserved to triumph. But Science was sometimes not
content unless she triumphed with somewhat of noise
and unnecessary brag. Finding herself disparaged by
some as Truth's youngest daughter, she occasionally
took a kind of pleasure in asserting her position against
her middle-aged sisters Literature and Theology.
They were older, she said, but she was married, and
had children. Science was right in taking herself
seriously; but sixty years ago she somewhat exaggerated the benefits she promised to mankind. What
wonder? Even now her rose-coloured visions are not
quite antiquated. Even in this very year (1891) Mr.
H .M. Stanley finds himself able to assure us that when
certain railways are completed in Central Africa,
"Moloch and Beelzebub will be utterly cast down, and all
the powers of darkness cannot restore them." If such a
man, with such an experience of human nature, both
black and white, and its portentous capacities of collapse, can hazard such a prediction, who can be surprised that, in the times of the Reform Bill, sanguine

souls anticipated that steam, and gas, and chemistry, would bring about something approaching to the Millennium ?

§ 13. *"The World" against "The Church"*

On this vast and complex movement, social, political, literary, scientific—not without its eddies, undercurrents, and backwaters, but flowing onward as a whole in a steady stream of national improvement—the Church looked down as an impassive or slightly uneasy spectator, having for the most part " formed no views." In urging some philanthropic measures, the Evangelicals, with the Nonconformists, had done good work : but the High Church had done almost nothing. Later on, perhaps, some members of the two parties might unite to protest against some desecration of the Sabbath ; or to propose a fast, or a day of humiliation, or to object to the performance of music in a cathedral ; but for the most part the Church sat with its hands folded, unmoved until something occurred to touch its temporalities ; or, if it moved at all, it was, first, to push itself forward as an opponent to national progress, and then to slink backward when frightened out of opposition.

The parochial system still sustained itself in small country parishes, but it threatened to break down among the masses :—so heavy was the strain caused by the crowding into manufacturing districts and into fast growing towns and cities, where there was no supply of churches or pastors to meet the increasing demand, and where old associations and neighbourly habits could no longer keep the flock together. In the parish there was no discipline ; between the clergy, no cohesion; in the whole ecclesiastical body, no leadership, no centre of control. What was there in such a national Church as this to gain the affections or the respect of the nation? In default of inner life, and spiritual guidance, and sympathy with the educational and political needs of the people, there remained one intelligible means by which High Churchmen might have maintained their position. They might have at least provided some fit and reverent expression for the devotional feelings of their congregations. But even this had been neglected. Take but one minor instance —selected merely because of its connection with the subject of this biography. Even in St. Mary's, Oxford, for some years after Newman had become vicar and had adopted Tractarian views, the Holy Communion was administered, not at the altar, but to communicants at their seats in the chancel, napkins being laid out for the purpose.

We may be sure that, wherever Newman was present, reverence must have permeated any forms, however outwardly irreverent they may now seem to us ; but in many places it can hardly be doubted that external neglect of forms led to internal irreligion. There was a general violation of seemliness and order. Pluralities abounded, honest work was rare. The Church was paid to do a certain minimum, which was supposed to be no more than the visible sign and symbol of an invisible priceless labour ; but even this minimum was not done. Hence arose louder and louder murmurs from some who took a common-sense non-legal view of things. No doubt the endowments of the Church might be alleged by legalists to be beyond the control of the nation, so far as they did not pro- ceed from the national purse, but from individual

benefactors. Yet, after the lapse of generations, such
gifts commonly come to be regarded as a collective
ancestral loan, made upon public conditions of interest
to be paid to posterity. That is perhaps not the legal,
but it is a natural view ; and hence we cannot be surprised that many people began to say that the nation
was not receiving from the Church its money's worth
for its money.

In Ireland there was even greater cause for mur-
muring. For there men saw bishops presiding over
dioceses in which the overwhelming majority refused
to be presided over ; pastors without flocks ; churches
with scarcely the two or three needed to make up a
formal congregation. \Tithes in some places could be
collected only at the point of the bayonet ; sometimes
weapons came to be used as more than a means of
menace, and the Established Church was thus associated in the minds of the peasants with the sense of
oppression, violence, and bloodshed.

Such were, or such were soon to be, the relations
between the Church and the State at the time when
Newman was ordained in 1824. Not that he himself
was at this period—or for a few years afterwards—
troubled with thoughts, or forethoughts, of politico-
ecclesiastical conflict. It was enough for him at present
to be thinking out the problems of salvation, as applied
to his own soul and to those of his parishioners. But
as soon as he came to work a parish, this logical, consistent, system-loving curate could not but be affected
by points of Church discipline and Church organization. Thus, by degrees, there must needs force itself
upon his mind the whole question of the relation between Church and State, and at last the question of
the Church itself—its essential character, and the part

to be assigned to it in his doctrinal scheme. What will be the consequence of these external forces upon the restless nature of one whose constant maxim it is to prefer holiness to peace, and who assumes, and interprets literally, the axiom that the Church must always contend against the world ? Must he not inevitably cast himself into the conflict, and come forward before long as a champion of the former ? So much is certain. The only question is as to the direction in which the champion will move, and the limits at which he will stop.

§ 14. *Idols*

The Idols of the Cave, says Bacon, are the Idols of the individual. They are the false images or phantasmal shadows that substitute themselves for the solid realities before the vision of those who sit captive, fast bound in the darkness of their own limited experiences and eccentricities. The metaphor, borrowed from Plato, represents mankind as seated in chains, with their backs to the opening of a cavern. Behind them pass various natural objects, and behind these objects is a fire ; thus the shadows, cast by the fire upon the inner wall of the cave, are accepted and seriously discussed by the poor prisoners, as if they were the realities.

All of us, more or less, sit under this servitude. Each one of us, says the *Novum Organum*, has a cave of his own. Sometimes it is the individual nature and peculiar temperament, sometimes a special rearing and education, or particular companionship ; sometimes the reading of special books, and deference to special authorities ; and thus, upon a mind preoccupied and predisposed, there may be produced impressions quite different from those received through the same object by a mind that is sedate and equable.

Hence, one man may incline towards novelty, another towards antiquity ; in one (and this is the most common of all errors in an imaginative mind) the faculty of discerning likenesses may overbalance the power of seeing differences ; some are so restless and so impatient of doubt that they cannot bring themselves to suspend their judgment ; some have no real thirst for knowledge, and no real trust in those faculties by which, in the course of nature, men seem to be intended to approximate to the highest truth. In others the "sedate and equable mind" is wanting ; they value knowledge, even the highest knowledge of all, not so much for itself as for its results in confirming their hopes or freeing them from fears ; and they do not so much hate imposture as they love and cling to safety.   In the search after religious truth, this is perhaps the most pernicious Idol of all ; but we all have our several Idols, against which there is no effectual remedy except to turn ourselves round from our own little world to the great world, from the Cave towards the Light.

Now concerning the future Reformer whom we are at this moment contemplating, must we not say that both his nature and his pursuits combine to brand him as one of those whom Heraclitus condemns of that most fatal fault of seeking truth in their own little world and not in "the great world." At first sight indeed it might appear that Newman's tastes and studies would be wide enough to correct, instead of confirming, any defects arising from a want of balance in nature.   An omnivorous reader ; a lover and writer of poetry, and a musician too ; an attempter of mathematics, not unwilling, as we shall see, to read two or three chapters of Conic Sections in a Long Vacation ; a student of Hebrew almost to the end of the Book of Genesis ; an attender of lectures on mineralogy and history ; one who had half a mind to study Persian, and who had cast thoughts towards German—may not such a versatile character as this claim, in his very versatility, an antidote against some of the idiosyncrasies of the Cave ?

More clearly viewed, however, these little literary digressions will be seen to be either wholly ineffective, or effective, if at all, in the wrong direction. Procrastinating, year after year, in the study of his own special subjects, he will be found attempting to compress the work of years into months, while he takes up subjects of outside knowledge merely to touch and drop them. Hence we shall find him, in his own province, justly distrustful of his own knowledge, worried, as he tells us himself, and " fagged," and " fussed." Not having mastered anything thoroughly by the intellectual faculties, he will never feel sure of anything he has approached through them. He will be skilled, not in things, but in the aspects of things. Hence all knowledge with him will be a " view," or an "intelligible position," or a " controversial basis." He will " throw himself generously " into a " system," that is to say, into other people's knowledge, rather because he distrusts the result of attempting to find knowledge for himself, than because he dislikes the labour. One thing he will know. His intellectual versatility and his knowledge of the weaknesses of educated humanity, will teach him how to write with effect ; how to say what will take with the refined ; and how to persuade almost all who desire to be

persuaded—except himself. On this very account he
will distrust his own appearance of knowledge, because,
while his followers lean on it, he knows it to be
hollow : " These people say *they* know it. But do I
know it myself ? Is there really such a thing as
knowledge ? "   Hence, while he will imagine ex-
cellently, he will always remain a very indifferent
knower. What men do well, they ljke to do ; and
they sometimes dislike and try to despise what they
cannot do. Newman, therefore, will like to imagine ;
and we cannot be surprised if he dislikes, and perhaps
despises, the attempt to know. Subtle and far-as-
piring though his thoughts may be, there is, between
him and " the Great World " an almost impenetrable
barrier, not visible at once, but impenetrable and
complete, like a crystal sphere.

On the forehead of such a student as this there will
be seen, not indistinctly, some of the very signs that
Bacon has described as the marks of the Idols of the
Cave. Permeating his life and thoughts, there will
be the predominating influence of the Imagination ;
but from this source, fed by external tributaries, there
will also flow other and minor influences. He will be
the servant of Antiquity (as against Novelty) ; the
servant of Synthesis against Analysis ; of the Subjective Whole (as against the patient attempt to
approximate to the knowledge of the Whole through
the Part) ; the servant of the Likenesses of things (as
against their Unlikenesses) ; the servant of Dogma
and Authority (as against Experiment and Induction).
Further, he will be under the dominion of ever-haunt-
ing terrors springing from the sense of unlikeness
between himself and an Almighty Super-human Being
whose main attribute it is to punish with super-

human severity. These imaginative fears will constrain him to believe what it is safest to believe, and will make a single superstitious impression more powerful than a thousand facts. He will leap to his conclusions first, and then resort to reason afterwards, simply to justify some predetermined action that has been dictated by ghosts of terror. Thus the logical faculty will become no longer a motive power at all, but merely, as it were, the quicksilver which tells us how heavily the mental atmosphere is pressing. Dominated by a hatred of "the world," he will find himself forced to try to hate not only worldliness, but everything in the world that does not conform to his pattern of sanctity. There are Two Volumes by which God reveals Himself to men, showing them how to end in loving Him by beginning with the love of one another : of these, one will be excluded from his vision by his indiscriminate abhorrence, or contempt, for visible things. And then when some outburst of bigotry compels him against his better nature to be cruel or unkind, he will call in logic to demonstrate his consistency ; and when he breaks with a friend or a brother he will "put his conduct on a syllogism."

Such a man may be respected for the sacrifice that he is sure to make for what he considers to be at once his highest interests and the highest truth, but he must not be trusted as a guide towards the highest truth. Many may be fascinated by the charm of his versatility. All must regard with a profound sympathy his long and weary struggle—a task so difficult in a mind so introspective—after conformity with the safest and most accurate dogma. Some, even of those who most differ from him, will not refuse their sympathy, when, after years of painful study, and anxious piety, and

growing forebodings of error, and increasing suspicions
of mortal sin, he finally floats into a haven of rest.
But, however deeply we may sympathise with his
spiritual anxieties, and however intelligible may appear
to some of us that surrender by which he found
his ultimate peace, he must end by doing what,
though honest for him, would not be honest for ordinary men ; he must sacrifice regard for facts to regard
for impressions. On the path towards that sacrifice,
common-place people will follow him at their peril. It
is not given to any to neglect facts with impunity. It
is not given to any but lunatics and lovers—and, in
some few instances perhaps, to poets and prophets—
to neglect facts and yet to remain honest and honourable men.

§ 15. *A forecast*

The *Apologia*, says Mr. E. T. Mozley, contained
some surprises for Newman's friends. So did his
political and theological development " contain surprises" for his mother. So did his life at Oriel " contain surprises" for the Provost and Fellows. So did
his leadership of the Tractarian Party, for the world at
large, and for the great mass of the Tractarians themselves. His whole life was full of surprises, even for
those who knew him best ; and, perhaps, among that
number, we may include Newman himself. But the
readers of a biography ought not to be taken by surprise. Before resuming, therefore, the chronological
order of events, it may be well to deduce, from the
statement of the internal forces at work, some kind of
rough forecast as to the direction of their resultant.

One reason why Newman's life was so full of surprises was, that he combined so many characteristics

often deemed incompatible. He combined a strong will with a timorous suspicion of his own wilfulness ; egotism with horror at himself; impulsiveness with distrust of his own feelings ; contempt for convention-alities with fits of remorse for outraging them ; resolu-tion to neglect facts and not be guided by reason with occasional doubts whether facts and reason ought not to be propitiated and might not be right after all ; keen taste for beauty with a belief that beauty is a mere temptation ; ambition for the highest and noblest tasks with a feeling that nothing human can be high or noble ; deep terror of the Eternal God with a still deeper sense that He must yet be trusted—for want of anything else to trust.

Such a personage, while really keeping on his own persistent course, will have all the more capacity for sur-prising his best friends, because—owing to the reserve which has rooted itself in the very depths of his solitary nature—he is unable to give to any of them more than a glimpse of his true self, and only now and then himself recognizes the most powerful of the complex influences at work within him. Beneath a pure, re-fined taste, a disposition that protects him from many sensuous temptations, a sensitive, impetuous, and highly poetic temper, a culture that has laid consider-able stress upon syllogistic and none at all upon inductive logic, and a passive and almost feminine affection for those who make advances to him, he conceals a depth of strong and retentive imagination, which often does duty for reason ; a strong disposition to take things as wholes though they are not wholes ; a mind of that kaleidoscopic nature which is con-stantly casting thoughts into patterns and making artificial unities out of them ; an excessive power of

seeing likenesses and of hammering them out for himself where they are not to be seen at first ; a will,
strong even to stubbornness against popular influences,
against incisive arguments, and against the logic of
facts ; a fierce instinctive recoil from masculine and
masterful minds ; a not inconsiderable faculty of
hating those who set themselves against any system
which he conceives to be authoritatively right ; an unlimited dread and hatred of sin, accompanied by constant doubts and misgivings as to what sin may be ; a
saintly aspiration after holiness without any adequate
sense of the eternal worth and religious bearing of fairness and justice in man, and consequently an inability
to approximate to an adequate conception of the
infinite justice of God.

And now suppose such a one grown up to manhood,
and a clergyman in the Church of England ; but still,
in manhood as in youth, detached from common
human nature, and from facts, and from the busy
world around him ; partly by the intensity of his concentration in his own eternal interests ; but partly—if
his parish duties throw him among a class of people in
whom he is not greatly interested—by the consciousness that he has no insight into their spiritual state,
and by a growing feeling that he is not adapted to get
on with them. Will he not strive, in proportion as he
finds his individual influence over them weaker, to make
his official influence stronger ? Will not his failure
tempt him to find fault, not with himself—for he has
done all he can—but with his system or no-system ?
And will he not aim at systematizing it still more, or at
finding another system altogether ?

Again, suppose our Reformer—at this critical point,
when he has done little more than commence his

ministrations—to find that the doctrine of Final Perseverance, in which he found peace and safety for his
soul, has been gradually growing weaker within him, and
is now on the point of fading away, if not already dead ;
so that he whose mission it now is to help others to
salvation has to confess that he is no longer sure of it
himself. Searching everywhere for some solid basis
of certitude, where is he so likely to look for it as in
the Primitive Church ; to which he was attracted even
in his childhood, and which exhibits, from a distance,
an ideal of Christian security and Christian consistency
contrasting painfully with the complexities, inconsistencies, and doubts, of modern Christianity ? Con-
ceiving a passion for the vision revealed to him in
these ecclesiastical studies—the vision of a living,
growing, victorious Church either contending against
or governing the World—will not the student be
detached yet more from modern needs and thoughts,
and conceive a still greater contempt for those
methods of investigating truth which have led to
schism and disorder in the Church of modern times ?
Distrusting his own nature, and having little knowledge of the sublime possibilities of human nature in
others, such a man must needs flee to books and papers
and authorities as his strong Rock and House of
Defence. He will begin to think that he has been
cruelly deceived and outraged ; led into an ambush of
schism ; wounded and taken captive by Private Judgment. With the festering sore still rankling in his
side, he will never—of so much he is certain, though
many things lie dim before him in the distance—no,
he will never trust his own feelings again. Authority,
in some shape, shall henceforth be his guide. Even
for a moment to have thought himself right will soon

appear to him a reason for immediately afterwards thinking himself wrong; and the use of judgment will become, in his mind, so identical with its abuse that the very faculty of judging will seem to him to savour of original sin.

And what will be the last scene of all in this eventful drama of spiritual agencies? Can common-sense allow us to doubt it? Beneath the strain of the solemn pulpit warnings "omnibus moriendum" we shall soon hear in louder and louder tones the sad refrain of Pascal, "je mourrai seul"; and the victory will rest with that imagination which can best pacify those terrors of solitude, by basing on the most definite system of act and doctrine the most definite and satisfying promises of ultimate safety. The Church of the Ante-Nicene Fathers in folio, even when identified or harmonized with the Church of the Anglican divines in quarto, cannot ultimately prevail against his conception of the living Mother whose words, throughout the ages, must needs be true because she holds in her own arms the living and growing Babe, the Eternal Truth. In a nature in which imagination is so deep, so strong, so retentive, so susceptible of spiritual hatreds and terrors, and so deficient in that sense of the Divine justice (perhaps also of the Divine love) which might have calmed those terrors—the craving for the early peace of youth must in the end prevail over opposing tendencies, such as love of consistency; sorrow for the inevitable pain that he must cause to friends; loyalty to a cause once loved; bitter regret for followers perhaps misled, and for the dream of a Mission that was no such Mission as he had supposed. Wherever fear of sin may lead him—fear, that is to say, of his notions of sin, and of his notions of punishment—there it must be his unalterable destiny to follow. Finally, his paper schemes being reduced to a blank by contact with realities, he will go continuously onward—however tortuous may be his path, while he dallies with the inevitable, determines to be guided by reason, plays at justifying himself on grounds of logic, and strives to convince himself that he is a free agent—to that ultimate shock which shall procure him peace by pulverizing his intellect ; so that at last, after long toil and tension, his mind may fall back once more at rest in the relaxation and easy calm of that sweet peace which he had lost as a youth almost as soon as he had begun to enjoy it.

CHAPTER IV

§ 16. *Groping*

WE return to Newman, recently ordained, and at once entrusted with the charge of a parish. Most men who are worth anything either change their minds a good deal after twenty-three, or, if they retain the same conclusions, base them on different grounds. It is one of the great trials of a clergyman ordinarily in the Church of England, and possibly in other Churches, that he is often induced by his own laudable impulses (strengthened sometimes by special circumstances as in Newman's case) to commit himself to a system first, and to realise it afterwards. Eager to do good work, he finds that the only path to the special activity to which he feels called is through a gate of Ecclesiastical Assent. Entering through this, he has —or had till lately—to pledge himself to the truth of a great number of propositions, touching on science and history, that is to say, on fact, to which a man ought not to be asked to commit himself without regard to evidence. About that evidence, he—as a rule—has had no time to form a permanent opinion. Recent modifications have somewhat lightened the burden. Still, even now, it is sufficiently heavy for those who

think. It was heavier in 1824, and Newman was
always thinking.

By thinking, I do not mean speculating. His
nature was even more legalistic and practical than
speculative. He tells us himself that he was not a
" philosopher," but a " rhetorician." He despised the
Cambridge men who wanted to make religion " nothing
more than a literature " : " Are they not Greeks," he
said, " and we like Romans ? " In that there was
some truth. He was Roman—at least in aspiration.
The Cambridge men, he complained, " cannot make
religion a reality." By " reality " he meant a " system," something to keep people in order. That was
true also. The Cambridge men could not do that.
Newman thought he could ; and, whether he was
right or wrong in thinking so, at least he had one
qualification for doing it, a highly practical mind.

Whatever he undertook to do he was not content to
pretend to do ; and in most business matters he had a
keen sense of cause and effect. Read his directions to
James Mozley as to the finding of a particular sermon
in a particular drawer in a particular cabinet, and you
will see that the writer could not be content to do anything except upon some principle, definite and clear as
he could make it. Later in life he blamed himself
for his want of system in controlling his followers, and
said he had not the art of managing men. And he
was right. He could influence and stimulate to action
many whose movements afterwards he could not keep
true to one pattern. But that was partly because, at
that time, he had not found his pattern, and was a little
uncertain where to find it. He was never lacking in
the love of regularity and discipline ; he believed that
men required to be kept very much in order, far more

by ecclesiastical than by secular control, and his heart
went out to the famous line of Virgil as describing an
essential duty of the Universal Church ;—

"Tu regere imperio populos, Romane, memento."

Consequently, the first thing Newman did, when he
took charge of St. Clement's, was to revive the disused
custom of visiting.   He determined to see every one
of the parishioners in turn.   His father disliked it, and
called it an invasion of an Englishman's castle ; but
Newman was not to be so deterred.   He had a duty,
not to the parish, but to the people in it ; the system
of the Church of England recognized no such thing
as a dissenter, and it was his business to work the
system.   If it failed, the responsibility rested with it,
and not with him.

It did fail ; but in part the failure was probably his.
Not that he did not show a good deal of tact and
sensible moderation in his treatment of his parishioners ;
but he had not those qualities which enable many an
Evangelical minister to do great things in a parish.
The secret of their success, so far as they succeed,
is that they themselves feel, and have the power of
imparting to others, a very deep sense of a personal
relation towards a Redeemer, for Whom they feel a
gratitude and a trust that constrains their lives towards
sympathetic affection for others.   A man who com-
bines this qualification with some degree of natural
sympathy and insight cannot help doing much to
enlighten and uplift souls that sit in darkness and the
shadow of death.   Now Newman, though sympathetic
with a few who loved and made advances to him,
was reserved to most men.   He had a keener insight

into the actualities than the possibilities of humanity ;
and his hatred of cant made him suspect both those
who seemed to talk it, and himself as well, lest he
should connive at it or re-echo it.   This increased his
reserve, and gave him a sense of perplexity and
helplessness.

Hence, when a sick man—with the memory of a
bad past, and with no present tokens of reform except
the inability to repeat his old sins—protested that he
had been, without any apparent cause, suddenly converted and blessed with peace, what could Newman
do ?   Could he throw himself heartily and sympathetically into a state of mind that he felt to be not
improbably a delusion ?   He might warn the man
against self-deception, and protest that words without
realities were dangerous.   And that is what he did.
But he must have done it with faltering lips ; for in
what else had he himself been trusting ever since his
own conversion, except in his own feelings and in the
ability to repeat certain words with sincerity ?   He
could not, at present, go against his own Evangelical
formularies as to conversion and salvation by faith
alone.   Here, then, he felt himself at sea, needing,
not giving, guidance ;   and he had too much good
sense and honesty to deny his failure.   He was
probably wrong in making the system wholly responsible for it ; but, in any case, the failure was indisputable.   It was probably in the course of 1825 that
he noted down, in memoranda made at the time, his
conviction, gained by personal experience, that the
religion which he had received from John Newton and
Thomas Scott would not work in a parish ; that it was
unreal ; that this he had actually found as a fact, as
Mr. Hawkins had told him beforehand ; that Calvinism

was not a key to the phenomena of human nature as they occur in the world.

Hawkins was at this time Vice-Provost of Oriel, and had been doing much to shake Newman's Evangelicalism. He it was who had protested against the assumption in Newman's first sermon which had divided Christians sharply into the two classes of saints and sinners. He had insisted on the recognition of the fact that men "are not either saints or sinners"; they were, he said, "more or less converted." He it was who, with his exact mind, had led Newman to weigh his words and to distinguish cognate ideas, and besides guiding him to the doctrine of baptismal regeneration, he had put into his hands Sumner's *Apostolical Preaching*, a book which, more than anything else, ultimately succeeded in rooting out Evangelical doctrines from his creed. But Newman found the process a gradual and a painful one.

"Lately," he writes (24 August, 1824), "I have been thinking much on the subject of grace, regeneration, &c. . . . Sumner's book threatens to drive me either into Calvinism or Baptismal Regeneration, and I wish to steer clear of both, at least in preaching. I am always slow in deciding a question; and, last night I was so distressed and low about it that the thought even struck me, I must leave the Church. I have been praying about it . . . . I think I really desire the truth and would embrace it wherever I found it."

"Slow in deciding" does not express the fact, or expresses it only superficially. Newman was quick, and almost instantaneous, in receiving into his imagination certain truths which commended themselves to it; and these, though he might struggle against them with the aid of logic, were seldom dislodged; so that, practically, he might be said, by anyone who could see the internal processes of his mind, to decide at once. And hence we cannot be surprised to hear that he was " taught" the doctrine of Apostolical Succession, about the year 1823, in the course of a walk round Christ Church meadows. Francis Newman is angry at the very notion of such a thing being " taught " so rapidly, but his brother explains it. " I recollect," he says, "being somewhat impatient of the subject at the time." The fact was that any doctrine of this kind, clear, definite, and falling in with the drift of Newman's progressive thoughts, was at once " received " ; but after the " reception " something remained to be done. " I alter ever, when I add," says Lord Bacon, describing his method of composition. So did Newman in composing his scheme of doctrine. Whenever he " added" he felt that the whole scheme required " altering " and readjusting. The adding was sometimes the affair of a moment, of a single imaginative flash ; it was only the altering that took time.

In the distraction caused by these painful misgivings Newman naturally turned for at least a temporary refuge to the Oriel or Noetic party represented by his friend Whately, by the Vice-Provost Hawkins, by Copleston, at that time Provost but soon to be Bishop of Llandaff, and by Arnold, a former Fellow, of whom Newman was destined to hear often, though he only met him twice. The unspiritual " High-and-Dry " Party, besides being intrinsically unattractive, did not encourage advances from an Evangelical. We have seen the good-humoured disdain with which Lloyd, their most intellectual representative in Oxford, though really liking Newman, affected to treat him as a perverse heretic. The rest of their party, who filled the high places in Oxford, were likely to be less good-

humoured and more disdainful.   It was Lloyd and his
friends whom he had in his mind as his opponents
when at this period he wrote down a suggestion for an
alliance between the Evangelicals and others: " It
seems to me that the great stand is to be made, *not*
against those who connect a spiritual change with
baptism, but those who deny a spiritual change altogether."

Between what seemed a lifeless Ecclesiasticism and
what had begun to seem mistaken Calvinism, the
Oriel School appeared for a time to present a middle
course ; the question was, whether it was a practicable
one.   No mention is made in the Letters about the
reception of this new doctrine of Apostolical Succession,
although its important bearing upon the problem now
before Newman must be manifest to all.   The Letters
are also silent as to another point of perhaps still more
interest—his attitude towards the Virgin Mary.   Francis
Newman, commenting on a passage in the *Apologia*—
" He (Hurrell Froude) fixed deep in me the idea of
devotion to the Blessed Virgin "—says : " But J. H. N.
knew him only in 1826.   Is not this inconsistent with
my statement about her in 1824 ? "   The " statement "
is as follows :—In 1824, when Frank was having his
rooms furnished, his brother, without his knowledge,
caused an engraving of the Virgin to be hung up in
them.   The younger brother ordered it to be removed,
and an altercation arose between the two, in which
the elder attacked Protestants, " saying that they forgot that sacred utterance, ' Blessed art thou amongst
women.' "   Afterwards he attacked " Protestants in
general, as ignorant and hasty."

This evidence cannot be rejected.   No one, even in
his old age, forgets, or misdates, conversations of this

sort connected with the furnishing of his first rooms
when he entered college as a freshman. It must be
true ; and a very extraordinary truth it is. But anyone
who is accustomed to Newman's nice use of words will
see that Frank's testimony, instead of impugning, confirms the statement in the *Apologia*. "*Fixed deep*"
is perfectly compatible with a *pre-existence* of "the
idea of devotion," only hitherto not "deep" and not
"fixed." We have therefore, in reality, two independent lines of evidence conducting us to this conclusion, that, as early as the autumn of 1824, while
Newman was in heart, as well as in appearance, an
Evangelical, he was so detached from the common
prejudices of his party, so open to new convictions, and,
presumably, so dissatisfied with his present religious
position, as to give his younger brother the impression
that he took an anti-Protestant view of devotion to
the Virgin. Strange though this is, it is by no means
inexplicable. If, as Newman tells us in a passage of
the poems apparently intended to be autobiographical,
he could not help, throughout his whole life, seeing
" the Judge severe e'en in the Crucifix," was it
unnatural that he should look about for some other
Person to intercede between him and the Severe One,
and should at least entertain on the surface of the
mind the notion that such a Person might be found in
the Mother of our Lord ?

The testimony of Francis Newman goes still further :—

" The more my brother argued about Invocation (not that I dare
say he ever urged me to *practise* it, I think *he stopped short* in refuting
my objections) the more uneasy he made me ; till, one day, wearied
with the topic, I broke out in clearer opposition than usual, saying,
' But, my dear John, what can be the *use* of invoking a Being who

cannot hear you? The Virgin is not omnipresent!' He replied by an argument under which I at once collapsed, muttering inwardly ' What is the use of discussion if he *will* be so *whimsical?* '"

§ 17. "*Pulling out his mind*"

The death of Newman's father in the same year in which he was ordained may have recalled to his mind a prediction made three years before, which at the time had passed unheeded, or rather, heeded but disbelieved. He had spoken very positively about the truth of the Evangelical opinions. " Take care," replied his father, "you are encouraging a morbid sensibility and irritability of mind which may be serious. . . . No one's principles can be established at twenty. . . . Weak minds are carried into superstition and strong minds into infidelity." On which Newman had set down this comment,—after prayer against delusion, pride, or uncharitableness—" How good God is to give me ' the assurance of life ' ! If any one had prophesied to me confidently that I should change my opinions, and I was not convinced of the impossibility, what anguish should I feel!" This prophecy was now being fulfilled. In the inevitable " anguish " which accompanied the breaking-up of old seeming certainties, he turned this way and that, seeking some middle course between the superstition which he disliked, and the infidelity at the thought of which he trembled. Butler's *Analogy* naturally claimed his attention. Now that he was learning, with the most acute pain, to distrust his feelings, the logical character of that able work naturally commended it to him as affording a more solid foundation.

We have read, above, his note, made in his youth,

about "the reality of conversion as cutting at the root of doubt, providing a chain between God and the soul, that is with every link complete ; I know I am right. How do you know it ?   I know I know."   It is difficult to discern the "links" in this chain of knowledge ; but undoubtedly the soul that has once "known" God to be a Father, is not disposed to give up that "knowledge" by reason of any so-called logical disproof.   For, in reality, such "knowledge" is of the nature of love and trust ; and although facts in nature and history may have suggested it, they could not prove it, and therefore ought not to disprove it when once suggested.   No man can be forced by logic to believe that any material or visible thing proceeds from a good God ; for he can always fall back upon the hypothesis of chance, or of a bad God pretending to be good, or of many gods.   But on the other hand, when he has once been impelled by his inherent or implanted love of order and righteousness and trust in order and righteousness, to believe that there is an orderly and righteous God, who will be in the end perceived to have subordinated evil to good and to have gained the victory which entitles us to call Him the King of the Universe—this belief, as it was not forced *upon* him by facts, so cannot be forced *from* him by want of facts.   To the question "How do you know it ?" he replies, "Because it is too good not to be true," or " Because I know it," or " Because it is a part of myself," or in some other wholly illogical, but (to himself) perfectly satisfactory way, and, it must be added, in a way that should commend itself even to the scientific and experimentalizing nature by the fact that it *works well*, and does not interfere with demonstrated truth.

In place of such a knowledge as this, Butler's *Analogy* seemed to Newman to suggest Probability —probability of a transcendent kind, but still probability. Probability, then, Newman accepted from Butler as the guide of life generally, and also as our guide towards God. To many—and especially to those who have worked mathematical problems in "Chances and Probabilities," and who are familiar with the statistical use of the latter term—this will seem an altogether lower level than that which the boy of sixteen occupied when he gave, as his explanation for "knowing," the answer, " Because I know." Even though, as Newman maintained, probability were transmuted by some special touch of the Divine hand from a great to a transcendent probability, still some would feel that they do not like this *word* in connection with their belief in a God. They would, of course, at once admit that whatever they believe in *is*, in a sense, probable ; but the word seems profane, and is perhaps fallacious. Speaking of such sacred subjects as the existence or attributes or acts of a Father in heaven, or even of the purity and interests of those who are dearest to them on earth, they prefer to use the words "trust" or "confidence" or "faith" —not "probability"; and, if it be replied that the last word may be used in some kindred sense to the former and not in its statistical meaning, they answer that, although such a distinction may be made by a single writer, he will find difficulty in observing it, and most people will find a difficulty in remembering it. It may mislead him and must mislead others.

However, it must be remembered that in Newman's case the belief in God was rather of an intellectual than of an emotional kind ; and his notion of faith

was, not personal trust, but belief in a great number
of dogmatic propositions to which the mind was
enabled by a special grace to give a full internal
assent beyond the assent that might have been
claimed by mere logic.

If Newman, at his conversion, had approached the
conception of God through the conception of the
Church, or through the conception of the family,
trusting in God with a trust the same in kind (though
infinite in degree) as that with which he trusted in his
parents, or in the best and noblest characters of his
human experience, then he ought never to have given
up, and perhaps never would have given up, his old
subjective faith ; for it would have been founded on
the facts of experience, the divine facts of human
nature. But as it was, his early faith in God was
altogether detached from any faith or trust in human
beings ; his mind ignored their existence, whenever
he stood in the presence of God ; it was "*my* Father,"
not "*our* Father," that was the centre of his system.
His faith was based, not upon facts, but upon texts
and such feelings as spring from texts, feelings about
which he could not feel certain that they had any
permanence or any basis in fact. His faith, in a
word, was a paper faith, except so far as self-
knowledge was concerned.

Even here he could not touch bottom ; he knew
enough about himself to know that he could not know
his own weaknesses or thread the labyrinth of his self-
introspective doubts ; and he was deterred, partly by
inherent self-suspicion, partly by Evangelical doctrine,
from recognizing the good within him. It speaks
much for the tenacity of his associations and the firmness of his nature, and perhaps for his determination

to believe *something*, that instead of collapsing like a
house of cards, his dogmatic structure did but dissolve
slowly under the touch of experience and the influence
of Oriel.   For there was nothing at this time to neutralize the impulses that were coming from the Noetic
School, and everything to aid them.   A high doctrine
of the Eucharist, for example, and frequent celebrations
of it, attract, in our days, many who are far from calling
themselves High Churchmen ; but how far Newman
was at present from attaching to it even what would
now be called a merely decent importance, and into
what neglect the most sacred ordinances of the Church
had then fallen, may perhaps be estimated from the
fact that, although he was ordained Priest the end of
May he did not administer the Communion till the
following August.   " I intend," he writes to his
mother, " to have a Sacrament, August 7, at St.
Clements ;" and he adds this note : " I administered
it as priest for the first time."

In the spring of 1825, Whately, having been
appointed Principal of St. Alban Hall, made Newman
his Vice-Principal, and at the same time induced him
to undertake an article on Miracles for the *Encyclopædia Metropolitana*.   Whately's treatise on logic
was meanwhile in progress, and Newman was playing
something more than the part of an " anvil " in the
contributions he made to it : he " composed," says
the preface, " a considerable portion of the work from
manuscript not designed for publication, and was the
original author of several pages."   With his parish,
with a new church rising and subscriptions to be
collected for it, a new Sunday-school, the general
management of a hitherto ill-managed Hall, his college
work, the Logic, and the article for the Encyclopædia,

all on his hands at once, Newman speedily worked himself (as he did for many years of his early life in almost every Long Vacation) into a complete nervous fever. A short holiday in the Isle of Wight combined with his marvellous recuperative power to bring him speedily back to something like his customary health ; and though he never quite recovered from the chronic indigestion which he contracted at this time, he writes in the autumn that he feels so strong that " parish, hall, college, and Encyclopædia go on together in perfect harmony. I have begun the Essay on Miracles in earnest and think I feel my footing better and can grasp the subject more satisfactorily. I can pursue two separate objects better than at first. It is a great thing to have pulled out my mind."

§ 18. *Inclining towards Liberalism*

It was not surprising that such a strain of work had caused a temporary collapse. The mere task of forming definite opinions on such a subject as Miracles was of itself a heavy one for a young man not yet five and twenty. In August 1825 Hawkins writes to Newman, " I hope by this time your essay on Miracles *à priori* and *à posteriori* parts, and all the contents of all the books in the window seat, are in a beautiful state of effervescence." Pusey, to whom Newman appeals for help from Germany, seems to be able to give him little ; and the Vice-Provost, when he re-places forty books for him in the University Library, finds that the essay writer, who ought to have been enjoying his holiday, has taken a good many missing volumes with him. It must have been a hard task indeed for an honest-minded man—under Whately's influence, too—to draw a clear line of demarcation between the Scripture Miracles, all of which were to be accepted, and the Ecclesiastical Miracles, all of which were to be rejected. No wonder that he calls Apollonius of Tyana "a crafty old knave," who makes him "poke into dusty books," who "asks questions about authorities for saying this or that," and whom he cannot despatch under ten days, whereas he had bargained for two. Evidence was to be, if not stated, at all events referred to, and, to some extent, weighed; the rules of reason were to be, at all events to some extent, observed; conclusions, orthodox in all respects, were to be arrived it. To do all this might very well have taken the youthful writer as many years as it actually took him months; and it cannot be surprising that the work, when done, was not regarded by him with satisfaction.

But now Newman was to be relieved from part of this strain of overwork. In the spring of 1826 he was appointed one of the four Public Tutors for Oriel. He looks forward with relief to the consequent relinquishment of his Vice-Principalship and of his curacy. "I have had," he says, "a continual wear on my mind, mislaying memoranda, forgetting names, &c." Now, all that was over, and he had leisure. But though he was absent from Whately, he was still to some extent Whatelyan. He sits down to write a sober view of his conversion and finds that there was nothing so very startling in it. "It was simply," he says, "a returning to principles under the power of the Holy Spirit, which he had already felt, and, in a measure, acted on when young." At the same time, in answer to his mother's birthday letter affectionately rejoicing over "a son who had ever been her greatest consolation in affliction and a constant delight at all times," he writes a line of tender warning. She had found in his sermons, she says, enlightenment, correction, support, and strength. "Do not be run away with," he replies, "by any opinion of mine. I have seen cause to change my mind in some respects, and I may change again."

Perhaps at this time he contemplated a Noetic goal for his theological course. Assuredly he had no thoughts, when taking tutorial work, of merging the minister in the scholar. In what spirit he undertook his new duty, his words show, written at the time : " Remembering that I am a minister of Christ, and have a commission to preach the Gospel, remembering the worth of souls, that I shall have to answer for the opportunities given me of benefiting those who are under my care." The undergraduates of those days, shepherdless, yet over-shepherded in name,—forced to subscribe the Thirty-Nine Articles in their youth and sometimes almost in their boyhood, as a preliminary to entering the University ; forced to attend spiritual teaching in which the use of "spigots by the Jews" might be the only information conveyed by a learned lecturer on the Gospel of St. John ; forced to attend the Holy Communion by Provosts and Vice-Provosts, who "did not want to know" that the sacred participation was closely followed by a riotous champagne breakfast—truly they needed "benefiting" under some one's care! All hearts must go with Newman in some of his protests against such abuses as these, and many will largely share his feeling that tutorial work in an Oxford college implied an aim at such a development of the character and the moral sense in his pupils as might fairly occupy a minister of the Gospel.

Newman was now on the point of making a new friend who would do more than any other human being—perhaps more than any other single external influence—to direct his course and to determine its final direction, " By the bye," says Newman to his mother, telling her of the election to the Oriel Fellowship, 31 March, 1826, " I have not told you the name of the other successful candidate—Froude of Oriel. We," *i.e.*, the Fellows of Oriel, " were in grave deliberation till near two this morning. . . . Froude is one of the acutest and clearest and deepest men in the memory of man." Clearly Froude had had not only Newman's vote but also his strenuous advocacy in that prolonged deliberation. And it was no bad preparation for the reception of Froude's influence into Newman's heart, that the latter should thus have favoured and befriended him. Of Froude, the time will soon come to speak more in detail. For the present, so much as this must suffice, that, in giving his vote, Newman could not have been swayed by any religious bias in favour of one whom, even as late as the winter of that year, he offended by asking whether he was not " a red-hot High Churchman." What took Newman, in Froude, was his originality and suggestiveness, his hatred of shams, his downright and aggressive earnestness, and perhaps, too, some glimpse of what was afterwards revealed in him—an anxious, ascetic, and almost superstitious aspiration after a medieval type of holiness.

Was it already Froude's influence—freshly impressed upon him—or was it an exalted sense of the new responsibilities of the Oriel tutorship, that made him write to his mother (29 April) in this high prophetic style ? " I have felt much that my engagements of late drive me from you, hindering my conversing with you, making me an exile, I may say, from those I so much love. But this life is no time for enjoyment but for labour ; and I have especially deferred ease and quiet for a future life, in devoting myself to the immediate service of God." Possibly it was neither of these things. Possibly it was simply that he had just sent off to the printer that famous Essay which had cost him so much fermenting of mind ; and now this restless worker was turning towards other labour. He was unwell, too ; and whenever he was unwell he was always forming vast plans. Accordingly, at this time (1 May) he tells his sister he is "about to undertake a great work perhaps."

The possible "great work" turns out to be nothing less than "the reading of the Fathers," about which his sister Jemima appropriately reminds him that Archbishop Usher took eighteen years in accomplishing it, beginning at the age of twenty. When Newman began it, and how long he took about it, we shall presently see. Meantime we note that at this point there vanish the last of the old dreams of missionary work. He now recognizes that his mission is in Oriel, and it is to be largely the mission of a theological student as well as that of a tutor. All his thoughts tend in this direction, for his family, as well as for himself. To his sister Harriett, anxious for "something to do," he sets the following task : " Make a summary of the doctrines conveyed in Christ's teaching, and then set down over against them what St. Paul added to them, what St. Peter, what St. John, and whether St. Paul differs from the other three in any points : whether of silence or omission, or whether they all have peculiar doctrines, &c. &c." Well might

E. T. Mozley—soon to be a pupil of Newman's and afterwards Harriett's husband—declare that no pupil could be with him for a quarter of an hour without having all his energies and faculties taxed to the uttermost. But this task set for his poor sister can, I think, only be explained by the fact that Newman must have been in one of his nervous fevers at the time. Just as when preaching, in appearance, to others, he was really often preaching to himself, so here, he seems to have been setting her one of the many tasks that he himself was longing to attempt, if only he had had the leisure. The same excitement, though much more calmly expressed, finds vent in a birthday poem (27 June) to Frank, who had just taken a double First.

" Frank," says Mrs. Newman to her eldest son, " is a piece of adamant. You are such a sensitive being." To the elder brother it seemed impossible that the now brilliant reputation and approved ability of the younger should not be placed at the direct disposal of the Church of England. Yet it is odd. For John Henry himself, until he failed in the Schools, had aimed at the Bar and not at the Church. But it was somewhat Newman's way to forget his own feelings when he had discarded them, and to make no allowance for them in others. He therefore assumes Frank's approaching ordination, reminding him that he himself was already " enrolled," and adding :—

> "and shortly thou
> Must buckle on the sword."

But there are no signs that any such intention had been formed by Frank, who tells us that for some time past he had felt a distrust of his brother's religious tendencies. He adds, " His affectionate verses to me

on my coming of age (June, 1826,) show that he expected me (by the force of sacred habit?) shortly to
take holy orders."

§ 19. *First Glimpse of Froude and the Via Media*

The Long Vacation of this year was one of the very
few in which Newman did not fall ill or originate a
great plan.   The reason was that he spent it with his
sister Harriett at a parsonage at Ulcombe, taking duty
for an old Oriel Fellow.   This began a close friendship
between him and the vicar, Rickards, a man of singular
goodness and kindliness ; redolent of a genial wisdom,
full of quiet humour ; prudent, but warm-hearted and
earnest for good causes ; learned in Anglican divinity,
but of still more judgment than learning ; and gifted
with a special insight into character.   Here Newman
was thoroughly happy.   He expanded.   He made the
poor people like him, and said things that stuck in
their minds.   " They were determined," writes Rickards,
" not to forget him, and they spoke of him as if they
were conscious he had done them good."   But " the
great work " was not yet commenced.   He tried learning Hebrew analytically ; he got as far as the end of
Genesis, far enough to see that he could never be a
scholar without understanding Chaldee, Syriac, and
Arabic ; and he resolved to make himself perfect in
the Pentateuch before proceeding further.   But there
is no evidence that he executed even this limited resolution ; and meanwhile " the Fathers " appear to have
remained unstudied.   All, or much of this, he relates
in a letter to Keble, the first of many.   At the end of
his visit, Newman pours out his heart in poetic sorrow
and passionate love for the scenes he is leaving.   It is

clear that there were times when he thought of Oxford as the poet Wordsworth did of Cambridge, that he was "not for that place" :—

> " I go where form has ne'er unbent
> The sameness of its sway ;
> Where iron rule, stern precedent,
> Mistreat the graceful day ;
> To pine as prisoner in his cell,
> And yet be thought to love it well."

On his return to the University some transient disgust at life in Oxford atmosphere (literal not metaphorical) expressed in a letter to his mother, contrasts with the tone of another letter written the same day to Rickards, in which he describes the new responsibilities likely to fall upon the Oriel tutors in consequence of the election of the Provost to the bishopric of Llandaff, and the departure of the Dean ; *"Nescio quo pacto,* my spirits, most happily, rise at the prospect of danger, trial, or any call upon me for unusual exertion ; and as I came outside the Southampton coach to Oxford, I felt as if I could have rooted up St. Mary's spire and knocked down the Radcliffe." Here we see the reserve of power in the strong will, beneath the fluctuation of the poetic temperament. A dangerous being, this, as a theologian in the Church of England, to be alone during Long Vacations, thinking to himself! The old Provost, Copleston, meeting him in the days when he was Junior Fellow, on a solitary walk, once saluted him with a gracious compliment as one who was "nunquam minus solus quam cum solus"; but there was more in this than a compliment. It was the mere truth. Newman was never alone. He always had his imaginations for company ; and, unless he had plenty to do of a distracting kind, there was no knowing whither his company might lead him.

For the present, however, he was not alone, and he had plenty of distractions. His pupils at Oriel, or some of them, finding a new coachman on the box, were trying, as Newman tells us, " to get the reins slack." He was more than a match for them ; but it took up all his energy, taming the tameable and chasing the absolutely untameable out of the college. Meanwhile, he was becoming intimate with Froude, whose rooms in Oriel were just above his own. There were walks, that Froude tells us of, in which the two talked a good deal together. Froude complains that he allowed himself to say to Newman more than he intended ; revealed too much ; suffered himself to be drawn into argument, and was puzzled. That they were not as yet of one mind is shown by Newman's remark, above quoted, about the " red-hot High Churchman " ; but, if the older beat the younger in argument, that would rather help than hinder the influence of the latter. Expert in logical fence, Newman could not help gaining victories which he disdained as soon as won ; but Froude was effective in protests, and all the more with one who, most vulnerable when victorious, had just achieved a dialectical triumph. His brother tells us that on one occasion John Henry challenged him to " a game of Sham Logic " ; " Of course, First Principles *cannot be proved;* therefore, in order to try what will come of it, we may assume anything. Let me, then, assume that the Pope is *our divinely-appointed leader* to Truth." To which Frank replied by suggesting that they might also, for a game, " Assume, as a First Principle, that the Grand Llama of Thibet is our

divinely-appointed teacher"; and nothing further
came of it. Some of his arguments with Froude
may have been, perhaps, like his battles with Frank,
"Sham Logic"; rather intended to feel the way towards, than actually to state, what might fairly be said
on this side or on that.

On 26 November Newman's pupils were off his
hands, engaged in the Schools, and he now had the
whole leisure of the Christmas vacation for the "great
work," the study of the Fathers. But though the
plan was still before him, his mind was now directed to
another project, in which we may perhaps already trace
the influence of his new friend. It appears that in the
previous autumn Rickards had asked Newman whether
he saw any useful application for the wide knowledge
which the former possessed of Anglican divinity. At
that time Newman had replied that he saw none.
But now he had become intimate with one who might
naturally suggest a different answer. Froude was
already a hater of Puritans. He knew, and was glad
to know, something about them ; because, he said, it
gave him a right to hate Milton, of whose fame he
"greedily desired to see a final demolisher." He was
also enthusiastic for the Anglican divines of the seventeenth century ; and though we do not know the extent
of his reading at the present time, it seems probable
that he, a high Tory of the Cavalier stamp, knew at
least much more of them than Newman did, and would
direct the thoughts of his elder friend towards them as
being the representatives of that "red-hot High-
Churchmanship" against which the latter was so ignor-
antly prejudiced. Accordingly, it is not surprising
that Newman took advantage of his first day of
freedom from college duties to write to Rickards the

following letter, in which he submits to him the first
sketch of the *Via Media* :—

"In our last conversation I think you asked me whether any use
had occurred to my mind to which your knowledge of our old
divines might be applied.   Now one has struck me—so I write. . . .
I begin by assuming that the old worthies of our Church are neither
Orthodox nor Evangelical, but intractable persons, suspicious
characters, neither one thing nor the other.   Now it would be a
most useful thing to give a kind of summary of their opinions.
Passages we see constantly quoted from them for this side and for
that ; but I do not desiderate the work of an advocate, but the result
of an investigation, not to bring them to us but to go to them.   If
then, in a calm, candid, impartial manner, their views were sought
out and developed, would not the effect be good in a variety of ways?
I would advise taking them *as a whole*—a *corpus theolog.* and
ecclesiast. ;—*the* English Church—stating, indeed, *how far* they differ
among themselves, yet distinctly marking out the grand, bold, scriptural features of that doctrine in which they all agree.   They would
then be a band of witnesses for the Truth, not opposed to each other
(as they now are) but *one*—each tending to the edification of the body
of Christ according to the effectual working of His Spirit in everyone
according to the diversity of their gifts, and the variety of circumstances under which each spake his testimony."

This plan of "taking *as a whole*" the Anglican
writers, and of finding in them "*the* English Church,"
is extremely characteristic of Newman, proceeding
from him, as it did, at a time when he knew extremely
little about them.   The reader can hardly fail to
see at once the immense and almost insuperable
obstacles.   It is easy to make a sentence about select-
ing "the grand, bold, scriptural features of that
doctrine in which they all agree" ; but, in practice,
who was to select ?   And then, who was to stamp the
selection with authority ?   Newman does not even
distinguish—as Froude probably had done, and as
Newman himself subsequently did — between the

divines of the sixteenth and those of the seventeenth
centuries.   To select, first the doctrine, and then "the
grand, bold, scriptural features" of it, implied what
some few might call a "discrimination," but what the
majority would be almost sure to call a "picking and
choosing," which would require the authority of nothing
less than a Church Council to give to such a compila-
tion any weight.   If we ask why the difficulty of the
project did not strike the suggester, the answer must
be that probably Newman regarded the scheme as so
essential to the Church of England, so useful (in other
words) to the cause of God, that it *must* be practicable.   He saw not one difficulty, but two ; the practical
difficulty of its succeeding, and the antecedent difficulty of its *not* succeeding.   The latter seemed the
greater.   He went by antecedent probabilities.

So far was he from being deterred by difficulties
that this was but one half of the plan which already he
seems to have marked out for himself, or for those
who would work with him.   Early in the spring he
had proposed to write about "the period between the
Apostolical Fathers and the Nicene Council, treated as
a whole, embracing the opinions of the Church, and
so much of Platonism and Gnosticism as may be necessary to elucidate it."   At that time he had not yet
begun the study of the Fathers, nor had he even
finished the Essay on Miracles, which was already six
months behind time.   Yet this piece of work he thought
he could accomplish for the Encyclopædia in two
years.   Combining in one view the work which he had
chosen for himself, and the scheme which he sketched
for his friend, we see that the one is the complement
of the other.   He was to draw out a scheme of the
"grand, bold, Scriptural doctrines" of the Primitive

Church; Rickards was to do the same for the Anglican divines; these two schemes were to be found to agree, at least so far as to allow of being harmoniously blended; and the resultant harmony was to lead to what all would recognize as "*the* English Church."

Rickards responds with his wonted geniality and discretion. He is "entertained" by the "magnificent" work with which his young friend designs that he should ennoble himself; but he does not agree that much can be done in these times through the weight of old authorities. He guesses—an ominous guess from one who really knew the Anglican divines—that "the material will be found too stubborn and discrepant to work well in the form in which you are naturally so desirous to see them. My impression is that our old writers are excellent men to keep company with if you wish to strengthen your powers by conversing with great and original thinkers; they will help you greatly to form a solid judgment for yourself. . . . We shall employ them to the most purpose by keeping them constantly in our sight and out of other people's."

It is tempting to speculate on what might have been the results, for Newman and for the Anglican Church, if he had spent the next six vacations at Ulcombe in the society of so prudent an adviser.

§ 20. *End of the Liberal Phase*

The year now opening (1827) will carry away with it the last remnant of Newman's Liberalism. It was perhaps the least eventful in his Anglican career. He is absorbed partly in college work and in chasing refractory men out of Oriel, partly in preparing for the work of an Examiner in the Schools. So busy is he that he laughs to scorn the very notion of having time to think about the great political question which was at this time distracting England. A certain Mr. W. had questioned his sister Harriett as to her brother's opinions on the "Catholic Relief Bill." He replies as follows : "As to Mr. W.'s absurd question about my opinion on the Catholic question, tell him that I am old enough to see that I am not old enough to know anything about it. It seems to me a question of history." A cautious answer! Yet if the great mass of educated Englishmen were content to give such answers it would be difficult to see the value of representative government. "If it were a religious question," he continues, "I might think it necessary to form a judgment ; as it is not, it would be waste of time." Justice, apparently, did not seem to him to enter into the question. He treats it as a matter that no more concerned him than a point of Greek or of Roman antiquity could concern a man unlearned in those subjects. "What would be thought of a man giving an opinion about the propriety of this or that agrarian law in Rome who was unacquainted with Roman history ? At the same time I must express my belief that NOTHING will satisfy the Roman Catholics. If this be granted, unquestionably, they will ask more."

In the summer of this year there had appeared Keble's *Christian Year*. It took Newman at once, but time was needed before its full influence on him could be manifested ; and, just now, he had no time. The first mention of the book is followed by details of college business relating to the dissipated men whom he was hunting out of Oriel. "Talking of hermits

puts me in mind of Keble's Hymns which are just out,
I have merely looked into them. They seem quite
exquisite. . . . We are having rows as thick as black-
berries."

In the vacation a second pleasant visit was paid to
Rickards at Ulcombe. R. Wilberforce was there too ;
and there was plenty of interesting talking and some
reading about various things ; including Keble's new
volume. But meantime he was neglecting to prepare
for his work as an examiner, and he began to have
forebodings about it : "What the Schools will say I
know not." Once more the fascinations of the country
were strong upon him ; but he is stronger. Longing
for the fresh and genial pleasures of village life and
shrinking from "man's haunts," he consoles himself
with a sense of a divine mission. In such a mood, no
wonder that the thought of the Schools and examinations repels him. Toward the end of his visit, the
charms of Ulcombe elicit from him a second burst of
poetry. In some lines written "for a flower-book," he
compares himself to the snap-dragon which he had seen
growing on the wall near his old rooms in Trinity.
He too, like that flower, was rooted in the wall,
"cas'd in mortar, cramp'd with lead ;" but he was
resigned to his fate.

> "Be it mine to set restraint
> On roving wish and selfish plaint ;
> And for man's drear haunts to leave
> Dewy morn and balmy eve.
>
> Mine the Unseen to display
> In the crowded public way,
> Where life's busy arts combine
> To shut out the Hand Divine."

At the close, he suddenly imagines the "breath of

Heaven" to give the scentless flower a fragrance not its own.

> "May it be! then well might I
> In college cloister live and die."

A few days afterwards, he moralizes again in poetry to the same strain. What though from the courts of the college the changes of Nature are banished and all discrimination of season is taken away? What though in Oriel "long days are fire-side nights, brown autumn is fresh spring"? His heart is fixed on the unchangeable, and he can antedate "heaven's age of fearless rest." Of all Newman's poems this perhaps is the one that most closely approaches the philosophic cheerfulness of " the just and firm-purpos'd man " in Horace: and he takes as his motto the well-known lines in which Virgil describes the triumph of philosophy over superstition :—

> " Felix, qui potuit rerum cognoscere causas,
> Atque metus omnes, et inexorabile fatum
> Subjecit pedibus, strepitumque Acherontis avari."

Term time recalled him to the long-neglected labour of preparing for the approaching examination in the Schools. For this duty he had been set at liberty from lectures by his colleagues. But the Schools were not destined to see him any more prosperous when examining than when examined. Perhaps it was now impossible to make up for the time lost during the Vacation ; perhaps the domestic anxieties of his mother (which as usual fell on him) may have worried and distracted him ; perhaps Frank's tendencies at this time to Nonconformity added to his troubles ; perhaps, with his acutely sensitive nature, he found it trying to

play an authoritative part for which he was conscious
that he was not adequately prepared, upon the scene
of his well-remembered failure as an undergraduate.
He completely broke down. He was seized by a
fainting fit in the Schools, while examining, was leeched
on the temples, and carried off as soon as possible by
a friend to consult a physician in London. From
town he writes to his mother that he has been at
Wilberforce's for some days finding himself tired with
his Oxford work ; that he is now quite recruited ; and
that, as he is so dutiful as to tell her all this at the risk
of her thinking him unwell, it will be a great shame if
his candour induces her to persist in thinking so. A
few days after this, Newman gave, perhaps, the last
proof of his being still under the influence of the
Noetics by supporting Hawkins against Keble for the
election to the Provostship. In answer to the protests
of Froude, Keble's former pupil, he said with a laugh
that if they had been electing an angel he would have
voted for Keble ; but it was only a Provost. He did
not believe that Keble could manage men, whereas,
about Hawkins he had no doubt. The interests of
the college just then demanded a specially strong and
firm Provost. Yet, five years afterwards, Newman
would probably have thought the interests of
religion paramount, or that the college itself required,
above all things, a Provost "of right principles."
But now we find him telling Keble that he also
agreed with Hawkins in his religious opinions and
habits of thinking, and that, although he did not
know Keble intimately, he suspected that he should
find that the latter did not approve opinions, objects,
and measures to which his own turn of mind has led
him to assent. Pusey followed Newman's lead, and

Keble withdrew. Next January saw Hawkins in Copleston's place, as the new Provost.

Anglicans and Romanists might speculate ingeniously and oppositely as to what might have happened had matters gone otherwise. Detached from the influences of action and reaction among poor and simple people, confirmed in celibacy, brought under Newman's strong, direct, and constant influence—which even at a distance was almost too powerful for Keble's Anglicanism, and, but for Keble's wife, would probably have been altogether too powerful when the crisis came—cut off from Nature, and cast upon the society of books and controversies, might not Keble have found himself so inseparable from Newman, that, in the issue, the two friends might have jointly composed the *Apologia*? On the other hand, if Keble had been elected, Hawkins would have remained Vicar of St. Mary's instead of vacating the post for Newman; Newman would have remained tutor of Oriel, throwing the best part of his life into college work, until he at last took a college living, where he would have thought out his problems quietly, trained the choir, taken an interest in the school, made poor people like him, perhaps married—and then there would have been no *Apologia* at all.

Passing speculations of this sort must not divert us from the significance of the close of this year. It leaves Newman, suffering under mental and physical prostration, and on the point of taking (in the election of the Provost) a last step towards a school of thought that was wholly alien from his inmost nature—a step of which he was soon destined to repent. Thus, though his motion was in one direction, his will was preparing to move him in another; and nothing was needed but a strong and sudden impulse of the heart to turn him irrevocably back from the alliance he had begun to form with intellectualism, towards new thoughts, new friendships, and new projects, that would soon place a great gulf between him and the Noetic School.

CHAPTER V

§ 21. *The Last Vestige of " Thankfulness "*

NEWMAN was ordained in 1824 and was supposed to be an Evangelical up to 1828 or longer. The reader may therefore naturally expect to find in his earlier sermons some traces of his Evangelical belief if not of his transient phase of Liberalism. But scarcely any of these are published, and among them, none of those (presumably Evangelical) which his mother specially commended. It is reasonable to infer that such of this period as are extant owe their publication to the fact that they were in harmony with the preacher's later thoughts. Nevertheless these early sermons are of great interest negatively as well as positively ; they show what in earlier days he omitted or subordinated as compared with his later doctrine ; and yet, running through the later and the earlier there is seen a thread of continuous thought.

In this period, while the Church is scarcely mentioned, the preacher lays his main stress, now as afterwards, on the great business of each man's life, the salvation of his own soul, the obstacles in the way, and the means of overcoming them. " Man goeth forth to his work and unto his labour till the evening "—this was the

text of his first (unpublished) sermon ; and a later one
on the same subject enables us to supply the outline of
his treatment of it.   "We see where we shall stop in
the evening," he tells us, "though we do not see the
road :" the "evening" is death ; the "work" is our
salvation ; this is to be each man's business till the
night cometh when no man can work.   From first to
last this remains *the* subject of Newman's Anglican
discourses.   There are subordinate questions variously
put and answered ; as to the means ; the certainty, or
uncertainty ; the time of accomplishment ; and, above
all, the test by which our prospects of safety may be
ascertained ; but, in some aspect or other, this is the
thought ever before the preacher—"that great work
in which all others are included, which will outlive all
other works, and for which alone we really are placed
here below—the salvation of our souls."

   "Salvation" may mean different things.   It may
mean a state of harmony and communion with the
Eternal Righteousness whom Christians call their
Father ; or it may mean deliverance from the penalties
and punishments attached by the Supreme Judge to
the violation of His Laws.   The latter aspect is predominant with Newman from the first.   He takes a
clear, definite and business-like view of the matter.
A certain absolutely priceless result is the object of
life.   Then what are the means for attaining this
object ?   That is the only question.   Let the means
be but made known and he will devote all his energies
to their employment ; what else in life is worth living
for ?   Such was his plain, sincere, and consistent view
of religion.   Other men *say* this, but he *acted on* it.
And it is this, in part, that gives to his sermons their
intense reality.   What most talk of, he sees and almost

makes you see. The following is from a sermon of
January 1832 :—

"Who is there but would be sobered by an actual sight of the
flames of hell-fire and the souls therein hopelessly enclosed? Would
not all his thoughts be drawn to that awful sight, so that he
would stand still gazing fixedly upon it, and forgetting everything
else ; seeing nothing else, hearing nothing else, engrossed with the
contemplation of it ; and, when the sight was withdrawn, still having
it fixed in his memory, so that he would be henceforth dead to the
pleasures and employments of this world, for their own sake, thinking
of them only in their reference to that fearful vision? . . . Yet to
this state of mind, and therefore to this true knowledge, the multitude
of men called Christians are certainly strangers ; a thick veil is drawn
over their eyes, and (in spite of their being able to talk of the
doctrine) they are as if they never heard of it."

"Thinking of" the "pleasures and employments of
this world only in their reference to that fearful vision"
—yes, this is "the state of mind" to which Newman
himself is no "stranger," and to which he strives to
habituate his hearers. But others have striven to do
this without much effect. One cause of Newman's
success—besides his graphic power—is that he sets
forth horrors with such an absence of excitement
that you might think you were listening to your
physician or legal adviser giving you a plain statement
of facts. You seem to hear him say, " I know you do
not like this. Neither do I. But can we deny that
it is fact ? And, if it is, why not look facts in the face?
Be like men. Do not talk, nor suppose you can alter
your doom by talking. Act ; and if you are willing to
act, I can at least tell you what to do under the circumstances. He does not often mention the *word*
hell. It is, for the most part, " too shocking to speak
of," or " too shocking even to think of" ; or, "fortunately" he is "not called upon to consider," or, he

"cannot venture to speak of," the consequences of such-and-such a course. But the horror, though unmentioned, is always there, and often more horrible for being kept in the back-ground.

Hostility to "the world"—or, at least, watchfulness against it—is another doctrine which Newman consistently preserves. "The world" may mean many distinct things, and Newman does not, on special occasions, ignore these distinctions. But, as a rule, and in his more natural mood, he teaches us that, though angels may learn something of the Creator from the order and harmony of the material Universe, man can learn *nothing*—nothing at least that is to the purpose, nothing that can avail him for the one important object, the salvation of the soul. The "good things of this world"—which are commonly called "blessings"—are, he admits, gifts of God. But so is wine. And, just as an invalid must abstain from wine, so it is to be with us as regards these "blessings"; our minds are weak and diseased, "so that we may be well content to be without them."

In his earliest extant sermon (23 January, 1825) he does go so far as to make mention of the word "gratitude" in connection with this world's gifts: "use them, as far as given, with gratitude for what is really good in them, and with a desire to promote God's glory by them; but do not go out of the way to seek them. They will not, on the whole, make you happier, and they may make you less religious." But this connection is not reproduced, so far as I remember —at all events, in the sermons of the next eight years. Indeed, in subsequent sermons he recedes from this position, and regards the pleasant things of this world as intended, not to make us thankful, but to "try" us.

In two other passages this sermon exhibits differences from all that follow for many years :—

"We shall be led habitually to pray that upon every Christian may descend, in rich abundance, not merely worldly goods, but that heavenly grace which alone can turn this world to good account for us and make it the path of peace and of life everlasting."

And again :

"For us indeed, who are all the adopted children of God our Saviour, what addition is wanting to complete our happiness? What can increase their peace who believe and trust in the Son of God? Shall we add a drop to the ocean, or grains to the sand of the sea? Shall we ask for an earthly inheritance, who have the fulness of a heavenly one ; power, when in prayer we can use the power of Christ : or wisdom, guided as we may be by the true Wisdom and the Light of men ?"

We may search in vain to find other such utterances as these in the later Anglican sermons. The sense of the profitlessness of the world does not diminish ; it increases. But the sense that he and those whom he was addressing could "all" be called "the adopted children of God" distinctly diminishes ; and, though "faith" becomes prominent, there is very little mention of "trust." God and Christ are regarded as parts of a system ; and "faith" means acceptance of that system. The preacher's studies and experiences will lead him to lay more and more stress upon the dangers of self-deception, and upon the need of the use of definite means for the all-important end ; and the questions, "What must we do to be saved?" and "How shall we know that we are in the way of salvation?" will leave him no time, no energy, and perhaps no desire, to repeat often such phrases of mere comfort. Nor will he publicly speak much about prayers for

" every Christian." Much more often, and more clearly, will he teach them that *not* all will be saved ; that it is only " the few who will be chosen " ; and that therefore it is the destiny of " the many," and indeed of all, to fear till their life's end.

§ 22. *" Self-Knowledge " the " root " of Religion*

Between the date (January, 1825) of the last quoted and that (June, 1825) of the following sermon, Newman was ordained Priest. His parochial experiences had begun to show him that some of his parishioners who seemed to have no right to the feelings of " conversion," nevertheless had them, or spoke as if they had them, and as if their feelings were everything and their actions nothing. One such case, at least, was at this time * coming under his constant notice.

Against such a violation of the rules of morality, Newman's heart and mind rose up in protest. Without actually breaking with the Evangelical doctrine of salvation by faith, he insists on the difficulty of salvation, and on the danger of finding that what we *call* faith has not been faith after all. " Self-knowledge " (he now preaches) is the root of all real religious knowledge ; and, in proportion as we search our hearts, we shall understand what is meant by an infinite Governor and Judge. God speaks to us primarily in our hearts. To know ourselves is the key to the precepts and doctrines of Scripture.

He does not mean that by studying ourselves we learn to know what is good in God, but that we learn to know the evil in ourselves, our alienation from Him, our need of His forgiveness ; and this is, of course, true. But it is very doubtful how far we can usefully learn much about ourselves without simultaneously thinking a good deal about others. Otherwise, we are soon drawn into a vortex of self-questionings. We want to know that we are sincere. How are we to know that? By doing this or that? But if we do this or that from the mere desire to gain heaven or escape hell, are we sincere except in being mercenary? The right course seems to be to give up such questions altogether, or rather to keep out of them by being interested in other things outside and above ourselves. But Newman, at this stage of his teaching, thinks it enough to bid his hearers compare Christ's precepts, or St. Paul's, or any other Apostle's, with their own daily conduct, and endeavour to act upon them. He points out how much we are the servants of our own habits, or of the customs of the age ; how many things there are that blind us to our faults ; and he protests that, even though a man may persevere in prayer and watchfulness to the day of his death, he will never get to the bottom of his heart. The ordinary, good-tempered Christian, he warns us, is in a dream ; and even to the true servants of Christ the prospect of the Judgment is awful :

"Then will the good man undergo the full sight of his sins which on earth he was labouring to obtain, and partly succeeded in obtaining, though life was not long enough to learn and subdue them all. Doubtless we must all endure that fierce and terrifying vision of our real selves, that last fiery trial of the soul before its acceptance, a spiritual agony and second death to all who are not then supported by the strength of Him who died to bring them safe through it, and in whom on earth they have believed."

The sermon concludes with an encouragement and a warning ; and other motives—besides the "fire"— are not altogether ignored :

" Many things are against us ; this is plain.   Yet is not our future
prize worth a struggle ?   Is it not worth present discomfort and pain
to accomplish escape from the fire that never shall be quenched ?
Can we endure the thoughts of going down to the grave with a load
of sins on our head unknown and unrepented of ?   Can we content
ourselves with such an unreal faith in Christ as excludes due self-
abasement or thankfulness, or the desire or effort to be holy ? . . .
Without self-knowledge you have no root in yourselves personally ;
you may endure for a time, but under affliction or persecution your
faith will not last. . . . To think of these things and to be alarmed
is the first step towards acceptable obedience ; to be at ease is to be
unsafe. We must know what the evil of sin is, hereafter, if we do not
learn it here. God give us all grace to choose the pain of present
repentance before † the wrath to come ! "

This and many other passages in the sermons, early
and late, reveal Newman's profound horror of sin.   In
his first University Sermon (July 1826), while identi-
fying, in many respects, " the philosophical" with the
Christian "temper," he lays a just stress on this difference, that whereas " the philosopher confesses himself
to be imperfect, the Christian feels himself to be sinful
and corrupt."   There would be no fault to find with
this if Newman consistently identified sin with that
"greediness" which, as St. Paul says, is essential idola-
try and aversion from God.   But he does not do this.
He takes various views of it, mostly arbitrary.   They
tend to make a weak mind horribly afraid ; but they
do not tell him what to be afraid of—not, at least, in
such a way as to commend the doctrine to the enlightened conscience.   Sometimes he regards sin as a
disease of the soul incurring the wrath of God, sometimes as a living thing, a beast of prey panting or
purring over its victim, sometimes as a foul monster
with flapping wings, restlessly beating against the bars
that for a time keep it from the human soul.   Such

passages are the more impressive because he never disguises his belief—forced on him, as he thinks, by the Scriptures—that, although the victory is to rest, somehow, with God and not with Satan, yet the majority of the human race are to fall for ever into the clutches of the Devourer.

§ 23. *Wandering from Evangelicalism*

Towards the end of the year 1825, in his Sermon on the "Inward Witness to the Truth of the Gospel," Newman is still occupied with the question of the means of attaining religious knowledge. Repelled by the case of sudden "conversion" just mentioned, he is now emboldened to say more distinctly that it is by *doing* we know : "When I see a person hasty and violent, harsh and high-minded, careless of what others feel, and disdainful of what they think—when I see such a one proceeding to enquire into religious subjects, I am sure beforehand he cannot go right." Here we have the germ of what might develop into a valuable truth or a pernicious falsehood, according to the sense attached to "religious subjects." If the phrase means the moral truths of Christianity and the revelation of the attributes of God, it is a valuable truth ; but the case is quite different if it means the details of historical narratives contained in the Scriptures and our inferences from these. Yet the doctrine might evidently be applied to these, even if it is not intended to be so applied in the following passage :—

"Do but examine your thoughts and doings ; do but attempt what you know to be God's will, and you will most assuredly be led on into all the truth, you will recognize the force, meaning, and awful graciousness of the Gospel Creed ; you will bear witness to the truth of one doctrine by your own past experience of yourselves; of another by seeing that it is suited to your necessity; of a third, by finding it fulfilled upon your obeying it."

During 1826, the year in which he was most under Whately's influence, inclining towards Liberalism, and working at high pressure, he was too busy to preach much. The single sermon of this period, preached in August 1826 (probably at Ulcombe) is entitled " Holiness Necessary for Future Blessedness." It is in large measure an attempt to show the reasonable necessity of the Christian scheme of salvation; and a protest that " blessedness " can no more follow where holiness has not preceded, than an effect can occur without a cause. He does not, in his first edition, define "holiness," but in later years he added a definition— " inward separation from the world "; and this negative idea pervades the whole of this, as every other, sermon. Taking the word in this meaning, he proceeds to show how a man who is not " holy " cannot hope for heaven, for heaven would be no heaven to him. " Heaven," he says, " is *not* like this world. I will say what it is much more like—a church."

Might it not be maintained that Heaven is more like a family? But perhaps Newman relied on a literal interpretation of the Apocalypse. Yet surely it might be urged that the " harps " and " songs " mentioned in that book can have no significance except so far as they express that kind of feeling which keeps families together. However, the passage is worth quoting as a sample of his incisive rhetoric, so careful to seem moderate; so mercilessly, though calmly, coercive in its apparent logic; entering the precincts of the thoughts so quietly and moving on so irresistibly till it plunges into the heart its point, tipped perhaps with some adamant of Scriptural allusion, leaving the reader (and how much more the hearer ?) smitten if not into assent at least into silence—until he has leisure to reflect that the proffered solution of one problem has raised others still more difficult :

" Nay, I will venture to say more than this ; it is fearful, but it is right to say it ;—that if we wished to imagine a punishment for an unholy, reprobate soul, we perhaps could not fancy a greater than to *summon it to heaven*. Heaven would be hell to an irreligious man. We know how unhappy we are apt to feel at present, when alone in the midst of strangers, or of men of different tastes and habits from ourselves. How miserable, *e.g.* would it be, to have to live in a foreign land, among a people whose faces we never saw before, and whose language we could not learn. And this is but a faint illustration of the loneliness of a man of unholy dispositions and tastes, thrust into the society of saints and angels. How forlorn would he wander through the courts of heaven ! He would find no one like himself ; he would see in every direction the marks of God's holiness, and these would make him shudder. He would feel himself always in His presence. He could no longer turn his thoughts another way, as he does now when conscience reproaches him. He would know that the Eternal Eye was ever upon him ; and that Eye of holiness, which is joy and life to holy creatures, would seem to him an Eye of wrath and punishment. God cannot change His nature. Holy He must ever be. But while He is holy, no unholy soul can be happy in heaven. Fire does not inflame iron, but it inflames straw. It would cease to be fire if it did not. And so heaven itself would be fire to those who would fain escape across the great gulf from the torments of hell. The finger of Lazarus would but increase their thirst. The very ' heaven that is over their head ' will be ' brass ' to him."

This sermon definitely severs Newman from the Evangelical school, for he now denies the general efficacy of a sudden " conversion " to secure salvation :

" It is plain then that, even with the influences of grace, no one is able to prepare himself for heaven, *i.e.*, to make himself holy, in a short time. Yet, alas! as there are persons who think to be saved by a few scanty performances, so there are others who suppose they may be saved all at once by a sudden and easily acquired faith."

In the main, this doctrine accords with Newman's later teaching, except that it is stated with less sombreness here—a fact that is curiously illustrated by one or two touches of gloom added in the later edition.*

These specimens of Newman's earliest preaching show both how, and why, he was breaking with Evangelicalism. It gave him no definite answer at all —it offered nothing but a vague subjective test—in answer to the question of questions, "How shall I be saved?" We have seen above that he referred such questioners to the Scriptures; men were to obey the precepts of Christ and the Apostles, and they would be safe. But, in the face of the immense variety of Scriptural interpretations, the impossibility of perfect obedience, and the difficulty of discriminating shades of imperfection, this was but a half-way refuge which could not long suffice. And this he was already feeling. He had already had experience of the manner in which some of his parishioners interpreted Scripture. Was each one, learned or unlearned, moral or immoral, to interpret Scripture for himself? What absurdities, what hypocrisies, what gross violations of morality, might not find shelter under such a system of private judgment! But if they were not to do this for themselves, was he to do it for them? That could not be. He himself was conscious of having been misled in the past, and of needing guidance for the future. The sermons show us that until he had secured such guidance and obtained at least an approximate solution of the Problem of Problems, he would not, and could not, take rest. In this perplexity, was it not natural that he should determine at least to ascertain whether there was not some stream of concordant and traditional interpretation of Scripture, handed down by the Primitive Church, from which he might obtain the teaching that he needed for himself and for others? After all, the great thing was sincerity, and, whatever the Primitive Church might not be, it was sure to be, at least, sincere.

CHAPTER VI

§ 24. *The Three Friends*

"GOD intends me to be lonely," so Newman wrote in later years, when he was sorrowing for his mother's death, and partly also, perhaps, for a certain estrangement that had separated him from her at the last. He often recognizes himself as an essentially solitary being. Such friends as came to him, if they came, came, he says, "unasked." He welcomed them as God's gifts,—sometimes, may be, looked on them a little too much as God's instruments,—but, if they strayed from what he deemed the path of duty, he could set his face as a rock against them, and finally, if they would not return, could wipe them out of his thoughts so as to leave scarcely a trace of the old love behind.

Such a man could not be, to any great extent, directly influenced by friends. Direct influence would find him prepared to resist it, or at least to argue about it, and to show cause why he should not admit it. Thus, it would pass into him, if at all, through the intellect, where it would merely touch the surface of the motive power within him. Influence on him, to be effective, must be indirect. To get at Newman, a friend had to appeal to him through the imagination ;

sometimes suddenly beating up his guard of logic by some means superior to all logic; but more often taking him off his guard, and quietly putting before him some unobtrusive suggestion, which would be at first hastily repelled, then recalled and reconsidered; presently welcomed; finally cherished and adopted. Still, we may learn much from a brief study of Newman's chief friends. Even if they had done nothing to change him, they might show us how he changed *them*, and help us better to understand the secret of his power over others. Besides, it is not easy to follow the history of Newman's development without some acquaintance with the lives and characters of his principal co-operators. To obtain this we shall have to deviate from our chronological order. But it will save space and conduce to clearness in the end; and indeed one of the friends whom we shall have before us, did actually, though indirectly, influence Newman's action at so many points in his career, that, if we omitted a sketch of him here, we should have to be constantly digressing for explanations afterwards. The three friends are Edward Pusey, John Keble, and—as a climax in respect of influence—Richard Hurrell Froude.

§ 25. *Pusey*

It seems, at first sight, one of the instances of the irony of Fame that Pusey should have been destined to give his name to the Tractarian Movement, although he did not originate it, took but little part in its early progress, and exercised but very little influence on the real leader. He was a few months older than Newman, though the junior of the latter in College standing. When the Tractarian Movement was on foot he was a Regius Professor of Divinity, a Canon of Christ Church and on easy terms with the University authorities ; known widely as a man of munificent charity and influential family connections ; and revered by all who knew him well for the height and purity of his character. These things had forced him before the world, while harder workers in the Movement remained in the background. Another accidental circumstance brought him publicity. Disliking anonymousness, he insisted on adding his well-known initials to such of the Tracts as he contributed.* This slight incident, together with the causes above mentioned, induced the public to select his name and not Newman's, as the means of satisfying the common craving for some new title to designate a new phenomenon ; and hence a member of the Tractarian Party became known not as a " Newmanian," but as a " Puseyite."

Yet the name was not wholly misplaced, for it was Pusey who first gave weight, and afterwards permanence, to the Movement. He was a man of learning, and (at a certain period at all events) recognized the teaching of history. To him the Movement owed the valuable Library of the Fathers, which in itself would claim our gratitude. Agreeing with Newman largely in point of doctrine, he disagreed from him in his historical views ; and although to Newman these appeared to present a frail barrier against the claims of the Roman Church, they sufficed for Pusey. Habitually sanguine, he had a strong belief in the past and future of the English Church, and being, at that time, a man of broad views and full of spiritual life and confidence, he was ready at all times to expand into good works and useful projects. He it was who suggested the establishment of Sisters of Mercy and other institutions in connection with the English Church. As to these, Newman could only mournfully say that if the spirit in the Church was sound, these would follow; but he felt himself unable to take action. But to Pusey the "if" did not present itself. Perhaps he had a keener sense than Newman had of the variety of ways and means by which Providence may teach its lessons to various ages and nations. Certainly he had not so keen a sense as Newman had of logical sequences and incompatibilities. His clearness of head seems to have been by no means equal to his goodness of heart. He felt able (in 1839) to include in his good-will even those Anglicans·who found their ideal in the sixteenth, and not in the seventeenth, century; so that, for example, he was quite ready to subscribe to a Cranmer memorial, and was amazed that Newman would not do so. He was disgusted and annoyed at the abuse levelled by some of the advanced Tractarians against the Reformers; he did not agree with Newman in calling Lutheranism heresy: nay, he would even (so Newman complains) have gone so far as to allow the use of the term "Protestant" as applied to the English Church, if he had not been checked in time. Taking all these facts together, we may perhaps feel that Fame, or popular instinct, or whatever else it may be called, was not so very wrong in giving the name of "Puseyites" to those who were really and honestly aiming at a Middle Course in the Church of England, without any covert inten-tion of ultimately reaching Rome. One special point that attracted Pusey in the *Via Media* was its "stationariness." To Newman, looking back, this was a matter of amazement. All the more reason—if the *Via Media* was to become stationary and to take root in the National Church—that it should be called by the name not of its actual, but of its adoptive, parent.

We have seen that Newman had been intimate with Pusey since 1823: and in 1834, when dedicating to him his first volume of sermons, he affectionately acknowledges the blessings of his long friendship and example. Why then did he say that from 1823 to 1826 he had, on the whole, no friend to whom he "could open his mind"? Why was it that, in after days, Pusey was so completely left in the dark about Newman's thoughts that even the younger Tractarians, such as Church and Rogers, were a little scandalized, and ventured to remonstrate?

The difference in temperament between the two may well have been one obstacle to unrestrained confidence. The one, so indomitably hopeful, so supremely confident, so free from intellectual perplexities—how could he fully sympathize with, or even quite understand, the weary spiritual solitude, the endless, restless, self-introspective doubts and worryings of the other? And the very fact that Pusey could *not* understand, and looked puzzled perhaps and disturbed when his friend made some half-confidence, would needs cause the latter to draw back and leave the essential thing unsaid. This, Newman himself tells us, was sometimes the case ; and Pusey's health was too often a good reason for not pressing troublesome confidences upon him. Again, regard for himself might also make Newman silent. It is not pleasant to reveal one's thoughts to a friend whom one loves and respects, but who is totally unable to understand them ; it gives one a painful suspicion of one's own insight into one's own thoughts, and makes one ask, "Can I really mean what I say when even my best friend does not under-

stand me ?"   Newman was wont to call Pusey " The
Great," and he seems to have been great in learning ;
still greater in simple devotion to what is good ; great
too, at that time, in width of sympathies.   To bring
• before such a man some thought that might suggest,
in some shape or other, *the little*—some petty doubt,
some over-nice scruple, some resolution or hesitation
as to some small asceticism, something that savoured
in any way of the subtle, the tortuous, the too indirect,
and to find his hinted disclosures so misunderstood
that he must either draw back in silence or blurt them
out with a brutal plainness that did no justice to the
fine shades of his meaning ; this might well, of itself,
have weighed for something in determining Newman
rather to go upstairs to Froude, or else to write to
Keble, instead of going to consult Pusey, who was
married and lived out of college.

Marriage, in itself, was of course, some impediment
too.   "We were not together" says the *Apologia*,
"under the same roof, we only saw each other at set
times; others indeed, who were coming in or out of
my rooms freely, and according to the need of the
moment, knew all my thoughts easily ; but for him to
know them well, formal efforts were necessary."   But
this would not explain the absence of confidential
intimacy in their earliest years of friendship while
Pusey was still unmarried and in Oriel.   Ill health
and absence abroad may in part account for it,
but some degree of mental separation must of necessity have existed on a point on which little might
be said but much felt.   Since 1817 Newman had felt
himself under some kind of religious call to celibacy :
since 1818 Pusey had been deeply in love with the
lady who was afterwards to become his wife.   Here,

then, was a whole province of thought and feeling which Newman and Froude could share in common, —strengthening one another in their informal vows— but from which Pusey would be quite shut out.

" May I lead him forward, at the same time gaining good from him," is the entry made by Newman on his first perception of the depth of Pusey's religious feeling.   That he gained from so good a man, whom he loved and respected to the last, is hardly more certain than that he "led him on."   Pusey had studied theology in Germany, and in 1828 he dedicated to his former teacher Lloyd (then Bishop of Oxford) a defence of German theology against the strictures of H. J. Rose in his Cambridge University Sermons.   In this he speaks of the " stiffness " and intolerable "orthodoxism" of his opponent's doctrine, welcomes Kant and Schelling; treats Lessing as " probably more Christian" despite his scepticism, than his orthodox opponent Göze, and as, "perhaps rightly, preferring Pantheism to the then existing systems."   In the change from this position we can see nothing in which he seems to have led Newman, but much in which Newman may have led him. This the *Apologia* confirms.   It tells us that Pusey so often took up and threw himself into what Newman said, that the latter felt the great responsibility he would incur if he put things before him just as he might view them himself.

§ 26. *Pusey " had no idea of Economy "*

But into one doctrine of Newman's Pusey did not —at all events during the period we are considering— ever " throw himself."   The former had revived or

Anglicized a term used by some of the Alexandrine Fathers to denote the gradualness of the divine revelation :—its progressive stages, implying rudimentary lessons at first, and advanced lessons afterwards, and consequently implying (since the Teacher was supposed to be all-knowing) reserves or suppressions of unfit truth and adaptations to particular classes of learners. Resorting to the metaphor of a steward or " *oeconomos*," in a large household (who does not waste his stores but metes out his rations with a wise frugality for their several purposes) these Fathers called such a system of teaching an " economy "; and the word was brought into use by Newman early in the Tractarian Movement.

To suppress a part of the truths he knows, is, of course, one of the first duties of a teacher ; and yet there is an ugly sound in the phrase, even when Latinized as a *suppressio veri*. The practice as well as the name, may be variously applied ; and how variously it was applied in the course of the controversy that is to be described may perhaps appear in future pages. Meantime we have to note the great difference in this respect between Pusey and Newman. The former altogether, at this time, abhorred suppression of facts in every shape. From St. Mary's pulpit, exhorting the undergraduates against luxury, he once let drop an audible though perhaps unconscious remark, that it might also be well if the older members of the University led simpler lives ; and as we have seen, he carried his liking for plain methods so far that he objected to the anonymousness of the Tracts. The latter had a distinct preference for indirect methods of acting and utterance. Pusey (said James Mozley) had " no idea of economy;"

Newman had to hear even from his chosen companions repeated protests against a habit so inveterate with him that one of them declared that he sometimes economized "just to keep his hand in."

Mutual respect united the two friends to the last ; but there are clear tokens that Newman never for a moment anticipated that Pusey would join him in his secession to Rome. When the world was put out of breath by Tract 90 Pusey loyally supported the author under the storm of popular reproach ; but he was annoyed by it, as well as by the results, which, he said, would leave on common people the impression of " Jesuitism" in the party as a whole. And against the advanced Tractarians who claimed to remain within the Anglican pale and yet to hold "*the whole cycle of Roman doctrine*," he did not spare strong and weighty rebuke. Great must have been his surprise when one of these replied that they had Newman's authority and that they were but giving clearer expression to Newman's words ; greater still when, on his questioning Newman himself as to whether he was entirely with this Romanizing section, the reply came back from the latter, " I do not know the limits of my own opinions." The leader of the advanced party, W. G. Ward, after his friend Oakeley had suffered from one of these rebukes, protested to Pusey that Oakeley was so deeply pained that he could never again ask his advice or sympathy when beset by public troubles. What Newman's followers felt so painfully, after experiencing it, Newman himself may perhaps have foreseen, without experiencing it, with a keenness of anticipation that prevented him from putting himself in the same position by consulting Pusey. True, Newman was of a very different calibre and stood on a very different

footing from that of Oakeley or any other member of
the Tractarian party. He was not one whom even
Pusey would bring himself easily to rebuke, however
much he might seem in the wrong. Yet the perplexity
with which Pusey would regard the leader's subtleties
would have much the same effect, proportionately, as
the indignation with which he denounced the inferences
that Newman's followers deduced from them. We
ought not therefore to be surprised if it should appear
that Newman never turned to Pusey for help in the
great crisis of his life. Younger men were at once let
into the secret of his trouble. Rogers, who occupied
Froude's rooms after his death and was, in some sort,
his successor in Newman's friendship, was at once
informed of it in the plainest language ; the amusing
and talkative Henry Wilberforce—the " scaramouch,"
as Newman called him—was not long left in ignorance ;
even to Keble some glimpse of the truth was given
after the interval of a year ; but Pusey " the Great,"
was too great, too distant, for Newman to make to him
—at least in any intelligible language—admissions so
painful to both, and all the more humiliating to the one
who would have to confess, because so mysterious to
the other who would have to listen. To the last,
between two such men there must have remained
affection—and sympathy too, of a kind ; but it was not
of that kind by which the franker could break down
the reserve of the less frank, and force him to open his
heart with the same free confidence which he gave
without effort to younger minds.

§ 27. *Keble*

While Newman was still a Scholar of Trinity preparing for the Schools, Keble, eleven years his senior,

was the admiration and almost the awe, of the under-graduate world. "Two First Classes" gained at the age of eighteen, "two Essays in one year, and a Fellow-ship at Oriel" were enough to induce young Newman to describe him to his father as "the first man in Oxford." When the Oriel Fellows with the usual shake of the hand welcomed Newman into their number, "I bore it," he says to a friend, "till Keble took my hand, and then felt so abashed and unworthy the honour done me, that I seemed desirous of quite sinking into the ground."

For some time after the election Keble seems to have been a little shy of the Junior Fellow, half Evan-gelical and half Liberal, who seemed to be leaning towards the Noetic School ; who was soon pronounced by Whately one of the clearest-headed men he ever knew, and who asked his old pupil Froude whether he was not a red-hot High Churchman. They were on friendly but not on intimate terms. Newman had consulted him in 1826 on his intended Hebrew studies ; and toward the end of 1827 during the election for the Provostship, Newman's protest that they were not electing an angel, but only a Provost—else he would have voted for Keble—must have convinced the latter how heartily he was respected and admired by the very man who refused to give him his vote. But it was not till the following year that the two came really to know one another ; "Do you know," says Hurrell Froude, "the story of the murderer who had done one good thing in his life ? Well, if I was ever asked what good deed I had ever done, I should say that I had brought Keble and Newman to understand each other." Hurrell Froude "brought us together," says the *Apologia* "about 1828."

Meantime the *Christian Year* (1827) had appeared, and was making way almost everywhere. But over and above Keble's reputation as a poet, and the portentous academical distinctions which had extorted such eulogies from Newman seven years before, he had personal qualities which, when once recognized, bound the latter to him in the bonds of an enduring friendship. He had the piety of Pusey, but a temper not so impenetrably sanguine ; so that he was better able to understand, and sympathise with, shades of doubt and religious misgivings. Freshness and force, deep religious feeling, lightened but not concealed by playfulness and quaintness, charmed those who resorted to him for spiritual counsel. At peace with all men and with himself, the author of the *Christian Year* appeared to present a spiritual haven to those who were seeking peace. His advocacy of " safe " doctrine did not indicate—not at least except during a subsequent phase of apparently brief duration—any unworthy timorousness as to the eternal destiny of himself or his fellow men. What he taught was, that between two religious courses, where both are lawful, if there is any difference in respect of reverence, the more reverent one is to be chosen, that which is farthest removed from self-seeking worldliness, or stubborn wilfulness, or empty conceit. It was a doctrine that might be easily carried to the length of superstition ; but there was nothing unworthy in aiming at such a "safety" as this. Quietly firm, and reverently confident, he did not find it needful for the attainment of holiness to proclaim a perpetual war against the visible world.

Flippancy and irreverence he did indeed hate, and sometimes he could speak his mind about them in brief words not easily forgotten. It happened once that his pupil Froude, on the point of leaving Keble's house, at the conclusion of a visit, let fall the expression that Law's *Serious Call* was "a clever book." Keble sat by his side, uneasy, yet silent. But just as they were bidding each other farewell, he burst out, "Froude, when you said that Law's *Serious Call* was a clever book, it seemed to me much as if you had said that the Day of Judgment was a pretty sight." Such flashes as these, issuing from a treasure-house of spiritual light within, would arrest Newman's attention more than any amount of argument. As an arguer, Keble was not excellent—sometimes, it is said, losing his temper, or committing himself hastily to the untenable, as when he maintained that fossil impressions must have been created ready-made in the strata. But to a supreme master of dialectic, like Newman, these would seem slight defects. *He* could do the dialectic. What he wanted was some one who could *see ;* and in Keble he seemed to find a sort of Seer, one who could rebuke with inspiration, teaching with some degree of originality, and seeing things with something of a divine insight. Hence, in moments of depression, comparing himself with the teacher Keble and the pupil Froude, he would pronounce himself inferior to both : *they*, he said, were the theologians and philosophers, *he* was a mere rhetorician ; they had thoughts of their own, he had none ; he, by their side, was unreal, "hollow."

Newman does not seem to have thus habitually compared himself unfavourably with Pusey, though he was touched (see p. 39 above) by his humility and devotion, However passively perfect, Pusey does not seem to have impressed his friend as possessing the same active in-

sight that characterized Keble. And yet in both there
were many of the same qualities that attracted Newman's admiration. Both were absolutely single-hearted;
both of great learning, though in different directions ;
and both, as compared with Newman, were stable in
their thoughts, and full of a devout faith or trust. But
in Keble there was what was not in Pusey—the poetic
temperament which can feel in itself, and realise in
others, the fluctuations of the spiritual surface ; and
this perhaps was the reason why, after Froude's death,
when Newman finally decided to submit his cases of
conscience to the deliberate and formal decision of
some friend, it was to the poet and not to the learned
student that he resorted as his confessor.

To Keble we shall find him hereafter referring a
trying dispute between himself and some of the more
moderate Tractarians, in which he avows himself ready
to do, or not to do, whatever Keble bids him do or
abstain from doing. When he is in doubt about the
lawfulness of remaining Vicar of St. Mary's, it is
Keble's leave to remain which he needs to satisfy
his conscience, and to Keble he resorts for it. To
Keble he goes again when the burden of remaining
is weighing still more heavily on his soul. Lastly, in
the final crisis, when he is on the point of joining the
Church of Rome, but doubts whether he may not be
under a judicial delusion, sent from heaven as a judgment for some secret sin, it is to Keble that he lays
bare his thoughts from day to day in a continuous
record that the latter may decide upon his spiritual
state.

Yet, though somewhat less solidly calm than Pusey,
and though (under the stress of the Tractarian Movement) occasionally driven to say harsh things, Keble

was never led by his sympathies with fierce or austere
combatants to the same lengths of austerity or "fierceness." Beneath the surface he remained essentially
peace-loving and human-hearted. It was far otherwise with Newman and Froude. The mottoes of the
Christian Year and the *Lyra Apostolica* well express
the contrast. That of the former is, "In quietness
and confidence shall be your strength"; the latter is
taken from the *Iliad*, out of the mouth of Achilles, and
it breathes conflict and the pride of the sword, "They
shall know the difference now I am back." On a
special occasion (such as that of the Hampden controversy) Keble was capable of renouncing an old
friend and pupil, who, after voting on the wrong side,
rushed across the High Street to shake hands with his
old tutor, and found himself repelled and reproached
aloud for having "sacrificed at the altar of Jupiter."
But in the main, when left to himself, he found good
in every one, and sought peace with every one. Instead of exulting, as Froude did, over Milton's slips
and indefensible faults, they made him "uncomfortable"; I have not found in his biography, and only
once or twice in letters to Newman, a harsh word
against Whately; and a "comfortable" Easter letter
from Arnold quite delights him. He was a Tory and
an avowed High Churchman; but, for all that, the
Evangelicals, from the first, recognized in him "a
spiritual man."

§ 28. *The "Christian Year"*

In a well known passage in the *Apologia* Newman
expresses himself as indebted to the *Christian Year* for
two intellectual truths which it "brought home" to

him. One of them was "the Sacramental system; that is, the doctrine that material phenomena are both the types and the instruments of real things unseen." The other was the explanation of our firmness of assent given to religious truth. This Keble ascribed, not to the probabilities that introduced it, but to the living power of faith and love by which we accept it. But both of these truths were transmuted in passing from the teacher to the taught. Newman, as we have seen above and shall see more clearly hereafter— accepted illustrations from Nature; but he did not, as Wordsworth did, and as Keble in less measure sometimes did, accept Nature as a teacher.

As to the second doctrine, that of Faith, Newman altered a poet's metaphor into a logician's scheme. There is a difference, Keble said, between slaves, and friends or children;—friends do not ask for literal commands, but from their knowledge of the speaker they understand his half words, and, from love of him, anticipate his wishes. So about God and God's will, we may be convinced of certain broad truths; and these, because of our trust in Him as a Father, we can apply in practice, so as to discern what is right, without seeking a new law for each particular occasion. This commends itself to all. But this would not settle questions of historical or scientific fact, such as whether the sun was stopped by Joshua, or whether the world was created in six days. Keble's theory, though it impressed Newman as beautiful and religious, did not satisfy him; "it did not," he complained, "even profess to be logical." So he worked it up into something new of his own, and gave it a varnish of logic. In his hands it became a formal scheme with laws of graduated probability. In accordance with these, we are to

recognize at the top of the scale a transcendent probability called certitude, about the existence of God ; then,
lower down, a medial probability about facts which,
though not certain, are highly probable ; and then, lower,
and after that, lowest, various degrees of probability
about other facts ; all, as it were, on the same inclined
plane of probability. It is perhaps with reference to such
symmetrical paper schemes as these that Keble wrote
to Newman : " You know I have always fancied that
perhaps you were over-sanguine in making things
square."

This leads us to a brief consideration of these two
points in the *Christian Year* to which Newman assigns
so great a part in shaping his theological convictions.

And first for the doctrine that "all material phenomena are both the types and the instruments of
things unseen." Such a doctrine might cover a wide
range. John Bunyan found in chickens, raising their
heads to heaven as they drank, a type and lesson of
thankfulness. But those who have once reflected that
the chickens do this to prevent the water from falling
out of their beaks, will find something distasteful,
grotesque, and almost insincere, in continuing to teach
others thankfulness by such a lesson. On the other
hand, to call Christ, with Keble, the " Sun of our Soul,"
and to recognize His type and His very presence in the
actual orb that sustains our material life is a less
arbitrary lesson. Those who look on Christ as
expressing, and incarnating, that principle of goodwill,
or spirit of fellowship, which binds together the world
of human nature—just as the law of attraction binds
together the material world—may yet feel that in
calling Him also the Sun (which is the source of light
and warmth and stable harmony for the whole of the

solar system) there is no more confusion of metaphor than in describing Him as a Word and yet as a Man, a Spirit and yet as a Law. The distinction between the two types, that of Bunyan and that of Keble, appears to be that the former is artificial, or seems so to all but mere children, the latter may seem natural even to full-grown men ; the former seems to sin against truth—at least for those who know the truth, the latter seems to interpret to us spiritual truth without violating scientific truth. If this is a true distinction, then to multiply religious types and to be ever seeking devout lessons in nature, seems a kind of snare for our souls, tempting us to find, during ignorance, types which we shall have to discard after knowledge, or to retain in some peril of hypocrisy. Likenesses between things on earth and things in heaven ought to be seen at a glance, if at all, and to be received, if at all, in a moment of spontaneous acceptance. Then they are the offspring of the poet or the prophet ; and the man who receives them in that spirit receives the poet's or the prophet's reward. But if they are hammered out with effort by the maker, and received upon authority by the learner, they are mere idols wrought by false prophets, who " teach for doctrine the commandments of men " ; and on him who makes, and on him who receives them, there falls the curse of the blighting spirit of conscious or unconscious falsehood.

Keble's types are most of them natural, derived from nature and not from books. Where he errs into artificiality and bookishness it is generally under the influence of the Old Testament, which leads him sometimes to confuse metaphors or to resort to very harsh and complicated imagery ; as, for example, when he calls on God to let His ear be pierced by the sad notes of His turtle-dove, teaching her to "unlock her heart" as suits a "soft returning spouse"; or, with an allusion to the Dove from the Ark, speaks of the same turtle-dove as "winning a leaf" from "the reconciling Tree"; or, worst of all, likening our Lord to Moses—who in his anger broke the two Tables that were said to have been written by the hand of God—implores the "offended Saviour" to

—"pause
"In act to break thine outraged laws."

In this occasional tendency there may have been something which confirmed Newman's already excessive readiness to find likenesses where there are none, and especially to utilize the Old Testament, as being hardly less applicable than the New both to the Church and to individual Christians.

Taken as a whole, however, the *Christian Year* is the utterance of one who loves and trusts Nature in the widest sense, that is to say, the world of men and things; which he regards from the point of view, not of an enemy or an ascetic, but from that of a humble recipient and loving learner, receiving through the world the teaching and gifts of God. Herein Keble was perhaps partly indebted to Wordsworth, whose poems he loved, when to love them was unfashionable, and continued to love till the last. But it is clear, too, that he loved Wordsworth because he had first loved Nature. Tokens of this abound in the *Christian Year*. Our guardian angel is said to mourn over our ingratitude when we look with hearts untouched on the first of the spring flowers; Christ Himself opens Nature's Book; the snow-drops bring Easter news; and shame is invoked on the heart that

can repine over lost blessings in the happy season
when—

> "Nature sings of joy and hope alone,
>   Reading her own sweet lessons in her own sweet time."

Nor does the poet fail to recognize that beyond, or
beneath, dogmatic theology there are vital truths of
which we need to be continually reminded by social
intercourse, and which the unlearned may sometimes
impress on those whose special business it is to teach
them.

> "And of our scholars let us learn
>   Our own forgotten lore ;
>   O guide us when our faithless hearts
>   From thee would start aloof
>   Where patience her sweet skill imparts
>   Beneath some cottage roof."

Solitude and fear are acknowledged in these poems
as teachers of divine truth ; but the social life is placed
above the solitary, and fear is mostly regarded as but
the beginning of love.   God's sunshine is said to be
ever behind the gloom.   He smiles on us even in His
wrath.   The unbounded potentialities of love are invoked to scatter the mists of perplexity which gather
round our very conception of time :—

> "Whole years of folly we outlive
>   In His unerring sight who measures life by love."

If sometimes, as we glide down the stream of life,
we seem at each turn of our course to be leaving
behind us withering hopes or aspirations, and to be
passing from the funeral of boyhood to nothing but
the deathbed of the man, we are roused from such

faithless gloom by an appeal to the Sun of life and gladness to enable us to see the glories of His world.

All this indicates a simple and trustful way of looking at men and things, which appears to spring directly from a living faith in God as the Father of men. This sort of " faith " or " trust," appears to be quite distinct from " believing " in great masses of historical or scientific assertions because they are supposed to be connected with religion. It is a sort of combination or tempering of human-heartedness, so to speak, with God-heartedness ; and this Keble appears to have in mind when—in his quaint way of expressing deep things by simple words, not sometimes without a touch of pedantry—he speaks of "good temper." By " good temper " he seems to mean that kind of temperament which, while deprecating *mere* enjoyment, countenances, and even inculcates, *thankful* enjoyment.

Not that he was free—indeed few poets are free—from fits of reaction and depression, and from temptations to causeless melancholy. Nor were there wanting, in his life, the causes that sooner or later justify sorrow in all of us. The loss of one sister and the suffering state of another weighed heavily upon him in his early manhood. But he refused to make these trials an excuse for persistent gloom. " They have furnished me," he says, " with too good an excuse for indulging a certain humour (calling itself melancholy, but I am afraid, more truly entitled proud and fantastic), which I find very often at hand, forbidding me to enjoy the good things and pursue the generous studies which a kind Providence throws so richly in my way . . . I have long known this to be very wrong, but I never felt the mischief of it so much as in the midst of your happy family party. I felt as if I was saddening everybody, and thousands and thousands of resolutions did I make that I would shake off this selfish remembrance of past and distant calamities, that I would enjoy myself wherever I went." This true unselfish faith enabled him not only to bear bereavements with singular patience and steadfastness but also to find consolations everywhere around him. A few days after the unexpected death of his younger sister, he declares that, were it not for his father and his sorrowing sister, he would feel "an unmixed though melancholy pleasure" in thinking of her whom he had just lost ; and his brother's little child, then in the house with them, is "like a little angel sent among us to shine in an over-clouded place."

§ 29. *Newman's influence on Keble*

Yet a cloud of that very melancholy against which he had fought in early life seems to have overspread a period, though but a brief one, in Keble's middle age. Many reasons might be given for it. He was impressed by the symmetry of Newman's grand conception of revived Anglicanism ; and this led him to give more weight to certain doctrines which laid stress on the depravity of human nature, on the difficulty of the attainment of salvation, and on the doom of the majority of mankind. The revelation of Froude's ascetic habits (which did not come to light till the publication of his *Remains* after his death) and the knowledge that Newman was in entire sympathy with these, may have forced him to contrast their gloom with his cheerfulness, and this to his own disadvantage. Still more, he may have been penetrated to the heart by Newman's conceptions of the Holy God, Whose eyes are too pure to behold iniquity, and before Whom mortal men, abased and abject, are but as "worms." Such thoughts as these, arising from his intimacy with Newman, appear to have darkened some years of his life, making him seem to himself a hypocrite and dissembler, causing him to pour forth confessions which astonish and bewilder his biographer, and eliciting from him the following condemnation of his own *Christian Year* :—" May it please God to preserve me from writing as unreally and deceitfully as I did then ; and if I could tell you the whole of my shameful history you would join with your whole heart in this prayer." This startling self-condemnation was not a casual or unique utterance. He repeats a similar avowal apparently in the same year.

Keble himself gives a partial explanation of the difference in tone between the *Lyra Innocentium* and the *Christian Year* as follows :—" When he wrote the latter," he says, he " did not understand (to mention no more points), either the doctrine of Repentance, or that of the Holy Eucharist, as held *e.g.* by Bishop Ken; nor that of Justification." But granting that these doctrines—some of which he probably received through Newman or Newman's system—influenced and altered his ecclesiastical convictions, we can hardly see why they should induce him to call himself deceitful.

The true or full explanation is probably very different. During the year (1845) in which he wrote these bewildering avowals, Newman was on the point of seceding to the Church of Rome ; his convictions in favour of Rome had been long clear ; but he feared that some secret sin might have subjected him to God's wrath and placed him under a "judicial delusion." In order to dissipate this fear, he was sending to Keble a record of continuous confession, laying bare, day by

day, his most secret thoughts.   A soul pure from serious
sin, sensitive even to morbidness, stung with fears of
insincerity, and on the other hand goaded with the
still greater terror of wilfulness and private judgment,
abasing itself before an ineffable Holiness, and regis-
tering every little infirmity of deed, word, and thought,
in the scrupulous resolve to be true and to attain truth
—might not the burden of such a mass of confidences
from such a source have caused the receiver as well as
the giver to turn *his* soul inward, to test himself on the
self-introspective rack, and to magnify his own slightest
faults, till every lapse appeared a sin and every falling
short of perfect veracity seemed a monstrous and deliberate hypocrisy ?

If this is a true explanation, Keble was at this time
far less influencing, than influenced by, Newman.
Indeed he was not merely influenced, he was bent and
well-nigh broken.*   But for the neutralizing power of
married life—all the more potent at that crisis because
his wife appeared to be on her death-bed and each
utterance seemed likely to be her last—there is much
reason to suppose that Keble in his usual passion for
whatever was self-sacrificing and safe from suspicion
of unworldliness, would have accompanied Newman in
his secession.   But his human-heartedness or "good
temper" came to his rescue.   The eyes that had
before discerned in a child "a little angel" sent "to
shine in an over-clouded place," now recognized in the
apparent death-bed of his wife, and in what seemed to
be her last utterances, a confirmation of what Newman
had himself taught in one of his last sermons, that the
Church of England was "a safe one to die in."   It
was not high doctrine; but it prevented him from
sinking lower.   Afterwards, looking sorrowfully back

on certain secessions to Rome, he attributed them to
a want of this same " good temper."   In 1853, he says,
" I really cannot imagine a person of his truthfulness,
learning and good temper, putting up with the Roman
system as a convert."   And in the following year he
writes about " poor dear R(obert) W(ilberforce) " after
the secession of the latter, " I thought he was too
good-tempered, besides his learning and truthfulness.
But he had got into an Utopian dream, and rather than
give it up, he shut his eyes and made a jump ; and
now he must, and, I suppose, will, keep his eyes shut
all his life."

On the whole, though Keble's share in determining
Newman's career was far more important than that of
Pusey, both must yield the palm in this respect to the
younger friend, who next claims our attention.

CHAPTER VII

RICHARD HURRELL FROUDE

§ 30. *Froude, the key to Newman*

RICHARD HURRELL FROUDE was two years younger than Newman. He went to Eton in 1816, and to Oriel in 1821. After obtaining honours both in classics and mathematics, he was elected Fellow of Oriel in 1826, and one of the tutors in 1827. In December, 1828, he was ordained deacon, and, in the following year, priest. He was attacked by consumption in 1832 and died in 1836. The first volume of his *Literary Remains* was published by Keble and Newman in 1838.

Newman describes himself as bound to him in the closest and most affectionate friendship from about 1829 till his death. Froude's opinions, he says, arrested and influenced him, even when they did not gain his consent; and among them he mentions admiration for the Church of Rome, for a hierarchical system, for sacerdotal power, and for full ecclesiastical liberty; hatred of the Reformers, scorn for mere "Bible Christianity," and an almost ostentatious acceptance of Tradition as a main instrument of religious teaching; high notions of the intrinsic excellence of Virginity, and devotion to the Mother of our Lord as its great pattern; a vivid appreciation of sanctity and delight in thinking of the Saints; an inclination, or something more, to believe in large miraculous interferences as occurring in the early and middle ages; a "devotion to the Real Presence" in which he had a firm faith; and a practical adoption of "the principle of penance and mortification."

In all these beliefs, then, he certainly preceded, and evidence will hereafter clearly prove that he also led, the friend who had been gradually disengaging himself from the Evangelical School. ·Even in other matters where at first Newman and he differed, Newman in the end came round to him. Froude was powerfully drawn to the Mediæval Church, Newman to the Primitive; but the Mediæval finally triumphed. He set no great store on theological detail, nor on the writings of the Fathers, but "took an eager courageous view of things as a whole. Omit 'courageous" (perhaps, also, the "eager") and the sentence will describe the nature of Newman's final decision. He, too, "took things as a whole"; it was the personified majesty of the vision of Rome that ultimately took him captive. Recognizing the difficulty of enumerating all the additions to his creed which Newman derived from a friend to whom he owed so much, the *Apologia* selects four: admiration for Rome, dislike of the Reformation, devotion to the Blessed Virgin, and belief in the Real Presence. But there is perhaps not one in the long list of Froude's opinions above mentioned, in which his influence on Newman is not perceptible. If not first planted, some of them were, at all events, fixed deep, and firmly rooted, by the friend who had previously received them. If therefore we would understand Newman's develop-

ment we should spare no trouble in attempting to understand that one of all his friends who is shown by
evidence, direct and indirect, to have contributed most
to it.

For this purpose, all the more pains are needed because the very friends who loved him best dealt somewhat hardly with his reputation. In his literary *Remains*
they gave to the world the most secret records of his
private life, in which, besides hinting at deeper "vile-
nesses," he sets down in detail with unflinching
severity, if not with exaggeration, the very smallest
infirmities of will and deed. The *Apologia* speaks of
"the gentleness and tenderness of nature, the playfulness, the free elastic force and graceful versatility
of mind, and the patient winning considerateness in
discussion, which endeared him to those to whom he
opened his heart"; and other testimony enables us to
believe that, in the small circle of those who knew
him well, he was really such as he is there described;
but, if we are to judge from his *Remains*, it is a
question whether this gentleness and considerateness
reached far beyond the close company of those who
were struggling for the religious cause which he had
at heart. Of this let the reader judge—making all
allowance for Froude's own self-condemning exaggerations—from some specimens extracted from his
Private Journal and Letters.

§ 31. *Froude's "Journal"*

The Journal is introduced by a remarkable letter
written by his mother, nominally to some correspondent, but really for her eldest son Hurrell, then
in his seventeenth year. In this she describes him

as being from his birth of very peculiar temper; pleasing, intelligent, and attaching, when he was undisturbed and kindly treated; but impatient when anything vexed him, and "very much disposed to find his own amusement in teasing and vexing others"; as one who, for the pleasure of what he called "funny tormenting," would keep his brothers screaming for nearly an hour under her window at a time when she was "wretchedly ill," and quiet was essential to her recovery; as recently frightening a baby brother after repeated promises not to do so, and this on a day when she was particularly unwell; as disturbing her health by these malignant pranks without the slightest feeling, "twenty times a day"; as telling a near relation, who had nursed him through a dangerous illness, that "she lied, and she knew she did"; as "almost entirely incorrigible when it was necessary to reprove him," and as having shown ostentatious indifference when she last remonstrated with him, on the very day on which she was writing, "whistling almost ever since," though she thought she had touched his heart.

The letter recognizes on the other hand, with affectionate pride, her son's admirable patience and even sweet cheerfulness under a dangerous illness followed by troublesome restraints, his pleasing conversation, manly and rational occupations, and his manner, at one time, kind and tender. But this last, she implies, was only a phase, and, she fears, a brief one. Yet she had noted in him many marks of a promising character; feelings just and high in all points of substantial principle; an admiration (deep for his age) of everything good and noble; a keen and refined taste for all the pleasures of the imagination;

he "was also quite conscious of his own faults and (*untempted*) had a just dislike to them." But all this promise of boyhood seems in danger of being blighted by the present outbreak of self-will. She has never found a successful mode of treating him. Harshness made him obstinate and gloomy ; calm and long dis-pleasure made him stupid and sullen ; and kind patience had not sufficient effect on his feelings to force him to govern himself. She concludes by saying that her son is now too old for any correction but that of his own reason ; and how to influence that she *knows not*. What is she to do ? Will her correspondent advise her ?

From this letter—which goes far to justify Keble's praise of Mrs. Froude's taste and imaginative power, while it makes us also readily understand why Froude revered the memory of his mother as if she were little short of a saint—we pass to the Journal, which begins six or seven years afterwards in the year (1826) when he was elected to the Oriel Fellowship. The second line is as follows :—" February 1, Oxford. All my associations here are bad and I can hardly shake them off." He determines to wrestle with his conceit, affec-tation, wandering of mind, lassitude. His mother is now dead, and his energies are partially quickened by the remorse he feels while reading passages in her journal ; " I did not recollect that I had been so un-feeling to her during her last year." Then follows an allusion which Newman,—devoted by a kind of in-ward vow to celibacy since the age of sixteen—would well understand, "The consciousness of having capacities for happiness, with no objects to gratify them, seems to grow upon me. Lord have mercy upon me." This is the mood which he elsewhere

describes to Newman as "sawney"—natural at times
to those who are under a kind of vow to serve a cause
without domestic distractions or encumbrances.

The problem exhibited in these pages of the Journal
is the old but never antiquated one "How to keep the
human machine in order." Roughly speaking, we
may say that there are two solutions. Men can be
delivered from the beast within them by love, or by
fear. The second may be called no deliverance at all
by those who have a keen appreciation of the first ; but
it *is* deliverance of a sort ; and Froude's Journal shows
us a man of immense strength of will, of acute intellect,
and of high imaginations, restless and masterful almost
to the extent of tyrannical malignity in his youth,
conscious of grievous lapses in the past and of something—he hardly knew what—terribly wanting in his
present moral condition ; now at last goaded by bitter
remorse, and urged by the pressure of new responsibilities, to reform his corrupt nature, and attempting to
work out his salvation through asceticism dictated, at
first, by something like terror.

Being perfectly free from cant, Froude makes no
profession at all of having found his salvation, or any
sense of peace and safety, in that Revelation of God
through Christ which Protestants, for the most part,
think the one thing needful. Of God as a Father, who
not only loves, but even (if one may so say) suffers
and sympathizes with repentant sinners, there is hardly
a word, or a trace of a conception. The name
of the Redeemer is not once mentioned in any of
the prayers that he commits to paper. There is
scarcely a phrase in them that might not have been
written by a man who had never read a page of the
New Testament, and had never heard of Christ.

Froude has always before him a Being of negative holiness, the access to Whom (we might almost say to Which) is through a course of obedience paid to precepts that we do not understand. The following extract from his *Occasional Thoughts* which was written in 1827, and before Newman's influence can have been very powerful, speaks of—

"A dignified and a manly course which may with patience be pursued ; of obeying precepts without affecting to understand the thing enjoined ; and waiting till we perceive their reason, merely from conviction that they have a good one. This is the only means of attaining any knowledge of the Most High. It is alone by long experience that we can build up within us that terrible idea. But the idea will never become terrible to us, unless the Name is long before kept holy."

In the previous year he had sent a poem to Keble in which—curiously tinging with his own gloom the language of the Psalmist who prays to be hidden " under the shadow of the wings" of the Divine protection — he speaks of God as a Being whose presence is mainly manifested by control and by a holy " terror " :—

"Lord of the world, Almighty King,
　Thy shadow resteth over all,
Or where the Saints thy terrors sing,
　Or where the waves obey Thy call."

Froude's religion, then, so far as it depended on his conception of God, was a religion of almost unmixed fear. So far as it was of something better, it was purified, first, by a love and admiration for the " holy men of old," such as the founders of the Oxford Colleges, in whose steps—after his election to his fellowship—he aspired to tread ; secondly, by his affection for Keble for whom, in the prayer written at the same time, he thanks God, as one who had convinced him in some degree of the error of his ways and in whose presence he tasted happiness ; but above all by his devotion to his mother, in whose recollection he found a consciousness of that blessedness which he had been taught to look for in the presence of Saints and Angels. These were feelings which were better than his religion, and which, if they could have developed and grown with the latter, might have delivered it from fears and have converted it into a source of peace as well as of activity : but, whether from the irremediable taint of the past, or owing to influence that proved too strong for Keble's, this growth did not go on.

Newman, as we have seen, taught at an early period that self-knowledge is the basis of all religious knowledge. Whether Froude adopted or originated this doctrine, it must have stimulated his fears : for it was a proverb with him that " everyone may know worse of himself than he possibly can of Charles II." In less than six months after the thanksgiving recorded above, we find him protesting (10 January 1827) that he dares not now utter the prayers of wise and holy men ; and that God has affrighted him with hideous dreams and disquieted him with perpetual mortifications. He prays for strength to look in the face the hideous filthiness of those ways, in which—for the sins that he has deliberately wrought—he has been permitted blindly to stray. But he has obtained relief by once more confessing to Keble, whom he thanks God for interposing—as his type upon this earth—between himself and the evils he has merited. Since his mother's death, he has been, he declares, " without God in the world." From Keble's previous letter, in answer to his first confession (October 1826), he had received something more like happiness than he had known since his mother died ; and now (8 January 1827) it is to Keble that he owes his release, for how long he knows not, from the misery in which he had been recently bound.   At the same time Keble advises him to give up his ascetic self-denial ; and Froude acquiesces.   Though it had the colour of humility, it now appears to him to have been in reality the food of pride ; self-imposed, it seems to him " quite different from when imposed by the Church."

What sort of self-denials they were, and what Froude's self-introspection implied, the reader ought to be informed for two reasons ; first, because they show the fierce determination and almost bitter self-hatred with which the young man turned against himself, in his resolution to suppress his own egotism and conceit, and secondly because Newman and Keble—or perhaps Keble instigated by Newman—thought it worth while to record the minutest of these details, and spoke of the Journal as a most valuable contribution to the Tractarian literature.   Froude sets down, for example —and they print—that he was ashamed on one occasion to have it known that he had no gloves ; that he was ashamed on another that he had muddy trousers (although he would not go to the length of concealing them) ; that he was pleased, on another, when there was no evening prayer ; that he felt an impulse of pleasure on finding that Wilberforce was not at chapel one morning ; that he ostentatiously hinted to S. that he got up at six o'clock ; that he read affectedly in evening chapel ; that he felt an inclination to make remarks with a view to showing how much he had thought upon serious subjects ; and that once, after accidentally breaking one of W(ilberforce's) windows, he felt a disposition to "sneak away."

Again, as to self-denials, Froude is permitted by his editors to record for posterity the offence, on Michaelmas Day, of "looking greedily round to see whether there was a goose" for dinner; on another occasion, that of "stuffing himself" with toast and tea after rejecting wines; on another, that of almost arguing himself out of his rule of sleeping on the floor; on another, his gratification that his meals on a particular day—"a bit of cold endings of dab at breakfast, and a scrap of mackerel at dinner—were the only things that diverged from the strict rule of simplicity," though he regrets that "in quantity, the air and exercise had such an effect" upon him that he "quite went up to the frontiers of moderation." He seriously argues the pros and cons—"bothering himself" about it for three days—concerning the purchase of a great coat; on the one side there is the fact that he "wants," *i.e.* needs it (which one would have thought would have been conclusive), but, against this, he sets the fact that he "wishes" it, and therefore it will be well to deny himself the satisfaction. Then, he tells how, at the Fellows' table in Oriel, he "was disgustingly ostentatious at dinner in asking for a china plate directly"— the meat was in those days served in College on pewter, so that "to ask for china" meant that ye would have no more meat—: "I did it on purpose, too, that the others might see I ate so much less than they did." Or again, "fell quite short of my wishes with respect to the rigour of to-day's fast, though I am quite willing to believe, not unpardonably; I tasted nothing till half-past eight in the evening. . . But I made a more hearty tea than usual, quite giving up the notion of a fast"— ; and so on, and this in the year 1826, the year before he became one of the tutors of Oriel.

By his own confession he occasionally made himself stupid and sleepy through these ascetic habits. But to the last he retained his admiration for them—at all events when they were imposed by external authority. Probably he shortened his own life—and the following extract from a letter of 1835 written about some lady of his acquaintance indicates that he may have induced others to shorten their lives—by practices of this kind, and that he regarded such a result with satisfaction :

"She died a few months back . . . . and from what W. tells me, must have been a little saint ; all last Lent she fasted so strictly as to hurt her health, in spite of being constantly ridiculed ; and where she got her notions from I cannot guess, except through T. and from her natural goodness . . . . To me it is humiliating to see how principles that stay in my own head find their way into one's pupil's hearts."

Why did the editors of Froude's *Remains* give to the world these extraordinary confessions ? Could it be that they brought themselves to hold up to the public gaze, not only their friend's faults, but also his method of attempting to rid himself of these faults, simply because they wished to teach the world that it was all a mistake, a mere beacon to tell others what to avoid ? It seems far more probable—and the Letters make it almost certain—that, besides giving a vivid picture of the man, they really wished to inculcate Froude's anxious, restless, self-introspective method as being on the whole right, for " young people," provided that it was conformed to the regulations of the Church. If indeed Froude had taken Keble's advice, they could not thus have made his secrets the property of posterity ; for he had advised his pupil not only to give up his self-imposed asceticisms but also to burn his confessions.   But this advice was given in 1826 ; whereas the *Remains* were published in 1838.   Are we wrong in inferring that, during this interval, Keble may have been pushed forward by Newman his co-editor, who taught that all religious knowledge must be based on self-knowledge ?   From the *Letters*, this seems probable.   Newman appears to have been the cause why what Froude's former tutor had once discouraged in his pupil, he was now induced to think likely to promote sanctity in others under a new Anglican system.   Here, at all events, is what Newman says about the Journal (31 August, 1837) :—

"Archdeacon Froude sent up within this last week Hurrell's private journal (1826–1827), of which I did not know the existence before, giving an account of his fastings, &c., and his minute faults and temptations at the time. . . . . They are more interesting than anything I have seen, except, perhaps, his letters to Keble. . . . . Does it not seem as if Providence was putting things in our hands for something especial? . . . . I want Rivington to have the volumes purchasable separately ; each will have separate interest for a different set of persons—the sermons for parsons, the first volume for young people. . . . . These new papers have quite made my head whirl, and have put things quite in a new light."

§ 32. *Points of similarity between Froude and Newman*

Froude's Private Journal has made it clear, that in one fundamental matter Newman and he were in agreement.   Their starting-points, or motives, were different.   The one was moved by an irrepressible sense of the aloofness and sinlessness of a perfectly Holy

Judge ; the other, in some measure by this feeling, but
still more by a remorse that made him turn upon himself as upon an enemy. But these different causes
produced the same result. Both " shuddered at themselves."

We now pass to other points of still closer
agreement, demonstrable, for the most part, by letters
written before his intimacy with Newman. Among
these must be reckoned a respect for power as power,
and a deficiency, almost amounting to absence, of the
sense of justice and fairness. This is curiously illustrated by one of Froude's letters to Keble in November
1826. He had been struck by a passage in Shakespeare's *Measure for Measure* in which the disguised
Duke—when reproved by his own officers and bidden
to pay respect to their position—bursts out with an
exclamation of bitter irony, that if *they*, judges of
injustice, are to be honoured, why then the devil
himself must claim the same deference :—

> *Duke.* " 'Tis false !
> *Escalus.* How ! Know you where you are ?
> *Duke.* Respect to your great place ! and let the devil
>   Be sometimes honoured for his burning throne ! "

It will be scarcely believed that Froude takes this
passage *literally* :—

> " I have just been reading your favourite play *Measure for
> Measure*, which gives me a much greater idea of Shakespeare than
> I ever used to have. There is a remark near the end of the fifth
> act, which I put down, not so much for its having had a chief share
> in exciting my veneration, as that it struck me there was a sublime
> wildness in it ; speaking of honouring high authorities, as such, he
> says, " Even let the devil be some time honoured for his burning
> throne.' "

The same insensibility to fairness is apparent in

many of his other thoughts. To disbelieve, for example that an unjust excommunication can have any such moral effect on the person excommunicated as can entitle it to be called an "evil," seems to him "heretical:" "I am shocked to see Jeremy Taylor so heretical about excommunication. He says that, when unjust, it is no evil." Elsewhere we find him asserting, not only that "there may be ecclesiastical ordinances which we have no business to repeal, though their consequence may seem to have no benefit" (a truism or a falsehood, according to the meaning of "seem") but also; "There may be Ecclesiastical Authorities to whom we are bound to submit, whether they are in conformity with, or in violation of, His will by whom they are delegated." And to such an extent does he carry his horror of his own self-will and conceit, his distrust of his own conscience, and his craving for some rule of authority, that he is in doubt "how far the certainty that an action is wrong, in itself, ought to be a reason for abstaining from it, when the better sort of people do not see the thing in the same light."

It follows, at once, that there is very little thankfulness in Froude's form of Christianity. The visible world seemed so full of delusion, mockery, and temptation, that a hostile or ironical attitude towards it was the only one possible. "This irony," says James Mozley, "arose from that peculiar mode in which Froude viewed all earthly things, himself and all that was dear to him not excepted." What was that "peculiar mode"? To define it briefly would be difficult. It must have recognized something of reality and goodness in those friends and allies towards whom his heart went out, and with whom he was ready to labour to the end for what he considered the "Truth,"

freely placing his fortune, his faculties, and his last
breath at their disposal. But still it was not the
"mode" of St. Paul, or of Keble; it was more like,
though not quite like, that of Newman. It was certainly not the "mode" of the author who wrote that
God "giveth us all things richly to enjoy."

Indeed "irony" is perhaps hardly the right word to
use of the superficial self-mockery—but more profound
self-hatred and self-contempt approaching sometimes to
despair—with which, in some of his self-introspective
moods, Froude smites and rends himself and his faults,
yes, and his resolves to correct his faults; sometimes
even pouring scorn upon himself for writing down his
own good resolutions and for thinking well of himself in
the act of doing it. "The chief reason," he says, "for
my being interested in any object is the fact that I
happen to be pursuing it," "nor can I look with serious
feeling on the miseries of any one but my own. The
blight of God is on me for my selfish life:" and again:—

"I use self-denial because I believe it the way to make the most
out of our (*sic*) pleasures; and besides, it has a tendency to give me
what is essential to taking my place in society—self-command. . . . .
I am driven to the attempt after piety as a last resource. I seek to
be hidden, and in the Lord's presence, not upon choice, but because
I have nowhere else to hide myself. I give up nothing, and ask for
everything. Can such an offering as mine have anything acceptable
in it? Can actions, originating in such a temper, have any tendency
to make me better, or to procure the blessing and grace of God?
And yet now I am proud of this that I have written, and think that
the knowledge it shows of myself implies a greatness of mind;
and I sometimes compare myself to Solomon in the beginning of
Ecclesiastes."

"I give up nothing and ask for everything" is the
very key-note of scores of Newman's utterances about
the "ventures" of a Christian, and the need of artificial

self-denials.   But would not such mental convolutions
and involutions as these bewilder even a firm faith ?
And is " irony " a term quite strong enough to denote
this savage, sarcastic self-laceration which, if persisted
in, would result in moral and spiritual suicide ?

So far, it would seem that the two friends resembled
each other in almost every one of their principles of
religious thought.   A religion of fear ; a profound
sense of an awful Holiness ; an absence of general
loving-kindness and human-heartedness ; a vast and
almost servile respect for power as power ; an inclination
to asceticism in the older of the two as a test of sincerity,
but, in the younger, rather as a means of suppressing
the passions ; a dread of wilfulness, and a rooted suspicion of self—these feelings appear to have been, in
both, so powerful and original that whatever influence
either might exert upon the other, would result, not in
changing, but in confirming and hardening ; or, at
most, in suggesting some new application of the
theories common to both.   We now pass to the only
principle in which the two seem first to have differed,
but ultimately to have agreed.

§ 33. *Froude learned "Economy" from Newman*

This "principle" (if it may be so called) is that of
tact or management—especially in the diffusion,
colouring, and sometimes in the reservation, or suppression, of religious doctrine with a view to sur-
mounting prejudice and instilling Truth.   To this,
Newman (though not the first to use the word in this
sense) gave the name of " economy."

There are many reasons for concluding that in this
one respect Froude was passive, a simple recipient from

Newman.   Froude had a natural directness and dislike of tactical concealments.   He was a straight rider across country, says the *Apologia*, and he went, or, if left to himself would have gone, equally straight towards theological or ecclesiastical objects.   Cautious Tractarians, who liked his objects better than his short cuts to them, told him with friendly sarcasm that he was " not afraid of his inferences : " and throughout the Movement we find him advising abrupt measures, and open collisions, where his older companions preferred the more quiet processes of gradual underminings or strategical ambuscades.

In the next place, few or none of his references to the method of " reserve " or " economy ", which he ironically calls " undermining," " poisoning," and the like—occur in his correspondence before his acquaintance with Newman ; but after their friendship was confirmed, these phrases became numerous, in his letters to other correspondents, as well as to Newman. Here are some specimens.   In February, 1832, he suggests a quarterly magazine " on a very unpretending scale " which might dispel the popular false notions about the Reformation, " to be at first only historical and matter of fact. . . . .   A thing of that sort might sneak into circulation as a book of antiquarian research, and yet, if well managed, might undermine many prejudices."   In 1833 he expresses to Keble regret that he will have " no chance to proceed with the undermining system."   To another friend he mentions a suggestion that biography is " the best means of infusing principles against the reader's will " ; and again, " Since I have been at home, I have been trying to proselytize in an underhand way."   Even a mathematical mastership, he tells Keble, may be diverted to what he has above called—and most people in this case will agree with him in calling—"underhand proselytizing." It is to be done in Codrington College, Barbados, under an Evangelical Principal.

"They are greatly in want of a mathematical instructor at Codrington College, where the next generation of West Indian clergy are now in embryo. So I mean to offer myself, on condition of having a room given me and being allowed to battell; and in that capacity shall endeavour to instil some good notions into the youths. . . . . —— is a nice amiable man, but rather Evangelical; I like him much. . . . . ; so will your worships have the goodness to get together a few sets of the ——* Tracts? . . . and mind to send lots of Tracts, for I shall try hard to poison the minds of the natives out here. . . . . It has occurred to me that something attractive and poisonous might be made out of a 'a history of missions.'"

Now, considering that the very same letter which describes these "poisonous" intentions, contains a request that parts of his "Breviary" may be sent to him; and that the preceding letter tells Newman, "In the preface to the Articles it is said that we are to understand them in their grammatical sense, which I interpret into a permission to think nothing of the opinion of their framers";—we must frankly admit that, if Froude received the principle of "economy" from Newman, he certainly developed it rapidly and carried it to extreme limits. But that really does represent precisely the relation between the two. Froude anticipated, and endeavoured to develop precipitately, the logical results both of the principles which they held in common, and of those which he instilled into his friend, and also of this particular principle which, alone, his friend seems to have instilled into him. Such a development may be often noticed, when a strong-willed man who sees only one side of a question,

takes up a plan invented by another who sees many.
The inventor may be moderate; the adopter carries
the invention to excess.   Froude was at that time
(1834) dragging Newman onwards toward Roman
doctrine; but he may have submitted to learn from
Newman the best method of diffusing it.   He did not
like the method and therefore he called it by bad
names, such as " undermining," " poisoning," and the
like.   Much, no doubt, depends upon the metaphor in
which we express such things.   " Undermining " is
justified by the rules of war; " poisoning " is not.
When Hurrell Froude took a mathematical mastership
under a " wise, amiable," but " rather Evangelical "
Principal (who, with his wife, by the way, was so kind
to Froude that he is " quite ashamed to think how
much trouble they have taken over him ") for the
purpose of " instilling some good notions" through the
Tracts, into the minds of " the next generation of West
Indian clergy," each reader must decide for himself
whether that particular process, under these particular
circumstances, is to be called " undermining " or
" poisoning."

It only remains to add a final proof that Froude, by
his own nature, was inclined to speak his mind freely,
plainly, and abruptly, without regard to consequences.
The *Apologia* tells us that almost the last letter Froude
wrote to Newman (1 November, 1835), contained a
protest against his " cursing and swearing " against
the Romanists.   But that was not quite the last.
The last on record was written to Newman on
27 January, 1836, a month before Froude's death;
and it contains a protest against his " economy."
The passage is printed differently in the *Remains* and
in Newman's Letters ; in the former, without any signs

of omission, and in the latter with the signs of omission
in the wrong place. I italicize the matter common
to both. In the *Remains* it is :

> " I do believe he (Rogers) hates the meagreness of Protestantism
> as much as either of us. *The other day accidentally put in my way
> the Tract on ' The Apostolical Succession in the English Church,'* and
> it really does seem so unfair that I wonder you could, even in the
> extremity of οἰκονομία (i.e. ' economy ') and φενακισμὸς (i.e.
> ' trickery '), have consented to be a party to it."

In the *Letters* it runs thus :—

> " It is very encouraging about the Oxford Tracts, but I wish I could
> prevail on you, when the second edition comes out, to cancel or
> materially alter several. *The other day accidentally put in my way
> the tract on ' The Apostolical Succession in the English Church.'*
> (This tract was in its *matter*, Palmer's, and I think in some parts of
> its writing J. H. N.). . . . Christie tells me, &c."

The reader will perceive that the marks of omission
in the latter version are attached by the Editor of the
Letters to the wrong sentence. Froude's *Remains* no
one now reads, so that posterity is almost dependent,
for its knowledge of him, on Newman's *Letters*. And
from these none would guess that his sentence about
the Tract was handed down unfinished, and that his last
dying protest against Newman's οἰκονομία and φενακισμὸς
was suppressed. It is much to be regretted that there
are several far more serious discrepancies between the
correspondence as printed in the published *Letters of
Newman*, and as printed elsewhere. It ought in fairness
to be added that Newman, in his reply (2 February),
as to his " economies " in his " first tracts," adheres to
his statements ; except so far as they are " revilings "
or " serious charges about which he has changed his

mind." But still this letter confirms the conclusion deduced above (p. 219) from Newman's correspondence with Rogers and R. F. Wilson, that the Tractarian leader was regarded by his own best friends as the originator, or reviver, of this Tractarian art, which, because he practised it so well, he sometimes practised to excess.

CHAPTER VIII

§ 34. *Froude was at first pronounced "sillyish"*

FROUDE—not Froude's opinions, but Froude himself
or his personality, Froude, first living, and then, as a
posthumous influence, still more powerful after death—
did more than any other external thing to make Newman
what he became, and to shape, through Newman, the
Tractarian Movement. Some of Newman's most important steps dated from the year of their intimacy. It
was in 1829 that the two became close friends—Newman the non-political and Froude the High Tory. It
was also in 1829 that Newman, severing himself from
Pusey, placed himself among the leaders of the Tory
agitation which turned out Sir Robert Peel; it was
from the same year that Newman dated the unshaken
resolution of celibacy in which the two friends confirmed each other; that year, in effect, began Newman's
war for the Church against the World in such a shape
as to prepare the way for the *Via Media:* and I have
already shown how, even before that date, Froude
appears to have indirectly turned Newman's thoughts
towards the Anglican divines, whose ideal the latter
afterwards attempted to blend with that of the primitive
Church. *A priori* we ought to be prepared to believe
that Froude pushed Newman on. Froude was a High

Churchman from the first, with an inclination towards the mediæval Church, and from this he never swerved. Newman was an Evangelical, extricating himself from Evangelicalism. The former had no doubts; the latter was at this time perpetually doubting. How could it be otherwise than natural that the former should take the lead of the latter? Properly to describe Froude's influence, one would almost need, at every turn of Newman's life, to break the narrative, by introducing some previous utterance of Froude's, recent or distant, bearing on the problem of the moment. But we are writing an account of Newman and not of Froude, so that such interruptions are out of the question. Hence, the reader may be glad to have before him here, though a little out of order, some of the points as to which Froude's *Remains* attest his controlling effect upon the course of things as a whole, and especially on Newman's action.

Even "the acutest, deepest, and clearest of men "— as Newman called Froude on his election to the Oriel Fellowship—may be perverse or have a twist in his intellect: and there is amusing evidence to show that, some time after Newman asked Froude whether he was not a "red-hot High Churchman," he still deemed the latter eccentric, or something worse. Rickards, the Vicar of Ulcombe, besides being a shrewd judge of men, was also very clever at conjecturing character from handwriting. One day in 1827 he gave a character of Froude, which Newman, who was present at the time, called "admirable." But here is what Froude says of it :—

"I should say of him what R(ickards) said of my handwriting. 'This fellow has a great deal of imagination in him, but not the imagination of a poet. So it leads him into all sorts of fanciful conceptions,

making him eccentric and often sillyish.' (To be parenthetical,
R(ickards) really wrote this as part of his commentary on my handwriting two years ago; and I think it, with divers others of the
remarks, not a little odd)."

When Newman found himself gradually approximating to Froude in his religious views, while Froude
remained the same, he perhaps took a different view of
this "sillyishness," and gradually learned to regard it
as an original insight, beyond that of the mere intellect,
into spiritual things. On Froude's side, the following
year (September, 1828) shows him more and more
drawn towards Newman himself—that is, the man and
his principles—but disliking his opinions. " N(ewman)
is a fellow that I like, the more I think of him ; only I
would give a few odd pence if he were not a heretic."
A few months more (during which Newman had
broken politically with the party of Whately by taking
the Tory side in the Peel election) seem to have so far
removed all barriers between them that we find Froude
confessing his faults to him with something of the
openness which he had used to Keble. Knowing
what we do of Newman's inclination towards anxious
asceticism, we can well believe that this frankness
(probably implying an interchange of confidences on
both sides) would go far—farther perhaps than the
pure, humble, and single-hearted piety of Pusey which
had made Newman feel an admiration not without
some tinge of shame—to bind the two friends more
closely than ever; and from that time forward they
seem to have moved on together, except that Froude
was always a little in advance. Here are a few instances in which (regard being had to the date) his
leadership appears to be made certain or probable by
a comparison of his *Remains* with Newman's Letters.

§ 35. *How Froude led Newman on* *

1. I have mentioned above that in 1829 Newman, somewhat to Whately's disgust, joined the Tory party (to which Froude belonged) against Peel. But afterwards it struck Froude that Anglicanism ought to be independent of politics; nay, ought to use politics for ecclesiastical objects; ought, perhaps, even to stoop to Radicalism, or something yet more extreme, if the Church could be served by it. Hence in April, 1833, he writes as follows :—

"I think that the only τόπος now is 'the ancient Church of England,' and, as an explanation of what one means, 'Charles the First and the Nonjurors.' When I come home I mean to read and write all sorts of things; for now that one is a Radical there is no use in being nice."

And again a month after to the same effect :—

"There is now in France a High Church party, who are Republicans and wish for universal suffrage, on the ground that in proportion as the franchise falls lower, the influence of the Church makes itself more felt. . . . Don't be surprised if, one of these days, you find us turning Radicals on similar grounds."

Newman (though in him it was a phase of brief duration) followed him a few months afterwards (18 September, 1833) :—

"Of late months, the idea has broken on me as it did a little before on yourself, that the Church is essentially a popular institution, and the past English union of it with the State has been a happy anomaly."

2. On 22 August, 1833, Froude writes to Newman :—

"It has lately come into my head that the present state of things

in England makes an opening for reviving the monastic system.
[† I think of putting the view forward under the title of 'Project of
reviving Religion in great towns.' Certainly †] colleges of unmarried
priests (who might of course retire to a living when they could and
liked) would be the cheapest possible way of providing effectively for
the spiritual wants of a large population."

This project was taken up in 1836 by his friend ; who
is now so generally credited with it that in recent times
people have been blamed for not knowing that this
was " a remarkable forecast of Cardinal Newman."

3. Again, he writes to Newman in August, 1833,
about a sermon he has composed of which the subject
is " The duty of contemplating the contingency of a
separation between Church and State, and of providing
against it, *i.e.* by studying the principles of ecclesiastical subordination, so that, when the law of the land
ceases to enforce this, *we* may have a law within ourselves to supply its place." He goes on to say that
the clergy must no longer presume on their social
standing : "We must come down in our notions about
being gentlemen." An echo of this will be found in
Tract No. 1 (bearing the date of 9 September, though
sent to Froude on 2 September). The Tract will be
given in full later on, but let the reader now merely
note the question with which the Tract starts :—

" Should the Government and the country so far forget their God
as to cast the off Church, to deprive it of its temporal honours and
substance, *on what* will you rest the claim of respect and attention
which you make upon your flocks? Hitherto you have been
upheld by your birth, your education, your wealth, your connections ; should these secular advantages cease, on what must Christ's
ministers depend ? "

Newman's Tract states clearly the grounds suggested by Froude's sermon. According to the Tract,

the priests are to be ecclesiastically subordinate to the
bishops—the successors of the Apostles, who have
imparted to them the power of absolution ; the laity
are to be ecclesiastically subordinate to the priests as
the possessors of that power.   Here we have those
very " principles of ecclesiastical subordination " which
Froude desired to see recognized by the laity, even
though not enforced by " the law of the land."   Thus
the Tract seems to follow precisely the lines of the
Sermon.

4. In 1833 (17 November) he thus writes to Newman
about " The Doctrine necessary to Salvation " :—

> " I am led to question whether Justification by Faith is an integral
> part of this doctrine.   I have not breathed this to a soul but you, and
> *express* myself offhand.   Is the denial of it anathematized directly
> or by implication ?   May one not broadly maintain, that no one has
> any right to call any opinion necessary, unless he believes its *necessity*,
> as distinct from its truth, to be revealed (I mean in Scripture or
> tradition) ?   If so, how liberal and how bigoted one may be at the
> same time without repining !   I could be content to waive the
> Articles,* keeping the Creeds, and so forth."

Here we find Froude suggesting (1) that no doctrine ought to be called necessary unless it is authoritatively declared to be so by Scripture, *or tradition, i.e.*
the Church ; (2) that the Thirty-Nine Articles might
be " waived " ; (3) that Justification by Faith (as he
understood it, and as he supposed it to be understood
by the Articles) is not a part of this " necessary doctrine."   In all these respects we shall find Newman
influenced by Froude ; and not improbably Froude's
difficulty as regards the last-mentioned doctrine was
the cause of his publishing (1838) a special treatise on
it (about which more will be said hereafter) which was
to Newman himself a source of great perplexity and

anxiety, and which bewildered, rather than enlightened, several of his most devoted admirers.

5. The following extract (8 February, 1834) from a letter to Keble is important because, although the suppressions in the text make the meaning obscure, the Editors, *i.e.* Newman and Keble, themselves indicated (in a foot-note) that what Froude proposed, the *Via Media* attempted to carry out :—

"You will see . . . the length I am being pulled on in anti-Protestantism. . . . Would not Hammond and Fell, and the rest of those humble men of God,* have altered ?"

6. The following is from a letter to Newman (2 July, 1835) :—

"The phenomena of the heavens are repugnant to Newton, just in the same way as the letter of Scripture to the Church ; *i.e.,* on the assumption that they contradict every notion which they do not make self-evident." He goes on to argue against Newman's "trumpery principle, about Scripture being the rule of faith in *fundamentals* (I nauseate the words)."

Carrying this suggestion a little further, Newman in 1843 maintained that the letter of the Scripture, where it is "repugnant," not to the Church, but to science,— *e.g.* to the Newtonian astronomy itself—may be susceptible of some entirely non-obvious interpretation ; and that nothing can be decided concerning the "repugnance" until something can be done which, in this world, we can never hope to do.

"Scripture, for instance, says that the sun moves and the earth is stationary : and science, that the earth moves and the sun is comparatively at rest. How can we determine which of these statements is the very truth, till we know what motion is ? "

(7) Tract 90 took a view of the Articles which Newman thus expressed in 1841 :—

" The only peculiarity of the view I advocate, if I must so call it, is this, that whereas it is usual, at this day, to make the particular *belief* of *their writers* their true interpretation, I would make *the belief of the Catholic Church* such."

The same " peculiarity of view" was suggested by Froude to Newman, seven years before (8 April, 1834) :—

" In the preface to the Articles, it is said that we are to understand them in their grammatical sense ; which I interpret into a permission to think nothing of the opinion of their framers."

8. The following was written to Keble (9 January, 1834 :—

" You will be shocked at my avowal that I am every day becoming a less and less loyal son of the Reformation.   It appears to me plain that in all matters that seem to us indifferent or even doubtful, we should conform our practices to those of the Church which has preserved its traditionary practices unbroken.   We cannot know about any seemingly indifferent practice of the Church of Rome that it is not a development of the Apostolic ἦθος : and it is to no purpose to say that we can find no proof of it in the writings of the six first centuries ; they must find a *dis*proof if they would do anything."

Possibly this letter may have been written to Keble by a kind of preconcerted arrangement with Newman, a sort of joint attack such as Froude suggests else-where : " Do keep writing to Keble and stirring his rage ; he is my fire but I am his poker."   In any case, such a stimulus, if it had not already reached Newman directly, would be almost certain to pass to him through Keble—letters from the sufferer at Barbados to one friend being naturally transmitted to the other.·   The same " poker " that stirred Keble would simultaneously stir one more easily moved to a religious " rage." And there are three distinct appeals here that would address themselves powerfully to Newman : first, the

mention of the "unbroken" tradition; secondly, the
argument that a statement is not necessarily untrue
because it is not proved to be true (it is only unproved,
it is not disproved) of which Newman made copious
use in his *Essay on Ecclesiastical Miracles;* thirdly,
the notion that many of the practices of the Church of
Rome, though condemned by Protestants, may possibly
be "developments." This last-mentioned doctrine
may have been present with Newman in his earlier
speculations, and he says that he introduced it into
the Arians in 1832 ; but in the application of it to the
Roman controversy in Newman's *Home Thoughts
Abroad,* published in 1836, we not improbably see
one of those doctrines of Froude, which, as the
Apologia says, "arrested" Newman even though he
did not give "immediate assent" to them. In the
dialogue entitled "Home Thoughts," it is the Roman
controversialist who uses the argument from Development and who is supposed to be beaten. The notion
seems to have taken Newman's imagination at once ;
and by battling against it with logical fence, he was
unconsciously doing no more than preparing himself
for surrender to it after a reasonable resistance.

9. One of the strongest barriers between Newman
and the Church of Rome was the belief of his youth
that Rome was Antichrist. Such a notion in such a
man was not to be dispelled by argument, but by the
substitution of some other more congenial belief. And,
remembering with what an increasing abhorrence
he regarded Rationalism, we shall probably not be
mistaken in supposing that the following suggestion of
Froude's, made in 1834 (26 December) may have been
pondered by Newman and kept on the surface of his
mind till at last it found admission :

"When I get your letter, I expect a rowing for my Roman Catholic sentiments. Really I hate the Reformation and the Reformers more and more, and have almost made up my mind that the rationalist spirit they set afloat is the ψευδοπροφήτης ('false prophet') of the Revelation."

§ 36. *Froude's General Influence*

As regards the subordination of Preaching to the Services of the Church, and the more frequent administration of the Holy Communion, Froude was wonderfully in advance both of Newman and Keble. A letter to the latter (9 January 1834) says, " I think that in the present state of religion, preaching should be quite disconnected from the Services, and looked on as an address to the unconnected (*sic*)," *i.e.* apparently to those who are not yet members of the Church ; and he seems to recommend the utilization of travelling lay-preachers under the name of " itinerant talkers." To another correspondent he says :—

" Preaching and reading the Scripture is what a layman can do as well as a clergyman. And it is no wonder that people should forget the difference between ordained and unordained persons, when those who are ordained do nothing for them but what they could have done just as well without ordination." He suggests to his friend even *doing without* a pulpit. But, "if you are determined to have a pulpit in your church, which I would much rather be without, do put it at the west end of the church, or leave it where it is ; every one can hear you perfectly ; and what can they want more? But whatever you do, pray don't let it stand in the light of the Altar, which, if there is any truth in my notions of Ordination, is more sacred than the Holy of Holies in the Jewish Temple."

The notion of putting the pulpit at the west end (the preacher, presumably, to preach over the backs of the people) must strike the reader as " sillyish," unless meant in jest. But the next suggestion to the same correspondent (22 August 1834) is of a very different nature. He urges the duty of every clergyman to give the serious members of his congregation the opportunity of receiving the Communion as often as he can without neglecting other parts of his duty. He himself would like it, if possible, daily. But he suggests to his friend the possibility of weekly, or at all events monthly, Communion. It is astonishing to us in these days, to find him apologizing for these suggestions as "overstrained." And that Newman and Keble should not have gone with him so far as this, is a curious sign of the prevailing ecclesiastical laxity.

> "I wish you would turn this over in your mind. I dare say you will think my view overstrained, and very likely it may be a little. Yet the more I think of it the less doubtful it seems to me. I know that neither N(ewman) nor K(eble) when I left England (Nov. 1833) saw the thing in the light in which it now strikes me; they thought that it was desirable to have the Communion as often as possible, but still, that the customs of particular places ought not to be changed without particular reason. But it really does seem to me that the Church of England has gone so very wrong in this matter, that it is not right to keep things smooth any longer."

Froude had not long to wait, however, before his protests received their due weight ; and not improbably he is accountable for the exaggerated expression inserted by Newman in the Advertisement to the first volume of the collected Tracts (published at the end of the same year (1834) in which this letter was written) : " The sacraments, and not preaching, are the sources of grace." Indeed, in this matter, Froude's influence is being to this very day exerted on the Anglican Church through the *Christian Year*. The

13th stanza on "Gunpowder Treason" formerly ran thus, but, of course, without italics :—

> "O come to our Communion Feast,
>   There present in the heart,
>   *Not in the hands*, th' eternal Priest
>   Will His true self impart."

Against this Froude protested to Keble (16 September, 1833) : " I should like to know why you flinch from saying that the power of making the Body and Blood of Christ is vested in the successors of the Apostles." This seems to him "simpler and less open to cavil" than the expression which Keble and others had used ! That Newman, prompted by Froude, did not "flinch" from these very words, we have good evidence. I italicize them in the following extract from a letter written to him by his friend Richards. Newman had used the words in an anonymous Tract. Rickards, not knowing the author, comments upon them (20 November, 1833), in these unfavourable terms : "What I most deplore is the language in which it speaks of some of the gifts bestowed upon the ministers of Christ and especially the expression "as intrusted with the awful and mysterious gift of *making the bread and wine Christ's Body and Blood*." It falls in with the supposition of Froude's influence here, that we have a subsequent letter from Newman to Froude in which, without actually blaming the latter, he tells him (15 December, 1833), that the " Transubstantiation passages" have "brought us into all sorts of trouble" and " Rickards has bullied me ὅσον ἀμήχανον" (*i.e.* "to any amount "). Subsequently, when Newman published (1835)—in his own name and not, as in the case of the Tract, anonymously—a second volume of sermons, he, without stating any opinion of his own, so far sacrificed to caution as to say in an Appendix, that Hooker was "known to be opposed to any formal doctrinal assertion of the presence of Christ in the sacred Elements, and especially on this ground, *lest* any such should withdraw our minds from His real presence and operation in the soul and body of the recipient." Those who appreciate Newman's nice use of terms, will see that the words "formal" and "on this ground" may well cover his own tacit adherence to the expressions which Rickards had condemned as being liable to give offence. However, Newman also quotes Hooker as saying, "The real presence of Christ's most blessed Body and Blood is *not* therefore to be sought for in the Sacrament, but in the worthy receiver of the Sacrament"—which seems equivalent to Keble's "*not* in the hands." It is not improbable that this is one of Newman's "economies" which would not have commended itself to Froude. How Froude ultimately beat both Keble and Newman, and influences high Anglicanism to this day, the curious reader will find detailed in an Appendix.

§ 37. *Froude, for " Holiness " against " Peace "*

The day after receiving news of Froude's death Newman wrote (2 March, 1836) to the bosom friend of his undergraduate days, J. W. Bowden, that he "can never have a greater loss," looking on for the whole of his life. Froude, he says, filled for him, at Oxford, in later days, the place that Bowden had filled in earlier, so that he from time to time confused him with Bowden, or called him by the name of the latter.

" I never, on the whole," he adds, "fell in with so gifted a person. In variety and perfection of gifts, I think he far exceeded even Keble. For myself, I cannot describe what I owe to him as regards the intellectual principles (*i.e.* philosophy) of religion and morals." Afterwards, as a tribute to his memory, he appended some lines to a poem composed in 1833 on the Separation of Friends. Originally it had ended with the description of a death-bed scene followed by the prayers of the survivor :

> " Fear startled at his pains and dreary end,
>   Hope raised her chalice high,
> And the twin sisters still his shade attend,
>   View'd in the mourner's eye.
> So day by day for him from earth ascends,
>   As steam in summer even,
> The speechless intercession of his friends,
>   Toward the azure heaven."

To these, after Froude's death, he made the following addition :

> " Ah! dearest, with a word he could dispel
>   All questioning, and raise
> Our hearts to rapture, whispering all was well
>   And turning prayer to praise.
> And other secrets too he could declare,
>   By patterns all divine,
> His earthly creed retouching here and there,
>   And deepening every line.
> Dearest ! he longs to speak, as I to know,
>   And yet we both refrain :
> It were not good : a little doubt below,
>   And all will soon be plain."

Such a tribute ought, of itself, to suffice to show that Froude is not quite fairly, or at least fully, represented

in the *Remains*. The Journal and even the Letters
fail, perhaps, to express some latent feeling which
might have softened apparent harshness. To those
who knew him well, his words were interpreted by his
personality, which all concur in describing as bright,
graceful, and even "beautiful." "Terribly thin"—
says one who saw him alighting from the coach amid
the greetings of his friends, on his last visit to Oxford
—"his countenance dark and wasted, but with a
brilliancy of expression and grace of outline which
justified all his friends said of him"; and Newman, in
recording their last farewell, tells us how "his face
lighted up and almost shone in the darkness" as if to
say that, in this world, they were parting for ever. It
was this brilliant and graceful embodiment in one so
earnest, so ascetically strict, so clear-headed, and so
confident—of definite, consistent imaginations about
spiritual things (which imaginations Newman describes
as "intellectual principles"), that first arrested, and
ultimately captivated, the older friend who was at first
disposed to smile at, even while admiring, the erratic,
"sillyish," "red-hot High Churchman."

This ought to surprise no one. Fundamentally agreeing with Froude, from the first, in the principles of
religious fear, obedience, and self-distrust, Newman
differed from him only in the expression and application
of them ; and on these points Froude's mind was settled
while Newman's was still in flux. No wonder that,
by degrees, Newman lost confidence in any utterance
of his own unless Froude first stamped it with his
approval. Did not Froude always take the lead,
experimenting, as it were, on himself? And had
not Newman repeatedly to confess that Froude was
right, and he himself wrong? One reason for this,

was, that Froude, being of an æsthetic bent, instinctively turned from the Primitive Church, which was, to him, an affair of books, and of which he knew very little, to the mediæval Church, with which he was in complete harmony, or to the Anglican non-jurors, about whom he had some sympathetic knowledge. This gave to his notions a naturalness and a practicableness in which Newman's were deficient. For this, and for other reasons, Froude seemed to be a seer in regions where Newman was only a groper ; and so, in time, the latter came naturally not only to depend on the former, but also to avow his dependence so far as to declare his unwillingness to commit himself to anything definite till the man who could *see* had given it his "imprimatur."

Still, the brighter and more pleasing side of Froude's character must not allow us to forget that his search after holiness implied not only something bordering on abjectness towards God, but also strife on earth and the appearance of ill-will towards a great multitude of men. These qualities explain, in part, the secret of his power over Newman ; who would not have allowed himself to be influenced by any but a detached soul, holding aloof from all the world, and especially perhaps from the rabble, that "knoweth not the law." But Froude was by far the more combative of the two, and appears to have acted on Newman, as on Keble, in the way of an inciting cause, or, to use his own metaphor. a "poker." A few hints of this have been given above, but, in the *Remains*, and elsewhere, there are abundant proofs.

"Hurrell Froude and I," writes Keble to Coleridge, ' took into our consideration your opinion that ' there are good men of all parties,' and agreed that it is a bad doctrine for these days : the time being come in which, according to John Miller, 'scoundrels must be called scoundrels.'" All who have studied Keble's life will recognize that Froude, and not Keble, must have been the main factor in "agreements" of this kind. But apart from that, the most cursory glance at the *Remains* would almost justify us in attributing it to Froude. On the same page for example on which we find "the wretched B.," we find also "that base fellow H. ;" and concerning a clergyman who in some political election had proposed "the health of those dissenting ministers who have laboured in the cause," it is suggested that he ought to be asked whether he recollected that the Prayer Book would translate his words into "the health of the founders of damnable heresy." Further, Philip Van Artevelde is "a rascally brewer ;" the Memoirs of Hampden are to be written by someone who "hates that worthy with as much zeal and more knowledge than your humble servant ;" he is glad to know the Puritans that he may have "a better right to hate Milton," whose fame he craves to see finally demolished ; and as to "the march of mind in France" he sincerely hopes that it "may yet be a bloody one."

Above all, Froude's attitude to the negroes taxes the ingenuity of his editors to extenuate and excuse it. Not of course that they would think any excuse necessary for the following extract. Froude was bound —so perhaps were Keble and Newman, though we find the latter afterwards playing with the notion of conniving at a Bible Christianity for elementary schools —to deny the name of "religious instruction" to anything that did not include High Anglican doctrine. But still, considering the difficulty of doing anything

for the poor creatures in Barbados without compromise, he ought (we might suppose) to have been
rather less harsh on the following attempt of the
Clergy to unite with the Nonconformists in some joint
system :—

"In —— the other day, in the absence of our friend P——, the
Rural Dean and the clergy 'went a-whoring' after the Wesleyans,
and the whole kit besides, to concoct a joint plan of general education : and very cozily they were going on together when he arrived
the other day.   Religious instruction here means marrying the
niggers, baptizing them, and teaching them to read.

> "'The age is out of joint.   O cursed spite,
> That ever I was born to set it right!'"

Apparently Froude and his friend P——, "set it
right," or tried to do so, by stopping this attempt, and
by leaving the negroes without any instruction at all.
For this, the Editors naturally make no apology,
because apology would not seem needed.   But it is
difficult for them to make, and impossible for the
ordinary reader to understand, such defence as they
make of the following passage :

"I think I have become even more uncharitable and churlish than
I was.   I have felt it a kind of duty to sustain in my mind an
habitual hostility to the niggers, and to chuckle over the failure of
the new system ; as if these poor creatures concentrated in themselves all the whiggery, dissent, cant, and abomination, that have
been ranged on their side."

Their excuse is little more than this, that he " re-
ceived the Communion with " negroes,* and that
Corporal Trim persisted in calling a French soldier a
" French dog," even in the act of giving him a penny !
This is not much.   Yet we must all agree with their
remark in the Preface : " The omission of what, to

some, sounds questionable, would have made the picture of him, as a Christian warrior, altogether less
complete and instructive."

This at least is true. Without this the picture would
have been indeed incomplete ; and, with this, it is
indeed most "instructive." For we find here depicted ⌐
a Christian in whose most secret records, self-examina-
tions, and prayers, there appears scarcely any mention
of Christ as a Person, and very little trace of any love
of Christ (who hardly appears at all in them except in
some reference to the sacramental Body and Blood); yet
one who with all his heart and soul is seeking after
that salvation which he supposes to be derivable
from Christ's Church : a man who obstinately detested, first in himself, then in others, the least
vestige of affectation, cant, or hypocrisy ; who spoke
what he meant, as he meant it, and would have always
gone, if his friends had allowed him, by the straightest
of ways towards what he deemed the best of objects ;
a man, therefore, of an essentially truth-loving disposition, searching for truth in all sincerity, but restricted
by a "system" to a search within certain limits and
through certain methods ; shut out from the great
world of men and shut into the comparatively small
world—not indeed as Newman was, of books, but—of
ecclesiastical traditions and imaginations ; by nature,
without any deep feeling of human-hearted sociality,
without love of man as a fellow-man ; by ecclesiasticism, led rather to hate than to love—loving indeed a
few, but only as a Spartan might love his companions
in arms, loving those select spirits by whose side he
could battle for the interests of " the Church."

Such a picture, though " instructive," is not pleasing.
Yet those who feel inclined to ridicule, or to give way

to disgust, as they peruse records of one whom they may be disposed to call "The Minute Ascetic,"—telling us of his shame at feeling ashamed that he had muddy trousers, or no gloves; or of his remorse for talking "flash," or for not finding it easy to keep awake during a sermon, or for wanting to win sixpences at cards—will, if they read on a little further, generally find other entries of a different character; as, for example, touching a certain Offertory: "intended £2 10s. but thought I should be observed, so vowed £5 to the —— Mendicity Society." We cannot smile at the man, who, beneath under-statements conveyed, half in slang, half in the language of Tractarian reserve, concealed a resolution, not only to deny himself, but even, so far as he could, to suppress himself; who so hated his own individuality, and was so alarmed at the least touch of the self-will of genius within him, that he "made it his great ambition to become a humdrum." Doomed to an early, lingering death, and to leave others to continue the religious conflict in which he, of all the combatants, took the keenest and most passionate pleasure, he drops no word of self-commiseration or repining; and in the last month of his life, having contributed the proceeds of his Fellowship to the Cause, he asks Newman to use it at his pleasure and to make people infer that the money was being contributed by a large number of subscribers. "Spend away, my boy, and make a great fuss as if your money came from a variety of sources." If this was "economy," it cannot at all events, be scoffed at. Nothing is here for contempt—least of all from common-place, compromising, half-way halting, semi-Christians or quasi-Christians. Manifestly we have here a man; no mere word-bag or lump of sensa-

tions; but a being with a will, and with a controlling
purpose; one who knew his own mind, and therefore
had a right to lead those who did not know theirs; a
fine specimen of the ecclesiastic militant; essentially a
champion of holiness, though essentially—if charity be
essential—not a Christian.

Such was Richard Hurrell Froude who while living,
influenced Newman much, and, after his death, more;
"retouching the faith," and "deepening every line in
the creed"—not, as Newman's poem suggested, of
himself, but of the poet, his survivor, his second self.
When he died, a book of his, by what most people
would call an accident, passed into Newman's possession. Newman deemed it more than an accident.
From that time forward, it lay on his study table; and
by it, though dead, his friend continued to speak and
to guide him—always in one direction. Rightly does
Newman record as one among nine important "events"
of the "cardinal" spring of 1836, "my knowing and
using the Breviary."

CHAPTER IX

§ 38. *Coming out of his shell*

WE return to Newman. " I was drifting," says
the *Apologia*, "in the direction of Liberalism.
I was rudely awakened from my dream at the end of
1827 by two great blows—illness and bereavement."
The illness which suddenly cut short Newman's work
as an Examiner in the Schools with a fainting fit,
has been mentioned above. It does not appear to
have been so long or so dangerous as to merit, at first
sight, the importance here attached to it ; but perhaps
its indelible effect on Newman may be due to its
peculiar circumstances. In the midst of a circle of
familiar faces, and familiar work, hedged round by the
little pomps and importances of a University official,
holding in his hands the fate of anxious aspirants for
First Classes, amid questions about this or that ancient
author, this or that little incident of antique history, or
this or that construction or idiom or peculiar usage of
some Greek particle,—thus suddenly with οὐ μή, or μὴ οὐ,
between your lips, to be pulled down, as it were, into
the very waters of the river of death, and to feel that
cold touch, and that sinking of the heart, which none
who have returned from them can ever forget—this,

though it may last but for a few seconds, is in truth
" a great blow " to those who in that short, sharp
plunge have realised how great and agonizing an effort
it was to throw themselves upon the Unchangeable
Rock, or the still greater agony, perhaps, of struggling
to touch bottom, and finding that they cannot feel it.

The " blow " of illness ought indeed to have been
heavy, to be mentioned in the same breath with the
" bereavement " which he endured in the death of his
sister Mary on 5 January, 1828, which made an impression on him the depth of which is attested for
years afterwards, by the Poems as well as by the
Letters.   Apparently his theological scheme did not at
this time allow him (as it did a few years afterwards)
to believe that the departed held any kind of communion with the loved survivors.   Hence, to his mind,
the only consolation, during life, appeared to be an
exact recollection of the dead ; and for this purpose he
bids his sisters treasure up every scrap of characteristic
word, or deed, and write it down at once before they
forget it.   " To think," he exclaims, " that all at once
we can only converse *about* her, as about some inani-
mate object, word, or stone."   And again, " To allude
to her as now out of the way and insensible to what we
are doing (as is indeed the case) is to me the most
distressing circumstance attending our loss."   It is
that doctrine of the " insensibility " of the dead—
evidently put forward with a sad deliberateness because
it " is indeed the case "—which seems to differentiate
him from Keble, even where he thinks he is in agreement with the latter in his views of the message conveyed to us through Nature from the spirit-world.
Both realise in Nature some presence of the dead ;
but Keble seems to have agreed with Wordsworth in

looking on Nature positively, as a kind of well-wrought
garment, through which we discern shape and motion,
while Newman regards it negatively, as a kind of veil,
a thick veil, that hides all that we most want to see ;
so that, to dramatize the difference between the two
poets, through Keble's Nature the Voice says, "Even
now, though far away, I am still near ; I am risen" ;
but, through Newman's Nature, "Though here, I am
far away ; I am hidden." An extract from a letter will
illustrate this. After a ride in the country, Newman
tells his sister that he has been impressed more than
he had thought possible by Keble's lines :—

> "Chanting with a *solemn* voice
> Minds us of our better choice."

And then he adds :—

> "I could hardly believe the lines were not my own, and Keble
> had not taken them from me. I wish it were possible for words to
> put down these indefinite, vague, and withal subtle feelings which
> quite pierce the soul and make it sick. Dear Mary seems embodied
> in every tree and hid behind every hill. What a veil and curtain
> this world is ! beautiful, but still a veil."

Among the dead, Newman was now to number one
whose death seems to have produced little impression
on him, yet to whom he had once thought he owed the
greatest debt any human being can owe to another.
The reader will remember that Walter Mayer, one of
his masters at Ealing School, is described as having
been, humanly speaking, the cause of his "conversion" ; and it was in his church, at Warton, that Newman, four years ago, had preached his first sermon.
The following letter, which is given entire, contains
the only allusion to his death in Newman's published
correspondence :—

" Last week, I did my exercises for my B.D. degree, merely to keep Arnold company, since one man cannot dispute with himself [and he could get no one]; and its (*sic*) being in Latin and in Collections week, I found it too hard work.

" I take most vigorous exercise which does me much good. I have learned to leap (to a certain point) which is a larking thing for a don. The exhilaration of going quickly through the air is for my spirits very good. I have a sermon to prepare for Warton to-morrow."

A footnote adds, " Rev. Walter Mayer's funeral sermon." And this is all. Possibly the writer may have been wishing to relieve his mother's anxiety as to his health, and, on that account, says little about a matter which might be supposed to cause him some distress. But still Mr. Mayer's *exit* is wonderfully quiet. Perhaps there is some omission in the Letters, or there may have been some estrangement between the teacher and pupil ; but, unless Newman's printed correspondence at this period does him grievous injustice, these very plain obsequies paid to his old Evangelical teacher appear to indicate a simultaneous death and burial of Evangelicalism itself, as of a former friend of whom the survivor was just a little bit ashamed, and about whom he perhaps felt, "the less said, the better."

In the spring of this year, Newman, as successor to Hawkins, was inducted into St. Mary's, and now recommenced regular preaching. His first extant sermon of this year treats of Infant Baptism, and marks an advance towards High Church doctrine. It declares that "though the Gospel is light, it is so only for " the children of the Church," that is, for those who accept the interpretation of it imposed by the Church ; and that " the blood of Christ is to be imputed to us by Sacraments, visible rites which represent to us the heavenly truth and convey what they represent." During the same year Froude achieved what he considered the great deed of his life by bringing Newman and Keble together ; and in the summer Newman paid the latter a visit at his home in Fairford. The impression made by Keble's friendship must have been deepened by the chronological study of the Fathers, which he now at last began.

Spring came, metaphorically, as well as literally, to the newly-appointed Vicar. He was doing good work in the college, and beginning to be a power in St. Mary's ; he was shaking himself free from a doctrine which, for some time past, he must have felt as a yoke upon his soul, and a restraint upon his utterance ; he was also gaining friends who could unreservedly sympathize with his aspirations. At this time, he says, he began to " come out of his shell." Never happy except when busy, he had plenty to do, about which there could be no doubt that it needed to be done, and that he was the man to do it.

The new Provost was supposed to be an invalid and had predicted that he would not live over forty ; on Newman, as the leading spirit among the tutors, the sadly-needed improvement of the College seemed to depend, and he threw himself into it. Who could refuse admiration to the combined versatility and thoroughness with which he discharged two tasks so distinct ?—in college, making war against ignorance, laziness, and luxury, and preparing the way for a better system of instruction and discipline ; quick at detecting, inflexible in punishing and eradicating ; alive to see, and ready to prevent, or suppress, lapses, negligences, tricks, and subterfuges ; so clever, so keen—one might almost say so worldly-wise in dealing with men of the

world and things of the world ; and yet, the same man,
in the pulpit of St. Mary's, absolutely detached from
the world ; close, as it seemed, to the very presence of
the Invisible ; with such an insight into the unseen
realities of things, with such a sense of spiritual per-
spective and proportion, and such a power of expressing what he felt and saw, that, under the spell of a
few sentences from his lips, the visible and tangible
crust of the material universe seemed to melt away,
and the listener's soul was left alone, face to face with
the awful and everlasting Judge.

Well might Robert Wilberforce, his colleague in the
Oriel tutorship, say that, after hearing him preach, he
felt he himself could preach no longer, but was altogether off the road ; well might his pupils in college be
captivated by the tutor who threw himself heart and
soul into their needs and work as though they were his
one object in life, and as if he would *make* them do
first class work by the mere power of his own volition ;
and well might his fellow-tutors look on with wondering
admiration, content to follow where he led, while even
the cautious Provost, for the present, forgot to be
alarmed, though perhaps occasionally pondering an
old saying about Newman in his undergraduate days :
" Here is a fellow who will not talk : but when you
have once got him to talk, you cannot get him to
stop."

§ 39. *The Peel Election*

In 1828 Newman was not a High Churchman ; in
1829 he was. That at least was the judgment of the
man who was now fast becoming his best friend.
" Newman," wrote Froude in September 1828, "is a
fellow that I like the more, the more I think of him ;

only I would give a few odd pence if he were not a heretic." The following year finds him writing to Newman himself, " I hope Pusey may turn out High Church after all : " and clearly he feels that Newman shares the hope with him. By this time, then, the latter—although both then and for long afterwards he declined to commit himself to any party—definitely belonged to the High Church. Yet everything, in the previous year, seemed to point to a quiet and gradual development. Even as an Evangelical, or (as Froude called it) a "heretic," Newman had come to attach an importance, unusual with Evangelicals, to the Sacraments. And that he had revolted against the shibboleths of his former party seems to be clear from a letter of 1828 (12 August) in which Froude claims his sympathy for a parson in the country who, he says, "is much disgusted with the cant that has been disseminated among his poor parishioners by silly women from ——, and complains that he can hardly go into a cottage without having religious affectation thrust on him." Why should he not have proceeded to work out his theological and ecclesiastical problems in a gradual way ? What happened to make 1829 the year of the decisive change ?

Politics seem to have been the moving cause—politics, around him for some years past, noisy enough, but hitherto not *in* him ; now however for the first time brought home to him, not improbably, by his Tory friend and fellow-tutor, who had his rooms above him, and who could come down in the evenings to talk over the shameful " Repeal of Dissenters' Liabilities " passed in 1828, and the possibility of a similar bill soon, in the interests of Romanists, ending the talk, perhaps, with execrations on the State for thus sacri-

ficing to political expediency the interests of the
Church. The last page but two of Froude's *Occasional Thoughts*, 1826-9, bears on the exclusion of
Dissenters. The last but one talks about the " ' array
of talent ' which has marshalled itself exclusively on
the side of the Romanists," and maintains that this
"array" should go for little as regards their political
claims. This phrase was used by the Peelites to
denote their intellectual superiority in the election
which turned Sir Robert Peel out of his seat for
Oxford University ; and Froude is manifestly writing
with reference to that contest. It would be interesting
to have some record of the conversation of the two
friends early in February, when the King's Speech
recommended Parliament to consider the disabilities
of Romanists, and Peel, with the view of taking the
opinion of his constituents, sent in to the Vice-
Chancellor the resignation of his seat for the
University.

Early in the month, at all events, Newman gave no
sign of action. He dates on 4 February one of his
longest poems on a theme unusual with him. Entitled
"My Lady Nature and her Daughters," the poem
says much about Nature, but a good deal more about
ladies, and about—

> " the robes they love.
> Silks where hues alternate play,
> Shawls, and scarfs, and mantles gay,
> Gold, and gems, and crispèd hair."

—protesting that there is nothing on earth so fair as
the graceful mirth of a lady, and that Nature herself,
with all her lofty aspirations, cannot so befriend " work-
day souls " as to answer their appeals for help. For

that, such souls must turn, not to Lady Nature, but
to "her daughters : "

> " High-born Nature answers not,
> Leave her in her starry dome,
> Seek we lady-lighted home,
> Nature 'mid the spheres bears sway,
> Ladies rule where hearts obey."

On that same day Peel had sent in his resignation ;
but it was known beforehand in the political world
that concessions to the Romanists would be announced
in the King's Speech. On the 17th we find Newman
already for some days engaged in the conflict. On
the 8th, three days after Peel's resignation had reached
the Vice-Chancellor, he is intending to do nothing.
What had happened in the interval to produce this
change ? An omen prepared the way for impelling,
but did not actually impel him ; for he writes (8 February) about it in perfect calm to his sister, clearly
assuming that Peel will have his way, and that there
will be no resistance :—

> " I was much struck with this evening's first lesson. It seemed
> to apply to the Church. You know I have no opinion about the
> Catholic question, and now it is settled, I shall perhaps never have
> one ; but still, its passing is one of the signs of the times, of the
> encroachment of Philosophism and Indifferentism in the Church."

The lesson was from Isaiah : the prophet appeals
to God to " rend the mountains and come down " ;
he laments for the desolation of the oppressed Church :
—" Our holy and our beautiful house wherein our
fathers praised thee is burned with fire ; and all our
pleasant things are laid waste. Wilt thou refrain
thyself for these things, O Lord ? Wilt thou hold
thy peace and afflict us very sore ? " What was it
that so interpreted this omen that it became the spark

to a conflagration ? Was it some sign ? or a supposed
answer to prayer ? Or was he goaded to action by
some exasperating boasts of the Liberals in Oxford ?
or did Froude come down stairs just after this letter
was finished, and reproach the writer with the pusil-
lanimous words he had written—"now it is settled"
—urging him to rise up and show Oxford, and through
Oxford, England, that it was *not* settled ? And was
it Froude that dispelled, now and for ever, the
distracting fancy of a "lady-lighted home," and
confirmed him in that resolution which, says the
Apologia, continued "with the break of a month now,
and a month then" *up to 1829, and, after that date,
without any break at all?*

To these conjectural questions the correspondence gives no answer ; but a letter, nine days
afterwards, exhibits Newman in the thick of political
conflict, in which he had evidently played a leading
part, throwing himself into it almost with the passion
and freshness of a boy, and all the more fiercely
because he was fierce for the Church. Others were
indignant, even those who were in favour of Peel's
measure in itself, at the suddenness with which the
political leader had changed his mind, and because he
expected his followers to change theirs as suddenly ;
but this indignation, although Newman felt it too, did
not sit well on one who had so ostentatiously proclaimed that the measure was an affair of history and
specialists, and that he did not intend to form an
opinion about it. Newman's main reason for resentment was that it seemed an attack upon the Church,
and this just at a time when the Church was beginning
to be the rock upon which he was basing much of his
new religious belief.

His excitement, though natural to one who was unused to such things, was very bewildering to his mother, who was perhaps annoyed at her son's calling his old friend Hawkins "the meddling Provost," for taking up Peel. The Peelites, too, "are mere sucking-pigs in their canvass and their calculations," strutting about like "peacocks." Peel himself is declared to be, in the opinion of the Oxford residents, "unworthy to represent a religious, straightforward, unpolitical body, whose interest he had, in some form, more or less betrayed." However, the result exceeded Newman's most sanguine hopes. The London lawyers, and the "array of talent," were beaten. " High Church and Low Church," said a Peelite newspaper, "have joined, being set on rejecting Mr. Peel." He was turned out by a majority of 755 to 609.

§ 40. *Newman prepares to do Battle for the Church*

Newman was not slow to see the lesson conveyed by this brilliant victory. This (he tells his mother) was the first public event he had been concerned in, and he thanks God from his heart both for his cause and its success : he and his friends have proved the independence of the Church and of Oxford ; "Well, the poor defenceless Church has borne the brunt of it, and I see in it the strength and unity of Churchmen." He does not add—but he seems to have added mentally—"Why should not Churchmen unite again for similar triumphs ?" A few days afterwards he writes again to his mother a couple of letters, almost amounting to a pamphlet, in which he sketches out a plan of campaign for the Church against the world, and tries to induce her to adopt his views. He begins by

urging that the laity must, even in these days, be
dependent on the clergy for religious truth. Here
he uses wonderful tact and tenderness in dealing with
what he must have deemed her prejudices. " Without
meaning, of course," that " Christianity is in itself
opposed to free inquiry," still he thinks it is "*in fact
opposed to*" free inquiry in the sense now understood
by the latter. The stream of opinion now tending
against the Church must, he says, be overcome, not
yielded to. He implies that the only hope against the
influx of unbelief is to be found in the promise of preservation to the Church, which, however, may very
probably be separated from the State : and he just
touches on the " Sacraments," together with " religious
education," in such a way as not to shock and yet
possibly to enlighten her, as to his own changed
position with respect to them :

" What a scribbler I am become ! But the fact is my mind is so
full of ideas in consequence of this important event, and my views
have so much enlarged and expanded, that in justice to myself, I
ought to write a volume.

" We live in a novel era—one in which there is an advance towards
universal education. Men have hitherto depended on others, and
especially on the clergy, for religious truth ; now each man attempts
to judge for himself. Now, without meaning of course that Christianity is in itself opposed to free inquiry, still I think it is *in fact*
at the present time opposed to the particular form which that liberty
of thought has now assumed. Christianity is of faith, modesty,
lowliness, subordination ; but the spirit at work against it is one of
latitudinarianism, indifferentism, and schism, a spirit which tends to
overthrow doctrine, as if the fruit of bigotry and discipline—as if
the instrument of priestcraft. All parties seem to acknowledge that
the stream of opinion is setting against the Church. I do believe it
will ultimately be separated from the State, and at this prospect I
look with apprehension—(1) because all revolutions are awful things,
and the effect of this revolution is unknown ; (2) because the upper

classes will be left almost religionless ; (3) because there will not be that security for sound doctrine without change, which is given by Act of Parliament ; (4) because the clergy will be thrown on their congregations for voluntary subscriptions.

"It is no reply to say that the majesty of truth will triumph, for man's nature is corrupt ; also, even, should it triumph, still this will only be ultimately, and the meanwhile may last for centuries. Yet I do still think there is a promise of preservation to the Church ; and in its sacraments, preceding and attending religious education, there are such means of heavenly grace, that I do not doubt it will live on in the most irreligious and atheistical times."

Then he enumerates the Church's "enemies" in six classes ; among whom, under the head of "Baptists," he seems to include, or at all events, to dispose of, the inconsistent Evangelicals, who would, in times of commotion, split, and go over to this side or that. After this, follows an interesting defence of "prejudice and bigotry" as the allies of the National Church. To appreciate this, we must remember that Newman had lately been rallying to his side the "two-bottle orthodox" as they were called by the Liberals. Whately, he says, taking a humorous revenge for his conduct in the recent election, had asked him to dine with a set of these men, the least intellectual in Oxford, and the fondest of port ; and, after giving him an evening between Provost This, and Principal That, had asked him "whether he was proud of his friends." This gave Newman something to think about. He was *not* proud of his friends, and yet—these were the friends of the Church. How came it so ? This was the question which, under the appearance of answering for his mother, he is really trying to answer for himself :

"And now I come to another phenomenon : the talent of the day is against the Church. The Church party (visibly at least, for there may be latent talent, and great times give birth to great men) is poor in mental endowments.   It has not activity, shrewdness, dexterity, eloquence, practical power.   On what, then, does it depend ?   On prejudice and bigotry.

"'This is hardly an exaggeration; yet I have good meaning and one honourable to the Church,   Listen to my theory.   As each individual has certain instincts of right and wrong antecedently to reasoning, on which he acts—and rightly so—which perverse reasoning may supplant, which then can hardly be regained, but, if regained, will be regained from a different source—from reasoning and not from nature—so, I think, has the world of men collectively. God gave them truths in His miraculous revelations, and other truths in the unsophisticated infancy of nations, scarcely less necessary and divine.   These are transmitted as 'the wisdom of our ancestors,' through men—many of whom cannot enter into them, or receive them themselves—still on, on, from age to age, not the less truths because many of the generations through which they are transmitted are unable to prove them, but hold them, either from pious and honest feeling (it may be), or from bigotry or from prejudice.   That they are truths it is most difficult to prove, for great men alone can prove great ideas or grasp them.   Such a mind was Hooker's, such Butler's ; and, as moral evil triumphs over good on a small field of action, so in the argument of an hour or the compass of a volume would men like Brougham, or, again, Wesley, show to far greater advantage than Hooker or Butler.   Moral truth is gained by patient study, by calm reflection, silently as the dew falls,—unless miraculously given—and when gained it is transmitted by faith and by 'prejudice.' Keble's book is full of such truths, which any Cambridge man might refute with the greatest ease."

It is, of course, undeniable that "moral truths " *e.g.* the government of the world by a righteous Ruler, and the duties of man to man, cannot be " proved " by any merely intellectual process ; they are suggested and recommended by experience, and received and retained by what we call "faith."   So far, Newman's last remarks are true.   But the danger is, that under the title "moral truths," priests of every religion inculcate truths that have no connection with morality. Here for example, when Newman speaks of the

"truths" which God gave men, "in His miraculous
revelations," and afterwards refers to Keble's book as
being full of " truths which any Cambridge man might
refute with the greatest ease," our minds pass naturally
to a story told in E. T. Mozley's *Reminiscences* about
Keble and Buckland.*   In the course of a somewhat heated controversy between the poet and the
geologist on the top of a coach, it is said that the
former finally took his stand on " the conceivability and
indeed certainty of the Almighty having created all the
fossils and other apparent outcomes of former existence
in the six days of Creation " ; in other words, he maintained that the fossils existed in the strata ready-made.
The same writer tells us that Newman " had, at this
time, nothing to say to such physical questions :" but
the words " at this time" are perhaps significant.
There is a danger of confounding " moral truth " with
" truth of fact," and it will be found that Newman did
not escape it.

To pass to the political part of the letter.   The
reader will note that in all that has preceded of this
long letter, there is no mention of justice.   What
follows will not supply the deficiency.   Once, indeed,
he will use the word (which for the most part he
studiously avoids) " expedient " ; but he will be merely
thinking of what is expedient *for the Church*, i.e. the
clergy, not for the nation at large.   In order to serve
the Church, he will avow himself willing, perhaps, not
only not to oppose, but even to favour Emancipation.
He looks at the matter simply as it may affect the
position of the clergy.   Emancipation is now necessary,
he admits, because all who have weight by their talent
or station, prefer " concession, to an Irish war."   But
the hatred of war, and the desire to secure the general

harmony of the United Kingdom, and the concentration of its energies on common objects, do not appear to weigh with *him*. Hurrell Froude expressed the hope not long afterwards that the " march of mind " in France might yet prove a " bloody one " ; and, about the time of the Reform Bill, Froude said that " the only war he could enter into with spirit would be a civil war." A similar spirit, though not yet so fierce, seems to breathe in Newman. It is agreed on all hands, he says, that the Emancipation will endanger the Irish Protestant Church ; some even say, it must ultimately fall :—

" All these things being considered, I am clearly in *principle* anti-Catholic ; and, if I do not oppose the Emancipation, it is only because I do not think it expedient, perhaps possible, to do so. I do not look for the settlement of difficulties by the measure ; they are rather begun by it and will be settled with the downfall of the Established Church. If then I am for Emancipation, it is only that I may take my stand against the foes of the Church on better ground instead of fighting at a disadvantage."

CHAPTER X

§ 41. *Newman's Sermons become "very High Church"*

IT would seem that Newman's letters to his mother had not the desired effect. Perhaps Mrs. Newman was still troubled at seeing certain of her son's old friends on the other side in the political contest—such as Pusey, Hawkins, and Whately—not to speak of Newman's former lecturer, Lloyd, now Bishop of Oxford. Not improbably she also suspected this introduction of politics into religious questions and was doubtful whither it might lead. Her son had assured her, in his first letter, that the Liberals were ridiculous in claiming for themselves the "talent" of the University Whately, he had then said, with perhaps Hawkins, was the only man of talent among them. But in his next letter he had admitted that "the talent of the day is against the Church." Which was she to believe? Was there no "talent of the day" on either side at Oxford? Perhaps she inclined to the latter of her son's statements and disliked his alliance with "the two-bottle orthodox." To assert that Peel was "unworthy" to represent "a religious, straightforward, unpolitical body" seemed perhaps a harsh thing to say about a man of whom Keble himself declared, not long afterwards, that he was "on moral grounds, disposed to respect and admire him." And this shrill tone of conflict may have seemed to her to be penetrating even her son's sermons, which had once given her so much comfort and spiritual help. In detaching himself from the world, had he not gone too far? Was he not in danger of isolating himself too much from the amenities and humanities of life? In preaching lately against "The Praise of Men" he had spoken as though it was impossible that a good man could be generally praised even in Christian society. And, in his recent sermon on "The World our Enemy," was it not a dangerous extreme to protest that the material world—even as framed by God and therefore good—is still "an enemy of our souls"? The exact causes may be uncertain, but the correspondence itself indicates, and the indication of it is confirmed from other sources, that Newman's mother found it hard to follow him into his new region of religious thought; and so did at least his eldest sister.

During leisure hours in this year of excitement the poetic spirit breathed again; but there is a difference of tone. The poet seems to feel, as before, that there is, if not a definite new work, at least a new path on which he is being led forward. But there is also a deeper sense of the mysteriousness of the way before him. "Still in my rooms at Oriel College," he writes on 7 September, "slowly advancing and led by God's hand blindly." The consciousness of his own blindness, the need of guidance, the new sense that he is living and working in a communion of Saints, as well as angels, to whom he must look rather than to men and women around him, seem to bring him comfort from above but somewhat more of isolation below. A

poem on his sister Mary shows the mourner now no
longer regarding the departed as insensible to what is
passing upon earth ; his sister, now, speaks to him in
"a voice from afar," watching the converse and even
"the blameless mirth," of those whom she still loved ;
hearing their "low prayers and musings sweet." The
Sea of Glass before the Throne reflects earth-scenes
for her ; yet she is at rest, sharing at once in God's
knowledge and God's peace. A sterner utterance
describes the mystery of the elect, "The Hidden
Ones," the unknown Saints of God, the indistinguish-
able "chosen few " :

> "The remnant fruit of largely scattered grace,
>   God sows in waste, to reap whom He foreknew
>   Of man's cold race."

Who can tell, asks the poet, praying for help lest the
frail heart should break in God's "annealing—"

> "Why pardon's seal stands sure on David's brow,
>   Why Saul and Demas fell?"

In "Thanksgiving" he prefaces his verses with
the words, "Thou in faithfulness hast afflicted me."
After proclaiming himself wholly God's, and praising
Him for the bright dreams and strange fancyings of
childhood ; for the bolder range of thought given by
the awful faculty of reason ; for the blessing of friends
"unasked, unhoped," and, best of all, for the "countless store of eager smiles at home"—he goes on to
offer his chief praise for the hours of affliction when he
had seen God's face "clad" in "kind austereness" and
has felt His pressure shaping the froward will. The
last words of the poem repeat what may be called the

refrain of this period, that faith thrives " in this world's shame." The year closes with a poem in a lighter mood, but with a clear under-current of ascetic melancholy, declaring that the plaintive and solitary life of a monk is "a danger-thwarting spell," and one well suited for him.

Many things contributed to make 1829 a turning-point in Newman's career and to decide him definitely for a life of asceticism detached from domestic ties. The Church seemed to need all his energies. Besides assaults from without, its own children were deserting it. "About this time," says Mr. E. T. Mozley, "not less than a dozen men of good University position and respectable abilities, went out of the Church of England in different directions, agreeing only in a hasty and presumptuous opinion, as we may certainly call it, that the Church of England was incurably wrong and finally doomed." For these and other reasons this was the year in which Newman irrevocably resolved on celibacy ; and at the close of it we find Froude writing to suggest that they should pledge themselves to it by a vow. To this Newman objects : " I have thought vows [*e.g.* of celibacy] are evidence of *want of faith* † [N.B. trust]. Why should we look to the morrow ? " But the resolution remained unbroken. We know, too, from the *Apologia* that in this year he contemplated—though it was not at that time carried out—" a life of greater religious regularity" than he had hitherto led. By these words he appears to mean the practice of fasting, meditation, and religious worship, to an extent that might very naturally remove him somewhat from the affectionate circle that had always greeted him with "eager smiles at home." Other domestic circumstances might at this time contribute to some degree of detachment from home life, although his mothers and sisters had now moved from Brighton to a cottage at Nuneham, close to Oxford.   Frank Newman had now begun to associate himself with Nonconformists and was soon to resign his Fellowship owing to religious scruples.   It could not be but that the High Church convert would resent an abandonment of the good cause just in the hour when it seemed to need help most.   His mother might regret it, but could not join in her eldest son's fierce resentment, and her feelings would seem to him so much too weak for the occasion as almost to amount to indulgence.

Apart from all surmises, taking known facts all together—Newman's recent excitement; his rapidly increasing tendency to ecclesiasticism as a policy, and to asceticism as a habit; his overpowering belief that a war was imminent between Church and State, and that it was his mission to help in preparing the Church for the conflict—we ought not to be surprised if, even with the purest affection on both sides, even between a mother so proudly and confidently loving, and a son so devotedly dutiful, there might naturally, and almost necessarily, reveal itself a rift of religious difference which might widen into something like estrangement. No longer therefore now must we expect to hear from Mrs. Newman the old heartfelt praise and gratitude once poured forth for her son's sermons which had done so much to give enlightenment and strength. They were still read by the family ; but the mother is silent about them.   Perhaps the titles in themselves— of those, at least, which he was preaching towards the end of the year—may almost suffice to explain her silence : " The Unity of the Church," and " Submission to Church Authority."   Perhaps, too, it was tacitly understood that the mother on this occasion spoke through her eldest daughter Harriett who, as on other occasions, expressed her dissent frankly, though without a trace of ill-feeling, " We have long since read your two sermons : they are very High Church. I do not think I am near so High, and do not understand them yet."

§ 42. *Failure of an Ambuscade*

On the last day of the year 1829, in answer apparently to one of Harriett's petitions for a quarter of an hour's quiet talk and a " decent lengthened call " —implying perhaps a little sense of being neglected— her brother replied, " I have nothing to say except that if I had but one-tenth part to do of what I really ought in various ways, I should have quite enough."

That was a sinister omen for 1830. It augured an insufficiently sane and sober estimate in the writer, first of what he *could* do, and then of what he " really *ought*" to do. In the latter class he included what we may call his first piece of ecclesiastical strategy. This was nothing less than a project for appropriating, and annexing to the High Church Party, the Evangelical Church Missionary Society, for which he had been elected one of the secretaries in the preceding spring. During the winter he had been very busy sketching letters and considering plans for this purpose. All through this business, his unusual want of tact—to describe his fault as mildly as decency will permit— can be explained only by supposing that his electioneering practice of last year had somewhat too much stimulated the desire to out-general his adversaries ; or else he was demoralized by the consciousness of a cause so

good as to justify means that in ordinary causes would
be called bad ; or his recent success had turned his
head, and he really did not quite know what he was
doing ; or, which is perhaps the most probable solution,
these three causes were all simultaneously at work
upon him.

His first object seems to have been to turn out of
office his colleague, the senior secretary. This man,
being an Evangelical of the old school, had interlarded
the draft of the Annual Report with Scripture phrases,
in the fashion apparently traditional with the Society.
With a view to his suppression, Newman moved in the
committee some two hundred and fifteen amendments
of his elder colleague's work. He must have had
strong support in the committee ; for his amendments
were only rejected by the casting vote of the chairman.
Besides this, he circulated anonymously " Suggestions"
to clergymen resident in the University, in behalf of
the Church Missionary Society. In this pamphlet he
protested that at present the Society interfered with
" the ecclesiastical system " by its arrangements generally, as well as by " its practice of addressing itself to
the multitude in public meetings " ; also, by sending
out missionaries for the propagation of the Gospel, it
encroached on the prerogative of the supreme Rulers
of the Christian Church ; practically, too, the doctrines
of some of its most active directors were Calvinistic ;
yet the Society spent in the previous year more than
£55,000 ; " Let me entreat you," proceeds the writer,
" to go on from considering these *mistakes,* to consider
the *evil.*" He then emphasizes the question, " How
should the clergy act in relation to this Society ?" In
answer, he points out that any clergyman could
become a member, not only of the Society, but also of

the committee, by subscribing half-a-guinea a year.
Let them become subscribers in order to "annex it to
the Christian Knowledge and Propagation Society, as
a sister institution in the work of evangelical charity."
Even if this involved "the temporary distraction of the
Society and the ultimate defection of a portion of its
members, still it would be supremely desirable."

"Very few indeed," writes Mr. E. T. Mozley, "approve of this plan or think it practicable." This was a
moderate condemnation, mild even from a zealous fol-
lower and future brother-in-law ; and all the milder
when we bear in mind that the writer himself admits
that, if Newman had been successful, "of course a
great secession of the Low Church party was to be
expected." An older friend of Newman's went a good
deal further and pronounced it unworthy of Newman,
and "really mean." * This was the verdict of Rickards,
whose conviction that the anonymous pamphlet could
not have proceeded from the Vicar of St. Mary's, had
been so strong that he had taken upon himself to deny
its authorship everywhere, and now had the mortification of going round to eat his words. In the abstract,
his judgment was just, much more so than Mozley's ;
yet it was severe, too. He did not realize that Newman was contending *for the Church* ; for which cause,
from time immemorial, men have felt justified in doing
sometimes the noblest of deeds, and sometimes the
most contemptible. Mozley, spite of his humour and
common sense, writes as follows to his sister under the
spell of the master mind, and the fascination of his
attractive ways—a fascination suggested in an interesting way by the word which he italicizes in the following extract :—

"Newman is not a man to be deterred by temporary failures. He is, indeed, better calculated than any man I know, by his talents, his learning, by his patience and perseverance, his conciliatory *manners*, and the friends he can employ in the cause—of whom I hope to be one—to release the Church of England from her present oppressed and curtailed condition."

There is a ring about these words which shows that there must have been rising at that time in Oxford a tide of party feeling which was likely to cause, and would partly excuse, unusual actions. Young men are generally very sensitive to the reproach of " meanness " in their leaders, and it is evident that this young man who hoped to be "employed" by Newman " in the cause " of the Church, had not the least sense that such a reproach was deserved. What in ordinary men and times would be called " mean," must, perhaps, in extraordinary men and times, be called " infatuated." Rickards himself perhaps, when he found *whom* he had been calling " mean," would have liked to correct the epithet. However, it could not be expected that the subscribers to the Church Missionary Society could draw these subtle distinctions : and they did not draw them. The collapse of Newman's strategical scheme was complete. It reminds us, in an amusing way, of his old experience at school with the *Spy*, in which a brutal majority spoiled everything. So it was, here, again. He had carried all before him in committee, so far as even to pass a resolution putting down public meetings for the future. But this was only a small body, clerical, or under clerical influence. Shortly afterwards the general meeting was held for re-electing officers, and here the lay element, or the Evangelical element, took its revenge. The re-election was generally formal. But they made it serious this time, turning Newman out of his secretaryship by an

immense majority.   A few weeks afterwards, the
expelled secretary withdrew from the Bible Society.

Almost the only link that now bound him to the
Evangelical School was the lingering belief that the
Church of Rome was, in some sense, Antichrist.
And even that—if Mr. E. T. Mozley's recollection is
correct as to the date, of which I feel some doubt—was
about this time being gradually loosened.   The Oriel
Common Room, says the latter, had been lately discussing the question, and had concluded in a compromise.   It was not the Church of Rome ; it was Pagan
Rome, as it were, in Christian Rome ; the spirit of
Paganism, partly possessing, and influencing through
local associations, the Christian Church—this was the
real Antichrist.   A conclusion of this kind was what
Newman and his friends, sixty years ago, used to call
a " view " ; and when they had talked about it for some
time, and got used to it, they were sometimes influenced
by it, and then they assumed at once that it would
influence others.   And this we shall presently find to
be the case with regard to this " view."   Only as the
old Evangelical " view " had been deeply impressed
upon Newman's imagination, we must expect to find
the new one somewhat slow in asserting itself.   The
new theory is, as it were, in solution.   It needs some
sudden shock to precipitate it and give it solidity ; and
for that we must wait till Newman sees Rome with
his own eyes and learns to recognize in it the City of
the tombs of the Apostles.

§ 43. *Out-generalled by the Provost*

Meanwhile tutorial business in Oriel had been
largely occupying Newman's thoughts.   The want of

method, the waste of effort, the constant failures in
the Schools, and the neglect to learn from failures
were all thorns to a system-loving mind always eager
for results. But beyond, and far above, these considerations, was the feeling that he was not influencing
his pupils as he had intended to do. Newman never
forgot that Origen had converted Gregory Thauma-
turgus to Christianity through his classical lectures.
Why should not he do the same ? " Men live after
death "—so he wrote to Rickards in the summer of this
year—" they live not only in their writings or their
chronicled history, but still more in that ἄγραφος μνήμη
[" unwritten memorial "] exhibited in a school of pupils
who trace their moral parentage to them. As moral
truth is discovered, not by reasoning, but by habitua-
tion, so it is recommended, not by books, but by oral
instruction. Socrates wrote nothing. Authorship is
the second best way."

From these words we might infer that he had persuaded himself that this was to be the work of his life,
and it is not improbable that he had done so. Yet at
the time when he wrote them, the vision of such a
work, at all events among the Oriel undergraduates,
had vanished. He had with great care elaborated a
plan by which the four tutors might divide the men
among them, each being responsible, to a greater
extent than was possible at present, for the moral as
well as mental guidance of those entrusted to him.
The scheme had been submitted to the three tutors
and approved by them ; but they seem to have taken
little account of what the Provost might have to say
about it. Perhaps Newman calculated on his zealous
support because, so far, he had gone unflinchingly with
them in enforcing discipline ; perhaps he had over-

rated the valetudinarian indifferentism to be expected
from a man who only gave himself forty years to live,
and who might now like to be still more quiet as Head
of a College.   Or had he underrated the alarm and
resentment that he had aroused in " the meddling
Provost" by his recent political action ?   In any case,
there was a miscalculation, and the Provost rejected
the proposals.   Hereupon the indomitable organizer—
who clearly regarded himself, and was regarded by his
fellow-tutors, as general in this campaign—determining to put pressure on the enemy, drew up and sent
in to the Provost what he afterwards called " his *ulti-
matum*," by which three of the tutors tendered their
resignations.

The threat that three tutors would simultaneously
resign was not a trifling one.   It was like springing a
mine upon the adversary, and there seemed every
hope that he would be forced to surrender.   But the
Provost was too clever for them.   He called in Hampden to give lectures ; and, though he could not compel
the three tutors to give up their present pupils, he
announced his intention of sending them no more, so
that, in time, they would " die with their existing
pupils," and cease to be tutors by having no one to
teach.   Thus this year saw a second collapse of
Newman's schemes.   He had been already turned out
of his secretaryship, and now he was to be slowly
starved out of his tutorship.   Not that he was in fault
here, or the Provost either.   The two men naturally
looked at the matter from quite different points of
view, and acted accordingly.   Hawkins—not unreasonably alarmed at a tutor who seemed likely to be too big
for his place, and whose theological developments it
was becoming difficult to predict—took the easy-going,

common-sense view of what was likely to be "safest" for
the college and for the men.   Newman thought a good
deal about what was best fitted to produce brilliant and
distinguished results for the college ; but a good deal
more about his duty to the religious purposes of the
founders of Oriel, and to the Church at large—not
without some dream also about shaping the pillars of a
new Anglicanism, to be erected in a new school of
young Anglican Churchmen.

The two views could not agree, one, the view of the
Head of a College, the other, that of a prophet who
was to be the trainer of prophets.   But if the prophet
had prevailed and linked himself for the next ten years
to the task of providing First Classes for his pupils in
Oriel, his own spiritual development would, not improbably, have been made less rapid, if not different in
its direction, by continual and wholesome contact
between his theories and the *facts* of healthy, bright,
and vigorous youth.   As it was, while calling the
result a " miserable " one for the college, Newman
welcomes the increase of leisure for himself, and immediately announces himself " full of projects " : " The
Fathers arise again full before me."

This sounds hopeful. Too long has " the great work "
been neglected, and now the reader may suppose that it
will be at last commenced.   But the next sentence fills us
with impatience and dismay : " This vacation, I should
not wonder if I took up the study of the modern
French Mathematics."   It seems, at first, as though
no excuse could possibly be offered for such deliberate
and incorrigible dilettanteism ; for he really knew
nothing about the subject, and, at the cost of much
precious time, could only hope to become a smatterer.
But it is not improbable that he regarded it as a means

of strengthening his mind to grapple with the problems of the theology of the first three centuries ;
and certainly some of those problems are more
remote from direct bearing on human affairs than
the problems of analytical geometry.

More than half of 1830 had now passed away—a
year of failures, disappointments, and worries. Everything had seemed to go wrong with him. He was
preparing a cottage at Littlemore—which was connected with the parish of St. Mary's and a part of his
cure—where his mother and sisters might be near him ;
but domestic troubles were rife. He was harassed—
"knocked up " he says—by the imminent departure of
his youngest brother Frank to Persia as a missionary,
and by a tedious religious controversy which had been
reopened by his second brother Charles, and in which
he had written over " twenty-four foolscap pages
about nothing." His young friend and ally, E. T.
Mozley, had for a time appeared to be on the point of
deserting him ; and he complains that, though he had
tried being frank and laying aside dignity with certain
people, it had not answered. " I am desponding," he
writes to Froude : " All my plans fail. When did I
ever succeed in any exertion for others ? I do not
say this in complaint, but really doubting whether I
ought to meddle." Rickards—who had perhaps been
alarmed by the affair of the Church Missionary Society
as an indication of an over-wrought condition of mind
—had apparently suggested to him, a month or two
before, that it would be well that he should leave
Oxford and take a living, and perhaps marry. In
Newman's reply he apparently regrets his shattered
Oriel project, but is content with the small sphere of
action before him : " I shall turn philosopher, rail at

the world and be content with a few friends who know me." As for leaving Oxford :—

"I will but say it is now many years that a conviction has been growing upon me (say since I was elected here) that men did not stay at Oxford as they ought, and that it was my duty to have no plans ulterior to a college residence. To be sure, as I passed through a hundred miles of country just now in my way to and from Brighton, the fascination of a country life nearly overset me, and always does. It will indeed be a grievous temptation should a living ever be offered me, when now even a curacy has inexpressible charms. And I will not so far commit myself as to say it must be wrong to take one under all circumstances. Is it not vastly absurd my talking in this way, when I have no more chance of such preferment, than of a living in the moon? Well, but this is the only great temptation I fear, for as to other fascinations which might be more dangerous still, I am pretty well out of the way of them, and at present I feel as if I would rather tear out my heart than lose it, though when once fairly caught, my views doubtless would change."

§ 44. *The Sermons of "a year of disappointments"*

This year of failure seems to have left its mark upon Newman's preaching, deepening in him the sense of the need of human self-denial for the reception and retention of religious truth. Disappointed at every turn, he found it more easy to think that God *meant* him to be disappointed—or rather, perhaps, to *disappoint himself*—by asceticisms, little as well as great ; by continually teasing himself, so to speak, as well as thwarting or crushing the larger and nobler instincts and desires of humanity. Self-denial he now enjoins, not only as a training morally expedient for man under the circumstances in which he finds himself placed, but also as a kind of imitation, on his part, of a Divine attribute. To the objections of those who urge that we are to be saved by faith, he makes a twofold

answer.   First, he urges that faith is, in effect, obedience ; which is true.   But then he goes on to maintain
that the obedience of one " who fears God as his
Maker, and knows that, as a sinner, he has especial
cause for fearing Him," and who rejoices " to find any
service which may stand as a sort of proof that he is
earnest," is " altogether one and the same " with
" faith."   This is not true.   Such " obedience " may
be based upon a servile fear wholly incompatible with
true faith.   It is a fundamental heresy to suppose that
faith can be thus defined.   But he has a reason for
thus grasping at " obedience " as a substitute for faith.
It is because the former is so much more definite than
the latter, and affords a man some " proof that he is
in earnest."   And his readiness to accept almost any
kind of " obedience " was probably increased at this
time by the increase of the mystery of the Divine
Personality, which must have grown more and more
perplexing as he read the Fathers, and toiled through
the Arian controversies.   Now also (for the first time
I think) there appears in the sermons the word
" economy " (explained above by anticipation) to express the dispensation of religious truth, not as it *is*,
but as it can be best accommodated to the understanding of those who are to receive it, and, in this
" economy," self-denial forms a prominent part.

There is a rational view of the Redemption of man
which supposes that Christ's self-denials were under-
gone for the purpose of bringing home to men's hearts
the image of God as a loving Father, and of exorcizing
that Evil Spirit of Slander which had too long possessed their souls and constrained them to turn away
from Him as from an enemy.   This gives a meaning

to all Christ's self-denials, as being, not self-lacerations
(such as priests of Baal inflict upon themselves to
propitiate their god), but wounds received for the sake
of the Good, in a stupendous conflict against Evil.
But Newman's view not of Redemption alone, but
even of God Himself, is tinged by the notion of the
divineness of—if I may so call it—an artificial self-
disappointment.   Man has to refrain from what is
lawful, not so much for the sake of self-control, nor for
the sake of helping his fellow-men, as because—this
at least is suggested—in God Himself, self-denial, *for
its own sake*, is seen shadowed forth in the incarnation.
Such seems the thought latent in the two sermons on
The Duty of Self-Denial, and Natural and Revealed
Religion.   In the former, after saying that fasting is
clearly a Christian duty, he asks, " Now what is fasting
but a refraining from what is lawful ? "   Then he
declares that other attributes of God are displayed in
Nature, " but self-denial, if it may be said, this incomprehensible attribute of Divine Providence, is disclosed
to us only in Scripture."   In the latter he asserts that
the Bible gives us " a life of the One Supreme God,"
and sets forth, as His most prominent attributes—

" Inherent freedom of will, power of change, long-suffering, placa-
bility, repentance, delight in the praises and thanksgiving of His
creatures, failure of purpose, and the prerogative of dispensing His
mercies according to His good pleasure.   Above all in the New
Testament, the Divine character is exhibited to us not merely as love,
or mercy, or holiness (attributes which have a vagueness in our conceptions of them from their immensity) but these and others as seen
in an act of *self-denial* . . . ."

The next words tell us that this "act of *self-denial*"
is a "mysterious quality, when ascribed to Him," but

that it impresses on us "the personal character" of
God ; and it is also added that " ' God so loved the
world,' that He *gave up* His only Son ; and the Son of
God '*pleased not Himself.*' " There is nothing here
that is not, in itself, justifiable. But then, when we
read on, and find that in the life of Christ "we are
allowed to discern the attributes of the invisible God
drawn out into action in accommodation to our weakness," the uneasy thought of an " economy " steals in ;
and—if we are familiar with the later sermons—we
cannot help asking whether the words " mysterious,"
" incomprehensible," " accommodation," " weakness,"
may not be (perhaps unconsciously) serving the purpose
of preparing us to be patient when we shall be told
that, in theology, "love" "does not mean love precisely " ; and that this also applies to the love of God ;
and that " we do not know and cannot form a notion
what is the real final object of the Gospel Revelation.
Men are accustomed to say that it is the salvation of
the world, which it certainly is not. . . .   Rather, as
far as we are told at all, that object is the glory of God ;
but we cannot understand what is meant by this, or how
the Dispensation of the Gospel promotes it.   Doubtless, this glory is set forth in some mysterious way in
the rejection, as well as in the reception of the
Gospel " !

If this be so, what becomes of the " method of
personation," which, says the preacher (as distinct
from the philosophic method), " is carried throughout
the revealed system " ? If God redeemed us for His
own " glory," and not for " the salvation of the world,"
and if His " glory " consists " in the rejection as
well as in the reception of the Gospel," then indeed

Newman will be justified in saying that His "love" "does not mean love precisely," but we shall also be compelled to say good-bye to the notion of a "Father in heaven." Then, too, we shall understand that, as Christian self-denial is defined as "a refraining from what is lawful," so God's self-denial may be—we know not what; for we know not His "real final object." For aught we know, the mere act of "refraining from what is lawful" may contain something divine; and for men on earth, all nature, with all its gifts and joys, may perhaps be something to abstain from; and God in heaven, instead of being really Love, or really our Father, or even our righteous Champion of good against evil, may be—who knows?—nothing but the Great Ascetic!

And the same uneasy feeling comes over us when we find a theologian impartially enumerating among the attributes of God, His "power of change," His "repentance," His "failure of purpose," and His "prerogative of dispensing His mercy according to His good pleasure;"—an impartiality, admirable, in one way, as showing the preacher's unbending and consistent determination to accept every statement about God in every book of the Old and New Testaments, and not to pick and choose the doctrines that he may prefer; but disastrous, in another way, as indicating that he will find an almost insuperable difficulty in putting aside these ancient and rudimentary notions about God in order to receive into his heart the one supreme revelation of the divine Fatherhood.* Hence, as we read the introduction of the Sermon where he describes Christ's "intended grant of a system of religious truth, grounded on that mysterious economy of Divine Providence in which His own incarnation occupies the principal place," we cannot help saying to ourselves, " Where will all this end ? How can he combine all these heterogeneous elements with one heartfelt belief ?   Is there not a danger that the ' truth ' will be stifled beneath the ' system ? ' May not the Divine Person be veiled behind the too obtrusive ' economy ' ? "

One of the sermons for this year appears to contain a specially vivid reflection of its " disappointments."   It is dated 12 September, and is entitled " Jeremiah, a Lesson for the Disappointed."   In the same month we have found him writing to Froude, " All my plans fail, when did I ever succeed in any exertion for others ? " But the same thing may be said, in various degrees, about most of the sermons of 1830.   They reflect the feelings of the preacher during the year, and it was a year of failure all the more depressing because it had followed a year of success.   The discourses on Old Testament subjects contain manifest references to the pending projects of political Reform, and to the growing antagonism displayed between the Liberal party and the Established Church.   But, in the depths of his perplexed and troubled heart, the problem of salvation (as presented from a new point of view) is still being tossed to and fro.   " By what, if not by faith, must I be saved ? "   As therefore the year begins with " Faith and Obedience," and " Steadfastness in the Old Paths," so it draws toward its close with " Obedience to God the way to Faith in Christ," and " Obedience the Remedy to Religious Perplexity."   Last of all, comes a very fine discourse on " The World's Benefactors " in which he consoles himself for his inability to do anything public and definite against the influx of public evils, by the reflection that others, too, have achieved in obscurity the most lasting benefits for mankind. Who, he asks, now knows the names of those primeval benefactors who have found out for us the simplest and most necessary arts and inventions ? Are not the Angels unknown to the world ? Is not God Himself hidden from mankind at large and but partially and rarely manifested ? How much more then may His servants endure to toil in obscurity, and to be unknown, and to appear to fail !

CHAPTER XI

§ 45. *The Reform Bill*

NEWMAN was now (February 1831) thirty years old. It was a common saying with him that, "by thirty," a man ought to have made up his mind : and those who know anything of his reverence for texts of Scripture, and of the importance he attached to "coincidences," can guess the reason for his choice of this particular number. At this age our Lord is said in the Gospel of St. Luke to have begun His public mission.* In this year, therefore, he prepared for a new departure, apparently expecting to receive insight into the means by which he was to discharge his appointed duty. He sent his friends, for their private reading, some of his verses on sacred and other subjects, and wrote to several of them letters of advice or warning.

Besides this Biblical omen or coincidence there were not wanting more substantial causes of unsettlement. The Reform Bill was now in actual progress through the House of Commons. In other words, the World —so it appeared to Newman—had now thrown off disguise and was rushing in full career against the defenceless Church. To these two factors—the Scriptural, and political—add weakness, deafness, and sleeplessness, resulting from over-work, and we can understand the condition of mind in which he preached on "The Secrecy and Suddenness of Divine Visitations," (2 February) :

"The present day bears upon it more marks than usual of pride and judicial blindness. Whether Christ is at our doors or not, but a few men in England may have grace enough safely to conjecture, but that He is calling upon us all to prepare as for His coming is most evident to those who have religious eyes and ears. . . .

. . . Yet granting things to be at the very worst, yet, when Christ was presented in the Temple, the age knew as little of it, as it knows of His Providence now. Rather, the worse our condition is, the nearer to us is the Advent of our Deliverer. Even though He is silent, doubt not that His army is on the march towards us. He is coming through the sky, and has even now His camp upon the outskirts of our own world. Nay, though he still for a while keep His seat at His Father's right hand, yet surely He sees all that is going on, and waits and will not fail his hour of vengeance. Shall He not hear His own elect, when they cry day and night to Him? His Services of prayer and praise continue, and are scorned by the multitude. Day by day, Festival by Festival, Fast after Fast, Season by Season, they continue according to His ordinance, and are scorned. But the greater His delay, the heavier will be His vengeance, and the more complete the deliverance of His people.

"May the good Lord save His Church in this her hour of peril ; when Satan seeks to sap and corrupt where he dare not openly assault! May He raise up instruments of His grace, 'not ignorant' of the devices of the Evil One, with seeing eyes and strong hearts, and vigorous arms to defend the treasure of the faith once committed to the Saints, and to rouse and alarm their slumbering brethren ! "

Others, besides Newman, took gloomy views of the national prospects at this time. To Arnold, also, the thought of the Last Day was sometimes suggested by what he saw in his fellow countrymen. But the former differed from the latter in this respect, that he saw most danger, not in the discord which was rending

the people in two, nor in the sense of injustice which
was setting class against class, and religion against
religion, but in the uprising against the Established
Church among those who called themselves philanthropic and who thought that a Church, like a Prophet,
is to be judged by its fruits among the people at large.
Against this philanthropic notion Newman, now, as
always, protests. Never, he says, can the Church of
Christ be popular ; since the " many " are rejected and
the " few " saved, whatever principles receive a hearty
reception from the masses are thereby convicted of an
earthly character ; the true " Light of the world " repels
more than it attracts ; we " compromise the dignity of
Christianity by anxiously referring unbelievers to the
effects of the Gospel of Jesus in the world at large."
Such is the doctrine preached in a University sermon
while (6 March) the Reform Bill was before the
House of Commons—culminating in a fierce aggression
upon those indirect resultants of religion, science, art,
literature, and social experience to which we give the
name of the fruits of civilization :

> " Let it be assumed, then, as not needing proof, that the freedom
> of thought, enlightened equitableness, and amiableness, which are
> the offspring of civilization, differ far more even than the piety of
> form or of emotion from the Christian spirit, as being ' not pleasant to
> God, forasmuch as they spring not of faith in Jesus Christ, yea,
> rather, doubtless, having the nature of sin.' "

To a friend who seems to have suggested a petition
against the Reform Bill, Newman writes in the same
bitter spirit. He will have no petition. The Church,
he says, was deserted by the State two years back (*i.e.*
when the Government relieved the Romanists of their
disabilities), and therefore the State has now no claim
on assistance from the Church (13 March) :

"Not that the Church should be unforgiving; but, if others think with me, *what* great interest has it that things should remain as they are? I much fear society is rotten, to say a strong thing. Doubtless there are many specimens of excellence in the higher walks of life, but I am tempted to put it to you whether the persons you meet generally are—I do not say consistently religious; we never can expect that in this world—but believers in Christianity in any true sense of the word. No, they are Liberals, and in saying this I conceive I am saying almost as bad of them as can be said of any one."

§ 46. *Reading for " The Arians "*

In the same letter he says that he is "thinking of writing on two theological subjects." One is a history of Church Councils ; the other, the Thirty-nine Articles. The latter was subsequently dropped, for the time ; but it was intended by Newman to be the more important of the two—the former being merely introductory to it. In fact, Newman was planning, not a mere defence or explanation of the Articles singly, but something very much like what he had suggested, nearly five years before, to Rickards. It was to be a great body of Anglican Divinity, which was to include a dissertation on the sources of proof and the terms of theology, together with a general view of Christian doctrines, to be proved from Scripture and referred to their several places in the Articles. Pusey rejoices that his friend has undertaken this work on the Articles. As to the Councils, he thinks that, here too, Newman may be of service in stemming heterodoxy : " Some of the Fathers, or rather parts of the Fathers, you must, of course, read ; but this will aid towards your great object. I should think this little essay will be of great use to yourself towards nerving you for that design." The meaning is clear :

the "great object" is to set forth a definite and comprehensive scheme of Anglican doctrine ; and this is to be connected with, and supported by, the doctrine of the Primitive Church, deduced from the Early Fathers.

Amid Reform discussions in England, and tithe-riots in Ireland, dissolution of the old Parliament and election of the new, Newman's tutorial work drew to an end with the departure of his last pupils ; and now he had leisure to gnaw his heart over the success of the Liberals. A summer spent by the delightful banks of the Dart in Froude's home, brought out once more his passionate love of the country, and his even more passionate resolve to close his heart against its fascination. " I should dissolve with essence of roses "—he writes to his mother, in his first rapture of delight at the colour and glow of the Devonshire scenery—" or be attenuated to an echo if I lived here " : and a poem records his shrinking from the temptation to love at all what Wordsworth felt that he could not love too well :

> " There strayed awhile amid the woods of Dart
>   One who could love them, but who durst not love.
> A vow had bound him, ne'er to give his heart
>   To streamlet bright, or soft secluded grove.
>   'Twas a hard humbling task, onwards to move
> His easy-captured eyes from each fair spot,
>   *   *   *   *
> Yet kept he safe his pledge, prizing his pilgrim lot."

Preaching to the congregation at Dartington, with its light-hearted contingent of young girls from the Vicarage, he takes as his subject, " Scripture a Record of Human Sorrow." The reason, he says, why Scripture omits such things as might be said in praise of this world, is because we are sure to find these out for ourselves, without being told of them. Our danger is on the side not of undervaluing, but of over-valuing them : " Only look upon the world in this light ; its sights of sorrow are to calm you, and its pleasant sights to try you."

Some of the circumstances connected with this sermon are particularly interesting. Writing to his mother, the day before he preached, he says, " I have had a sermon to write for to-morrow, which I do believe to be as bad a one as I have ever written, for I was not in the humour ; " and, commenting elsewhere on it, " Influenza was about, the forerunner of the cholera. It went through the parsonage at Darting-ton. Every morning, the sharp merry party, who somewhat quizzed me, had hoped it would seize on me. But I escaped and sang my warning from the pulpit." Afterwards, looking back on the early deaths of four or five of the young " merry party " who then listened to him, he speaks of himself as of a prophet of evil omen. On other occasions he describes himself as unconsciously—and sometimes unreasonably, to an extent that shocked him on reconsideration—dropping ominous forebodings in the presence of friends who afterwards found them realised. But, passing over this touch of prophetic egotism, may we not ask whether his words were wisely chosen to strengthen those who heard him in bearing what they were destined to bear ? Would those young girls be more able, or less, to endure sorrow, when it came, for having enjoyed, with a full, free, and grateful delight, the pleasant sights of Nature, as proceeding from God, not to "try " them, but to make them thankful ?

Back at Oxford and plunging into the Fathers

again as a preparation for the History of Church
Councils—which ultimately narrowed itself down to a
history of the Arians of the first three centuries—he
already sees the prospective toil in a lengthening vista.
" My work opens a grand and interesting field to me ;
but how I shall ever be able to make one assertion,
much less to write one page I cannot tell. Any one
pure categorical would need an age of reading and
research. I shall confine myself to hypotheticals ;
your 'if' is a great philosopher as well as a great
peace-maker." This is significant, but not satisfactory
in the projector of a great body of systematic divinity
in which theological terms were to be used scientifi-
cally. It seems to have led Newman into a bad habit
of caution ; which he cannot wholly throw off—even
where he can hardly be intending to " confine himself
to hypotheticals " because he is not " able to make one
assertion." Take, for example, almost the last page
of the last of the University Sermons where—after
asserting that " not even the Catholic reasonings and
conclusions " most thoroughly received among us " are
worthy of the Divine Verities which they represent
but are the truth only in as full a measure as our
minds can admit it "—he continues thus :—

" It is true that God is without beginning, if eternity may worthily
be considered to imply succession ; in every place, if He who is a
Spirit can have relations with space. It is right to speak of His
Being and Attributes, if He be not rather super-essential ; it is true
to say that He is wise or powerful, if we may consider Him as other
than the most simple Unity. He is truly Three if He is truly One ;
He is truly One, if the idea of Him falls under earthly number. He
has a triple Personality, in the sense in which the Infinite can be
understood to have Personality at all. If we know anything of Him
—if we may speak of Him in any way—if we may emerge from
Atheism or Pantheism into religious faith—if we would have

any saving hope, any life of truth and holiness within us—this only
do we know, with this only confession, we must begin and end our
worship—that the Father is the One God, the Son the One God,
and the Holy Ghost the One God, and that the Father is not the
Son, the Son not the Holy Ghost, and the Holy Ghost not the
Father."

Grant that the context here indicates that Newman
is not here using "if" as a "*peace-maker*" between
himself and his conscience. Grant that he is not, as it
were, personifying and worshipping Hypothesis, pay-
ing homage to "If" as if it were a Benefactor who
bestowed on him a dogmatic scheme that is philosophical only as long as it is hypothetical. Grant that our
regard to Newman's nice choice of words need not
lead us to draw any subtle distinctions of shades of
doubt, implied in the subjunctive "if He *be* not
rather super-essential," and the indicative "if He *is*
truly One." Grant that he really does feel the truth,
in some sense, of the Personality (or perhaps we
should say, the untruth of the impersonality) of the
Infinite God. Yet many will ask uneasily. "What is
the *result*—we do not say the *purpose*—of all these
'if's'? What but to make religion a vacuum and call
it a peace?"

It seems inevitable that Newman's moral and spiritual
appreciation of what he deemed to be the highest truths
of religion should be greatly weakened by the feeling
that no plain statement about them could be hazarded
without vast "reading and research." Christianity, at
this rate, seems to become an affair of bibliophiles.
But if this was so, Newman's neglect of the study
necessary to attain to some provisional conception of
these fundamental truths becomes almost inexplicable.
How he had procrastinated, will be seen at a glance,

when we remember that he conceived his "great work" of reading "The Fathers," in April 1826. Yet after three years, reading them chronologically, he was still "hungering for Irenæus and Cyprian" in June 1829, not having finished even the comparatively non-voluminous authors of the second century. Was it the toil, or its possible resultlessness, from which he shrank? In any case, as he had prepared himself for a failure as an Examiner in the Schools, so he is now preparing for a failure as a writer on Church History.

§ 47. *Newman "intends to be a hot-headed man"*

The Long Vacation had not come to an end when an event occurred which seemed likely to call Newman away from Oxford to a sphere in which the *Arians* would needs have been dropped altogether; and perhaps the *Via Media* would never have been written. Whately was appointed Archbishop of Dublin. At first Newman expected an immediate summons to accompany his old friend, whom he had served so well at St. Alban Hall: and this is proof enough that, although the two had taken opposite sides in the Peel election, they remained on excellent terms. But a far less keen mind than Whately's must have discerned that, if any attempt was to be made to tranquillize Ireland by giving up some of the endowments of the Established Church there, and if the new Archbishop was to take part in such a policy, Newman was not the sort of man on whose help he could count. At this distance, it may seem strange to us that Newman himself should not have seen this, but he was not alone in his blindness. Both Keble and Froude at first rejoiced in the elevation of their old Oriel friend, although the former puts in a *caveat :* "If they (the Whigs) have made no truckling bargain with him to sacrifice the temporalities to a reformed Parliament, if such be their good pleasure." "It was no surprise to Mr. Newman," says the autobiography, when Whately manifested no desire to gain his co-operation in his new sphere of action. This is a lapse of memory. On the contrary, Newman *was* "surprised" that he was not asked to go to Ireland, as is shown by the words italicized (not by Newman) in the following letter to his sister, written about a fortnight after Whately's departure (4 October) from Oxford :—

"For some time Whately's promotion teased me much and in a selfish way . . . . *I foresaw he would ask me some time or other* to join him in Dublin, and not only did I feel it would seem selfish and ungrateful and cowardly not to do so, but I feared it might turn out to be my duty on direct grounds, and had even thought (that is, for some time) that a post in Ireland was the one thing which seemed to have claims enough to draw me from Oxford ;—perhaps you have heard me say so.

"However, by this time I think my mind is quite made up that it is my duty to remain where I am ; so remain I shall. (*Is it not good to answer before I am asked ?*)"

This letter exhibits Newman's habit—mentioned once or twice before—of reasoning with himself, while writing to a friend. He doubts whether he is right. Yet he does not like exactly to confess that he is in doubt. But, by soliloquizing, on paper, to a correspondent, he achieves the treble object, first, of reopening a question without appearing to re-open it ; secondly, of putting his case strongly before himself while putting it before a friend ; and lastly, of obtaining assent without seeming to ask for it. In this case, the friend selected is his sister Harriett—which seems strange, until we find that she is staying with Rickards, with whom he had previously discussed the question of leaving Oxford. It is therefore really to Rickards that he is giving his reasons for remaining. They are these : 1st, his engrossing work on the Church Councils (which ultimately became *The Arians*) ; 2nd, the utility of that work and its incompatibility with work in Ireland ; 3rd, his influence on the much-neglected study of theology in Oxford :—

"Fourthly, if times are troublous, Oxford will want hot-headed men, and such I mean to be, and I am in my place ; fifthly, I have some doubt whether my health would stand an Irish engagement. Many minor reasons might be added to the above. *I dread Whately proposing something* [He never did—he knew me better than I knew myself—J. H. N.], but expect nothing *immediate :* though at first *I did."*

This completely disproves the statement that it " was *no surprise* to Mr. Newman " when Whately passed him by.

In order to understand Newman's feelings, and perhaps also his inaccurate recollection, we must bear in mind what was going on in Parliament. Three days after the announcement of Whately's appointment, the Reform Bill passed through the House of Commons. It was anticipated that it would be rejected by the Lords, and especially by the bishops, and on 3 October the discussion began in the Upper House. Newman, who could not conceive that a bishop could support Liberalism in Ireland, looked forward to a conflict there in behalf of the interests of the Church. To him the archbishopric seemed a perilous outpost, and he felt chivalrously moved to give up everything that seemed to him so precious at Oxford, in order to serve his old Principal and the Church at the same time by strenuously maintaining an ecclesiastical policy of resistance. On 7 October the Lords rejected the Reform Bill by a majority of 41, of whom 21 were bishops ; and in the letter above quoted Newman says, " I am thankful the bishops have lately played so bold a part, but I fear they will still give way, a large number of them being frightened 'at the sound themselves have made.'"

This explains everything. Whately seemed to Newman to have accepted the post of a fighting archbishop; and Newman was prepared to fight by his side. When he was not summoned to do so, he felt surprised, and perhaps hurt, though—so far as his own work and prospects were concerned—not disappointed. But when it turned out that Whately preferred conciliation, even at the cost of some sacrifice of Church temporalities, to the possibility of civil war, his feeling of personal surprise changes to bitter resentment on public grounds ; and in a few months we shall find him saying that " poor Whately " must be disowned by his friends ; " of course, to know him now is quite impossible." Then, in later life, looking back upon the whole providential, and as it were predestined, tenour of things, he found it difficult to realize that he was ever so void of prescience as to the turn events would take in Ireland, or so blind to the ultimate incompatibility between himself and Whately; and hence (in accordance with his habit, imagining that what was *fit* must needs be *historical*, and that what *ought* to have occurred, *did* occur), he imagined, and put down on paper, that Whately's passing him by was "no surprise to him." Yet we have it from his own hand that, at first, he "expected something immediate," and, six weeks afterwards, had not ceased to "expect."

We shall return to this subject hereafter, for the *Apologia* completely misrepresents the facts and casts an unmerited blot on the archbishop's reputation. But, even were there no further proof, this would suffice to prove that the estrangement between the two friends began with Newman. As for Whately—who, as Newman confesses, knew him better than he knew himself—he, though regretting the breach, continued to regard his former Vice-Principal—the "anvil" of days gone by—with cordial good-will. At first he did what he could, in spite of Newman's unconcealed hostility, to maintain their friendly feeling. But in 1836 an event, which will be mentioned in its due place, altogether reversed the position of the two men. Then it became Newman's turn to make advances, and Whately's absolutely to repel them.

We have now, however, to think merely of the immediate effect on Newman produced by Whately's appointment. The reaction from this temporary unsettlement combined with everything else to concentrate him more zealously, perhaps more fiercely, on his mission. Rejected, as he thought, by Whately, he naturally threw himself with more vigour than ever into his visions of a reformed Church. There was much at this time to irritate and exasperate one who reverenced episcopal authority. There were Reform riots in London against the bishops. Scarcely one of them could go into the streets without the danger of being hissed and hooted. If a bishop was asked to preach, there was a possibility that, when he entered the pulpit, the congregation would leave their seats. All this, so far from tempting Newman to go with the

tide, increased his determination to go against it.
Everyone was for Reform, but in what they called a
forward direction. Since Reformation was so fashionable, he also would be in the fashion : he too would
reform, but *backwards :* "You may assure Rickards
from me that I am a reformer as much as he can be.
. . . I should like (as far as I can understand the
matter) to substitute the First Prayer Book of King
Edward the First for the present one; but such
reformers are not popular, that is the worst of it ; so
that practically I do become an anti-reformer in the
modern sense of the word."

§ 48. *"The Christian World, so-called," a "Witness
for Satan"*

The cholera now showed signs of visiting Oxford.
A letter from Mrs. Newman, the last from her pen in
the correspondence, makes an offer to be his "head
nurse" in the event of such a visitation. She has
thought out all her plans, and wishes to take the strain
of such work from off his shoulders : "Your usefulness
is before you, I trust, for the comfort of many, for
many years." It is pleasing to note that, even if there
was some sense of religious difference between the two,
it did not affect their deepest relations. In fortitude
and self-devotion, how worthy the son was of the
mother, is attested by an amusing story of an absentee
Oxford clergyman during the epidemic. He left with
his churchwardens a list of those of his clerical friends
or neighbours to whom they might apply in a case of
danger. Of Newman, he knew little or nothing; but
Newman's name was first on the list.

Thus the year 1831 drew towards its close, in gloom,
and tumult, and fear of the plague, and alarm for the

Church. Writing about the Irvingite "gift of tongues" at this time, Arnold says, " If the thing be real, I should take it merely as a sign of the coming of the day of the Lord. . . . My sense of the evil of the times and to what prospects I am bringing up my children, is overwhelmingly bitter." To Newman the whole of modern society, the nation itself as a whole, nay even Christian society, appeared identified with evil. " The Christian world, so called," he asks in St. Mary's,—" what is it practically but a witness for Satan rather than a witness for Christ ? " He is now so completely converted from his old doctrine of *laissez-faire* that he declares clergymen to be, above all men, bound to form and pronounce an opinion on " events of the day and public men," but it is because what happens in nations must affect the cause of religion in those nations. Hence it is that it becomes the duty of the clergy " to cry aloud and spare not, to lift up our voice like a trumpet and show the people their transgression and the house of Jacob their sins."

Preaching shortly afterwards before the University on " The Usurpations of Reason," he asserts that these " may be dated from the Reformation": " theories of Government that exclude Religion from the essential elements of the State " are perhaps " off-shoots of the same usurpation " ; and he emphasizes the " danger " of " surrendering customs and institutions which go far " to make the Church " the pillar and ground of moral truth." But in these " customs and institutions " does he include tithes levied from nine out of ten people to pay for the religion of the tenth ? As for the " danger," the Government of the day could have retorted that the greatest " danger " to religion would be a connection with oppressive injustice. But to that

Newman would (no doubt) have replied that human
notions of justice did not apply to religious matters,
and that the Government, from its very nature, was
disqualified from judging what was right : " Consider in how mysterious a state all things are
placed ; the wicked are uppermost in power and name,
and the righteous are subjected to bodily pain and
mental suffering as if they did not fear God."

For Newman's depreciation of his own times, and
especially of those fruits of justice, humanity, and
philanthropy, which were then appearing in the nation,
and which the English Church seemed to have done
so little directly to develop, some extenuation may
perhaps be found in the provoking complacency of the
party of progress. This was, in his eyes, the sin of
sins. It was almost a sin not to be anxious, not to be
timorous ; to be gratefully happy was a suspicious,
dangerous, condition of mind ; but to be self-satisfied,
betokened a crass, vulgar blindness, intellectual as
well as moral, which filled him with unutterable
contempt. Another explanation is, that he made it a
principle to ignore one half of history. " We have no
business," he used in effect to say, "with the faults
of former times, but only with those of our own.
When we find a stick bent one way, let us bend it
the other ; by saying a little too much, where there is
a certain defect, you often succeed in producing an
impression that is a kind of mean between the letter
of your words. and the previous impressions of your
hearers, so that your exaggeration produces a result
that is not exaggerated." This method results ultimately in some sacrifice of progress as well as of truth.
Neither a nation, nor a man, would make much way
by ignoring all errors except those of the present, and

simply attempting to avoid these. Still, for the purposes of immediate result *—for which Newman was
always craving, even when trying to repress the
craving—his method was a successful one ; and for
rhetorical purposes it is truly admirable, as may be
seen from the following denunciation of the self-
adulation of the age :—

"We can scarce open any of the lighter or popular publications of
the day without falling upon some panegyric on ourselves, on the
illumination and humanity of the age, or upon some disparaging
remarks on the wisdom and virtues of former times. Now it is a
most salutary thing under this temptation to self-conceit, to be reminded that, in all the highest qualifications of human excellence, we
have been far outdone by men who lived centuries ago; that a
standard of truth and holiness was then set up, which we are not
likely to reach ; and that, as for thinking to become wiser and better,
or more acceptable to God than they were, it is a mere dream.
Here we are taught the true value and relative importance of the
various gifts of the mind. The showy talents on which the present
age prides itself fade away before the true metal of Prophets and
Apostles. Its boasted ' knowledge ' is but a shadow of 'power'
before the vigorous strength of heart which they displayed, who
could calmly work moral miracles as well as speak with the lips of
inspired wisdom. Would that St. Paul or St. John could rise from
the dead ! How would the minute philosophers who now consider
intellect and enlightened virtue all their own, shrink into nothing
before those well-tempered, sharp-edged weapons of the Lord ! Are
not we come to this? is it not our shame as a nation, that, if not
the Apostles themselves, at least the Ecclesiastical System they
devised, and the Order they founded, are viewed with coldness and
disrespect? How few are there who look with reverent interest
upon the Bishops of the Church as the Successors of the Apostles ;
honouring them if they honour, merely because they like them as
individuals, and not from any thought of the peculiar sacredness of
their office. Well, let it be ! the End must one time come. It
cannot be that things should stand still thus. Christ's Church is inde-
structible ; and, lasting on through all the vicissitudes of this world,
she *must* rise again and flourish, when the poor creatures of a day
who opposed her, have crumbled into dust."

Now (1832) Newman was more than the sacred age—"thirty years old." Yet he had received no further insight into the special means by which he was to fight the good fight for the Church. All the more need was there that he should, at least in St. Mary's, lift up his voice—as he had recently proclaimed it to be the duty of the clergy to do—and "cry aloud and spare not" to show the people their transgressions. His first sermon in the new year is on "The Lapse of Time." Thoughts of his own personal salvation, and of the work he ought to do, press heavily on him ; and "works of penance" are—I believe for the first time—mentioned as characteristic of a true Christian. In the autumn of the preceding year, his pupils had combined to make him a present of the works of "the Fathers," so much talked about by him since 1826 and so little read. Henceforth they confronted him in his rooms and goaded him to labour. In the December following the gift, he writes, "resumed opusculum [*Arians*] after many weeks' interruption [I was working too hard at the *Arians*. It was due the next summer, and I had only begun to read for it or scarcely so, the summer past.]"

Every circumstance, as well as feeling, at this time tended to make his difficult subject more difficult, and the work more anxious. Desirous always of leaning on authority in religious matters, he was forced back upon it still more by the spectacle of the results of "free inquiry" around him in England. No wonder he declared himself "fussed" and "fagged" with the work. Froude—who went at truths, so to speak, by

intuition, and had no taste for antiquarianism—scarcely
disguises his impatience at his friend's worry, and
warns him that if he goes on "fiddling" any longer
with his introduction, he will certainly "get into a
scrape." Yet, what was he to do? About truths
so hard to fathom as the Triple Personality and
Divine Unity what did he know of his own knowledge? What *could* he know except through books?
His perplexity expresses itself in a sermon preached
in January on "Personal Influence the Means of
Propagating the Truth," in which we seem to hear
him asking himself how he could know that this or
that doctrine, or even this or that way of expressing
this or that doctrine, might not have an importance
that was hidden from the natural man. Might not all
truths alike in the Divine scheme be equally important,
all alike to be accepted on authority as parts of an
"economy" or "accommodation" adapted to the weak
intellects of men?

"For instance, for what we know, the Episcopal principle, or the
practice of Infant Baptism, which is traceable to Apostolic times,
though not clearly proved by the Scripture records, may be as necessary in the scheme of Christian truth as the doctrines of the Divine
Unity, and of man's responsibility, which, in the artificial system, are
naturally placed as the basis of religion, as being first in order of
succession and time."

One knows not whether to marvel at the simplicity
or audacity of a statement of this kind, which at one
stroke—under the cover of a "for what we know"—
disables us from judging, or testing (and the Scriptures
from supplying us with the means of judging, or
testing) the relative importance of any practice or
doctrine "traceable to Apostolic times"; and which
describes as an "artificial system" that mode of

thought which attaches greater importance to the doctrine of "the Divine Unity" than to the "Episcopal principle."

A few extracts from this sermon will show us that, at this time, Newman was persuading himself of two things; first, that it was needful for him to commit himself to his present far-reaching course of study in order that he might bring himself into harmony with the doctrine "traceable to Apostolic times"; and, secondly, that he was doing right for the present in remaining comparatively quiet, contenting himself with testifying from the pulpit of St. Mary's, while he was kindling his torch at the fires of the Early Church. A summary of it will make the sentences that are important for our purpose easier to understand.

True Christians have ever been a small minority even in the primitive Church, although that has been as near an approach to the pattern of Christ as fallen man will ever attain, being, in fact, a Revelation in some sort, of that Blessed Spirit, in a bodily shape, who was promised to us as a second Teacher of Truth after Christ's departure. It is because the *Church was intended* thus to teach us certain things, that the Scripture has *not* taught us these things. It was the work of the Scripture to secure the formation of a certain character, it was the further work of the Church to unfold a system for our intellectual contemplation as well as for the preservation of spiritual truth. There may be a kind of genius for moral truth as well as for art and for action; reason cannot attain to such truth; and, even if it could, reason could not communicate it to others, because language itself is too defective and artificial for such a purpose; one can no more "write and read a man" than "give literal depth to a painted tablet." But "we shall find it difficult to estimate the moral power which a single individual, trained to practise what he teaches, may acquire in his own circle, in the course of years. While the Scriptures are thrown upon the world, as if the common property of any who choose to appropriate them, he is, in fact, the legitimate interpreter of them and none other; the Inspired Word being but a dead letter (ordinarily considered) except as transmitted from one mind to another." "A few highly-endowed men will rescue the world for centuries to come. Before now, even one man [Athanasius] has impressed an image on the Church, which, through God's mercy, shall not be effaced while time lasts." "Such men . . . . light their beacons on the heights; each receives and transmits the sacred flame. . . . . "

"Such considerations lead us to be satisfied with the humblest and most obscure lot; by showing us, not only that we may be the instruments of much good in it: but that (strictly speaking) we could scarcely in any situation be direct instruments of good to any besides those who personally know us, who ever must form a small circle, and as to the indirect good we may do in a more exalted station (which is by no means to be lightly esteemed), still we are not absolutely precluded from it in a lower place in the Church."

Writing on the Incarnation in the *Arians*, he was necessarily led to the consideration of the relations between our Lord and His mother; and hence, perhaps, this subject is for the first time brought forward in the sermons. Newman frankly acknowledges that the question cannot be pursued; we must not think of her apart from her Son; if we did, and if the Scripture had given us a more vivid picture of her life and character, he feels that the purely human nature of the Mother would so far carry away our sympathies that we should pay her undue reverence:

"What must have been her gifts who was chosen to be the only near earthly relative of the Son of God, the only one whom He was bound by nature to revere and look up to; the one appointed to train and educate Him, to instruct Him day by day as He grew in wisdom and stature? This contemplation runs to a higher subject, did we dare follow it: for what, think you, was the sanctified state of that human nature of which God formed His sinless Son, knowing as we do, 'that what is born of the flesh is flesh,' and that 'none can bring a clean thing out of an unclean?'"

Newman's perception of logical sequence led him thus to the verge of acknowledging that since the

flesh of Jesus was by the orthodox admitted to be
clean and sinless, the same admission must be made
about that of His mother. But "he dares not follow
it." He recognizes that there may be a meaning in
the Scriptural silence about that wondrous relation-
ship on which—

"It is perhaps impossible for us to dwell much without some perversion of feeling. For, truly, she is raised above the condition of
sinful beings, though by nature a sinner; she is brought near to God,
yet is but a creature; and seems to lack her fitting place in our
limited understandings, neither too high nor too low. . . . . Hence,
following the example of Scripture, we had better only think of her
with and for her Son." . . . .

Every word here recognizes a difficulty and no solution
of it except through authority. But there is also
manifest an avowal of incompleteness and of inconsistency which must have troubled one who believed
that the Primitive Church communicated to mankind a
"system" of Divine Truth. The position is one of
unstable equilibrium.

CHAPTER XII

§ 50. *Divine Justice*

THROUGHOUT the year 1832 we hear the note of alarm in the sermons growing louder and fiercer. On previous occasions he had deliberately attacked the fashionable philanthropic principles of the day, by contrasting them with the principles and precepts of Scripture. Now he directs our attention to the nature of God Himself, as being inconsistent with such modern notions. In a University Sermon (8 April) he deliberately controverts the theory which maintains " benevolence unlimited and absolute to be the attribute of the Divine governance and the end the general good." The sermon is entitled, " Justice as a Principle of Divine Governance."

If "benevolence" meant "indulgence," and if "good" meant "comfort" or "enjoyment," no true Christian could dispute Newman's position. But he ignores the fact that " benevolence unlimited and absolute" must mean wishing for each person that which *is* best for him—not that which *seems* best, or is *physically* best, but that which is *really*, *i.e.*, *wholly*, best. The highest definition of justice to individuals is "giving to each man that which is best for him," whether praise or blame, reward or punishment, pleasure or pain. Of course, the limited intellects of men cannot hope to succeed perfectly in combining this ideal justice to individuals, with ideal justice to society. But if we are to speak of Divine Justice, as Christians, we can hardly be content to fall below the standard held up by Plato. Consequently, unlimited benevolence would appear to be not inconsistent, but at one, with unlimited justice. A writer whom Newman regarded as an Apostle, and as the nearest of the Apostles to Jesus, has preferred to say that God is "Love," although he might have said, with equal truth, God is "Justice." That writer knew well how men have degraded the name of Justice, so that, perhaps in most civilized nations, even our legal vocabulary—not to speak of countless proverbs about Law —bears witness to the degradation ; for if Justice had been what it should be, there would have been no need of Equity, still less of Mercy. Therefore he preferred to say God is Love, implying by it that He is also supremely just.

If St. John was right, the title of Newman's sermon must be pronounced misleading, except upon an interpretation of the word "justice" in the high and noble sense that it bears in Plato ; and, thus interpreted, "justice" is not incompatible with "unlimited benevolence." In truth, however, Newman seems to have been carried away by some purely legal notion of Justice as a kind of *lex talionis*, not effectively corrective, nor remedial, nor even deterrent. Sheltering himself under the least satisfactory portion of Butler's *Analogy*, he justifies the supposed Scriptural disproportion between offence and penalty, by pointing to a similar disproportion in the penalties inflicted by Nature. As if the fact that Nature, sometimes, first tortures, and then murders, a little child for playing with a box of matches, or crushes another to atoms for playing near a precipice, is to lead us to entertain for a moment the diabolical suggestion that the punishments of the Righteous Judge are equally disproportionate—so we should have to call them if we regarded Nature as a human person punishing as we punish—useless, and cruel ! Yet this is only by one step more immoral than to argue about the possible disproportion of the ultimate penalties of God from the fact that " a solitary act of intemperance, sensuality, or anger, is often the cause of incalculable misery." For what is this but, in effect, to argue that, *because* there is such disproportion in the *present*, in which God's kingdom has *not* yet " come," *therefore* there will be the same, or worse, in the *future*, in which, as we trust, God's kingdom *will have* " come ? Are not these so-called " punishments " of innocence or slight carelessness, and acquittals of gross recklessness or vice, just the wrongs and inequalities which we trust that the Supreme Justice will hereafter set right and make plain ? However, the whole of this sermon is to the same purpose, teaching us that, since there *is* evil in *this* world, God himself *may* work evil in the *next*, and that, since almost all natural religions have supposed Him to be a Tyrant, therefore our mouths are to be stopped in contradicting a proof of His tyrannical nature which some would derive from Revelation itself.

Now, too, there appears, perhaps for the first time in the sermons, a quasi-materialistic view of the Eucharist, connecting the gift of immortality to the human body with participation in the Bread and Wine of the Holy Communion : as if in our material frames there were a material something which can be made immaterial and eternal by the Sacrament. The teacher implies that God can indeed sustain us, as He sustained the saints of the Old Testament, without that Sacramental food, but if He does, it will be, as it were, by a miracle. Sustenance, and life immortal, are conveyed by the sacred Bread and Wine in a natural way, this being God's regular and appointed means : " We have no reason for thinking we shall live for ever unless we eat it, no more than we have reason to think our temporal life will be sustained without meat and drink."

What further step was needed to prepare Newman to receive any doctrine whatever on the basis of sufficient " authority " ? The one thing needful now to quicken his religious development was that he should *find* such a basis somewhere and not be driven to hunt for it here and there or to put it together in pieces for himself—illogically constructing Authority with the aid of Private Judgment. A spectator of his mental processes might have safely predicted that he would find the required " basis," long before he had read a tenth part of " the Fathers." How indeed, could he bear to wait, with Archbishop Usher, eighteen years ?—or more probably, with his procrastinating disposition, twice eighteen ?

And meanwhile, excitement in the political world was fast growing more intense, and at any time something might be expected which he would look on as a " sign " enjoining immediate action. The bishops had given up their opposition to the Reform Bill, and the king, under pressure, had promised to make peers in order to ensure its passage. On 7 June the Bill became law.   All this while Newman was concluding *The Arians*, the result of little more than six months of continuous work, which ought to have taken him more than as many years : " Tired wonderfully "—so he describes himself—" continually on the point of fainting away, quite worn out." And now, free from this crushing burden, and at the same time also giving up his last pupils, he was left at leisure to brood over the darkening prospects of the Church, and the insults and spoliations that it was likely to endure at the hands of the reformed World ; and this, in the solitude of the Long Vacation, during which he was left to himself, and therefore never alone :—never, because there was nothing now to protect him from the gathering crowd of fears and fancies within him, which his faith was not strong enough to control, nor his judgment to keep at a distance.

§ 51. *" The Spirit of Whiggery," " the Sin of Saul"*

The cholera now came again and in earnest.   In London the gentry were flying in all directions. Henry Wilberforce was not allowed by his mother to risk a visit to Oxford ; a cousin of theirs—she writes to Newman—had been seized at noon while on her way to church ; by midnight she was dead.   Froude was summoned home ; and he and Newman parted as if possibly not to see one another again.   Alone in deserted Oxford, Newman remained to grapple with the disease as best he could, and to resist the folly of his parishioners, who would neither use their own brains nor the brains of others for their self-deliverance.   It is curious to see how, even here, Newman's political contempt for the multitude flashes out, just

when he is doing his best for them.   Some of his
people had dug up the bed furniture of a cholera
patient, which they had buried instead of burning.
" Is not this," he writes, " the very spirit of Whiggery
—opposition for its own sake, striving against the truth
because it happens to be commanded us : as if wisdom
were less wise because it is powerful!"   Under all
this pressure, Newman very nearly broke down ; but
he just prevented a collapse by giving up all work and
making his violin, for a time, his only care.   Traces of
this extreme tension are perceptible in a sermon on
"The Religion of the Day," in which he heaps condemnation on those who profess religion, even more
lavishly than on those who assail it.

The former, he says, expecting a millennium, have
been hailing every evidence of improved decency,
every wholesome civil regulation, every beneficent and
enlightened act of state policy, as signs of their coming
Lord ; they have allied themselves, for what they considered good purposes, with bad men : " They have
accepted and defended what they considered to be
reformations and ameliorations of the existing state of
things ; though injustice must be perpetrated in order
to effect them, or long cherished rules of conduct,
indifferent perhaps in their origin, but consecrated by
long usage, must be violated.   They have sacrificed
truth to expedience."   It is seldom indeed that Newman appeals to justice ; but here, where he does appeal
to it, he appears, by means of an " or," to connect and
almost identify it with " long-cherished rules of conduct"!   He altogether leaves out the questions,
" ' Cherished ' *by whom ?* " and " Were those ' rules '
just or *unjust ?* "   To bring such an accusation as this
against men who certainly believed that "justice" was

their leading motive, seems an abuse of the privilege of
the pulpit, only extenuated by the plea of violent
nervous tension in the preacher.

Deeper than ever, now, is the theological gloom
with which he invests his doctrine of the opposition
between the Church and the World. At first sight it
suggests downright Manicheeism. He is (in a sense)
justified by orthodox theology in saying that the world
is Satan's instrument to break our moral strength ; but
it is, of course, also true (and, so to speak, far truer) to
say that the world is God's instrument to increase our
moral strength. Yet, while ignoring, and almost
appearing to reject, the latter, Newman so insists on
the former statement, as sometimes to give a reader
the impression that he really believes the visible world
to be the legitimate kingdom of the Devil. To an
angel, or a departed saint, the glorious harmonies of
the material world may, he thinks, convey some lesson ;
to *us*, none, or at least, none that is of any practical use.

"Religion, it has been well observed, is something *relative to us :*
a system of commands and promises from God *towards* us. But
how are we concerned with the sun, moon, and stars ? or with the
laws of the universe ? how will they teach us our *duty ?* how will they
speak to *sinners ?* They do not speak to sinners at all. They were
created *before* Adam fell. They 'declare the *glory* of God,' but not
His *will.* They are all perfect, all harmonious ; but that brightness
and excellence which they exhibit in their own creation, and the
Divine benevolence therein seen, are of little moment to fallen man.
We see nothing there of God's *wrath*, of which the conscience of a
sinner loudly speaks. So that there cannot be a more dangerous
(though a common) device of Satan, than to carry us off from our
own secret thoughts, to make us forget our own hearts, which tell us
of a God of justice and holiness, and to fix our attention merely on
the God who made the heavens ; who is *our* God indeed, but not
God as manifested to us sinners, but as He shines forth to His
Angels, and to His elect hereafter."

If he had contented himself with saying that certain aspects of philanthropy are sometimes subtle forms of selfishness—as when people desire to make a neighbour comfortable merely because the sight of discomfort makes them uncomfortable ; or if he had urged that the mere thrill of almost physical expansion which we feel in the enjoyment of high and noble thoughts is consistent with habitual slavery to selfishness—all this would have been true ; but it would not have been the truth that Newman wished to convey. He is putting in practice his favourite precept—"bending the stick the other way." He found his countrymen exulting in a complacent religion, pleased with themselves, and disposed to do the best thing they could to make the world comfortable to everyone. He will therefore treat them as heathen, and "put them in fear that they may know God." He extols, as the best medicine for *them*, those gloomy views of religion which they all discard. Even the errors of what are called the dark ages, *e.g.* a persecuting spirit, fear of religious inquiry, bigotry, were, after all, he says, but perversions and excesses of *real virtues* ; conscience *is* necessarily a stern, gloomy principle, and therefore modern Christians have silenced it ; better to torture the body all one's days, and to make this life a hell upon earth, than to remain tranquil in the life that *is*, over the eternal pit that *is to be*. He admits that we ought to think of God rather than ourselves ; but, he adds, when we do look within, we ought to think of ourselves "with a certain abhorrence and a contempt at being sinners." To "point to any particular time" when we "renounced the world (as it is called) and were converted," is "a deceit" ; we can never be sure of salvation while we are here ; "Dare not to think you have got

to the bottom of your hearts ; you do not know what
evil lies there. How long and earnestly must you
pray, how many years must you pass in careful obedience, before you have any right to lay aside sorrow,
and to rejoice in the Lord !"

Previous divergences from his old Evangelical
doctrine have prepared us for this declaration, that
the distinct consciousness of a formal "conversion" at
"any particular time" is a "deceit" ; but he goes
much further now. He does not hesitate to proclaim
that we are still under "Law," and that Christians
need detailed precepts in religion now as much as
Israel did. The world, he maintains, is not changed
by Redemption, as a whole ; viewed, as in God's
sight, the world *can never become wiser or more enlightened than it has been;* we cannot "mount upon
the labours of our forefathers" ; is it to be supposed
that we are better than the Jews ? The conclusion of
the discourse almost amounts to this, that our yoke is
heavier, and our chances of everlasting punishment
greater, than it is for those whom St. Paul describes as
being under the "beggarly" elementary lessons of the
Law of Moses ; and that, even when we have faith in
Christ, we can never be sure that we have it.

"Let us then approach God, all of us, confessing that we do not
know ourselves ; that we are more guilty than we can possibly understand, and can but guess † whether we have true faith or not."

His University sermons, till the end of the year,
continue to proclaim an ecclesiastical crusade against
"public opinion." There is always something attractive in the Coriolanus-like attitude of the solitary
champion of an unpopular cause whose "thoughts"
are so "informed with nobleness" that he is —

> "To shame unvulnerable, and sticks i' the wars
> Like a great sea-mark, standing every flaw,
> And saving those that eye him."

But it is essential to our hearty admiration for such a warrior that "nobleness"—and not the interests of a clique, not even the interests of a class or order—should "inform" his "thoughts." This is not quite the case with Newman. In his sermon on "Human Responsibility as Independent of Circumstances," preached before the University on 4 November, he has some very fine censure on fatalism, and servility to public opinion; but it is too much like an ecclesiastical shriek; it is not "noble." He appears to ignore the fact that God, not Satan, may, in some vast popular movements, be swaying the minds of men and teaching His lessons. His hatred of what is popular degenerates into a narrow and perverse authority. So far does he go with Horace's "firm-purpos'd man," who stands unmoved by "civium ardor prava jubentium," that he bends all his energies in thwarting *everything* that is suggested by the popular enthusiasm. Having no high standard of justice, he forgets that the poem couples "*just*" with "firm-purpos'd". The "civium ardor" will not move *him*, even when it is "*justa* jubentium." Parodying the Scriptural precept, "Thou shalt not follow a multitude to do *evil*," he would refuse to go with the "multitude" at all, even "to do *good*." He is vehement and contemptuous against the philosophers who represent society as moving by a certain law through different stages, and who then, not content with stating the fact (which is undeniable), go on to speak as if what has been, and is, ought to be, "as if, forsooth, Satan could not work his work upon a law and oppose God's will upon system." But when

we analyse his notions of what "ought to be," we
generally find that, instead of meaning righteousness,
or justice, or beneficence, or anything that men can at
once accept as Divine, he has in his mind some ideal
founded on his interpretation of Scripture, which may
possibly be altogether unjust, unrighteous, and oppressive. This fault underlies the following splendid
passage, in which the preacher uses first the word
"innocent," and then "Scripture Truth," to mean the
same thing, *i.e.* "consistent with the temporal interests,
or predominance of the Established Church":

"Nothing, for instance, is more common than to hear men speak
of the growing intelligence of the present age, and to insist upon
the Church's supplying its wants, the previous question being entirely
left out of view, whether those wants are healthy and, legitimate, or
unreasonable,—whether real or imaginary,—whether they ought to
be gratified or repressed, and it is urged upon us, that unless we
take the lead in the advance of mind ourselves, we must be content
to fall behind. But, surely our first duty is, not to resolve on satisfying a demand at any price, but to determine whether it be innocent.
If so, well; but if not, let what will happen. Even though the
march of society be conducted on a superhuman law, yet, while it
moves against Scripture truth, it is not God's ordinance,—it is but the
creature of Satan; and, though it shiver all earthly obstacles to its
progress, the gods of Sepharvaim and Arphad, fall it must, and
perish it must, before the glorious fifth Kingdom of the Most High,
when He visits the earth, who is called Faithful and True, whose
eyes are as a flame of fire, and on His head many crowns, who
smites the nations with a rod of iron, and treadeth the winepress of
the fierceness and wrath of Almighty God."

The last sermon of the year is on "Wilfulness, the
Sin of Saul." The subject lends itself readily to a
political application, and Newman availed himself of
the opportunity. He draws a picture of the wilful
king ashamed of the "illiberality" of the institutions

of Israel. The conduct of the lower classes shows, he says, that we too, as a people, are as wilful as the Jews. He implies that what the nation needed was not reformation of laws that were so obsolete or so injurious that they created irreverence for law, but an increase of readiness to obey *any* laws, simply because they were laws. This too, he says, is the tendency of Revealed Religion: "it absorbs into its province even those temporal ordinances which are, strictly speaking, exterior to it. It gives the laws of men the nature of a divine authority."

Towards the conclusion he utters the following rather hysterical condemnation of English society as at present constituted, in which he inserts a defence of "party religion," suggesting that our Lord Himself originated religious partisanship. Apparently he has no other reason for this, than a play on the word "party," because Christ employed, as His immediate emissaries, a small group, or "party," of His countrymen:

"The present open resistance to constituted power, and (what is more to the purpose) the indulgent toleration of it, the irreverence towards Antiquity, the unscrupulous and wanton violation of the commands and usages of our forefathers, the undoing of their benefactions, the profanation of the Church, the bold transgression of the duty of Ecclesiastical Unity, the avowed disdain of what is called party religion (though Christ undeniably made a party the vehicle of His doctrine, and did not cast it at random on the world, as men would now have it) the growing indifference to the Catholic Creed, the sceptical objections to portions of its doctrine, the arguings and discussings and comparings and correctings and rejectings, and all the train of presumptuous exercises, to which its sacred articles are subjected, the numberless discordant criticisms on the Liturgy, which have shot up on all sides of us; the general irritable state of mind which is everywhere to be witnessed, and craving for change in all things; what do all these symptoms show, but that the spirit of Saul still lives?—that wilfulness, which is the antagonist principle to the zeal of David,—the principle of cleaving and breaking down all divine ordinances, instead of building up. And with Saul's sin, Saul's portion awaits his followers,—distraction, aberration, the hiding of God's countenance; imbecility, rashness, and changeableness in their counsels; judicial blindness; fear of the multitude: alienation from good men and faithful friends; subserviency to their worst foes, the Kings of Amalek and the wizards of Endor."

Such were the thoughts which Newman was now to carry with him to foreign lands. For some months, Froude had been at home ill, and a journey had been planned to take him from England during the coming spring. Pressed by his friend to accompany him, Newman had at last consented, partly on grounds of health: " Not that I ever expect to be regularly well as long as I live. It is a thing I do not think of; but still I may be set up enough for years of work, for which, at present, I may be unequal"—this he had written in a long self-persuading letter to Froude, giving his friend (or himself) eight good reasons why he *should* accept the invitation pressed upon him. In the end, the reasons had prevailed. As the time for the voyage drew near, he was more and more unwilling to tear himself away from Oxford, and from the excitements of St. Mary's; but on 5 December—three days after " Wilfulness, the Sin of Saul "—he is at Falmouth, waiting for the Froudes, and for the vessel, hourly expected, that is to take him and them to the Mediterranean. His anticipations he describes in a letter from Whitchurch to his mother two days before starting. He has had " no time to think," but " at times it seems miserable to be going away for so long;" yet hereafter he will, he doubts not, look back to it with pleasure:

"I really do *not* wish (I think) that it [this present cessation] should be anything else than a preparation and strengthening time for future toil ; rather I should rejoice to think that I was in this way steeling myself in soul and body for it.

" In the afternoon service yesterday, the second Psalm [for singing] was Ps. 121 Merrick's version. Now I cannot think that the organist chose it on purpose, yet chosen on purpose it must have been by someone or other. So it seems like an omen or a promise."

Is this egotism to be called sublime or otherwise ? The organist chose a Psalm, which describes how " He that keepeth Israel will neither slumber nor sleep. The Lord Himself is thy keeper ; the Lord is thy defence upon thy right hand." What then ? May not the Whitchurch organist have had a son, or a friend's son, abroad, and needing " defence upon *his* right hand " ? Might not the Whitchurch congregation like to think that " the Lord Himself was *their* keeper"? Might not even the organist himself, for his own sake, be glad to remind himself that he was under the protection of One who will " neither slumber nor sleep " ? And yet Newman cannot think " the organist chose it on purpose." Is not his imagination —at least in contemplating his fellow-men—somewhat barren, as compared with his exuberant imaginations about himself and God ? " Chosen on purpose it must have been by someone or other :" by whom ? Clearly by that God who, even from Newman's childhood, had " ever answered " his, i.e. Newman's " prayers." " So," it seemed like an " omen," or " promise," i.e. to Newman. But why not to the organist ? Why should the organist be regarded as a mere instrument —unconsciously overruled by this " interposition " of Providence for the special purpose of choosing a Psalm that should afford a " promise " to the Lord's

Servant—the Champion, that was to be, of the Anglican Church?

Newman gives us an alternative. He does not compel us to think that he called it a "promise"—a word rather too closely associated with Christian thoughts; let us, then, prefer the Pagan term which he allows us to use; and let us conclude that, in circumstances of special tension and excitement, he was even more ready than usual to succumb to superstition and to find in everything "an omen." This is neither sublime nor ridiculous; it demands pity. Yet it is necessary to try to fix our thoughts steadily on little incidents of this kind in Newman's life: for they are (to use Bacon's illustration) the small stars in the Milky Way, representing some of the minute habits that go far to make up the man, and, at once, to explain and excuse him. They also give us a key to the influences that will be exercised on him during the next few months. Go where he will, he will be—shall we say "prophet" or shall we say "egotist"? Let us say "self-centred." Seldom has a traveller left his country who was more likely, on returning to it, to verify the adage that such people "change their climate but not their mind *."

CHAPTER XIII

THE PAUSE

§ 52. "*Delighted but not interested*"

NEWMAN'S first letter to his mother describes "the most pleasurable day—as far as externals go—I have ever had that I can recollect." Everything charms him, but especially the sea and its colours; first the "rich indigo" of the surface at rest, then the white edges of the waves, breaking into foam under a freshening wind, and "turned into momentary rainbows;" the changes in the wake of the vessel into transparent green, white, white green, &c.; then (as the day went on) brightening to a glowing purple, inclined to lilac, over which, "the sun set in a car of gold," "succeeded by a sky, first pale orange, then gradually heightening to a dusky red, while Venus came out as the evening star with its peculiar intense brightness." The coast of Portugal is a vision tantalising him that he cannot land to determine that it *is* a country; the rocks pass before him like a pageant, with the lines of Torres Vedras high above them; "the cliffs a greenish-reddish brown, very sober;" at their base the dashing waves, the foam rising like Venus from the sea: "I never saw more graceful forms, and so sedate and deliberate in their rising and falling."

Yet these " pleasurable days " teach him nothing so clearly as the danger of being too much pleased. Through all these glorious works of Nature, which struck the unsophisticated eye of the Psalmist of Israel, as having been created in a divine Wisdom, and as declaring a celestial Glory, Newman moves as one discerning in them the craft and subtlety of the Tempter of mankind. Such might be the feelings of some timorous, superstitious mind, fresh from hearing the mocking music in Berlioz's *Faust*, in which the sylphs and gnomes combine with Satan to lull the misguided soul to a slumber that shall lure him to his ruin and end in the Ride to Hell : " Dream, dream, happy Faust ! " Under this stress of watchful alarm, he writes as follows to his mother :

" . . . I have good hope I shall not be unsettled by my present wanderings. For what are all these strange sights but vanities, attended too, as they ever must be, with anxious watchfulness lest the heart be corrupted by them, and by the unpalatable necessity of working up oneself to little acts of testifying and teaching, which mere indolence, not to say more, leads one to shrink from ! "

And then, not quite sure of his own feelings, and half afraid that he really *is* enjoying Nature too much, *for its own* sake, he adds :—

" I really do think that the hope of benefiting my health and increasing my usefulness and influence, are the main considerations which [cause me to] absent myself from you and Oxford."

The typical ecclesiastic has *a priori* views about men and things. It displeases him if, on experience, he finds facts varying from his pre-conceptions ; but still worse, he is uneasy and troubled if he is forced to recognize that these variations are not so bad as they

ought to be on his hypothesis. These perturbations of
mind, which he ought to accept as proofs that he has
something to unlearn, he is inclined to reject as
temptations, and to say that they have a "corrupting"
tendency :—

> " I no longer wonder at younger persons being carried away by
> travelling, and corrupted ; for certainly the illusions of the world's
> magic can hardly be fancied while one remains at home. I never
> felt any pleasure or danger from the ordinary routine of pleasures,
> which most persons desire or suffer from—balls, and pleasure parties,
> or sights,—but I think it does require strength of mind to keep the
> thoughts where they should be while the variety of strange sights—
> political, moral, and physical—are passed before the eyes, as in a
> town like this."

Besides this negative feeling of uneasy antagonism
to the beautiful and glorious world, the positive sense
of a divine mission was never absent, and drove the
traveller constantly into himself when he might have
learned more from things outside himself. At no time
does the innate solitariness of his nature come out
more clearly than in this Mediterranean tour. From
a child he had been a recluse in soul, and every
appearance of sociality in him had been merely
superficial. His first poem—on "Solitude"—written
before he was seventeen, indicates that, even then,
to be alone in the company of his own thoughts
about the vast scheme of things, was a kind of
heaven to him. Now, as then, he was self-centred,
but in a different fashion ; concentrating himself, now,
not (so far as he could avoid it) on his own feelings,
but on some dimly discerned vision of a mission in
which he might avoid self-will. Still, the effect was
much the same. Instead of thinking about his conversion and his assurance of salvation, he was now

thinking partly about the difficulties in the way of salvation, and the impossibility of attaining any assurance of it ; but partly, and more often, about the work God was calling him to do, and the manner in which God intended him to do it, and how God had shaped the course of his life that he might be prepared to do it : and the result of this was that, amid all the stir and liveliness of his sea-voyage, amid the brightest splendours of the Protean deep, or the glories of the southern sky when the stars were at their brightest, he was in spirit always alone, always compelled by his principle, as well as by his nature, to think about himself. Out of himself not even Homer can drag him. Even when he is on the track of Ulysses, gazing on Ithaca, his mind flies back to the scenes of his own childhood, the shrubberies in his father's house at Ham, near London, where he first read Pope's *Odyssey* and made acquaintance with the dog Argus and the swine-herd Eumæus :

"When I was for hours within half a mile of Ithaca, as I was this morning, what did I not feel! Not from classical associations, but the thought that what I saw before me was the reality of what had been the earliest vision of my childhood. Ulysses and Argus, which I had known by heart occupied the very isle I saw. . . . .

". . . . I gazed on it by the quarter of an hour together, being quite satisfied with the sight of the rock. I thought of Ham, and of all the various glimpses which memory barely retains, and which fly from me when I pursue them, of that earliest time of life when one seems almost to realize the remnants of a pre-existing state. Oh, how I longed to touch the land, and to satisfy myself that it was not a mere vision that I saw before me ! "

It must have been hard, at times, for a scholar and a poet to maintain so consistent an egotism amid the classic scenes of the Mediterranean ; but he confirms himself in it by his poetry itself and sometimes by a

special eulogy on solitude, as for example in his sonnet
on Melchizedek "without father, without mother, without descent" :

> "Thrice bless'd are they, who feel their loneliness ;
> To whom nor voice of friends nor pleasant scene
> Brings aught on which the sadden'd heart can lean ;
> Yea, the rich earth, garb'd in her daintiest dress
> Of light and joy, doth but the more oppress,
> Claiming responsive smiles and rapture high ;
> Till, sick at heart, beyond the veil they fly,
> Seeking His Presence, who alone can bless."

Yet is "egotism" the right name for that state of
mind which—though it finds nothing to lean on in
friends or earthly scenes—flees beyond the veil to the
Divine Presence? Are St. Paul and Moses to be
called "egotists" because they too had their sense of
mission and went into the wilderness? At this rate, are
not all prophets, and perhaps most poets, "egotists"?
It may be so. Perhaps we ought to say that egotism—
which is a kind of insurrection against conventional gre-
gariousness—is, like all other insurrections, justified
by success. Such love of solitude, and such sense of
missions, as in the end bring the solitary thinker into
sympathy with mankind, and into harmony with the
drift of things, so that he insensibly falls into a scheme
tending to some ultimate and permanent good—these
succeed ; these are from above ; these are from the
Great Common World, from the Creator and Inspirer.
But sometimes they are unsuccessful. Then they are
proved to have sprung from one's own Little World,
not from the quickening Spirit, but from created,
restless, and rebellious matter, the uninspired. The
alternative put by Virgil should always be before the
minds of all Reformers: is it "Deus" that we hear?
or is it our own "dira cupido"?

Cynics may say that the whole affair is clear. Newman was an ambitious ecclesiastic. When Whately attributed Newman's leaving him and the Liberals in 1829 to a wish to be the head of a party himself, he was, they will say, not far wrong in his surmise, and Newman was quite right to add the word "think" in replying "I do not think that this charge was deserved." To them, Newman's detachment from everything in which he ought to have taken an interest during all this voyage, will seem to have arisen from a morbid and exaggerated notion both of his own capacity and of the part that Providence intended him to play —all based upon a narrow conception of human life quite inadequate to the vast and varied facts of its actual history. But though there is some truth in this, it is only a part of the truth. Newman was, no doubt, at this time, quite an obscure person. Indeed some strangers who met him in the course of his tour were interested in making the acquaintance of "the brother of Mr. Frank Newman of Balliol who had gone out as a missionary to Persia." Doubtless in him, as in other young self-introspective, shy men of capacity, the consciousness of the contrast between what he was in the eyes of the world, and what he was in reality and intended to be, could not but have been occasionally present. But the fact cannot be overlooked that Newman was largely justified by results, and that in his conduct of the Anglican Movement—at all events in its later phases—there are scarcely any symptoms of a "wish to be the head of a party," and a great many of a desire to avoid such a responsibility, and to do anything that seemed likely to please God. This is not an ordinary token of ecclesiastical ambition.

Nevertheless that he saw things with an ecclesiastical

eye is undeniable. Instances will be given hereafter. But the following passage will show how much he was shut up in himself and his work, even when Nature did her utmost to draw him out :

"No description can give you any idea of what I have seen, but I will not weary you with my delight ; yet does it not seem a strange paradox to say that, though I am so much pleased, I am not interested ? That is, I don't think I should care—rather I should be very glad—to find myself suddenly transported to my rooms at Oriel, with my oak sported, and I lying at full length on my sofa. After all, every kind of exertion is to me an effort : whether or not my mind has been strained or wearied with the necessity of constant activity, I know not ; or whether, having had many disappointments, and suffered much from the rudeness and slights of persons I have been cast with, I shrink involuntarily from the contact of the world, and, whether or not natural disposition assists this feeling, and a perception almost morbid of my deficiencies and absurdities—anyhow, neither the kindest attentions nor the most sublime sights have over me influence enough to draw me out of the way, and, deliberately as I have set about my present wanderings, yet I heartily wish they were over, and I only endure the sights, and had much rather *have* seen them than *see* them, though, the while, I am extremely astonished and almost enchanted at them."

§ 53. *The ecclesiastical eye*

What Newman was really interested in, while his superficial being was being delighted with the colours of the Mediterranean, may be inferred, not only from passages here and there in the Letters, but also from the series of dated poems which he composed during his tour. These poems were part of an ecclesiastical project—to set up a verse-department "for all right purposes" in the *British Magazine*. Almost all Newman's contributions spring directly from the thoughts or experiences of the moment. Thus, the first of them,

" Home," records the impression produced by a visit to the home of his friend Rogers, shortly before going abroad ; beautifully describing the " love-encluster'd columns " of the Temple of domestic Affection, which meets him everywhere in his native land, and the likeness of which he will miss in his " weary round " abroad. Those which follow, before he left England and a little after, speak of the necessity of "hate " as a preparation for " love," and of " holiness " as a training for " zeal." Others—and these are scattered through the whole of the series—exhibit the poet's doubts whether he ought, or ought not, to protest against this or that violation of strict Christian rule which he experienced in his voyage. Some represent his prayers for guidance. Through all, there breathes the feeling that Christianity, if it is to be a reality, must be an austere, hard, and militant religion. This feeling is sometimes intensified by a special incident so recorded in the Letters as to interpret the Poems.

Take, for example, the poem on Christmas in which he declares that he cannot " keep " his " feast," because though he hears " the tuneful bells " around him, he is " bereft of the sight of the High Priest " (he means, I suppose, Christ upon the altar, Christ as the Body and the Blood), from whom come the glories of the season —followed by a declaration that Christmas will lose its mirth for Britons when Christ calls the Bride away from them. Comparing this with Newman's Christmas letter to his sister, we find that they are in the harbour at Malta, " taking in coals on a holy day," and that as the captain's orders are precise, there is no alternative. But what provokes him is, " that the coal will be got in by the afternoon, and they are making preparations for a Christmas dinner, which seems incongruous." He is also put to confusion because he sees a poor fellow in the Lazaret saying his prayers with his face to the house of God in his sight over the water, and he adds, " it is a confusion of face to me that the humblest Romanist testifies to his Saviour, as I, a minister, do not." However, the poem indicates that he would not touch the Christmas dinner. The bells, he says, " peal a fast" for him, and this perhaps is the meaning of the following passage in the letter : " I do what I can, and shall try to do more ; for I feel very spiteful."

The earliest of the series are of individual rather than public application ; but by degrees, as England is left behind, the thought of the battle from which he is retreating for a time brings him back to political and ecclesiastical subjects. Thus, the " poor wanderers " who are the victims of "Private Judgment" are exhorted, in the poem thus entitled, to obey the voice of the Church who is now lifting herself from the dust to reign as in her youth ; Liberalism and Worldliness are attacked in a somewhat screaming note, as "infidel Ammon and niggard Tyre" ; Gibraltar calls forth a warning to the " Tyre of the West" that wields " Trade's master-keys," to dread her own power, and not to defy the Bride of Heaven ; and in " The Patient Church" the Bride herself is bidden to " bide her time." Many of these are above the level of mere political poetry ; but some are spoiled by a shrillness of tone suggesting that the mood of the writer is, to use his own word, quoted above about himself—when he grudged the poor sailors their dinner on Christmas afternoon because they had been obliged to work all Christmas morning—rather " spiteful."

True to his leading thought that " our business is

with our own faults and not with those of others," and full of the conviction that England would be a great deal better for a somewhat more gloomy and almost timorous religion, he says very little indeed about the darker side of the Greek or Roman Churches ; but in "Superstition," he makes his position clear. The "children of the South," he says, "shudder" at Christ, and seek charms and rites to avert His wrath. He confesses that he himself fears Christ as much as they do ; but still he will go to no other for help, for in no other can he find it :

"O Lord and Christ, Thy Children of the South
　　So shudder, when they see
The two-edged sword sharp-issuing from Thy mouth,
　　As to fall back from Thee,
And cling to charms of man, or heathen rite
To aid them against Thee, Thou Fount of love and light !

But I before Thine awful eyes will go
　　And firmly fix me there,
In my full shame ; not bent my doom to know,
　　Not fainting with despair ;
Not fearing less than they, but deeming sure,
If e'en Thy Name shall fail, naught my base heart can cure."

In contrast with the poems of personal religion and with the somewhat acrid and narrow political productions, take the poem on Corcyra. Here, for once, the thought of antiquity was almost borne in upon him by special circumstances. There had been a great ball at the palace, and the spectacle of so many Greek faces with Greek names, amid dress-coats and English uniforms had set Newman first on the question, "What would Thucydides have thought if he could have seen this ?"

—and then on the antecedent "improbability" of the change that had, after all, come to pass. This was a congenial thought. He always exults in speaking of the passing procession of " this world's " sights as the mere shows of a magic lantern in which there is no law or order. And so here—with an abuse of a word that he is constantly abusing—he " sets it down in his books," as a proposition settled and indisputable, that no change is so great as to be "*improbable*." Then too he meditates on the eternal fate that attends the actors in the great tragedies of Greek and Roman history, and from the combination of these thoughts arises one of the best specimens of his poetic power :—

> " I sat beneath an olive's branches grey,
>   And gazed upon the site of a lost town,
>   By sage and poet raised to long renown ;
> Where dwelt a race that on the sea held sway,
> And, restless as its waters, forced a way
>   For civil strife a hundred states to drown.
>   That multitudinous stream we now note down
> As though one life, in birth and in decay.
> But is their being's history spent and run,
> Whose spirits live in awful singleness,
> Each in its self-form'd sphere of light or gloom ?
> Henceforth, while pondering the fierce deeds then done,
> Such reverence on me shall its seal impress
> As though I corpses saw, and walk'd the tomb."

Only perhaps in one other poem does he allow himself (not without an apology borrowed from Terence) to be carried away by classic scenes ; and still it is with the same feeling that is expressed above—that the great Greeks and Romans to whom we owe so much, were but as " corpses " ; that when we read their history we " walk " over a " tomb," and that the shores of the storied Mediterranean are but the sepulchre and

record-stone of a "course without the prize." This
was written at Messina :—

"Homo sum ; humani nil a me alienum puto."

" Why, wedded to the Lord, still yearns my heart
    Towards these scenes of ancient heathen fame ?
    Yet legend hoar, and voice of bard that came
Fixing my restless youth with its sweet art,
And shades of power, and those who bore a part
    In the mad deeds that set the world on flame,
    So fret my memory here,—ah ! is it blame ?—
That from my eyes the tear is fain to start.
Nay, from no fount impure these drops arise ;
'Tis but that sympathy with Adam's race
Which in each brother's history reads its own.
So let the cliffs and seas of this fair place
Be named man's tomb and splendid record-stone,
High hope, pride-stain'd, the course without the prize."

For the most part, however, his mind passes over
the most obvious historical associations to fly to ecclesiastical or Biblical thoughts.   If the former rise to the
surface for a moment, he soon suppresses them as in
the following extract :—

" What has inspired me with all sorts of strange reflections these
two days is the thought that I am in the Mediterranean.   Consider
how the coasts of the Mediterranean have been the seat and scene
of the most celebrated empires and events which are in history.
Think of the variety of men, famous in every way, who have had to
do with it.   Here the Romans and Carthaginians fought ; here the
Phœnicians traded, here Jonah was in the storm ; here St. Paul was
shipwrecked ; here the great Athanasius voyaged to Rome.   Talking
of Athanasius, I will give you some verses about him :

    " When shall our Northern Church her champion see,
        Raised by Divine decree,
    To shield the ancient Truth at his own harm ?
        Like him who stayed the arm
    Of tyrannous power, and learning's sophist-tone
    Keen-visioned Seer, alone."

where it will be noticed how even Athanasius is only
introduced with a reference to the needs of the English Church, perishing for want of a champion.

§ 54. *"Satan let out of Prison"*

From the coast of the Morea the friends sailed to
Messina and thence to Naples, which they took on
the way to Rome. Their experiences of the Greek
Church and the Roman, hitherto, had impressed them
rather in favour of the former—at least so far as concerned the earnestness of the clergy. What they saw
of the latter in Sicily and Naples shocked them not a
little. Froude writes thus from Naples to Keble :—

"I remember you told me that I should come back a better
Englishman than I went away; better satisfied not only that our
Church is nearest in theory right, but also that practically, in spite of
its abuses, it works better; and to own the truth, your prophecy is
already nearly realized. Certainly I have as yet only seen the surface of things, but what I have seen does not come up to my notions
of propriety. These Catholic countries seem in an especial manner
. . . κατέχειν τὴν ἀλήθειαν ἐν ἀδικίᾳ, ('hold down the truth in unright-
ousness'). . . . . Monasticism is said to be going out of fashion
fast; hardly anyone goes into the convents, and those who are in
already are subjected to no discipline; at least, O.'s friend, Mr.——
who went into a Benedictine convent at Monreale, is now in Naples
without permission, leading a gay life, and the Church has not proceeded to any severe measures against him. I have seen priests
laughing when at the Confessional : and indeed it is plain, that unless
they habitually made light of very gross immorality, three-fourths of
the population would be excommunicated. . . . . The Church of
England has fallen low, and will probably be worse before it is better ;
but let the Whigs do their worst, they cannot sink us so deep as
these people have allowed themselves to fall while retaining all the
superficials of a religious country. I hope when I get to know something of the language, and to see more of the people, that I shall see
reason to retract my present views."

Newman's letters are at first to the same purport. The state of the Church, he says, is deplorable :

> "It seems as if Satan was let out of prison to range the whole earth again. As far as our little experience goes, everything seems to confirm the notion received among ourselves of the priesthood, while on the other hand the Church is stripped of its temporalities and reduced to distress."

Besides the poverty and contempt into which the clergy have fallen, he deplores the "infidelity and profaneness as if the whole world (Western) were tending towards some dreadful crisis." He begins to hope that England, after all, is to be "the 'Land of Saints' in this dark hour, and her Church the salt of the earth" :—

> "We heard of one man—at Messina, I think—who, while bearing his witness against the profligacy of the priesthood, rigidly attends mass, and, on being asked why, answered that the altar is above the priest, and that God can bless His own ordinances, in spite of the instruments being base. This seems very fine, but the majority of the laity who think, run into infidelity."

Naples confirmed the bad impression which Sicily had given him, and almost cast into the shade the recollections of the fascinating ruins at Egesta. Indeed this Roman Brighton was, in every respect, the best possible preparation for one who was to see Rome itself immediately afterwards, and to take the Eternal City into his heart. Naples seems to him what he most detests, "a watering-place," with watering-place scenery—inferior altogether to that of Sicily and the Greek islands—and to be admired chiefly by watering-place people ; nothing but a retirement for the purposes of animal gratification. Fresh from Sicily—that battle-field where ancient nations, Greeks, Carthaginians, Romans, Arabs, and Normans, had each left its mark and passed away— he finds himself in what he thinks an overrated, noisy, and vulgar place, suited for luxurious Romans once, and for lazy pleasure-seekers now; but not for him. The silly Saturnalia of the Carnival, the pictures on the walls representing souls in the flames of Purgatory, and what he saw there generally, both of priests and people, disgusted and repelled one who could not but contrast them with recent visions of the Genius of ancient Greek worship, seated in her enchanting solitude on some Sicilian hill-top, grand in the midst of error, breathing her inspiration through the perfect beauty and proportion of her simple and unadorned architecture,—visions to which his mind flies back again and again as to the fragrance of some sweet flower. "The sooner," he says, "we are out of so bad a place, the better." Its badness spoils for him even his recollections of the neighbourhood: "Pompeii and Herculaneum are wonderful places, but they do not move me."

From frivolous Naples he approaches Rome, as one should best approach that city of Divine visitations, as St. Paul approached it: "through ancient towns, full of ruin, along the Via Appia;" then the Pontine Marshes; then, through a region of rocks and woods, to the desolate flat of the Campagna, once thickly populous, now the haunt of malaria; then ruins, isolated at first, of monuments, arches, aqueducts; "you think it never will have done; miles on miles the ruins continue; at length the walls of Rome appear; you pass through them; you find the city shrunk up into a third of the space enclosed. In the twilight you pass buildings about which you cannot guess wrongly. This must be the Coliseum ; there is the arch of Constantine ; you are landed at your inn ; night falls ;" and—you have leisure to dream about it.

§ 55. *Rome, "the City of Divine Judgments"*

The dreams that night must have been all the more vivid because there was a conflict, so to speak, between dreaming and undreaming. It had been the dream of Newman's youth—not yet quite dispelled by the conclusions of the Oriel common-room—that the Pope, or the Church of Rome, was Antichrist ; and as he walked alone along the Via Appia, over the Pontine Marshes, going on before his carriage while the horses were changing, and making a poem on what he was soon to see, he could not but have revolved in his mind his youthful application of those passages in the Apocalypse which speak of the Beast that stamped men with its mark, and the Great Harlot who "made drunk the kings of the earth." Even this first impression, made, not by Rome, but by the mere approach to it, seems to have shaken his soul so that he halts, in doubt whether to reverence or to censure. The thought in the poem is double, first of Rome as an empire, then of Rome as a Church. The first stanza speaks of her as one of "the hateful four" on the scroll of the prophet Daniel : the second is as follows :—

> " And next a mingled throng besets the breast
>   Of bitter thoughts and sweet ;
> How shall I name thee, Light of the wide West,
>   Or heinous error-seat ?
> O Mother, erst close tracing Jesus' feet,
>   Do not thy titles glow
> In those stern judgment-fires which shall complete
>   Earth's strife with Heaven, and ope the eternal woe ? "

On reaching the city itself and moving amidst its
ruins, he feels the presence of a conflict of ideas that
task all his symmetrizing power to reduce to some
sort of harmony.   On the one hand, he beholds the
great enemy of God, the Beast, "dreadful and terrible."   The Jewish candlestick, sculptured on the
Arch of Titus, the arena where Ignatius suffered, and
the columns with their proud heathen inscriptions still
visible, repeat, as it were, the rebellion of Babel
against heaven, and mark the place as the vile tool
of God's wrath and Satan's malice.   And yet he has
felt almost at the first glance that Rome is the first of
cities and has absorbed into itself his interest in all
others : "All that I ever saw are but as dust (even
dear Oxford inclusive) compared with its majesty and
glory !   Is it possible that so serene and lofty a place
is the cage of unclean creatures ?   I will not believe it
till I have evidence of it "—so he writes to his sister
after two days' experience.

It is not the museums and galleries and works of
art that captivate him—though here too he speaks of
himself as "subdued" by the Apollo, so different in
the original from all copies that he had seen, and
touched by "the strange simplicity" which Raffaelle
has the gift to bestow upon his faces ; it is the Rome
of the Apostles, the city of the tombs of the martyrs,
that overpowers his imagination.   The power of the
Church is also here brought home to him by the vast
size and beautiful proportion of the buildings which make
him feel "little and contemptible."   Characteristically
also he notes "the Sunday kept so decorously," so
different from things at Naples.   Here there are no
trumpery inscriptions in the streets profaning the most
sacred subjects, and the look of the priests is superior.

It is the city of St. Gregory, too, whose church, he has visited, reading the inscription which records the names of some of the earliest English bishops, including "the monk Augustine," who went forth thence to convert England to the Catholic faith. Thus, by degrees, he is turned round to a new view altogether, which contemplates the Eternal City as suffering indeed under the Judgments of God, yet not as it were for her own fault, but as bearing the sins of the world, "smitten of God and afflicted" as the Prophet, or as Jerusalem, is described in the Scriptures :—

"There is such an air of greatness and repose cast over the whole, and, independent of what one knows from history, there are such traces of long sorrow and humiliation, suffering, punishment, and decay, that one has a mixture of feelings, partly such as those with which one would approach a corpse, and partly those which would be excited by the sight of the spirit which has left it. It brings to my mind Jeremiah's words in the Lamentations, when Jerusalem, or (sometimes) the prophet, speaks as the smitten of God. Oxford, of course, must ever be a sacred city to an Oxonian, and is to me. It would be a strange want of right pride to think of disloyalty to it, even if our creed were not purer than the Roman ; yet the lines of Virgil keenly and affectionately describe what I feel about this wonderful city."

Thus he writes to Rogers, whom, next to Froude, he loved best and trusted most of all his younger followers ; and to whom, first, in later days, he was destined to reveal the earliest symptoms of secession to the Church of Rome. Even at this early date, we can perceive that there had been stamped upon his heart an image that may be covered for a time, but not effaced. Rome, he tells the same friend, is "like Aaron's rod," and has "swallowed up" the memories of other cities. We have read his protest that "it would be a strange want of right pride to think of disloyalty to Oxford": and yet—between it and Rome, how can he express the difference! He recalls the verses from the Eclogues, in which a simple rustic of Northern Italy confesses that he had been foolish enough once to suppose that Rome was like his own city; but now he knows the former to be as superior to the latter as a cypress tree to a bramble bush; he bids Rogers repeat every word of these lines and dwell on each word :—

> " *Urbem quam dicunt Romam, Melibœe, putavi*
> *Stultus ego huic nostrœ similem,*" &c.

—he tells him his recollections of the cypresses of Corfu; of "the graceful, modest way in which they shoot up with a composed shape, yet boldly in their way, being landmarks almost for miles round;" and then he adds that " these lines keenly and affection- tionately describe what he feels about this wonderful city." Alas, poor Oxford! It is curious how, in a single flash of imaginative insight, he predicts, almost as though he were inspired with a spirit of prophecy, the contrast that henceforth he is doomed to carry about in his heart, between the two cities of his love. " Right pride" inclines him to Oxford; but passionate overpowering devotion carries him towards Rome. Which of the two is likely to prevail? "Pride"— even as "right pride"—would not be a strong point in one who, like Newman, carried humility (in matters of religion) to the verge of abjectness.

To enhance the serenity and repose of the Eternal City, what he had heard from time to time of the state of things at home served as a foil: " How awful," he wrote, "seems to me (here) the crime of demolition in England! All one can say of Whigs, Radicals, and the rest is, that they know not what they do"; and again, "We have just heard of the Irish Church Reform Bill. Well done! my blind Premier, confiscate and rob, till, like Samson, you pull down the Political Structure on your own heads." A few days later, after commenting ironically on Arnold's scheme, (of which he had just heard) for allowing to Protestant Denominations the use of Anglican churches, he just contemplates, and apparently not quite in irony, the possibility of Rome as a residence for himself, if the time should come to shake off from his feet his native dust :—

"The air is too soft perhaps to suit me for a permanence, otherwise I cannot conceive a more desirable refuge, did evil days drive one from England. But this is impossible of course, because one's duties bind one there, even were we cast out as evil; and besides, I cannot quite divest myself of the notion that Rome Christian is somehow under a special shade, as Rome Pagan certainly was, though I have seen nothing here to confirm it."

He adds, however, a protest: "not that one can tolerate for an instant the wretched perversion of the truth which is sanctioned here." Still, Rome, he assures us, even in this respect, is not worse than other places; and once more the contrast between it and Naples suggests itself: "The clergy, though sleepy, are said to be a decorous set of men. They look so, except the canons at service, who laugh and talk. Far otherwise at Naples, which is a wretched place." What he means by "perversion of the truth" is expressed elsewhere as "superstitions, or rather, what is far worse, the solemn reception of them as an essential part of Christianity." By this distinction, he seems to imply that he was ready to condone a good

deal that he called " superstitious," if only it could be
recognized as non-essential, adapted perhaps for Rome
but not for England ; and this, as well as his change
of feeling towards Rome itself, may prepare us to find
him now making some effort to ascertain what were
the fundamental differences between the two Churches
and whether they were so great as to prevent all hope
of union.

§ 56. *Rome " The Cruel Church "*

For an account of the manner in which Froude and
Newman endeavoured to obtain from Cardinal (then
Monsignor) Wiseman an answer to the question raised
at the end of the last section, and for the result of their
attempt to ascertain from him what possibility there
might be of bridging the gulf between the Anglican
and Roman Churches—we shall search Newman's
letters in vain.   The *Apologia* indeed tells us that
Froude and he made two calls on Wiseman, but gives
us no hint as to the nature of their conversation with
him.   Fortunately, however, Froude fills the gap.
The interviews took place about the first week of
April ; and he wrote the following description of them
on the 13th :

"It is really melancholy to think how little one has got for one's
time and money.   The only thing I can put my hand on as an
acquisition is having formed an acquaintance with a man of some
influence at Rome, Monsignor ——, the head of the —— College
who has enlightened —— and me on the subject of our relations to
the Church of Rome.   We got introduced to him to find out
whether they would take us in on any terms to which we could
twist our consciences, and we found to our dismay that not one step
could be gained without swallowing the Council of Trent as a whole.
We made our approaches to the subject as delicately as we could.
Our first notion was that the terms of communion were within

certain limits under the control of the Pope, or that in case he could not dispense solely, yet at any rate the acts of one Council might be rescinded by another ; indeed, that in Charles the First's time it had been intended to negotiate a reconciliation on the terms on which things stood before the Council of Trent. But we found to our horror that the doctrine of the infallibility of the Church made the acts of each successive Council obligatory for ever, that what had been once decided could never be meddled with again ; in fact, that they were committed finally and irrevocably, and could not advance one step to meet us, even though the Church of England should again become what it was in Laud's time, or indeed, what it may have been up to the atrocious Council, for M—— admitted that many things, *e.g.* the doctrine of mass, which were fixed then, had been indeterminate before.

"So much for the Council of Trent, for which Christendom has to thank Luther and the Reformers. —— declares that ever since I heard this I have become a staunch Protestant, which is a most base calumny on his part, though I own it has altogether changed my notions of the Roman Catholics, and made me wish for the total overthrow of their system. I think that the only τόπος now is 'the ancient Church of England,' and as an explanation of what one means, 'Charles the First and the Nonjurors.'"

The Editors of the *Remains* are a little scandalized at Froude's blunt way of putting things. They append a foot-note, saying, "All this must not be taken literally, being a jesting way of stating to a friend what was really the fact, viz., that he and another friend availed themselves of the opportunity of meeting a learned Romanist to ascertain the ultimate points at issue between the Churches." Doubtless there is in Froude's account a certain element of ironical and almost mocking exaggeration. He always likes to exaggerate his failures ; and this was a failure. But this does not prove that the interview was not seriously meant. When the editors speak of "meeting" and Froude, of "getting introduced," we see at once that—in this respect at all events—it is the former and not the latter who "must not be taken literally." They do not like quite to suppress the narrative, as they do not suppress others of Froude's Romanizing utterances which they think will tend to good; but they wish to minimize the deliberateness with which two Anglican clergymen sought an interview with a Roman Prelate in order to ascertain on what terms the Church of England could be reconciled to the Church of Rome.

The impression made upon Froude himself by the failure is manifest. He looks on Rome in a much more practical way than Newman does. He has no dreams about the Fourth Empire, or the Beast, or Antichrist. Not that he cares about its classical associations either. "St. Peter's itself is," for him, "the great attraction of Rome, worth all the classics put together." His main delight is, to see the old Roman force and splendour absorbed into the service of Christianity—"St. Peter and St. Paul standing at the top of Trajan's and Antonine's columns, and St. Peter buried in the circus of Nero." With such spectacles around him, he cannot help desiring to know how his own insular Church can be reunited to this Church, so manifestly triumphant over her ancient foes, so independent of the State, and so complete, definite, and satisfactory to the æsthetic taste. Repelled by Rome, he is turned, as a last resource, to the Church of the Nonjurors; but he does not attempt to conceal his disappointment.

On Newman the impression may perhaps be inferred to be all the greater because he is almost entirely silent about it. Let the reader note how, in the extract which will next be given, a bare mention of "the conversations with Dr. Wiseman and Mr.

Bunsen "—the only allusion, I think, in the whole of the correspondence, to this most important part of their visit—is wedged in between other matters of mere sight-seeing or casual interest, and succeeded by an aspiration after "union" and a complaint of the "cruel" inflexible Church which will be content with nothing short of their submission or destruction. Reading between the lines, he will easily recognize a close connection between the "conversations with Dr. Wise man" (*not* with " M. Bunsen") and the passionate outburst that follows :—

"I ought to tell you about the *Miserere* at Rome, my going up St. Peter's, and the Easter illumination, our conversations with Dr. Wiseman and with M. Bunsen, our search for the Church of St. Thomas of Canterbury, my pilgrimage to the place of St. Paul's martyrdom, the Catacombs, and all the other sights which have stolen away half my heart, but I forbear till we meet. Oh that Rome were not Rome! but I seem to see as clear as day that a union with her is *impossible*. She is the cruel Church asking of us impossibilities, excommunicating us for disobedience, and now watching and exulting over our approaching overthrow."

§ 57. *Rome "where the Church sits in sackcloth"*

A day or two after this interview Froude and his father quitted Rome on their return to England. Newman, who intended to make a short visit to Sicily, was left for some hours in the Great City wandering about the place alone "with a blank face," to dream his ecclesiastical dream in the presence of far vaster ecclesiastical realisations. A few hours afterwards he sits down by himself to dinner in detested Naples, and his heart flies back to the grave melancholy of the City which has cast him out and will not hear of reconciliation: "How shall I describe the sadness with which I left

the tombs of the Apostles ?   Rome, not as a city, but
as the scene of sacred history, has a part of my heart,
and in going away from it, I am as if tearing it in
twain."   The hateful presence of this City of Pleasure
brings him to a truer recognition of the hidden and
mysterious grandeur of that other which he imagines
he is leaving for ever.   No longer is Rome now to
him the Beast great and terrible, nor even the City of
God's Judgments, in the ordinary sense which applies
judgment to guilt.   Nay, even the memory of her, as
the City of the Cruel Church, is for the time blotted
out by the thought of her unutterable sorrows, as if
she were judged indeed, but by no common judgment ;
smitten, but smitten of God ; afflicted, but after the
manner of the Messiah : being indeed a kind of
Mediator for all other cities, and bearing, under the
veil of her serene sadness, the burden of the sins of
all her frivolous and rebellious sisters throughout the
unrepentant earth :

"The town is essentially a watering-place, and more like Brighton
than any place I know ; the same glare, the same keen brightness of
the hills, the same disposition of houses opening upon the sea, the
same boisterous wind, the same stimulating air, the same sparkling
water, the same bustle, or rather tenfold, and the same apparent
idleness of the people.   Oh, what a change from the majestic pen-
siveness of the place I have left, where the Church sits in sackcloth
calling on those who pass by, to say if any one's sorrow is like her
sorrow !"

This view having captivated his imagination, he
proceeds to supply himself with a logical basis for it ;
and this he does in a letter to the sober theologian
Rickards.   He had not written to him before, since
leaving England, but on the question now at issue he
feels that his friend's judgment will be useful.   He wishes

to rid himself, by argument, of the belief which his imagination has not yet been able quite to shake off, that the Church of Rome is in some sense Antichrist ; and he selects Rickards as the friend to whom (as well as before himself) he may set forth his reasons. To him he suggests that the real Antichrist may not be the Church, but "a sort of *genius loci* which enthralls the Church which happens to be there." He adds that, " Even were the old spirit dead, the City would be under the curse by which children suffer for their fathers' sins ; but the spirit lives to show they are the children of those who killed the Prophets." A notion has struck him, he says, on repeatedly reading the Apocalypse, that " the Rome there mentioned is Rome, considered as a city or *place*, without reference to the question whether it be Christian or Pagan " ; and again, " I am a great believer in *genii locorum*. Rome has had one character for 2,500 years ; of late centuries the Christian Church has been the instrument by which it has acted—it is its slave. The day will come when the captive will be set free." " How a distinction is to be drawn between two powers, spiritual and devilish," he cannot understand ; yet " that it is incomprehensible is no objection to the notion of God's doing it."

The argument is difficult to make out. He says that, for 2,500, *i.e.* 670 years before Christ, till the time at which he was writing, Rome has had one character. I know of nothing that occurred in the history of Rome precisely 2,500 years ago, that could induce us to suppose that Newman meant this number exactly. Presumably he means to go back (in rather rough numbers) to the supposed date of the foundation of the City. Does he then believe that,

from that time to this, a Genius of the Seven Hills has
influenced the people on them, whether Pagans or
Christians? No other inference as to his meaning
seems possible. If so, he would appear to have
believed that a *place*, in itself, may be under a curse
which affects all who are in it. But how this could
affect a city *at its foundation*—unless he laid stress
upon the legend of the murder of Remus by Romulus
—is hard to see. But perhaps, for us, the point of
importance is, not to explain the belief; but simply to
state it, as Newman's; and to realise how it might
gradually lead to a practical surrender of his old
identification of Antichrist and the Church of Rome.
The Roman Church will be, henceforth, for him,
under a curse perhaps, but a curse for which she was
not herself responsible; wrestling in behalf of the
world, against that Evil Beast which claims the City as
its prey ; a captive for the sake of Christendom ; and
"the day will come when the captive will be set free."

The letter ends as it begins, in a conflict between
passionate gratitude and passionate reproach. The
memory of Rome, he says, will ever be soothing to
him ; Jerusalem alone could impart a more exalted
comfort and calm. And then he sums up his travels.
In point of interest, he has seen nothing like Ithaca,
Messina, and Egesta (he puts aside Rome) ; in point
of scenery, nothing like Corfu ; but as to Rome, he
" cannot help talking of it ; " he enumerates again its
Apostolic memorials, the churches founded by the chief
of the Apostles himself; the house and table of St.
Gregory, who gave Christianity to England ; the place
of the martyrdom of St. Peter and St. Paul ; "but the
catalogue is endless. . . . O Rome! that thou
were not Rome!"

Great must have been the charm of the cities and valleys of Sicily to have drawn Newman away to them from his returning companions. At the end of their interview with Dr. Wiseman, Newman had said solemnly, in answer to his courteous hopes that the two friends might pay him another visit, " We have a work to do in England." It was at this time too that Froude and he had chosen the fighting motto for *Lyra Apostolica,* " They shall know the difference, now I am back." With his heart thus full of future battle, he half regrets, just before crossing over to the island, that he was going to travel in those wild solitudes, " and to sleep in dens of the earth—and all for what ? for the gratification of imagination, drawn by a strange love of Sicily to gaze upon its cities and mountains." By way of excusing himself to Rickards, he says that the expedition, he hopes, will " set him up," and that bad times are at hand, so that it may be well for him to learn to travel alone as Wesley and Whitefield did.

Of Sicily he saw little. Fever was already making its approaches on him, and its intermittent attacks may be traced in the varying tone of his letters. Yet before he succumbed to it, he saw the climax of all the scenery in his tour in Taurominium, the only place (as far as I remember) of which he speaks as though he could be bettered by its beauty : " It was worth coming all the way, to endure sadness, loneliness, weariness to see it. I felt for the first time in my life that I should be a better and more religious man if I lived there." As he left the place, he caught a view worth mention-ing because it supplies an interesting instance of the

way in which the Letters illustrate the Poems : "Etna,"
he writes, " was magnificent. The scene was sombre
with clouds, when suddenly as the sun descended upon
the cone, its rays shot out between the clouds and the
snow, turning the clouds into royal curtains, while on
one side there was a sort of Jacob's ladder." It was
this sight which suggested to him a parallel (expressed
in the poem called " Taormini," and prefaced with the
text " And Jacob went on his way, and the Angels of
God met him ") between himself and " the Saint " who
was nerved by sights from the third heaven " for fourteen trial years." The *Apologia* tells us that it was
when he was thus left to himself that the thought came
upon him that deliverance is wrought not by the many
but by the few, not by bodies of men but by single
persons. Now, too, it was that he repeated to himself
—applying it of course to the Church and the Liberals
—the famous lines of the *Aeneid* in which Dido
invokes curses on her enemies and prays that her
avenger may arise. So strong was the feeling with
which he turned to play the part of this "avenger"
that the author of the *Apologia*, looking back upon his
life thinks that now *for the first time* he " began to
think that he had " a mission !

On the serious illness which befell him in Sicily he
dwells with a minuteness of detail into which we need
not follow him. Again and again—in the summer and
winter of 1834, in the spring of 1835, and lastly in the
spring of 1840—he recurs to the remembrance of it,
and writes page after page about it as being " pleasant
and profitable." The explanation given by " a friend
whose judgment may be relied on " is, that Newman
looked on this crisis as providential : " he so plainly
always looked on the fever in all its features as *a crisis*

in his life, partly judgment on past self-will, partly a sign of special electing and directing favour, that the prominence given to it is quite accounted for by those who knew him, and explains why all these strange pictures of fever are given." By "self-will" Newman meant his yielding to the deceitful fascinations of the Sicilian mountains instead of returning at once to his mission in England. The Froudes had returned, and the natural course for him was to do the same; but he had turned aside to see the strange sights and beautiful scenes of antiquity, and for this he was now being chastised : "I felt God was fighting against me, and felt at last I knew *why*—it was for self-will."

Amongst the details which he afterwards wrote down concerning his illness, is one of which some of his biographers have taken little account. They have some justification for neglecting it ; for it is a very heavy self-condemnation, in which Newman complains of his want of "love" and calls himself "hollow" ; and it is obvious to remark, 1st, that it is a way with some saints to esteem themselves, at times, the vilest of sinners, and 2nd, that Newman, at this special time, was on the verge of delirium, if not actually delirious. The first of these remarks has some force. Several of his poems, at this very time, show that he exaggerated thoughts that but rested on the mind's surface, as though they were almost sins. Thus, the poem called "Dreams" deplores the mere recurrence to the nightly imagination of the wild fancies of "youth's twilight hour," and of "the revel or the scoff in Satan's frantic train," apparently referring to the time when, as a boy of fourteen, he had bragged to his father of having read Hume's Essay on Miracles and had rebelled against the doctrine of everlasting punishment. And

again, after seeing at Frascati certain pictures which
contrasted strangely with those of the Holy Family—
pictures of which he says in his letters that he is
amazed how men of any religious profession and
clergymen can admire them, we find him, in " Temptation," praying to the Son of Mary that His Mother's
smile may rest upon his frail being—

> " Till I am Thine, with my whole soul, and fear,
> Not feel a secret joy, that Hell is near."

For exaggerations, therefore, I think we must be prepared ; but it does not follow that his self-censure,
though wrong in degree, should be wholly wrong in its
direction.   That would be to attribute to him a
dulness and obtuseness quite inconsistent with his
character.   And as for the objection of delirium, that
would be absolutely futile.   Those who make it forget
that the verdict which will now be laid before the
reader was delivered, *not at the time*, but nearly *two
years afterwards*.   Such a remand was surely long
enough to secure a deliberate and judicial sentence.   It
was written at Oxford in the Christmas Vacation of
1834 :

> " Next day the self-reproaching feelings increased.   I seemed to
> see more and more my utter hollowness.   I began to think of all my
> professed principles, and felt they were mere intellectual deductions
> from one or two admitted truths.   I compared myself with Keble,
> and felt that I was merely developing his, not my, convictions.   I
> know I had *very* clear thoughts about this then, and I believe in the
> main true ones.   Indeed, this is how I look on myself ; very much
> (as the illustration goes) as a pane of glass, which transmits heat,
> being cold itself.   I have a vivid perception of the consequences of
> certain admitted principles, have a considerable intellectual capacity
> of drawing them out, have the refinement to admire them, and a
> rhetorical or histrionic power to represent them ; and, having no

great (*i.e.*, no vivid) love of this world, whether riches, honours, or anything else, and some firmness and natural dignity of character, take the profession of them upon me, as I might sing a tune which I liked—loving the Truth, but not possessing it, for I believe myself at heart to be nearly hollow, *i.e.*, with little love, little self-denial. I believe I have some faith, that is all; and, as to my sins, they need my possessing no little amount of faith to set against them and gain their remission."

The good qualities which Newman here attributes to himself, he has—and in abundance. And he depreciates himself in speaking of his "self-denial" as "little"; for there is nothing that he would not do, no sacrifice, no self-abasement, that he is not ready to make for the good of his soul. "Faith" too—if by "faith" he meant, not trust in a Person, but belief in the truth of a great mass of Biblical facts—he had in such large measure that he was always ready to believe (so far as he could *make* himself believe) anything that appeared likely to be acceptable to God; and for such large "faith" as that, "some" is a poor epithet, and "that is all" is a disparaging under-statement. But when he condemns himself for having "little love," it is not so easy to contradict him.

Affectionate though he was to his relations and intimate friends—as long as they were in religious agreement with him—it is impossible to say that his sympathies with men in general were wide or deep. As for his love of God, it was not of such a kind as even to contemplate in this life an approach to the "casting out" of fear. Hence, since God can only be known by loving Him, came at times a terrible consciousness that he was placed in a position where he did not know so much about Him as he was obliged to seem to others to know. He thought indeed that he knew enough about the Truth to enter on a course of conflict as its champion ; yet whenever he had time to reflect, he was haunted by the conviction that the Truth was not in him. Such a man—and there are many such among those whose profession it is to deal with sacred things—is right in calling himself "hollow," although to a man of the world he will appear guilty of gross exaggeration. He *is* hollow—not absolutely, but by comparison with many less highly-endowed, less actively-religious, less saintly-living, less self-deny-ing souls, who may not perhaps feel certain of many things, but are certain at least of one or two things— as, for example, the Fatherhood of God, and the ulti-mate and perfect triumph of Good over Evil—of which they can speak, and on which they can act, without the thought of an "economy," and without the faintest trace of any kind of fear except that reverence which is essential to the profoundest love and trust.

§ 59. *End of the Poetic Period*

During Newman's solitude in Sicily, the thought of Rome—though subordinated for a time to thoughts of his own mission, with intermittent flashes of conviction as to his own deficiencies—was by no means entirely absent. A passage in the *Apologia* makes a signifi-cant distinction between two kinds of impressions which he had received from the Roman systems when abroad ; one he says affected his "imagination," the other his "heart" ; and it was in Sicily that he received the latter :

"When I was abroad, the sight of so many great places, venerable shrines, and noble churches, much impressed my imagination. And my heart was touched also. Making an expedition on foot across some wild country in Sicily, at six in the morning, I came upon a small church. I heard voices and looked in. It was crowded, and the congregation was singing. Of course it was the Mass, though I did not know it at the time. And in my weary days at Palermo, I was not ungrateful for the comfort which I received in frequenting the churches; nor did I ever forget it."

These and other remarks about Palermo point to the suggestion that in after times Newman attributed his indelible recollections of these influences, and their profoundly tranquillizing effect, to the Presence of the Sacred Elements on the Altar, although at the time he was ignorant of this : " I began to visit the Churches, and they calmed my impatience, though I did not attend any services. I knew nothing of the Presence of the Blessed Sacrament there." But, whatever he may have deemed the cause, or causes, we can well understand his statement that he never did forget the result. Possibly when he wrote of " not attending the services," he did not mean to exclude being present as a sympathetic spectator. For the effect of the " varied round of service " in " soothing the heart " is described in a poem written at Palermo while the scenes were fresh in his recollection :

" I cannot walk the city's crowded streets,
  But the wide porch invites to still retreats,
  Where passion's thirst is calm'd, and care's unthankful gloom.
     There, on a foreign shore,
    The home-sick solitary finds a friend ;
      Thoughts, prison'd long for speech, outpour
    Their tears ; and doubts in resignation end.
  I almost fainted from the long delay
  That tangles me within this languid bay,
  When comes a foe, my wounds with oil and wine to tend."

Naturally, however, as he draws homeward, most of

the poems take their colour from the conflict that
awaits him. " Day-labourers " encourages the warrior
whose task it is to deliver the Church from " her
present chain " ; " Warfare " reminds him that, if Paul
had remained in peaceful retirement, " men had not
gnashed their teeth nor ris'n to slay," but—England
would have remained in heathen darkness. " Sacrilege,"
and " Liberalism " speak for themselves.

The period of poetry will soon end, making way for
the period of action. From the time of his return to
England his Muse is almost silent—so far at least as
concerns any original utterances—until we come to the
Dream of Gerontius, written at the end of his sixty-
fourth year. But we cannot pass from this aspect of
his life without remarking to what a sweet translucent
purity, or to what a height of genuine poetic vigour he
can reach, when he does not feel bound to be ecclesiastically " spiteful," and allows himself to sing of those
simpler wider truths which look a little beyond
the " verse department in Rose's magazine for all
right purposes." He is perhaps at his very best when
recalling the image of the sister prematurely taken
from him, or when describing the feelings of separated
friends ; but he takes a high flight, too, when he suffers
himself to remember that he has read and loved the
great Greek tragedies. The poet who has told us how
" Eli's feebleness, Saul's black wrath, may aid Ahito-
phel's spite," hardly prepares us for the following noble
comparison between the Jewish race and blind Œdipus
in his old age :

> "O piteous race !
> Fearful to look upon,
> Once standing in high place,
> Heaven's eldest son.

O aged blind
Unvenerable ! as thou flittest by,
I liken thee to him in pagan song,
  In thy gaunt majesty,
The vagrant King, of haughty-purposed mind,
  Whom prayer nor plague could bend ;
Wrong'd, at the cost of him who did the wrong,
Accursed himself, but in his cursing strong,
  And honour'd in his end."

Too, far too rare, are such utterances as these. As
he approaches home, the poems show more and more
traces of a mind conscious of a mission, and doubtful
about the means. His work looms before him with a
vagueness which sometimes deters him by the fear
that he may be presumptuous, sometimes encourages
him by the hope that he may be helpful. In "Pusil-
lanimity," for example, he reminds himself that it falls
on men sometimes to claim "powers that" they
"dread, or dare some forward part"; and that we
must not shrink as cravens from the imputation of
"pride." "Uzzah and Obed-Edom," on the other
hand, teach an opposite lesson—to avoid presumption,
and to remember that the Ark of God is to be aided
by us not "as patrons," but "as sons." The "Power
of Prayer" is a warning that those who would give
great gifts to the world cannot hope to gain this high
privilege "at once," but only through a long course of
trials ; and the "Path of the Just" ("Semita Justorum")
recognizes that, through his past life, grace has been
generally conveyed to his soul, not through the quiet
routine of life, or through joys, but through "grief, or
pain, or strange eventful day"; and even so, now :—

"—whene'er, in journeying on, I feel
The shadow of the Providential Hand,

Deep breathless stirrings shoot across my breast,
Searching to know what He will now reveal,
What sins uncloak, what stricter rule command,
And girding me to work His full behest."

All through these poems—and especially in those in which the thought of strife, rather than mere effort, is predominant—the poet is definite when he tells us what he is fighting *against*, but not so clear when we wish to ascertain what he is fighting *for*. "Sacrilege" means obviously that the attempts to despoil the Church of her temporalities and endowments are to be resisted ; but, when he speaks of releasing the Church from "her present chain," it is natural to ask whether he is simply repelling Disestablishment, or wishing to revive the independent power of the Mediæval Church.

It is as an illustration of his present vagueness of plans, as well as for its pathetic beauty, that a special interest attaches to "The Pillar of the Cloud," better known by its opening words, "Lead, Kindly Light." The title suggests the Exodus of Israel, and it is natural to think of Newman as the Anglican Moses. But that law-giver claimed also the title of a leader and prophet ; and the plaintive prayer, "I do not ask to see the distant scene—one step enough for me," hardly reminds us of the prophets of Israel. With them it was customary to describe themselves as standing upon a tower or upon a hill, like watchmen seeing what was afar off and proclaiming it to the people. Perhaps, however, the poet felt that the analogy between Judaism and Christianity—the former so much more joyous and free from responsibility, *in spite of* its scantier privileges ; the latter so much more tremulous and anxious, *because* of its ampler privileges hedged round with still more ample responsibilities and punishments—necessitated in a Christian leader a more timorous tone, and a contentedness to adopt the attitude of one not in the Light, but groping his way towards it.

Doubtless, too, Newman was writing under the painful recollection of the former delusive lights—the firebrands of his own Evangelical feelings, or the Will-o'-the-wisps of the Noetic School of Oriel—which had led him so long and wearily astray. Never henceforth would he yield to such deceitful phantoms—all of them, in various shapes, representing the Arch-deceiver, Private Judgment. Under Whately's influence he had "loved to choose and see his path." Suppressing the recurring fears of the wrath to come, he had allowed "Pride" to "rule his will"; but it should be so no longer. Henceforth he would follow whithersoever the Lord might lead him. It might be "o'er crag and torrent," but no obstacles should keep him back. It might be through the darkness, but still he would grope onwards. What though he no longer had the peace of his childhood? What though the "angel-faces" that once smiled on his youth had now for a time departed from him? Still, if led, he would follow.

What—we may ask—can be more manifest self-surrender than this? Did it not deserve to succeed? It deserved; and it succeeded. It succeeded in bringing to the poet, at last, a peace of mind almost approaching to that which he had enjoyed when he had lived in the doctrine of Final Perseverance; and perhaps that was a goal that he would in after days have deemed sufficient. But to do more than this, to prepare himself to be a guide from the Lord for a great nation, to make a highway for his countrymen

toward the Truth, to cast down the mountains and
exalt the valleys so as to make rough places plain for
the wayfaring multitude—this was a task that mostly
implies long years of patient waiting, often among
simple people, or even amid distasteful drudgery, in
which the eye of the prophet learns to see and his heart
to feel, and the simple truths that join the human
and the divine flow into him, he knows not how nor
whence, filling him with a force that is not his own,
until the moment comes when the celestial messenger
touches his lips with "the coal from the altar," freeing
him from doubt, self-consciousness, and fear, and
fitting him to deliver a message of eternal truth :

> "All may save self ;—but minds that heavenward tower
>   Aim at a wider power
>   Gifts on the world to shower.—
>   And this is not at once ;—"

"And this is not at once." In these words Newman
has directly hit one blot in his career—the haste with
which he committed himself to a far-reaching enterprise, about the nature of which he knew, and was
contented to know, so little that he could not even
discern how unprepared he was to take an active part
in it. But the following words, perhaps, throw even
more light upon the causes that gave his career its
ultimate direction. They describe the means by which
a prophet is to gain his power :

> "And this is not at once ;—by fastings gain'd,
>   And trials well sustain'd,
>   By pureness, righteous deeds, and toils of love,
>   Abidance in the truth, and zeal for God above."

Can this power be thus "gained" by *all* "minds that
heavenward tower"? Is it not a *gift* that may be

directed, but not created, by such preparation ? and, without the gift, can all the training of all the schools of the prophets avail anything ? The very mention, too, of "fastings" along with "righteous deeds" and " toils of love,"—does it not show a misappreciation of the difference between the work of the drudge and the work of the genius ; between the man who is under law and the man who is under grace ? It is as though a great artist were to tell his pupils that none of them could become what he himself was, except by grinding colours and—painting pictures of genius. " Fastings," in themselves, are but colour-grinding and palette-preparing ; a toil of love is a work of genius, that is to say, of spiritual genius, not to be reached —or compensated for if absent—by any number of " toils of penance." A man cannot achieve "righteous deeds " unless he has the spirit of righteousness in him ; and a man cannot guide a nation or a church unless he has in himself and feels that he has, an intuition—for which he never dreams of taking credit, for he feels that it is not his own—into a few simple truths of which he feels absolutely sure. Again, as to " abidance in the truth ": for a prophet, this is not enough. A layman, or an ordinary ecclesiastic, may be content to *abide* in the Truth ; but the Prophet, besides abiding in it, must *possess* it—some of it, though it be but a grain of it. Furthermore, he must feel that he possesses it in such a living and expanding form that he is irresistibly moved to impart it to others. It is no reproach to a man that he is not thus moved. A man may not have the gift of prophecy or of guidance ; yet he may have his gifts for all that. He may be a critic, or a rhetorician ; and in either of these provinces he may do good work and feel himself honest. But it is at his peril that he trespasses into the region of the prophet. If he does that, he has mistaken his vocation; he has not reached that stage in the development of one devoted to great deeds, where—

"—doubt is not, and truth is more than truth."

What he thinks the voice of God is the voice of a restless self; his kindly light is a meteor of the marsh; and though he may remain good and true as a man, yet, as a prophet, however long the dismal hour may be averted, it must come at last when he will look into his own soul and pronounce himself "nearly hollow."

CHAPTER XIV

§ 60. *The Period of "fierceness"*

On 14 July Keble preached in the University Pulpit the Assize Sermon, afterwards published under the title of " National Apostasy." " I have ever considered," says the *Apologia*, " and kept the day, as the start of the religious movement of 1833." This introduces us to what may be called Newman's "aggressive period" which, in later years he included in the happiest portion of his life. His wonted anxious piety suddenly gave place to what he himself describes as a mixture of " fierceness and sport," which gave offence to many, and which he himself does not attempt to defend. After many weeks of illness and home-sick anxiety, an extraordinary re-action of health and exuberant energy and an absorbing sense of mission, carried him for a brief season altogether out of his ordinary self. " My health and strength," he says, " came back to me with such a rebound that some friends at Oxford, on seeing me, did not well know that it was I, and hesitated before they spoke to me." The feelings of a prophet seem to have overcome, for the moment, the feelings of the man. He lost his balance as he had done before in the

political excitement of 1829. "Agitation," he writes,
"is the order of the day," and, "the Apostles did not
sit still." But neither did the Apostles exactly
"agitate"; whereas Newman threw himself into "agitation" with a vehemence for which even those who
knew him best were unprepared.

Not more than two or three weeks elapsed after his
return to England before he started a society. This
almost immediately took, as its main object, the
diffusion of tracts advocating "right principles."
Here Newman's faculty of rapid, incisive, and versatile
composition gave him immediate pre-eminence. He
had not thought of the plan himself at first. Possibly
he was still brooding over his Sicilian dream, that
great things are accomplished not by bodies of men,
but by single persons. And, besides, he was not
naturally inventive. But what others originated, he
could at once take up, and could see in it more than
was seen by the authors themselves, and could develop
it to the utmost. And this he now did when "one
whom" he "will not name" (all we know is that it
was not Froude) suggested an association for Church
purposes. Having once begun he went fast. Even
Keble could not keep pace with him and doubted, at
first, whether to join the new Society. At that time
Newman and Froude *were the only members of it;*
but the former wrote brusquely back to Keble that
"he might join it or not but the league was in existence." Upon this, Keble seems to have joined at
once and to have raised no further difficulties although
the Tracts soon began to startle moderate persons.
Newman himself admits that he intended to shock
people : * "we are bringing out a stinging *Lyra* this
September — moderate well-judging men will be

shocked at it. I am pleased to find we are called
enthusiasts—pleased, for when did a cause which could
be so designated fail of success?" His old friend
Rickards, who had begun by promising the proposed
Association cordial support, soon complained of the
"irritating and irritated" tone of some of the Tracts
and threatened to withdraw from the movement
altogether.

It is certainly a fact—whether it is an extenuation,
is not quite so certain—that this "irritating and irritated" tone was the result of deliberate calculation.
For all the purposes of controversy Newman understood human nature very well indeed; and among
other effective controversial devices is that of silencing
an adversary by audacity. This he could do so
neatly that some of his friends compared his style to
a blow on the face, or in the stomach, or taking an
adversary's breath away. Another device, and this
too Newman mentions as one on which he acted, is
that—known in commerce as "haggling"—of asking
more than one hopes to get in order to get more than
one's commercial adversary expects to give. Above
all, he was a master of what may be called the legitimate arts of literary advertising and literary polemics.
It is said that the *Times* tried to induce him to join
their regular staff: and the effort did credit to the
editor's judgment. None knew better than the
founder of the Tractarian Association how to get
up a controversial stir; how to put a case clearly
before the public with every advantage of force,
variety of illustration, brevity and general attractive-
ness, extending even to printers' devices of paragraph
and type; and since, according to his favourite
proverb, men like to do whatever they do well, he

naturally liked to do all these things. On one occasion he distinctly avows his desire to irritate the editor of a certain newspaper *usque ad insaniam;* and what he avows once he frequently puts in practice.

But this is not the whole of the explanation of his "period of 'fierceness'"; for this cannot explain the painful break which now occurred in his domestic relations. And besides, he showed himself unnaturally harsh in small matters that subserved no definite object. He tells us himself that he dissuaded a lady from attending the marriage of a sister who had seceded from the Anglican Church ; and that he answered the remonstrance of a friend of Evangelical and Liberal opinions by saying that he and his friends "would ride over him and his as Othniel prevailed over Chushan-Rishathaim." Newman dearly loved those friends of his who were co-operating for the common good : but it was perhaps as co-operators, rather than friends, that some of them came closest to his heart. If they thwarted his action, or even disappointed his hopes of their actions, he could be extremely austere, or, as one of his best friends described it "flinty." After seven years spent under the same roof with him, one of his pupils describes him as "a good hater," and says that "any one who disappointed or thwarted him found him to an extraordinary degree implacable." To the same effect, though expressed with studious kindness and moderation, is the testimony of his brother-in-law and old ally in the Tractarian movement : "Had Newman been less hopeful, he might have been more forgiving ; for it is the most generous and confiding who most feel ingratitude*."

An amusing instance, showing how some of his closest friends dreaded this "flinty" humour, occurred

soon after the start of the Tractarian Movement.
Henry Wilberforce came to Oxford with the intention
of telling Newman of his approaching marriage. Now,
to marry, appeared to Newman a kind of falling away
in any of his coadjutors except such seniors as Pusey
and Keble.* Wilberforce therefore came in alarm.
And the alarm did not diminish. He actually dared
not break the news : " I did not tell Neander*," he says,
" (as who would) but yet I did tell his sister and gave
her leave to tell him . . . . I suppose however he will
cut me." Rogers became the mediator ; " He came
to Oxford," so he explains to Newman, "with the
intention of breaking the matter to you ; but when he
came near and saw how fierce you looked, his heart
failed him and he retreated ἄπρακτος."

The "fierceness," in this instance, and even before
such mediation, disappeared, and Newman afterwards
became godfather to one of Wilberforce's children : but
it was not always that these ascetic heats passed so
easily away in such humorous and harmless evapora-
tions. At home, for example, his conduct was painfully
and persistently austere. Francis Newman complains
of the unnatural stiffness and dignity of his elder
brother when they met after some two years of absence
in July 1833, and he adds that his elder sister also
(either now or afterwards) had to experience similar
estrangement, in which Mrs. Newman herself was to
some extent included and which lasted till the death of
the latter. The cause, we are told, was their refusal to
accept Newman's high claims to be the prophet of a
national revival of religion. Of this sad domestic
trouble there are but few traces in the Letters ; but we
shall see, in due course that Newman felt it as a great
sorrow though not entirely of his own causing. With

Harriett, after his mother's death, the correspondence
would indicate that he retained friendly, but hardly the
most confidential relations; and it is almost pathetic
to note how, sometimes, in writing both to her and to
his mother, he avoids some subjects and chooses
others, often those not nearest to his heart. It is for
his sister Jemima that he reserves, for the most part,
his religious confidences : his letters to his elder sister
remind us of the condemnation he is said to have not
unfrequently passed on her independence of thought.
"Harriett has that in her *which I cannot permit.*"
As for the heretic Francis, his elder brother would have
nothing to do with him; until the pulverization of
the *Via Media*, and the appearance of the majestic
phantom of the Church of Rome, tamed his spirit and
taught him milder counsels.

In his account of the rupture with his brother,
Newman treats himself unfairly. His custom of calling
in reason, as *he* thinks, to advise him, but, really, to
justify a course predetermined by the feelings, makes
him appear to superficial readers (as no doubt he
appeared to himself) coldly and dispassionately logical.
He seems to speak as though he were compensating
for his usual application of feelings to the subjects of
reason, by applying reason, for once, to the subjects of
feeling : " I would have no dealings with my brother,
and I put my conduct upon a syllogism. I said St.
Paul bids us avoid those who cause divisions : you
cause divisions ; therefore I must avoid you."

But let us do Newman the justice he did not do himself. The reason he gives here is not the true reason.
I would no more believe that Newman cut his brother
under the influence of a "syllogism" than that Hamlet
refused to kill his uncle at his prayers for fear he should

not send him to hell. The parallel is more than a
mere casual one. Newman was very like Hamlet in
many ways; as much a dreamer, with fits of violent
action, followed by fits of depression, and then by
dreams again; as much, or more, given to studying
signs and omens; as much, or more disposed to believe
in a Divinity that shapes our ends, spite of our rough-
hewing; as much led by—and as much given to
distrust—his own feelings, impulses, and imaginations;
as self-introspective, and as much puzzled by the
complex problems of self-introspection and the difficulties of discerning between conscience, reason,
cowardice, and the thousand other voices that a man
may hear within himself when he cuts his nature into
two parts and makes one part try to listen to another;
as fond, as femininely fond, of intimate receptive
friends in a refined circle, and as contemptuous of
bad taste, brute materialism, and the vulgar common-
place multitude; as impatient of pomposity and con-
ventionalism in others, and suspicious of hollowness and
effusiveness in himself. Nor must we omit that both
were passionate admirers of the Roman type of character that speaks little and does much; both, at once
despisers and masters, of the Grecian arts of rhetoric
and histrionism; so that they did not hesitate to play
with language in order to deceive prying people and
bewilder self-complacent fools; and sometimes, under
the stress of trying circumstances going half unconsciously beyond the lawful rhetorical limits, they were
led, in their contempt of words and in their contempt
of self, to throw out wild and whirling utterances,
as to which, afterwards, not even they themselves
could exactly tell us whether they meant what they
said, or what had been their reason for saying it.

Lastly—which is the most important point for our purpose—the power of thought in both was so much too subtle and too swift for the stiff, chilled faculty of deliberate resolution ; both saw so many aspects of a question, running off into so many discursive side-issues and possibilities and doubts, that they could never take any important action except with the eyes of the reason momentarily closed. Then, when they opened them again, and the cold fit of self-distrust and self-judgment came back upon them, they could not bear to think in cool blood upon what they had seen, leaving it unexplained, but felt a passionate necessity, either to discern a special Providence in it, or else to explain it by logical rules, and to invent for it rational, but non-existent, motives. And so terribly afraid were they of depending upon their tortuous, shifting, fluctuating selves, and so wonderfully ingenious in inventing causes and motives, that—between the stimulus of fear and the aid of ingenuity—they never failed to satisfy their imaginations for a time that, in whatever they did, they had either been led by a Supernatural guidance, or else had acted calmly, deliberately and judicially, on some scheme of their own, and for the very best of reasons.

Hence neither Newman nor Hamlet is to be taken at his word when either makes himself out to be cynically or diabolically bad. To recur to the instance given above, when Hamlet catches his uncle on his knees at prayer, and refuses to take advantage of the opportunity for exacting vengeance from the murderer, he excuses himself to himself aloud on the ground, that his uncle, if killed at that moment, may perhaps go to heaven, whereas he wishes to send him to hell! Who, upon thinking it over, can believe that excuse? No one who knows anything of human nature in itself, and of human nature "methodized" in Shakespeare. It is simply—as Coleridge long ago pointed out—the self-deception of the dreamer who could persuade himself of anything. Hamlet's nature, always doubting, always procrastinating, and always shrinking from committing itself to action—revolts from the tremendous step to which he is urged by what, after all, "may be the devil"; and he excuses that which in his heart he is half disposed to condemn as the sickly sample of a coward, on the plea of the unseasonableness and inadequacy of the revenge, that he may pose to himself as a cold-blooded schemer of the finest Italian type: "See how cool I am! How logical! How consistently and deliberately cruel! Could Machiavelli have done it better?" Who has not known even kindly sheep or gentle gazelle-like natures, deck themselves out as wolves after this fashion? Newman was no gazelle; but neither was he a wolf. When he cut his brother, and "put his conduct upon a syllogism" it was no logic, it was prophetic fervour that goaded him to the transient harshness; the syllogism was only the excuse, the after-thought, the cloak of wolf-skin devised by his tortuous imagination.

This "period of fierceness" was at once the happiest and the most deplorable period of his life: happiest, because the fervour of his zeal for the Lord freed him for the time from anxieties about his soul; most deplorable, because he was now actively, not passively, violating the laws of human nature and preparing the way for a heavy retribution. This was the time when, as James Mozley tells us, he was exclaiming against the Liberals twenty times a day, "We'll *do* them." This was the time, too, when he was re-writing a large part of that labyrinthine work, the *Arians*, in which he thus speaks his mind freely about the teachers of heresy. A heresiarch, he says, " should meet with no mercy ; . . . he assumes the office of the tempter, and, so far forth as his error goes, must be dealt with by the competent authority, as if he were embodied evil. To spare him is a false and dangerous pity. It is to endanger the souls of thousands, and it is uncharitable towards himself." Newman confesses that this is a " fierce passage," but does not add much to soften it. All he says is that he himself " could " not " have even cut off a Puritan's ears." *Could not* means, of course, no more than that it would have been a very repellent task. He adds that " Arius was banished, not burned." But he does not deny, nor is it easy to see how he logically could deny, that if he could have stopped Arius from being a heretic and from making heretics, by burning, or decapi-tating, or otherwise getting rid of him, it would have been his duty to God to do so. Prudent heresiarchs, who appreciated the effect on Newman of a sense of duty to God, would have been wisely unwilling to place their earthly fate in his hands.

§ 61. " *Impossible*," *now, to know* "*poor Whately*"

Newman's general confession of the fierceness that characterized this period of his life encourages the supposition that other particular charges of " fierce-ness," not admitted by him, may nevertheless be true. His old friend Blanco White, for example, with whom he had once had rooms in common, and played the violin, and discussed religious questions, declared in

1839 that Newman, on the outbreak of the Tractarian Movement, " would have nothing to do with him." Newman, in his *Apologia*, " very much doubts " this. But, the doubt being expressed in 1864, and the positive statement being made in 1839, the presumption, so far, is in favour of the statement. Again, Blanco White, if cut, would be more likely to recollect it than Newman, if the latter was cutting old friends all round him. Lastly, we have evidence to show that, in another and far more important instance of the same kind, Newman's memory was inadequate to the facts. I am referring to the final disruption of friendly relations between Newman and Archbishop Whately, which will suitably find its place here. The account in the *Apologia* is so very misleading that it is necessary to give details. They speak for themselves.

The *Apologia* throws all the blame on the Archbishop : " From the year 1834 he made himself dead to me. He had practically indeed given me up from the time that he became Archbishop in 1831." No evidence is given in support of this statement ; yet there were in Newman's possession some documents bearing on it, and absolutely inconsistent with his account. These, however, were not published in the *Apologia*—not at least in the first edition. Subsequent editions contain, in an !Appendix, and in small print, four letters, with the following preface :—

"On application of the Editor of Whately's correspondence, the following four letters were sent to her for publication. They are here given entire."

Few read Appendices in small print. Yet these letters are essential to a comprehension of the facts ; and they confirm the impression derived from Newman's printed correspondence, that the rupture was begun, not by Whately, but by Newman.

To begin, first, with the correspondence: we find Newman himself, in August, 1833, declaring, though with regret, that it is necessary to give up Whately's acquaintance :—

"As to poor Whately, it is melancholy. Of course, to know him now is quite impossible, yet he has so many good qualities that it is impossible also not to feel for him. I fear his love of applause, popularity &c., has been his snare; for a man more void of what are commonly called selfish ends does not exist."

We may remark, in passing, that—considering the difficulties that attended an Archbishop of Dublin at a time when his clergy were reduced to straits for want of their tithes, and the tithes could often only be collected by military force—love of "applause and popularity" is not a mild or lenient accusation to bring against him. With Newman's accusation we may compare Whately's own statement that he was far from possessing a heroic invulnerability against the opposition of enemies and the perversion of friends; "The process of mental case-hardening is more pain than Aladdin's lamp and ring would repair"; and again, "my present appointment—a call to the helm of a crazy ship in a storm—is one which nothing but an overpowering sense of duty would have induced me to accept. Let me hope for your prayers, that I may be supported in my appalling task, and enabled to bring at least some fragments of the wreck into haven." As regards his vote for the "Church Temporalities Act," he says, "These very men [who attacked me] knew, if they took the trouble to make even the least enquiry, that this very Act was framed

by the then Ministry under the sanction and approba-
tion of the Primate, long before I had ever even heard
of it." These facts, and Whately's nature, and Newman's knowledge of Whately's nature, being all considered, I do not see how we can find Newman guilt-
less of a harsh, hasty, and uncharitable censoriousness.
Had he accused Whately of weakness, of sacrificing
principles to expediency, of preferring sacrilegious
peace to a civil war for the " rights of the Church "—
this would, at least, have been an intelligible and par-
donable charge : but it is unpardonable in an old friend
and fellow-worker, who must have known the stuff of
which Whately was made—under cover of acquitting
him of "what are commonly called selfish ends"—to
impute to him one of the most contemptible crimes of
which an ecclesiastical statesman can be guilty, "love
of applause and popularity." Truly if Newman could
say of Whately, "he made himself dead to me," the
other might have retorted with far more justice, " *You*
made yourself blind to *me*."

In the second place, so far from the Archbishop's
having really "made himself dead " to Newman from
the year 1834, the correspondence shows us one of
Newman's friends apparently accusing him of cutting
Whately among others, and Newman himself apparently admitting it. "A friend," says the Editor of
the Letters, "looking back to a day when Whately,
then Archbishop of Dublin, was in Oxford, remembers
accusing Mr. Newman to his face of being able to
cast aside his friends without a thought, when they
fairly took part against what he considered the truth.
And he said, 'Ah, Rogers, you don't understand
what anguish it was to me to pass Whately in the
street coldly the other day.'" But the Editor adds,

" Possibly Whately's alienation from Newman may also
have had its touch of anguish, never allowed to trans-
pire." This last sentence appears to indicate that
the Editor had never read*—as indeed probably few
have read—the small-print correspondence published
in the Appendix to later editions of the *Apologia*.
The substance of these will now be given.

In October, 1834, possibly after finding himself
" passed coldly in the street" by Newman, Whately
brought to the notice of the latter "a most shocking
report, confidently and long asserted," that Newman
had absented himself from Oriel chapel in order to
avoid receiving the Communion along with him. He
protests that, on the ground of their "long, intimate,
and confidential friendship," it would have been
Newman's "right and duty" to remonstrate with him,
if he had done anything to offend the latter, or anything that Newman " might think materially wrong" ;
but he has based his denial of the report on Newman's
general character, and he now begs for permission to
deny it on Newman's own authority.

In his reply, while explaining that he had been
absent from the chapel for other reasons, Newman
adds : "Yet, on honest reflection I cannot conceal
from myself, that it was generally a relief to me, to
see so little of your Grace, when you were at Oxford ;
and it is a greater relief now to have an opportunity
of saying so to yourself;" and he proceeds to justify
this expression by a bitter attack on the Archbishop's
political and ecclesiastical action. In answer to this,
the Archbishop while gently complaining that many of
his accusers had not taken the trouble to ascertain the
facts on which they based their charges, reminds
Newman of the old times when they "took sweet

counsel together, and walked in the house of God
as friends," and adds, "If you had freely and calmly
remonstrated with me on any point where you thought
me going wrong, I should have listened to you with
that readiness and candour and deference, which, as
you well know, I always showed." He continues, "I
for my part could not bring myself to find relief in
escaping the society of an old friend—with whom I had
been accustomed to frank discussion—on account of
my differing from him as to certain principles, whether
through a change of *his* views, or (much more) of
my own—till I had made full trial of private and affectionate remonstrance and free discussion. . . . But
though your regard for me does not show itself such as
I think mine would have been under similar circumstances, I will not therefore reject what remains of it."
Finally, though he fears Newman will read, "with a
jaundiced eye," if he ventures to read at all, any
publication of his, "yet for auld lang syne" he encloses
his last two addresses to his clergy. Against these
reproaches, Newman makes really no defence at all—
except that "good very seldom comes of volunteering a
remonstrance," and that the full character of "Whately's
policy came on him "almost of a sudden." He adds
that, when the suppression of the Irish Sees was irre-
trievable, a "bitter grief" prompted him to "hide
himself" from the Archbishop, then, after professing
the delight it would give him to stand forth as the
Archbishop's friend, if he could feel he "had a call
that way," he concludes thus, "But may God help me,
as I will ever strive to fulfil my first duty, the defence
of His Church, and of the doctrine of the old Fathers,
in opposition to all the innovations and profanities
which are rising round us."

In the face of this evidence, who can doubt which of the two friends " made himself dead " to the other, or "gave up" the other ? the one who expostulates upon an unfriendly silence ? who declares that he " will not reject what remains" of his old friend's regard though he could have wished it had been more, and sends him a token "for auld lang syne" ? or the one who avows that it was a " relief" to see so little of the other, and a " relief" to make this avowal, and confesses, in effect, that he made no remonstrance with his friend, because " good very seldom comes of volunteering a remonstrance " ? Surely the contrast between the facts as shown in these letters, and Newman's remembrance of the facts as set forth in the *Apologia*, shows that Newman's rooted self-distrust as to his own feelings was largely justified by the occasionally irresistible bias of his mind. There were times with him, so it would seem, when he *could not help believing that he remembered—whatever he wished to remember ;* and in that mood, he could persuade himself of the truth of almost any aspect of facts that seemed in harmony with the fitness of things.*

In later days Whately did undoubtedly manifest an intense resentment against Newman ; and the latter seemingly ignorant of the cause for it, expresses his consciousness that he had "annoyed" the Archbishop. How far the " annoyance" was justified will be considered hereafter. Suffice it to say, now, that it had no connection with any sense, on Whately's part, of Newman's present conduct in casting aside an old friend.

Some words, prefixed by Newman to the four letters published in the Appendix of the *Apologia*, seem intended to extenuate the harshness of his tone by suggesting that he wrote under the provocation caused by what we shall presently describe as the Hampden controversy. "It will be observed," he says, "they are of the same date as my letter to Hampden at p. 57." On turning to p. 57, we find that the letter to Hampden is not dated; and the context merely indicates some time in November. But the Letters give the date of Newman's letter to Hampden as 28 November. Now the first two letters in the correspondence between Newman and Whately were written in October, and the two last on 3 November and 11 November respectively. The words therefore "of the same date" are not true either in the letter, or in the spirit. For the "provocation"*, if it can be so called, arose *after* the correspondence.

On the whole, the conclusion of any one who cares to weigh the evidence must be, 1st, that Newman is quite inaccurate in his facts, and, 2nd, that Whately compares favourably with him in temper and charity. But, further—besides confirming us in the belief that we must accept Blanco White's positive statement, against Newman's "doubt," as to the disruption of the friendship between the two—the result will also oblige us for the future to pause before accepting in detail *any* statement of Newman's about facts, and perhaps even about his own feelings, if it appears to be suspiciously liable to the charge of being coloured by his wishes.

In parting from this, the most polemical period in Newman's development, what impresses us—even more than the violent outburst of hot zeal against his opponents—is the lamentable absence of that spirit of pity which (one would suppose) ought never to abandon a Christian teacher, and seldom to remain

long unexpressed in his teaching. St. Paul is
vehement against Judaizing Christians ; our Lord
Himself against bigoted Pharisees who call good evil ;
but Newman is uselessly vehement, and foolishly
harsh, against those who are guilty of nothing worse
than an exasperating inquisitiveness, or sometimes
against dull, common-place people, who are not versed
in the Fathers and are mystified by the vocabulary of
his Revival. He seems to be vehement for the
Anglican system rather than for Christ ; or, if for
Christ, then for Christ regarded as the mere centre of
the theology upon which he had been recently writing
in his *Arians.* As a consequence, there is little
outward manifestation of whatever Christian loving-
kindness there may have been within him. Zeal for
God, and hatred of sin, he has in plenty ; but he shows
no compassion at all for matter-of-fact people who are
not of his way of thinking. Why should he have left
in the dark, for example, the poor fellow who assumed,
as a matter of course, that " sacrifice," when applied
to the Eucharist in the *Tracts for the Times* must be
a misprint for " sacrament " ? Might not Newman
have assumed the same thing in his old Evangelical
days ? Against antagonists of his own calibre he
might be allowed to be ferocious. Born controversialist as he was, he could not help taking a
pleasure, for the moment, in dialectic triumphs ; and
when James Mozley tells us that during this period he
was in the habit of exclaiming twenty times a day
against the hated Liberals, " We'll do them," we ought
in fairness to remember that the game he was playing
was partly of a political nature, and that to " do "
or to " dish " one's adversaries, is a political temptation difficult for human nature (even in a prophet)

always to resist. But this does not excuse the
pleasure he took in leading slightly foolish opponents
into intellectual absurdities and leaving them to find
their way out as best they could. In discussing
religious questions this is unpardonable, and in after
life he himself did not defend this conduct. It is
all the more difficult to defend because many of those
whom he thus despised and took pleasure in bewildering, must have appeared to him to be suffering from
grievous, perhaps even from dangerous spiritual error.
What healthy man would mock at the halt, the
maimed, and the blind ?

But the right course is to treat this phase as a false
and quasi-religious inflation, which would soon pass away
and leave him a great deal less confident about himself
and a little less hard towards others. A man of so
pure and delicate a taste—so sensitive to the attractions of refined and sympathetic friendships ; always
despising the coarse rough ways of controversy, and
disliking them, too, except in the heat of battle ; keenly
alive to the possibilities of error everywhere, and more
than half disposed to think that real truth is attainable
nowhere—could not throw himself heartily into polemics without an effort : but, having so far done violence
to his nature as to plunge into the conflict, such a one will
often be more logically austere, more consistently unkind, sometimes even more insolently aggressive, than a
cool, deliberate, and, so to speak, professional controversialist—and all the more because he is contending
not merely against external foes, but sometimes
against the growing rebellion of his own self-suspicions,
which he would fain distract and forget by " throwing
himself generously" into all the violent gestures and
actions of profound conviction. Such a state of mind

may be no more than a short insanity ; yet of course it must leave its mark upon the inward man. Bigotry is a kind of spiritual profligacy that needs—almost as much as sensuality itself—the well-known warning of Burns. It "hardens all within." It hardens the heart against the natural affections, the mind against evidence, and the whole human being against the manifold teaching of God.

CHAPTER XV

§ 62. *The Dream, as a Vision*

EVEN after the Declaration of War, nay, even after Tractarians had actually taken up arms and begun to advance, they still had no definite plan. In the very act of moving forward, they will be found asking one another what their goal was to be. What one of their number humorously confesses—"for my part, I never knew where it was all to end, except somewhere in the first three centuries of the Church, and I have to confess that I knew very little about them "—is repeated in various forms by most of their prominent members. But still, though the Leader himself had nothing that can be called a plan, he had something that may be called a " view," a Dream of the Campaign.

This may be regarded in two ways, first as a vision in the mind of the dreamer, and then as a " view," reduced to writing. When he thought of it as the former, he mostly had before his eyes the mediæval Church. As the latter, it presented itself to him as a mass of extracts from the Fathers and the Anglican divines, supporting, interpreting and supplementing the Prayer Book. The Primitive Church affected him mainly in the second form, as being a

voice identical with Patristic authority; he did not
realize it as a picture with sufficient distinctness to
enable it to compete, in point of picturesqueness, with
the mediæval Church to which his friend Froude had
long inclined.   Or perhaps he soon perceived that the
Church of the first three centuries was too antique,
too unpractical; did not keep the world enough in
order; did not trample enough on kings and princes of
the earth.   In any case, we may say roughly that,
while the Fathers (of whom he knew very little), and
the Anglican divines (of whom he knew still less),
influenced his mind, the mediæval Church—as he had
recently witnessed its power, majesty, and beauty even
under terrible modern corruptions—appealed to his
imagination and had found the way to his heart.

The Letters and the *Apologia*, together, enable us
to trace the part played by the Church of Rome in the
first shaping of Newman's vision.   He would not go
to Rome for doctrine, for its "creed" was not
"sound"; but he would go as close to it as he could
in imitating the strength of its government, its
practical assertion of superiority over "the world," its
visible representations, and material channels, of sacramental grace, its "varied round of service," its
soothing influences, its definite assurances of absolution from sin, and of salvation for the anxious soul.
He was confident that "there was a visible Church
with sacraments and rites which are the channels of
invisible grace"; but, in order to find this doctrine and
this Church, it was not necessary to go to Rome.   The
doctrine was to be found in the English Prayer Book
—especially, he felt sure, when people came to
interpret it in the light of the Anglican divines of the
seventeenth century—and it could be supported by

reference to the Fathers and verified from the Scriptures. The visible Church at home—though it had
preserved the sacraments and channels of grace—was
indeed, at present, scarcely recognizable in the existing,
worldly, torpid "Establishment"; but it was there,
and would be recognized by all when the revivified
frame shook off its lethargy and sprang up to the
beauty of holiness in a new and consecrated activity.

Taking Newman's own description of his object,
at the time when he had confidence in the attainment of it—"a living Church of England . . . . .
made of flesh and blood, with voice, complexion, and
motion and action, and a will of its own "—we gather
that what he wanted at this time to borrow from Rome
was, not so much the "voice, motion, action, and
will," but the "flesh and blood, and complexion."
"I considered," he says, "that to make the *Via
Media* concrete and substantive, it must be much
more than it was in outline; that the Anglican
Church must have a ceremonial, a ritual, and a fulness
of doctrine and devotion, which it had not at present,
if it were to compete with the Roman Church with
any prospect of success. Such additions . . . . .
would be confraternities, particular devotions, reverence for the Blessed Virgin, prayers for the dead,
beautiful churches, munificent offerings to them and
in them, monastic houses, &c." These outward,
picturesque developments he seems to have at times
been almost disposed to accept as a substitute for life
and growth. It is true that, in April 1839, he writes
more carefully that "by the *Via Media* . . . . . was
not to be understood a servile imitation of the past,
but such a reproduction of it as is really new, while it
is old." But elsewhere he says, as if it were a noble

aspiration, that, "saving our engagements to Prayer Book and Articles, we might breathe and live and act and speak, as in the atmosphere and climate of Henry III.'s day, or the Confessor's, or of Alfred's": and this passage seems more accurately to describe the early spirit of the Movement. It was not to be a progress, but a return—such as indeed he elsewhere describes it; but there he speaks of it as a "return," not to the mediæval Church of England, but to "the seventeenth century." Probably, like his brother-in-law, who at that time was his ally, he did not know quite how far back he was to "return," and varied between "the first three centuries," "Henry III.," "the Confessor," "Alfred," and "the seventeenth century." He had only made up his mind that it was to be "not the sixteenth"—not the Church of the English Reformation.

The dream that was floating before Newman's mind is painted in bright colours in a sermon of his Roman period preached in 1850, in which he gives a florid description (vivid certainly, but spoiled by blank verse, and not up to the level of his pure Anglican style) of Religion in England in the century after its conversion:

"The fair form of Christianity rose up and grew and expanded like a beautiful pageant from north to south; it was majestic, it was solemn, it was bright, it was beautiful and pleasant, it was soothing to the griefs, it was indulgent to the hopes of man; it was at once a teaching and a worship; it had a dogma, a mystery, a ritual of its own; it had an hierarchical form. A brotherhood of holy pastors, with mitre and crosier and uplifted hand, walked forth and blessed and ruled a joyful people. The crucifix headed the procession, and simple monks were there with hearts in prayer, and sweet chants resounded, and the Holy Latin tongue was heard, and boys came forth in white, swinging censers, and the fragrant cloud arose, and mass was sung, and the saints were invoked ; and day after day, and in the still night, and over the woody hills and in the quiet plains, as constantly as sun and moon and stars go forth in heaven, so regular and solemn was the stately march of blessed services on earth high festival, and gorgeous procession, and soothing dirge ; and passing bell, and the familiar evening call to prayer : till he who recollected the old pagan time, would think it all unreal that he beheld and heard, and would conclude he did but see a vision, so marvellously was heaven let down upon earth, so triumphantly were chased away the fiends of darkness to their prison below."

The man who, in an advanced period of life, could write down such a description of a "brotherhood of holy pastors" blessing and "ruling a joyful people," and apply it to the times of the "battles of the kites and the crows" before the Heptarchy, is obviously capable of being led on a long way by dreams, and of confronting with audacity the obstacles of intervening facts.

If, therefore, we wish to understand Newman's course in the Tractarian Movement, while carefully studying the views that he reduced to writing, with all their developments and variations, we must never lose sight of the vision that possessed his imagination. It was not till 1834 that he began to study systematically the Anglican divines ; but we are dealing with the projects that floated before him in 1833 : how then could the latter be modified by the former ? How can a man's plans be influenced by information that he does not possess, or by books that he has *not* read ? Almost all that he knew at this time about the Anglican system was through Laud. He had received the impression that Laud's system was intended to keep the laity in better order, and was characterized by closer adherence to antiquity and more ornateness of ritual, than were found in the English Church after the accession of William III.

But he did not know that this would be in harmony with the general consensus of Anglican divines, for he had not studied them ; and he did not know whether it would work out in practice, for he himself admitted it had not been tried ; it was a mere paper theory.

It is not to the Anglican divines, then, that those must turn who would grasp, as far as it can be grasped, Newman's conception in 1833 of the new Anglican system that was to be—and who would prepare themselves to realize how much, and how soon, and in what directions, he would modify it.   They must rather fix their attention on those characteristics of an Ideal which would impress the imagination of a recent and hasty but admiring student of the Primitive Church ; of a poet who had been captivated by the picture of the triumphs of early Christianity over the world, and who believed that it was his destiny to help forward the repetition of such conquests in his own country ; of a wilful, impulsive, imperious, and passionate zealot panting for "holiness" and contemptuous of "the world" and worldly peace ; of an anxious seeker after salvation in whom morbid fears and self-distrusts—which in ordinary times clouded his heart, suspended his action, and forced his imagination to fall back ever and anon upon reserves of syllogistically-arranged words—were only for a brief season kept down by the transient consciousness of a high prophetic task.   Nor must they forget that they have before them a born dogmatist ; born simultaneously to religion and to dogma ; one who, from his youth, approaching the Creator intellectually, and as an isolated creature seeking to save his own soul, and not concerning himself with, nor even luminously realizing, the souls of others, had taken dogmas whole into the intellectual side of his imagination ; one who—putting aside all thought of human love, human trust, and human reverence whenever he strove to enter into communion with God—had trained himself to feel that all salvation depends upon belief, that all belief consists in the assent to propositions, and that the propositions of Christianity are of little worth till they have been collected into a complete, consistent, and symmetrical system, and accepted as a whole.

To all these aspects of this many-sided nature we must add—however great the superficial incongruity between this and the character of a dogmatist—that he was a seer of visions, a noter of "signs," and observer of "omens" ; one who seldom received religious truth into his inmost being except through indirect avenues, momentary flashes, involuntary recollections, chance utterances of friends, suppressed panics of his own heart, and whose stubborn outward resistance to the world of fact and argument concealed a ready inward receptiveness to whatever was not fact, provided only that it appealed imploringly to faith, and threw itself upon the mercy of devout imagination. Last, and most important factor of all, we must never forget that this dreamer of ecclesiastical dreams had recently seen them, or many of them, majestically realized in that City of the Apostles, to which he had given, as he had confessed, half his heart, and in truth more than half; so that now he could scarcely step forth into the street from his rooms in Oriel without muttering to himself "*inter viburna cupressus*," and wondering distrustfully whether he was indeed disloyal to his beloved Oxford.

For such a Reformer, in cool moments, sketching—
or as he would express it, apprehending—the ideal
Church, the first and foremost condition would be that
it should be based on "sound belief," and the second
and subordinate condition would be that its expressions
of devotion, and the forms by which it conveyed the
Divine grace should touch the heart and should convey
to it the sense of an obedience paid to Divine ordinances and of a consequent security to the obeyer.
But in times of trouble and depression it was almost
certain that this order would be reversed. The former
condition satisfied the Reason, the latter the Imagination ; and, if it came to a contest between the two, the
claims of the latter were certain to prevail : Oxford
would succumb to Rome and the " view " would vanish
away in the splendour of the vision.

§ 63. *The Dream on paper*

To all this, it may be objected, that Newman was
not either "dreaming" or "sketching," a new Anglican
system, but simply reviving the old ; that he consistently represents himself as " taking his stand on
the Prayer-Book"; that he merely wished to recall
(as he expressed it himself) " a forgetful generation
to the theology of their forefathers," and "to build
up what man has pulled down in, some of the questions connected with the Church ; and that, by means
of the stores of Divine truth bequeathed to us in the
works of our standard English authors." Why then
should he be convicted of haste, since he was not
introducing novelties, but simply exhorting his countrymen to stand in the old paths ? And why should we
suggest that he was deceiving himself when he was

merely attempting to throw himself generously into that form of religion which was providentially put before his nation, and before him as a member of it ?

The answer is, that the old Anglican system, as he conceived it, had never existed except on paper. The English Church, in practice, had always been anomalous and inconsistent. To prove this from history would be tedious and superfluous; to prove that Newman knew this, and acted on this, is easy, and brief, and all that we need. In his treatises on the *Via Media* there is ample proof of it. He does not deny, there, that many of the Rubrics had become so obsolete, and were so generally deemed impracticable, that there was need of what he emphatically describes, in capital letters, as " A SECOND REFORMATION," Church discipline, excommunication, ecclesiastical imposition of penance, had been all, from the beginning, not so much forgotten as non-existent, in the Reformed Church ; they were remnants of an older system and had been left by the Reformers in the new ; but they had never worked. It could hardly be said that they died out ; they never really lived in the Anglican Church. Some may maintain that the Reformers would soon have swept away these anomalies, if they had been allowed a free hand by the royal power. Newman assumes in his *Via Media* that the Reformers deliberately retained this anomalous element ; he claims to agree with them, so far ; and, with a scarcely concealed irony, says, " It is hard indeed that, when I share in the opinions of the Reformers, I should have no share in their (*i.e.* people's) praises of them." But, for whatever reason they may have been retained in the Prayer Book, they had practically perished for the people.

Nor is it only in respect of discipline that the *Via Media* was a mere theory. It was theoretical, or perhaps we should say tentative and provisional, as regards doctrine also. "What the doctrine of the Church is, what it has been for three centuries, is a matter of fact, which, without reading, cannot be known"—so he writes (1834) in the first *Via Media*, and this "reading" was to be "in the works of our standard English authors." What else is this but to commit himself and his party provisionally to believe in a great body of divinity about which he has merely the vague and general notion * that it is, in the main, orthodox, while trusting to Providence and the efforts of friends to eliminate any heretical or heterodox element? Yet so well aware is he that the Anglican Divines have not always harmonized in one consistent doctrine, that, even as regards the Reformers, with whom just now he professed agreement, he is careful to state that he agrees with them only so far "as they speak in the formularies of our Church"; and he adds, "That they should have said different things at different times, is not wonderful, considering they were searching into Scripture and Antiquity and feeling their way to the truth."

With a discipline and government on paper that had never "worked," and with a doctrine that had to be ascertained from a careful sifting of "a vast inheritance" from authors, who, during three hundred years, "said different things at different times"—the new Anglicanism must surely be called essentially *new*, and not a mere revival of the old. In saying this, we simply repeat what the *Via Media* calls "plausible" and almost admits; "It may be argued that the Church of England, as established by law and existing in fact, has never represented a doctrine at all, or been the development of a principle ; has never had an intellectual basis"; and again "until we can produce diocese, or place of education, or populous town, or colonial department, or the like, administered on our distinctive principles, as the diocese of Sodor and Man in the days of Bishop Wilson, doubtless we have not as much to urge in our behalf as we might have." "Not as much to urge as we might have." That is surely an under-statement * of the adversary's objection. Does not the *Apologia* better express it : "I trusted that some day it would prove to be a substantive religion " ? and again, " The *Via Media* was at present a paper religion"? If so, ought not the "paper religion" to have been drawn out before proclaiming the NEW REFORMATION ?

The term "paper system" is indeed too favourable to describe such a dream. The Anglican rubrics, it is true, existed as an authority, on paper; but the contemplated body of Anglican doctrine was not only devoid at present of any authoritative existence at all (even on paper), but would also need many years, much toil, and even more judgment—some would say nothing short of a special inspiration—in the Tractarian compilers who were to elicit it from the profuse theological stores of three centuries of Anglicanism. In the first place, who was to define the circle of the " standard English authors " from whom the doctrine was to be extracted, and to decide the exclusion, or inclusion, say of Jewel, Tillotson, and Hoadley ? This done, who was to distinguish, in the selected authors, between individual opinion, fundamental principles, and the guesses of uninstructed genius ? And

how justify all this exclusion, inclusion, and discrimination without an appeal extending beyond the Anglican
divines themselves to the Early Fathers?   Much of this
Newman, and Newman's friends, frankly confess that
they were not able to do when they began their
campaign.   In the *Via Media,* for example, where
" Laicus" and "Clericus" are conversing on the
" irreconcilable differences" between the English and
Roman Churches, after " Laicus" has admitted that
he hardly knows how to find his way through it, we
find " Clericus," making this admission, " I have but
a smattering of reading in Church history.   The more's
the pity ; though I have as much as a great many
others : for ignorance of our historical position as
Churchmen is one of the especial evils of the day."
Keble, as well as Newman, we shall presently hear
making similar confessions.

The result of all this was, of course, that he committed himself, in his statement of the controversy
between England and Rome, to positions from which
he had afterwards to recede.   As " Clericus," in 1834,
he is confident that " no party would be more opposed
to our doctrine, if it ever prospers and makes noise,
than the Roman party": but writing in his own name,
in 1837, and endeavouring to meet the objection that
the High Church party might pass into Romanism,
what answer does he make ?   Simply this—that Ken,
Collier, and the rest, did not join the Church of Rome
at the era of the Revolution.   But he makes up for
its inadequacy by calling it " irrefragable : *   " If nothing more has accrued to us from the treatment
endured, this at least has providentially resulted, that
we are thereby furnished with irrefragable testimony to
the essential difference between the Roman and Anglican

systems." Thus, in order to prove the essential difference between the system of Rome, and another
which he admits never to have worked as a system,
and to be a mere paper theory, both in discipline and
detailed doctrine, he thinks it sufficient to point out
that, in a certain period of the Anglican Church, a
small number of Anglican High Churchmen did not
secede to Rome, in spite of circumstances that might
have tempted them to do so!

Nor must we omit—among other proofs that Newman generally admitted the real novelty of this nominal
revival of what was old—his avowal that the New
Reformation, though it would not change the Prayer
Book, would substantially change the whole of its
interpretation and application. The Church, he says,
" should not alter the Articles, she should add to
them ; add protests against the Erastianism and latitudinarianism which have incrusted them. I would
have her append to the Catechism a section on the
power of the Church." Those who are familiar with
Hurrell Froude's correspondence, and who know how
often he contemplated and apparently desired such a
position of things as might justify the orthodox
Anglicans in excommunicating the heterodox, will
regard this proposed " addition " as very ominous.
It seems to mean that Newman desired ultimately to
appropriate the Church of England for his party, as he
had once striven to appropriate the Church Missionary
Society. Those parties which, in Newman's time,
were dominant, and which, ever since the Reformation, had enabled a large, if not the larger portion, of
the nation to remain within the pale of the Anglican
Church, were now, it would seem—so far as the clergy
were concerned—to be turned out ; High Churchmen

alone were to remain, not merely (as they had hitherto done) to play and theorize about High Church doctrines, but to carry them into practice, by reviving, for instance, ecclesiastical excommunication, imposing ecclesiastical penance, and insisting on a public ecclesiastical reconciliation before re-admission to the Holy Communion. Well may " Laicus " say of part of the new scheme—if not the whole of it,—" It is visionary to talk of such a reformation ; the people would not endure it," and well may " Clericus " reply, " It is ; but I am not advocating it, I am but raising a protest. I say this† ought to be, ' because of the angels,' but I do not hope to persuade others to think as I do."

§ 64. " *Supreme Confidence* " *in the Dream*

In the fervour of the earlier portion of his Roman period, Newman compared his *Via Media* to the basking whale in the *Arabian Nights*, upon which the sailors disembarked, taking it for an island ; and just when they were making themselves comfortable and cooking their dinner upon it, the creature began to frisk about, and finally swam off. The simile was fair enough, always provided that whenever he used it in his lectures, he lectured in a white sheet, doing penance for having misled others as the captain of those unhappy mariners. But he seldom or never repents in a satisfactory way. When he confesses himself to be in the wrong, he generally takes a quarter of the blame, and casts the other three-quarters upon those who are not in the wrong at all, or more often (as in Whately's instance) on those whom he himself has wronged. And so it was with the poor Anglican divines, whom he desired to make responsible for his "new Reformation." He tells us that they deceived him ; that he read the Fathers through their eyes ; that they requited his desire to say what they said, and to fight their battle with a generous partisanship, by completely taking him in, so that he afterwards felt inclined to "bite off their ears." All this passionate —it would be a libel to call it feminine—querulousness is vented upon the poor Anglicans for no other offence than this, that their works were so voluminous that Newman could not, or would not, find time to read them carefully before he committed himself to their general orthodoxy, and based upon it his Dream of a New Anglicanism, in which he "felt a supreme confidence."

It is clear that Newman had not attempted to study the Anglican divines in a systematic way till after he had begun his campaign. In the spring of 1826 he conceived the "great work" of reading the Fathers ; and, so far as he did any reading steadily, this was his occupation for the next eight years. How little he knew about the Anglican divines at that time is seen from the letter to Rickards written in the winter of that year, in which he "assumes that the old worthies of our Church are neither Orthodox, nor Evangelical, but intractable persons, suspicious characters, neither one thing nor the other," and invites his friend to summarize their doctrine. It was to Laud's work on Tradition that he owed his special inspiration. But when he had read this, instead of taking up the Anglicans, he began (after long procrastination) the study of the Fathers. " Newman," says E. T. Mozley, "so often spoke of Laud as seeing and hearing all that was going on, and actually walking about Oxford, that he seemed to realise it as a fact." This suggests the kind of influence Laud's theory exerted upon him. He did not wait to read or reason about it. He received it into his imagination. Then, finding it in himself, he thought he "found himself in it," and determined to try to revivify it. Thus he afterwards (1844) describes his feelings :

"The case with me, then, was this, and not surely an unnatural one :—As a matter of feeling and duty I threw myself into the system which I found myself in. I saw that the English Church had a theological idea or theory as such, and I took it up. I read Laud on Tradition and thought it (as I still think it) very masterly. The Anglican Theory was very distinctive. I admired it and took it on faith. It did not (I think) occur to me to doubt it. I saw that it was able and supported by learning, and I felt it was a duty to maintain it. Further, on looking into Antiquity and reading the Fathers, I saw such portions of it as I examined, fully confirmed (*e.g.*, the supremacy of Scripture). There was only one question about which I had a doubt, viz., whether it would *work*, *for it had never been more than a paper system.*"

No mention, the reader will perceive, is made of any systematic study of the Anglicans. After Laud, the student "looked into Antiquity" and "read the Fathers," *i.e.* some few "Fathers." How little time he had found for reading "the Fathers," and how little he had read of them, we have repeatedly seen. Leisure to spare for the Anglicans he had absolutely none ; and, having regard to the immense inferences that he proposed to base upon their writings, we are not exaggerating in saying that he knew practically very little about them. In a sanguine nature, ignorance of the facts is quite compatible with "supreme confidence" in a "cause" based on the facts, especially if the mind has been long engaged in "dreaming about" the cause, and finds it "momentous and inspiring." That it was so here the *Apologia* testifies.

" I had the consciousness that I was employed in that work which I had been dreaming about, and which I felt to be so momentous and inspiring. I had a supreme confidence in our cause ; we were up-holding that primitive Christianity which was delivered for all time by the early teachers of the Church, and which was registered and attested in the Anglican formularies and by the Anglican divines. That ancient religion had well nigh faded away out of the land, through the political changes of the last 150 years, and it must be restored. It would be in fact a second Reformation—a better reformation, for it would be a return not to the sixteenth century, but to the seventeenth."

Having felt this " confidence " in 1833, he began to study the Anglican divines systematically in 1834. This we gather from the *Apologia :* " I am as certain now upon this point as I was in 1833, and have never ceased to be certain. In 1834 and the following years I put this ecclesiastical doctrine on a broader basis, after reading Laud, Bramhall and Stillingfleet and other Anglican divines on the one hand, and after prosecut-ing the study of the Fathers on the other." The next sentence shows that, as we might have anticipated, the Anglican divines in 1834 confirmed the belief he had held about them in 1833 : " The doctrine of 1833 was strengthened in me, not changed." Expressed simply, does this not mean, " In 1834 and the following years I read the Anglicans in the hope of supporting a certain ' confidence ' ; and my ' confidence ' was sup-ported " ? The only objection to this view of the matter is that elsewhere Newman declares that he read the Fathers " through the eyes of," and therefore *after*, " the Anglican divines." But this is only one of Newman's many self-deceptions. He believed this because he wished to believe it. His own direct evidence, and the indirect evidence of circumstances, shows that this was not true—except so far as he may have here and there accelerated his too hasty and excited study of the originals by means of quotations and translations.

These, then, so far as they can be deduced from the collective evidence, appear to be the stages in the Dream of the *Via Media*. First, on the collapse of Newman's Evangelicalism, seeking for a definite basis of faith, he found it in the Church as set forth by Laud ; second, he read a few of the Fathers hastily, and— as it would appear from his own confessions—through translations and quotations contained in the English Apologists ; third, he sketched a hazy Anglo-Primitive system out of his Patristic knowledge and his Anglican imaginations ; fourth, he set about proclaiming this as " A NEW REFORMATION," in 1833 ; fifth, he began to read the Anglican divines systematically—in the hope of finding this system in them—in 1834 ; sixth, he found it ; seventh, he discovered, before ten years had passed, that what he had found was a mere " paper-system," which never had lived nor could live ; and that the work " which he had been dreaming about " was nothing but a dream.

To be complete, we should add an eighth stage, in which he accused the Anglican divines (whom he had never seriously studied) of having " taken him in ; " and threw upon them the blame that was wholly due to himself.

CHAPTER XVI

§ 65. *The Hadleigh Meeting*

NOT six weeks had elapsed since Keble's signal, the Assize Sermon on National Apostasy, before Newman began the advance. Toward the end of July, Froude and two others had met at Hadleigh, in the Rectory of H. J. Rose; but had agreed upon only two points, (1) Apostolical Succession, and (2) the integrity of the Prayer Book. There followed a decided difference of opinion whether the cause would be best served by a public Association, or by the issue of Tracts written by well-wishers favouring the common principles but not pledged, or pledging one another, to details. Newman, though willing to join an Association, was strongly for the Tracts, and the result proved that he was right. A tract or pamphlet had more chance of unity of style, concentration, and force, than a collaborated document. A little eccentricity, or want of individual judgment, in one or two of the contributors might be almost an advantage in a Movement which was at present of an exploring or skirmishing character; and the objection that anonymous pamphlets would have no weight was met by the special circumstance that they were notoriously written by Oxford

men, issued from Oxford, and, though nominally
"Tracts for the Times," were called by their supporters "The Oxford Tracts." Newman anticipated
the great advantage that would come from this, and
prepared to trade on it. They ought to make much,
he said, of their situation at Oxford, and of the deference paid to the University through the country ; no
party was likely to be active in Oxford but themselves,
so the field was before them : "all their acts, as coming
from the University, might have the authority of Convocation almost, in such cases as when Convocation
could not be expected to speak out." His anticipations were justified to the utmost. The public adopted,
not the ostensible title, but the inference from the
familiar name. Thus the name of the University gave
a popular stamp of authority to the leaflets of Newman
and his associates, and the Tractarian scheme became
known as "The Oxford Movement*."

The *Apologia* tells us that the leaders put forth
"views and principles for their own sake, because they
were true," without having any distinct notion of the
practical results that would spring from them. As to
"principles," the Hadleigh Meeting defined two of
them. But Newman can hardly have intended to
convey the impression that he had ascertained *all* his
"principles" at the time when he began the campaign.
What he means he expressed elsewhere, "We knew
enough to begin preaching upon and there was no one
else to preach." Hence we find him writing (5 August)
to Keble not only to settle "on some uniform plan of
talking as to principles," but even begging for a
"sketch of principles" themselves, "*e.g.*, that by the
Irish Bill the Church's liberties are invaded." Ought
not they (he continues) to stir up the clergy of Water-

ford to disobey a Bishop of Cashel, or to stir up the bishops to consecrate a Bishop of Waterford? And will Keble supply him with his promised paper on "virtual excommunication"?

In his reply (8 August) Keble shows that he, too, is at present uncertain about his "principles." As to any statement about the Church, "if the Hadleighans could not agree, where, *inter quatuor muros*, will you find six men to agree together?" He only wishes a bishop would give them a hint! It would be so much more satisfactory to be acting under bishops. For himself, he cannot (he thinks) take the *Oath of Supremacy* in the sense now put on it by the Legislature, and therefore cannot *accept* any office in the Church of England, but is disposed to believe himself not bound to resign the office he already holds. He is also ready to prepare his flock for some trial of their Church principles. Rose had been deprecating agitation for repeal of the *Praemunire*, and had been suggesting that they might get a Synod, lay and clerical, and that a reaction from the present anti-Church feeling might be expected. Keble's comment is that, if the reaction will re-establish the ten bishops in Ireland, and make the nation pay the Church rates, it may be waited for; if not, he would say, "Take every pound, shilling, and penny, and the curse of sacrilege along with it; only let us make our own bishops, and be governed by our own laws"; of what use, he asks, will be a Synod in which the ruling members will be "nominated by an infidel Government"? Yet, perhaps, the sacrifice of Church rates and even a greater amount of property might be desirable if that would purchase "the bishops' nomination" for them. In all this, however, Keble feels

"terribly unlearned"; and so, too, as regards the
"*Excommunicables*": he would like to try the subject,
but, he adds, "I fear I ought to know my books better."

Froude, throughout, had made up his mind that the
right course was to agitate for the appointment of
bishops by the Church and for the abolition of the
Praemunire. Rose, in advising delay, had predicted
that a few years would bring either a republic or "a
repetition of the rotten borough-system" and a return
to things as they were. The latter prospect,
apparently welcome to Rose, was by no means so to
Froude. This plain-spoken Church Reformer declared
bluntly that it would be "the worst calamity they could
dread," nor did he conceal his contempt for the old
prejudice that the clergy must be "gentlemen," and
that the Church must have prizes to tempt men of
talent. However, all but Froude agreed that for the
present they must avoid expressing advanced views
and must "begin by laying a foundation." Even
Newman, for the present, sides with the party of
caution. "Froude," he says, "wishes to break with
Rose, which must not be, I think," and he tells Keble
that his old pupil requires "a bit of advice." Yet
Froude so far carried Newman with him that the
latter, while not advocating disestablishment, was
ready to prepare people for it, and to urge Keble to do
the same. Pressing forward on this line, Froude informed Newman in August that he had written a
sermon "on the duty of contemplating the contingency
of a separation between Church and State and of providing against it, *i.e.*, by studying the principles of
ecclesiastical subordination, so that, when the law of
the land ceases to enforce this, we may have a law
within ourselves to supply its place.†"

This seems to have suggested to Newman the subject of the first of the famous Tracts. Suppose the
Church were disestablished, what, he asked himself,
would be the position of the clergy? Stripped of
their endowments and livings, perhaps even of their
churches and cathedrals, how would they differ from
the Ministers of the Nonconformists?   On   what
" principle," sharply distinctive from that of Dissenters,
could they take a firm and definite stand ? Beyond
supporting the Prayer Book as it was, the one " principle" on which the Hadleighan Conference had been
able to agree was that of " Apostolical Succession."
Let this then be taken as the basis of action for the
clergy in the New Movement, this be their justification for differentiating themselves, whether established
or disestablished, from mere Protestant sectarian
ministers. The former were "the successors of the
Apostles," the latter were not. To some this might
not seem much, in the way of a " principle " ; but it
might work up to a great deal, and, at all events, it
was something to begin upon. It was perfectly clear
and definite, or at least it *looked* clear—till you came
to distinguish between the fact (if proved to be a fact)
and the inferences from the fact. It also had the
merit (for clergymen) of appealing, not to disputable
interpretations of New Testament texts but to the
Prayer Book of the Church of England.

§ 66. *Tract No.* 1

Regarded as a specimen of Newman's sympathetic
rhetoric the paper is admirable, and for this, as well as
for its historical interest, it is here presented to the
reader entire with all those advantages of italics and

capitals which Newman so skilfully utilized, that in comparison with his art, the more effective because restrained, that of modern sensational advertisers becomes contemptible.

To my brethren in the sacred ministry, the presbyters and deacons of the Church of Christ in England, ordained thereunto by the Holy Ghost and the imposition of hands †.

Fellow-Labourers—I am but one of yourselves a Presbyter; and therefore I conceal my name, lest I should take too much on myself by speaking in my own person. Yet speak I must; for the times are very evil, yet no one speaks against them.

Is not this so? Do not we "look one upon another," yet perform nothing? Do not we all confess the peril into which the Church is come, yet sit still each in his own retirement, as if mountains and seas cut off brother from brother? Therefore suffer me, while I try to draw you forth from those pleasant retreats, which it has been our blessedness hitherto to enjoy, to contemplate the condition and prospects of our Holy Mother in a practical way; so that one and all may unlearn that idle habit, which has grown upon us, of owning the state of things to be bad, yet doing nothing to remedy it.

Consider a moment. Is it fair, is it dutiful, to suffer our bishops to stand the brunt of the battle without doing our part to support them? Upon them comes "the care of all the Churches." This cannot be helped; indeed it is their glory. Not one of us would wish in the least to deprive them of the duties, the toils, the responsibilities of their high office. And, black event as it would be for the country, yet (as far as they are concerned) we could not wish them a more blessed termination of their course than the spoiling of their goods and martyrdom.

To them then we willingly and affectionately relinquish their high privileges and honours; we encroach not upon the rights of the Successors of the Apostles; we touch not their sword and crozier. Yet surely we may be their shield-bearers in the battle without offence; and by our voice and deeds be to them what Luke and Timothy were to St. Paul.

Now then let me come at once to the subject which leads me to address you. Should the Government and the Country so far forget their God as to cast off the Church, to deprive it of its temporal honours and substance, *on what* will you rest the claim of respect and attention which you make upon your flocks? Hitherto you have been upheld by your birth, your education, your wealth, your connexions; should these secular advantages cease, on what must Christ's Ministers depend? Is not this a serious practical question? We know how miserable is the state of religious bodies not supported by the State. Look at the Dissenters on all sides of you, and you will see at once that their Ministers, depending simply upon the people, become the *creatures* of the people. Are you content that this should be your case? Alas! can a greater evil befall Christians, than for their teachers to be guided by them, instead of guiding? How can we "hold fast the form of sound words," and "keep that which is committed to our trust," if our influence is to depend simply on our popularity? Is it not our very office to *oppose* the world? Can we then allow ourselves to *court* it? to preach smooth things and prophesy deceits? to make the way of life easy to the rich and indolent, and to bribe the humbler classes by excitements and strong intoxicating doctrine? Surely it must not be so;—and the question recurs, *on what* are we to rest our authority when the State deserts us?

Christ has not left His Church without claim of its own upon the attention of men. Surely not. Hard Master He cannot be, to bid us oppose the world, yet give us no credentials for so doing. There are some who rest their divine mission on their own unsupported assertion; others, who rest it upon their popularity; others, on their success; and others, who rest it upon their temporal distinctions. This last case has, perhaps, been too much our own; I fear we have neglected the real ground on which our authority is built—Our Apostolical descent.

We have been born, not of blood, nor of the will of the flesh, nor of the will of man, but of God. The Lord Jesus Christ gave His Spirit to his Apostles; they in turn laid their hands on those who should succeed them; and these again on others; and so the sacred gift has been handed down to our present bishops, who have appointed us as their assistants, and in some sense representatives.

Now every one of us believes this. I know that some will at first deny they do; still they do believe it. Only it is not sufficiently, practically impressed on their minds. They *do* believe it; for it is the doctrine of the Ordination Service, which they have recognised as truth in the most solemn season of their lives. In order, then, not to prove, but to remind and impress, I entreat your attention to the words used when you were made ministers of Christ's Church.

The office of Deacon was thus committed to you : "Take thou authority to execute the office of a deacon in the Church of God committed unto thee : In the name, etc."

And the Priesthood thus :

"Receive the Holy Ghost, for the office and work of a Priest, in the Church of God, now committed unto thee by the imposition of our hands. Whose sins thou dost forgive, they are forgiven ; and whose sins thou dost retain, they are retained. And be thou a faithful dispenser of the Word of God, and of His Holy Sacraments : In the name, etc."

These, I say, were words spoken to us, and received by us, when we were brought nearer to God than at any other time of our lives. I know the grace of ordination is contained in the laying on of hands, not in any form of words ;—yet in our own case (as has ever been usual in the Church) words of blessing have accompanied the act. Thus we have confessed before God our belief that the bishop who ordained us gave † us the Holy Ghost, gave us the power to bind and to loose, to administer the Sacraments, and to preach. Now *how* is he able to give these great gifts? *Whence* is his right ? Are these words idle (which would be taking God's name in vain), or do they express merely a wish (which surely is very far below their meaning), or do they not rather indicate that the speaker is conveying a gift? Surely they can mean nothing short of this. But whence, I ask, his right to do so? Has he any right, except as having received the power from those who consecrated him to be a bishop? He could not give what he had never received. It is plain then that he but *transmits ;* and that the Christian Ministry is a *succession.* And if we trace back the power of ordination from hand to hand, of course we shall come to the Apostles at last. We know we do, as a plain historical fact ; and therefore all we, who have been ordained clergy, in the very form of our ordination acknowledged the doctrine of the APOSTOLICAL SUCCESSION.

And for the same reason, we must necessarily consider none to be *really* ordained who have not *thus* been ordained. For if ordination is a divine ordinance, it must be necessary ; and if it is not a divine ordinance, how dare we use it ? Therefore all who use it, all of *us*, must consider it necessary. As well might we pretend the Sacraments are not necessary to salvation, while we make use of the offices in the Liturgy ; for when God appoints means of grace, they are *the* means.

I do not see how any one can escape from this plain view of the subject, except (as I have already hinted) by declaring that the words do not mean all that they say. But only reflect what a most unseemly time for random words is that in which ministers are set apart for their office. Do we not adopt a Liturgy *in order to* hinder inconsiderate idle language, and shall we, in the most sacred of all services, write down, subscribe, and use again and again forms of speech which have not been weighed, and cannot be taken strictly?

Therefore, my dear brethren, act up to your professions. Let it not be said that you have neglected a gift; for if you have the Spirit of the Apostles on you, surely this *is* a great gift. "Stir up the gift of God which is in you." Make much of it. Show your value of it. Keep it before your minds as an honourable badge, far higher than secular respectability, or cultivation, or polish, or learning, or rank, which gives you a hearing with the many. Tell *them* of your gift. The times will soon drive you to do this, if you mean to be still anything. But wait not for the times. Do not be compelled, by the world's forsaking you, to recur as if unwillingly to the high source of your authority. Speak out now, before you are forced, both as glorying in your privilege and to insure your rightful honour from your people. They think they have given and can take it away. They think it lies in the Church property, and they know that they have politically the power to confiscate that property. They have been deluded into a notion that present palpable usefulness, produceable results, acceptableness to your flocks, that these and such like are the tests of your divine commission. Enlighten them in this matter. Exalt our Holy Fathers the bishops, as the representatives of the Apostles, and the Angels of the Churches; and magnify your office, as being ordained by them to take part in their Ministry.

But, if you will not adopt my view of the subject, which I offer to you, not doubtingly, yet (I hope) respectfully, at all events, CHOOSE YOUR SIDE. To remain neuter much longer will be itself to take a part. *Choose* your side; since side you shortly must, with one or other party, even though you do nothing. Fear to be of those whose line is decided for them by chance circumstances, and who may perchance find themselves with the enemies of Christ, while they think but to remove themselves from worldly politics. Such abstinence is impossible in troublous times. HE THAT IS NOT WITH ME IS AGAINST ME, AND HE THAT GATHERETH NOT WITH ME SCATTERETH ABROAD."

A few words are needed on this splendid piece of rhetoric, partly that we may do justice to its rhetorical merit; partly, because of its bearing on Newman's subsequent course. To prevent misunderstanding, it should be stated at once that Newman's doctrine is not assumed to be identical, in several respects, with that of orthodox Anglicans or of the medieval Church.

I do not know whether Newman relied on the words "the Holy Ghost . . . now committed," for his statement that "the grace of ordination is contained in the laying on of hands, not in any form of words." If so, it should be noted that the words, by themselves, are ambiguous. It is still more curious, under these circumstances, that in some Prayer Books published by authority,† the punctuation (which is important, as there is no Latin original to help us to dispel the ambiguity) is different (1) in the Prayer Book ordinal for the priest, (2) in the Prayer Book ordinal for the bishop, (3) in Newman's version of the ordinal for the priest :—

(1) "Receive the Holy Ghost for the office and work of a Priest in the Church of God, now committed unto thee by the imposition of hands," &c.

(2) Receive the Holy Ghost, for the office and work of a Bishop in the Church of God, now committed," &c.

(3) Receive the Holy Ghost, for the office and work of a Priest, in the Church of God, now committed," &c.

The American Office provides an alternative form free from all ambiguity, making it clear that it is the "authority" or "office," and not "the Holy Ghost," that is thus "committed" :—

(4) " Take thou authority to execute the office of a Priest in the Church of God, now committed," &c.

and this is unquestionably in accordance with the language of Scripture. In the Bible, a " message," or " stewardship," or " charge of preaching the Gospel," is " committed " or " entrusted " ; the " Holy Ghost" is not " committed " or " entrusted," but " given." It should be added that a well-known passage in Scripture speaks of the imposition of hands, not as being *instrumental*, but as *simultaneous* (Tim. iv. 14), " Neglect not the gift that is in thee, which was given thee † *by* " [perhaps " under the influence of "] " prophecy, *with* the laying on of the hands of the presbytery." In the face of these facts, Newman is too positive in asserting that the " words " are nothing, and the " hands " everything : " I know the grace of ordination is contained in the laying on of hands, not in any form of words."

These points are touched on, not, of course, to settle a question about which volumes might be written without settling anything, but merely to show the complexity of a subject which nevertheless, in Newman's hands, is made to appear transparently clear and simple. And further difficulties are obvious. Is it meant (1) that even an impenitent man's sins are forgiven if a priest " forgives " them, and that a penitent man's are retained, if the priest " retains " them ? (2) or is the actual forgiveness, though uttered by the priest, yet *conditional* on the sinner's penitence ? (3) and, in that case, is not the penitence in itself sufficient, and does it need the priestly absolution ?

Some readers might ask yet further, " Was this power of insight and forgiveness intended by Christ to be imparted to *all Christians*, so that every one of His disciples, so far as he or she *was* a disciple, should have this divine power of forgiving ? and was this His meaning in teaching us to call ourselves 'a nation of kings and priests'? and, if this be so, were the words of Christ, referred to in the Ordination Service, intended to set forth a divine pattern and ideal to which *all*, both laity and clergy, are to strive to approximate ? To those who are set apart for clerical work, the solemn service of Ordination ought, of course, to be a means of special grace and help ; yet must not some of the clergy confess, that they have known persons, not clerical, who surpass them in that divine power of lightening the burden of sin to which we technically give the name of 'absolution'?"

Of this view it must suffice here to say that neither Newman nor High Anglicanism would recognize it*. But other difficulties present themselves of a very different nature ; and to omit these would be to leave ourselves unprepared for those very doubts which, though Newman now passes over them so lightly, treating them as if dead, and propitiating them as it were, by a graceful burial, will presently rise up as spectres and scare him Romewards. When Tract No. 1 tells us that, if we trace the succession "from hand to hand," *of course we shall come to the Apostles at last*, and *we know we do, as a plain historical fact*— it is slurring over the very serious danger from the author's point of view—that Romanists might deny him the right to say "of course" in the case of Anglican Orders. Even at that point in his career, Newman might have known that (in his and Froude's view) certain degrees of heresy—such, for example, as he would probably have imputed to Bishop Hoadley— might go some way to invalidate ordinations by such

heretical hands.*   Again, the "of course," and "we
know," ignore the well-known facts that, in certain
periods of the Church, there have been grave irregu-
larities which might lead to an omission, or fatal mis-
adventure, even in that simple act of imposition of
hands, which (as Newman asserted) of itself conveyed
the divine grace.   It is distasteful to touch on details
here, but a physical theory of this kind necessitates
entering into physical questions.   What, then, if a
lapse of thought, or sudden faintness, on the part of
the bishop, caused only one hand, or only a part of
one, say the tip of one of the fingers, to be laid on
the candidate?   Or what if it were, in such circumstances, laid, not on the head, but on the shoulder or
temples?   Or, if the candidate wore some covering
on his head, say, a skull-cap or a wig, would that
invalidate the ordination?

To those who accept the rite as a spiritual one, the
symbolism seems to preserve the sense of continuity,
to stimulate the imagination, and to quicken the
faith, and therefore to be by all means worthy of retention, but still not absolutely essential to the inner act.
To them, Absolution seems a spiritual healing, and the
Holy Communion a spiritual nourishment, so that some
external irregularity in the ordination of a Minister of
Christ, however much to be regretted, would not
amount to an invalidation of these sacred ministrations.
And—whatever it might be to others—to them at all
events, it would be a blasphemy to impute to God what
they would call a physical system of sacramental grace.
For upon Newman's* theory of transmission, absolutions, when administered by such an irregularly-ordained
priest, would be no absolutions; and the Body and
Blood of Christ would not be received by those

who (in all good faith and perfect devotion of heart)
supposed that they were partaking of them.   One or
two irregularly-ordained bishops might produce scores
of such non-bishops and thousands of such non-priests
in the next generation ; and these, as time went on,
would be indefinitely multiplied.   Thus, an unwilling
imposture in bishops that were no bishops, and in
priests that were no priests, would produce a spiritual
starvation and death (all the more irremediable because invisible and unknown) in generation after
generation of the unconscious laity.   These poor deluded creatures may suppose that they are Christians,
but they are not ; they are spiritual corpses.   The
channels of grace to which they resort with pious
fervour for the supply of God's best gifts are, though
they know it not, mere empty conduits, leaving them
unblessed, unsanctified, unforgiven, cast on His "uncovenanted mercies."   Newman himself has taught
them that they have no more reason—apart from His
power to whom all things are possible, and who may
intervene in their behalf to save them· by special
miracle—for supposing that their souls can attain
eternal life without the Sacrament of Holy Communion, than for supposing that they can drink without water or eat without food.   Without the Apostolic Succession of physical contact traced from hand
to hand, what are all the graces and gifts of the most
saintly pastors, what the most ennobling utterances
of the most heart-felt worship ?   They are all hollow,
all deceptive ; the worse for being good.

Such, and so terrible, are the spiritual evils which
(according to the strict theory of Tract No. 1)
must befall any Church in which, through any cause,
accidental or otherwise, there has been a break in the

chain of physical contact which should unite Christian
priests and bishops now with the Christian Apostles
of eighteen centuries ago.   Some of my readers may
disbelieve in the necessity of such a physical succession ; some may deny it with indignation, and may be
impatient that their attention to it should be, as it
were, importuned at such length.   But that is unreasonable.   They are not asked to agree with Newman : they are only asked to try to understand him ;
and how can they do that if they refuse to put themselves in his position ?   And, if they put themselves
in his position, how can they choose but be afraid ?
How can they do otherwise than walk in terror all the
days of their life, with fear and trembling, lest perchance the Apostolic link be snapped, though they
know it not, and their faith be all in vain, and they be
cast adrift from Christ, tossed, though unconsciously,
on the vague and doubtful seas of " uncovenanted
mercies " ?   Let them realise what Newman glossed
over so gracefully in 1833 and they will understand
what drove him out of the English Church in 1845.

§ 68. *The Effect of Tract No. 1 on the Clergy*

Yet to many a common-place clergyman in out-of-
the-way country parishes, Tract No. 1 may have
indirectly conveyed a real moral stimulus, in spite of
its apparently non-moral doctrine.   Compared with
Nonconformist Ministers, they would often find themselves in some respects not superior, sometimes inferior,
to the latter : what then could they say to their people
if they were disestablished to-morrow, in order to
assert a superiority of position ?   Newman gave them
something to say, and something that was at least

less base and worldly than a mere claim to superior
social standing and "gentlemanliness." Doubtless, he
did some of them harm. Some of the grosser sort,
conscious of moral, as well as intellectual inferiority to
the average "Minister," and having really no *raison
d'être* in their parishes at all, might grasp greedily at
this new official grandeur of their own, now first
revealed to them. These might be made arrogant,
superstitious, and more morally callous than ever.
But another type of parson might be quite differently
affected—"Have I really,"—he might say—"these
divine powers though I never knew them? And
were they given me not for my own virtue, but through
a special grace? Then surely this is a somewhat
awful responsibility. I must reconsider my position."

Reconsidering it, such a man would find that his
principal use in the parish was to be a channel of
sacramental grace, and that his labours were more
definitely prescribed than he had supposed. To
administer baptism to an ailing child, or the Holy
Communion or Absolution to a dying man, he felt
before to be a solemn duty. But now it is a matter of
more than life and death. On such an errand he will
now feel bound to go forth, to the sacrifice (if need be)
of any other duties, and without counting any risks,
much less discomforts, believing that he is carrying
with him a medicine far more efficacious for eternity
than the country doctor's is for time. Nor is it likely
that many will stop at the mere formal duties of alms-
giving and visiting the sick and needy. If a man
makes it his business to do such things at all, then,
even though he does them at first simply because
they are prescribed duties, he cannot always (one
would think) resist the spiritual promptings that such

deeds naturally suggest.   Again on the other hand, as regards the services of the Church, he will henceforth be independent.   None of the laity need come, yet he can send up the incense of intercessory prayer ; none of the congregation need communicate, yet he can offer at the altar for the parish and for the whole world the Sacrifice of the Eucharist ; no day can pass without his having performed efficacious duties— efficacious, because their efficacy depends not upon his own mental or moral faculties, but upon his power of accurately uttering prescribed words and performing prescribed motions—assuming, of course, that he has himself received the imposition of hands from a bishop who could trace his succession, by a similar experience, back to the Apostles themselves.

In all this, what a satisfying definiteness !   Contrast it with the painfully limitless toil of a pastor who regards all the rites of religion, and the sacraments themselves, as but means to an end ; who conceives himself bound to keep his eyes open to what is in the hearts of men and women around him ; to adapt his labours to their needs ; to persuade, rebuke, argue, guide ;—who furthermore, besides these spiritual works, feels it his duty to do what he can to improve the physical and material circumstances of those who are in his charge, not by mere alms-giving, but by all useful means, sometimes perhaps by *stopping* indiscriminate almsgiving, and who cannot regard with any satisfaction crowded services, or even well-attended administrations of the Holy Communion, or the universal habit of baptism if he finds these outward manifestations accompanied by a low standard of morality.   Who can fail to see that the simplicity, directness, and if I may so say, achievableness of what may be called the materialistic method of religionizing the masses, possess great advantages over what may be called the spiritual method—if only the former is thoroughly believed in ?

But we must not be led by these thoughts to digress from our immediate subject : the skill with which Newman throws himself into the position of the clergy, realizes their isolation and their dejection, and helps them out of both.   As in the days of his boyhood we noted the dramatic art with which he threw himself into the character of a fisherman, and realized a fisherman's view of virtue, so now, on a different plane, he sympathetically throws himself into the clerical view of ideal clerical life.   And, like a consummate teacher, he refrains from teaching his pupils too much.   He has ulterior designs on them which he will not at present bring forward.   He intends to draw them out of their insular, cold, stationary, High and Dry Church position, into a closer union with the Church Catholic ; to kindle in them an affection for the Primitive Church from which they have degenerated, to stimulate them to self-denial, asceticism, celibacy, detachment from the laity over whom they ought to rule, as they cannot rule if undetached.   Thus his object is to prepare a chosen army of Catholically-minded Anglicans who shall, if possible, leaven and appropriate the National Church, or else, if need be, secede from it in such numbers as to constitute a New Anglicanism, under happier auspices than those of the Nonjurors.

But, of all this, how little he says ! And, what he does say, how simple it is, how easy to perform, how admirably adapted for persuading them to commit themselves at once to a first step forward !   How skilfully, too, he avails himself of the words of Scripture! "Stir up the gift of God which is in you"—that is a Scriptural phrase. But it is questionable whether the Apostolic "stir" meant *make a stir about* —in which sense many would be led to interpret his precept by the word which he himself italicizes in it : " Make much of it . . . Keep it before your minds as an honourable badge, far higher than that secular respectability . . . . which gives you a hearing with the many. Tell *them* of your gift." How immediately attractive, all this, to clerical human nature ! And at the same time how ultimately adapted to make thousands of them in their country solitudes meditate on all the powers implied in this "gift," and especially to prepare them to consider that awful faculty of which he was intending soon to remind them—" of making the Bread and Wine the Body and Blood of Christ"! Teaching them in this way by line upon line and precept upon precept, Newman appears to have been leading them on, as he prayed that he might "lead on " Pusey, with that kind of "economy" which formed a prominent part in his doctrinal method.

CHAPTER XVII

§ 69. *Who?*

For some time after the advance, it was doubtful who would lead. The disagreement which manifested itself in the Hadleigh meeting did not cease when the meeting had agreed on its two " principles." The steadier portion, alarmed at Froude's progressist tendencies, were against the Tracts, and nearly succeeded in suppressing them. Newman, after almost yielding, at last recalcitrated. The annoyance of composing, recomposing, and watering down addresses and petitions, so as to make everyone sign what no one liked, combined with his own sense of the efficacy of the Tracts to decide him in permanent resistance ; in which, of course, Froude stoutly supported him. The Tracts continued. Through the Tracts, Newman's literary power naturally exerted a predominant influence ; the " Z.'s," as Froude called the steady-going Establishment section, sank a little into the background ; the " Apostolicals," as he called his own section, came to the front, and Newman among those who were at their head.

Several things helped to keep him in this position, and to push back others. Pusey was ill at this time ;

and, though he was "more or less" with the
Tractarians, and was willing to circulate the Tracts,
his adhesion, at all events in the earliest stages of the
Movement, was to be kept a secret.   Great as was
the influence of his character, learning, and position,
his married life kept him from seeing so much of the
younger men in Oxford as Newman was able to do.
Keble, too, was soon to be married ; and, even now,
his distance from Oxford disqualified him, even more
than Pusey, from being a centre of action.   Rose was
a Cambridge man, out of touch with the rising gener-
tion of Oxford, and he had neither the health, nor the
vigour of mind, nor perhaps the clearness of head,
needful for the task.   There remained Froude, who
was too young ; younger than his years in impulsiveness and disregard for the feelings of others ; active
rather than a source of action (except to a few) ; not
magnetic ; repelling the many, rather than attracting ;
and he too, like Rose, was soon to be called by death
from the conflict.   Newman, on the other hand, was
at the very heart of the position ; always (throughout
this period) healthy and vigorous ; always busy, but
still always at leisure to see everybody ;   anxiously
conciliatory in language and manner to every one who
would work for the cause ; ready to make allowance
for them and their failures, and even for their
infirmities, provided they were not fatal to his objects ;
not known as yet to the world as a High Churchman
or as a man of any party ; but supposed by many to
be still a pious Evangelical, with high sacramental
views, who seemed to be aiming at a union of serious
people in all parties for the common good of the
Church ; a man who could persuade and controvert
to perfection on paper, could bring heaven nearer to

earth when preaching in St. Mary's, and could exercise a marvellous attraction on those young men in Oxford of the intellectual sort who thought about religion.

And yet, in spite of all these manifold gifts, he was not a good leader. Those whom he could attract, he could not keep in order. He was wanting in persistence. Everything, with him, depended upon system ; and he was not *always* sure of his system. Hence came an occasional inward fluctuation which, although he concealed it (as a good general must) from most of his subordinates, nevertheless could not be wholly hidden from those who were closest to him, and this affected his public acts and utterances. Like the young warrior in Tennyson's *Princess*, he was liable to palsying fits of visions revealing to him the unreality of all things, which, sometimes in the very height of his victories, slackened his hand, unnerved him for effort, and half disposed him to turn his back and flee, not from his enemies but from himself. To help him against such attacks he needed a friend who could revive his confidence, and who could see his way with a clearness not vouchsafed to himself. Such a friend he had in Froude, whose very deficiencies helped him to help Newman.

Wanting human-hearted imagination, and not realizing difficulties and obstacles arising from men's infirmities, inconsistencies, or virtues, Froude could see no position but his own—not even Newman's ; and he was absolutely certain of his own convictions. He looked at men and women from the architectural or engineering point of view, as so much human stuff, stone, rubble, and mortar, to be made up into a projected structure of which he possessed a plan made out to scale ; and, as soon as things were ready for building, he wanted to build, dealing with his materials as materials, and having no more hesitation in running counter to prejudices, or colliding with habits, than he would have in running a railroad through a cutting or across a morass. We compared Newman above to Hamlet, the man of dreams, and doubts, and scruples, and talks, and delays, interspersed with fitful actions. His affectionate friend Rogers, cool, composed, collected, thoughtful, the model of honour, we might compare to Hamlet's friend Horatio. Proportionately, Froude (having passed through his self-questioning period) is Laertes, the man of action and violence, who likes straight courses, abominates tricks and procrastinations, and is always burning for the sake of the good cause to "sweep to his revenge." Hamlet—who, while talking, abuses himself for talking, and, in the very heat of his passion, despises himself for being passionate, and because he is scrupulous, calls himself a coward—avows himself ready to give anything for a friend who "is not passion's slave," and is drawn towards the man of deeds and straightforward purposes, who knows no scruples, and entertains no delays. So Newman is drawn towards Froude. In the play, circumstances make Hamlet and Laertes enemies, and the hero had to be content with Horatio; but in the drama we are considering, fate was not so unkind; and our Hamlet was fast friends with Laertes, till the latter died and made way for Horatio to take his place.

Thus the two friends, Newman and Froude, supplemented one another. Newman supplied conciliation, dexterous management, apt and versatile utterance, the power of rousing attention, and skill in making combinations, as well as that far higher faculty

of personal influence without which the Movement
could not have gone on. Froude supplied intuition
and force ; over-rode obstacles and delays ; and having
(almost from the first) determined the direction of
advance, kept up a steady pressure which prevented
any permanent deviation. The point on which the
two differed longest and most seriously was the propriety of combining an advance toward Rome with an
attack on Rome. Froude thought that they ought to
be influenced, in this matter, by a consideration of the
steps which they had already taken towards the
Roman position. Already they loved Rome in their
hearts more than mere Protestantism, and each year
of study had revealed to them fresh infirmities or
iniquities in the Reformers ; they were prepared
(Newman as well as Froude) to disseminate about the
Holy Communion a doctrine popularly indistinguish-
able from Transubstantiation ; they were both in
favour of a celibate clergy, and both wished to intro-
duce monachism into the English Church. Primitive
Tradition seemed to both needful to interpret the
Scripture, and Newman was not very far behind
Froude in being prepared to go on towards accepting
the Tradition of the Church as an independent
authority where Scripture was wanting. Having
gone so far as this together towards Rome, might
they not possibly go yet further before long ? Was it
fair, was it not misleading to others, might it not divert
both themselves and others from their goal—thus to
attack bitterly and publicly a Church to which they
already owed so much and might yet owe more ?
This was Froude's view.

The progress of the Movement will show us Newman, at first resisting, but finally yielding to his friend;

and in answer to the question, "Who was to be leader?" will point to *both* as joint leaders. Some might assert that it would be more correct to speak of one as leading by means of the other : Froude the Moses, Newman the Aaron, of the Anglican exodus : only in this case Moses, the man of action, has been eclipsed, in the eyes of posterity, by Aaron, the man of literature. But such an estimate ignores the spell of Newman's personal influence. It seems better to adhere to the statement that the two friends led together. Or we may say Newman led the Movement and Froude led Newman ; and this, in spite of the fact that the younger died in 1836. For if unity of action implies indivisibility of souls, there are few friends of whom it would be truer to say than of Froude and Newman that "in death they were not divided."

§ 70. *Whither?* (1) *"I think our system will be very taking"*

Three other Tracts were issued almost simultaneously with No. 1. Newman wrote them all. Their object was "to make the clergy alive to the situation, to enforce the Apostolical Succession, and to defend the Liturgy." Politics were to be avoided ; innovations, for the present, to be discouraged. He also drew up a paper "for the use of our Propagandists." They were to form local associations ; instruct the corresponding member ; to sound men on certain questions ; to be of no party and to interfere with no party questions. "We have nothing to do with maintaining the temporalities of the Church, much as we deprecate any undue interference with them by external authority." This last sentence carries out the general intention to unite the party on broad issues. "Our object is to get together immediately as large a body as we can, in defence of the *substance* of our spiritual rights, privileges, our Creeds, &c. ; but we wish to avoid technicalities and minutenesses as much as possible." Under the head of "Queries in Prospect" the same paper gives some useful hints as to reticence. While suggesting "petitions against lax men about to be appointed bishops," it deprecates intemperance of language ; yet it permits mention of any *facts* illustrative of the tyranny exercised over the Church. This caution follows : "If men are afraid of Apostolical ground, then be cautious of saying much about it. If desirous, then recommend prudence, and silence upon it at present. Everything depends on calmness and temperance. Recollect that we are *supporting* the bishops ; enlarge on the unfairness of leaving them to bear the brunt of the battle."

Great were the obstacles in the circulation of the Tracts under the postal and travelling arrangements of sixty years ago ; but the energy and enthusiasm of Newman's agents surmounted them all. Publishers raised difficulties ; "the Z's" objected and protested ; some moderate men were shocked ; more were bewildered ; but, on the whole, the brevity, force, novelty, plausibility, and earnestness of the Tracts arrested attention and compelled the religious world to know that some movement was being originated by men of learning, culture, and sincere piety, who had definite convictions of the need of Church Reform. At first, there was no indication of Romeward tendencies. There was no appeal even to the High and Dry against the Evangelicals. On the contrary,

Newman expressly anticipated that the latter would be attracted by some of their writings, as they actually were. If any of their contributors advocated extreme views, Newman maintained that this would "*strengthen* the Association by enabling it to take high ground, yet seem in the mean"—a view which he mentions elsewhere with approval. Condemned by some, approved by others, but read with interest by almost all who had a chance of reading them, these efficacious leaflets grew in number and in size, and sounded on all sides the Tractarian trumpet.

Toward the end of 1834 the first forty-six Tracts were collected into a volume prefaced by an " Advertisement" explaining their nature and objects. This preface complains that, whereas " the Apostolical Succession and the Holy Catholic Church were principles of action in the minds of our predecessors of the seventeenth century," the present ministers of the English Church, finding her maintenance secured by law, "have been under the temptation of leaning on an arm of flesh instead of her own divinely provided discipline." If "the awakened and anxious sinner, who goes to a dissenting preacher because (as he expresses it) he gets good from him," had " been taught as a child that the Sacraments, not preaching, are the sources of Divine Grace ; that the Apostolical ministry had a virtue in it which went out over the whole Church, when sought by the prayer of faith ; that fellowship with it was a gift and privilege as well as a duty, we could not have had so many wanderers from our fold, nor so many cold hearts within it." " Methodism and Popery," it continues, " are in different ways the refuge of those whom the Church stints of the gifts of grace ; they are the foster-mothers of abandoned children. The neglect of the daily service, the desecration of festivals, the Eucharist scantily administered, insubordination permitted in all ranks of the Church, orders and offices imperfectly developed, the want of societies for particular religious objects, and the like deficiencies, lead the feverish mind, desirous of a vent to its feelings and a stricter rule of life, to the smaller religious communities ; to prayer and Bible meetings and ill-advised institutions and societies, on the one hand ; on the other, to the solemn and captivating services by which Popery gains its proselytes. Moreover, the multitude of men cannot teach or guide themselves ; and an injunction given them to depend on their private judgment, cruel in itself, is doubly hurtful as throwing them on such teachers as speak daringly and promise largely, and not only aid but supersede individual exertion." It concludes with the following expression of opinion on the part of the leaders of the Movement : " While they consider that the revival of this portion of truth is especially adapted to break up existing parties in the Church and to form, instead, a bond of union among all who love the Lord Jesus Christ in sincerity, they believe that nothing but these neglected doctrines, faithfully preached, will repress that extension of Popery, for which the ever-multiplying divisions of the religious world are too clearly preparing the way."

Style, as well as thought, stamps this Advertisement as Newman's handiwork. " The Sacraments, not preaching, are the sources of Divine Grace "—*implying* that preaching is not among *the* sources, and conveying to most readers the meaning that it is not *a* source, of Divine Grace—is just one of those

audacious "blows in the stomach" which characterize
Newman's controversial compositions, and it effectively prepares the mind of the reader for that depre-
ciatory view of preaching which Froude had expressed
nearly twelve months before : " I think that in the
present state of religion, preaching should be quite
disconnected from the Services and looked on as an
address to the unconnected." Again, the concluding
sentence, with its aspirations for a new and comprehensive union of Church parties, reminds us of a letter
written a month or two before :

"To become a Romanist seems more and more impossible; to
unite with Rome (if she would let us) not impossible ; but she would
not, without ceasing to be Rome. Somehow my own confidence in
my views seems to grow. I am aware I have not yet fully developed
them to myself. There are opinions, as yet unknown to me which
must be brought out and received ; inconsistencies, too, perhaps to
set right ; but, on the whole, I seem to have a grasp of a system,
very comprehensive. I could go on a great way with Rome, and a
great way with the Evangelicals ; nay, I should not despair of religious Dissenters. I think our system will be very *taking* from its
novelty, its sublimity, and its argumentative basis."

Already, in the previous March, he had declared,
" I see a system behind the existing one, a system
indeed which will take time and suffering to bring me
to adopt, but still a firm foundation." As the confidential expression of temporary exaltation and excessive sanguineness to a friend, such an utterance is
easily explained (though it sounds a little like a
dramatist's exultation over his as yet unwritten
tragedy) ; but the repetition of it first in a letter, and
then publicly in the Advertisement to the Tracts,
shows that Newman's temporary successes, and perhaps,

too, the mere pleasure of activity, were confirming him in that "supreme confidence" with which he had begun his campaign.

§ 71. *Whither ? (2) "I expect to be called a Papist when my opinions are known"*

In his description of the effect produced by the early Tracts, "They were intended," says the author of the *Oxford . Movement*, " to startle the world, and they succeeded in doing so." Their " strong and peremptory language," their " absence of qualifications or explanations," " frightened " even "friends" who "had no ground to quarrel with their doctrine." Those whom they did not frighten they often bewildered. The story went " that one of the bishops, on reading one of the Tracts on the Apostolic Succession, could not make up his mind whether he held the doctrine or not." They " fell on a time of profound and inexcusable ignorance on the subjects they discussed, and they did not spare it." As to the cry of Romanism raised by their enemies, he continues thus :

"The cry of Romanism was inevitable, and was soon raised, though there was absolutely nothing in them but had the indisputable sanction of the Prayer Book, and of the most authoritative Anglican divines. There was no Romanism in them, nor anything that showed a tendency to it. But custom, and the prevalence of other systems and ways, and the interest of later speculations, and the slackening of professional reading and scholarship in the Church, had made their readers forget some of the most obvious facts in Church history, and the most certain Church principles : and men were at sea as to what they knew or believed on the points on which the Tracts challenged them. The scare was not creditable ; it was like the Italian scare about cholera with its quarantines and fumigations ; but it was natural."

To whom was " the scare " " not creditable " ?   Apparently the Dean means to the *scared*.   But was it quite creditable to the *scarers* ?   They " intended " to " startle."   Did they intend to " startle" without " scaring " ?   Was their " strong and peremptory language " calculated to soothe false or exaggerated fears ?   And if " friends," who " had no quarrel " with the Tractarian " doctrine " were " frightened " by the " absence of qualifications or explanations," might not " frights " and " scares " be expected in ordinary people ?   It is more than probable that in the early Tracts there was nothing that could be called distinctively Roman, but, after all, those who prefer to " startle" and even " frighten" people for the sake of making them listen, ought not to be surprised if this sort of advertising ends by frightening some of their audience, not into listening but into recoiling.   The Dean adds that the teaching impugned by the Tracts was really Calvinistic, or Zwinglian, and not Anglican : but under which category comes Bishop Jewell ?   The answer is important ; for we know that Froude wrote to Keble in this very year about this generally recognized bulwark of the Church of England, " He is what you would in these days call an irreverent dissenter."

Contrast with this criticism that of Newman's wise, thoughtful, and learned friend Rickards.   It refers to one of the Tracts—Newman's, but not known to him as Newman's—entitled " Heads of a Week-day Lecture."   It has been mentioned before but needs special attention here :

" I do not dwell so much upon the points (which yet I think are most objectionable), that it makes too rapid an advance upon events which may or may not be coming on, and that it is calculated to bring on the evils it alludes to rather than avert them ; but what I

most deplore is the language in which it speaks of some of the gifts
bestowed upon the ministers of Christ, and especially the expression
'as intrusted with the awful and mysterious gift of making the
bread and wine, Christ's Body and Blood.'

"Of course I do not quarrel with the expression when I meet
with it in writers who lived before the controversies introduced into
the world upon the subject, through the errors of the Church of
Rome; but to use it now, and moreover to use it in a set of tracts
which at any rate will be read at first with a good deal of suspicion,
and in most instances with a view to ascertain what sort of men write
them, and what the real objects of the Association are, appears to
me to be nothing less than tossing firebrands into our own work."

This reproach Newman answered at once, with perfect
temper, but with a distinct intimation that he could not
condemn the opinions expressed on "the Lord's
Supper," and that he "expects" his opinions to be
condemned as Papistical when they are known.   His
words indicate a curious combination of self-distrust
and confidence ; a desire to express his opinions simply
and directly, and yet a doubt whether they could
catch the popular ear (without reckless exaggeration).   "Energy," he says, "is ever incautious and
exaggerated"; yet "energy gives the edge to any
undertaking."   He knew that his own energy was, at
that very moment, "giving the edge" to the Tractarian
enterprise ; and therefore this practically admits the
charge of exaggeration.   Yet to admit, exaggeration is
inevitable, and to add that it has the advantage of
carrying people on to the right point (just as asking too
high a price induces a purchaser to give a fair price)—
what is this but to imply that some little deliberate
mis-statement is justifiable, if in the end it brings
people to the desired haven ?   Not that Newman here
definitely admits the charge.   Indeed he could not
admit it as regards the words condemned.   For, insti-

gated by Froude, he had reached opinions on the
Lord's Supper which, in popular estimation, could not
be distinguished from Transubstantiation.

> "Lastly, I must just touch upon the notice of the Lord's Supper.
> In confidence to a friend, I can only admit it was *imprudent*, for I do
> think we have most of us dreadfully low notions of the Blessed
> Sacrament.   I expect to be called a Papist when my opinions are
> known.   But (please God) I shall lead persons on a little way, while
> they fancy they are only taking the mean, and denounce me as the
> extreme.   Thus all good is done (I do not say *kept up*) by going
> before people, and letting them fancy they are striking a balance.
> Let others be doctors of the Church.   I do not aim at being such
> (though I think myself right) ; let me be thought extravagant, and
> yet be copied."

With his intimate knowledge of the strength of prejudice, and of the deterrent power of shibboleths upon
the multitude, Newman ought to have been prepared,
in serious and sober earnest, to be called a " Papist " ;
and we can only treat as one of many inconsistencies
the sense of injury which he soon expresses when he is
taken at his word.

§ 72. *Whither ?*   (3) *Away from the Reformers*

If there were as yet no definite instances in the Tracts
of distinctive Roman doctrine, there were clear indications, in the correspondence between the leaders, of a
tendency to reject the doctrine of the Reformation.
The stress laid on the quasi-materialistic efficacy of the
sacraments, and on the materialistic Apostolical Succession as the sole channel of Eucharistic grace, would
naturally cause some of the new Anglicans to look
with envy at the great and continuous Church of
Rome, in which the material transmission was less

disputable than in their own.   Were the Reformers
wise, they might ask, in cutting themselves off, so to
speak, from that vast spiritual aqueduct ?   True, they
claimed that the Roman waters had been corrupted,
and that they had re-established communications up
above the tainted spot with the original stream : but
then such statements as these, though easily made
about invisible things that do not necessarily produce
any outward visible result, are as easily denied ; because
neither assertion nor denial can be verified by present
fact.   It was natural therefore that in many of the
Tractarians, at a very early period, there should be an
uneasy feeling about separation from Rome ; and this
in some would produce an anti-Reformation tendency.

In Newman and others, if they had been left to
themselves, this might have only made itself felt by
degrees.   But in the former it was at least stimulated,
if not largely produced, by Froude, who during the
whole of the critical year 1834, though absent in Barbados owing to ill-health, was very active in prompting
his friends by letters.   This was just the time when
the Tractarian scheme was beginning to take shape,
and the plastic leader was himself needing to be led.
Accordingly Froude did lead ; sometimes towards
Rome, but always away from the Reformation.   Against
the Reformers he avows a hostility that never varies
except to grow more intense.   In things indifferent, he
says, they ought to conform to " the Church which has
preserved its traditionary practices unbroken " ; Bishop
Jewell, he complains, " laughs at the Apostolical suc
cession both in principle and as a fact," and is no better
than an " irreverent dissenter " ; the Council of Trent
" had no fair chance of getting at the truth if they saw
no alternative between transubstantiation and Jewel-

lism"; and he declares that the English Colonial
Bishops are just as much exonerated from their oath of
canonical obedience, by proving that there is no
universal bishop recognized in Scripture, as ever
Cranmer was. All this came to Newman commended
not only by its force and logical consistency, but also
by the special circumstances through which Providence
seemed to claim his attention. His suffering and solitary friend, in whose face he might never look again,
spoke with an influence which even Keble, at home,
could not have exerted. That this was so, is attested
by a sermon preached in the autumn of this very year :
" When a man in whom dwells God's grace is lying
on the bed of suffering, or when he has been stripped
of his friends and is solitary, he has, in a special way,
tasted of the powers of the world to come, and exhorts
and consoles with authority."

Newman's replies indicate deference varied by tender
protest ; but he always ends by deferring. Here and
there he speaks as though he had deferred too much
already, and his tone is that of one half resisting, half
desiring to be overcome. He complains of his hard
fate in being attacked for Popish expressions (especially
about the Eucharist), for which, seemingly, he is half
disposed to make Froude responsible ; " Here, as you
well know, it was you who were apt to be unguarded—
not I." The position appears to have been this.
Froude knew his own mind, and was for transubstantiation. Newman did not quite know his own mind.
Sometimes he was not quite with Froude ; he was for
what may be called " transubstantiation with a difference "—the difference being not of a nature to be
popularly intelligible. At other times (and seemingly
at this time) he went entirely with Froude, only he for

the most part expressed his mind "guardedly," so as to conceal his quasi-Roman opinions beneath a decent veil of High Anglicanism or Primitive Patristic language. Recently, however, it would seem he had slipped into Froude's "unguarded way of speaking, and had suffered for it." In the same letter he communicates to Froude his intention to have daily prayers, even though they may be solitary, at St. Mary's. On reading this, one who is familiar with Newman's Correspondence feels a slight shock of surprise. "How is this?" we ask. "Is it possible that one so naturally un-inventive and non-innovating as Newman suddenly assumes the part of an innovator? Ought not this suggestion to have come first from Froude?" It ought, and it did, though Newman (as often) had forgotten the debt. While writing, he refers to one of Froude's old letters, and adds, " I see this agrees with a notion of yours."

On Froude no protests had any effect. Newman's concessions he accepts grudgingly, as not enough; but he never makes any in return. His persistency is irrepressible. The inconsistency of Keble's and Newman's practice and language, with their high Eucharistic views, calls forth excessive remonstrance. He complains that neither of them, at the time when he left England, saw the necessity of frequent communion in the same light in which he did; he quotes Bishop Bull as recognizing in the ancient Fathers generally the Eucharistic doctrine of quasi-transubstantiation; he quotes the Preface to the Articles as "a permission to think nothing of the opinion of their framers "; he accuses Keble of wishing to "back out of the conspiracy," and in the same letter, protests he thinks "worse and worse" of "the Reformers," and asserts—as he had to Newman (only now more strongly)—that "the Preface to the Thirty-Nine Articles was certainly intended to disconnect us from the Reformers." A little later he suggests that it would be more satisfactory to have received one's orders from a Scotch bishop. "The stream is purer, and besides, it would have left us free from some embarrassing engagements"; and he tells his correspondent not to speak of the "Mass Book" but of the "Liturgy of St. Peter." The last letter of the year is from Newman, from whom he anticipates a "rowing" for his "Roman Catholic sentiments"; he has a theory about the Apocalypse which conflicts with Newman's, and has almost made up his mind that the False Prophet is the rationalist spirit set abroad by the Reformers whom he "hates more and moret." The whole "set" of Reformers is, in his judgment, so contemptibly base that they have "dirtied" such innocent phrases as "the Lord's Supper," "the Lord's Table," and the like, and he will never hereafter use any phrases which could "connect him with such a sett." He will never "even abuse the Roman Catholics as a Church for anything except excommunicating us." He regrets that the High Church party had not set up for themselves more than a hundred and thirty years before; but unluckily, they "cut the ground from under their feet by acknowledging Tillotson": "Would that the Nonjurors had kept up a succession! and then we might have been at peace, proselytes instead of agitators." "I can see no other claim," he writes to Keble, "which the Prayer Book has on a Layman's deference, as the teaching of the Church, which the Breviary and the Missal have not in a far greater degree."

Such were the opinions impressed upon the Tractarian leaders in 1834, adopted by them and largely acted on, in 1835, and destined to obtain their avowed sanction and approval by their publication in 1838.

CHAPTER XVIII

§ 73. *" You seem to be finessing too deep "*

THE difficulty of Newman's position in 1835 was far greater than that of the average religious Reformer. Few honestly assume such a part without having at least two or three new, definite, and vehement convictions, in the strength and light of which they seem to see their way clear, at least for a long distance, and no choice but to proceed upon it. Such men have, or think they have, a spirit within them which so quickens their faculties that they feel a new trust in themselves and have no need to pause and look round after each new incident in order to consider the next step. For right or wrong, they do what they do without consulting committees, or resorting to books, precedents, and authorities. With Newman it was far otherwise. He had the three-fold task, first, of impelling others violently onwards ; secondly, of constantly and anxiously consulting the Fathers and the Anglicans—the maps, and charts, and guide-books, so to speak—as to the right course to take ; thirdly, of keeping an eye upon his own motion lest he himself should either go too fast or perhaps lose the way and go altogether wrong. Dependent

as he was upon the convictions of others, he was sorely
perplexed and troubled, as soon as the bright and
eager period of "fierceness" had passed away, between the danger of saying too much and the
cowardice of saying too little, between the merits of
reserve and unreserve in the communication of
religious truth.   In his intellect and judgment, he
inclined to "economy" ; in his heart, suspecting his
own subtlety, he admired those who could say out
straightforwardly just what they meant, and, at rare
intervals, he paid them the tribute of imitation.
Hence came an inevitable oscillation between two
methods of warfare, ambush and open battle, feints
and attacks, marching straightforward and tactical
countermarching.

Early in the year Newman confesses to Froude in
a letter full of touching affection, how helpless he feels
without the lead of that straight rider across obstacles :
" No one can enter into one's mind except a person
who has lived with one.   I seem to write things to no
purpose as wanting your *imprimatur*.   Perhaps it is
well to cultivate the habit of writing as if for unseen
companions, but I have felt it so much that I am getting
quite dry and hard."   Yet, even while Newman was
making this affectionate avowal, Froude was inditing
more rebukes.†   Why had Newman praised Ridley ?
Why had he allowed Pusey to call the Reformers the
Founders of our Church ?—" You seem to be finessing
too deep.   'Why publish poor Bishop Cosin's *Tract
on Transubstantiation ?*   Surely no member of the
Church of England is in any danger of over-rating the
miracle of the Eucharist."

This accusation of "finessing" demands a little
attention, if we are to do Newman justice ; and we

shall have to speak about his views of the Eucharist. That he did *not*, in 1836, believe in " Transubstantia-tion *as held by Rome*," will be seen from a letter quoted further on (p. 386.) But the words I have italicized indicate (or else why add them ?) that he *did* believe in that doctrine *in a certain sense*. We have seen (p. 168) that, under Froude's influence, in 1833, Newman spoke of the ministers of Christ as intrusted with the " gift of *making the bread and wine Christ's Body and Blood*"; that Rickards protested against such words ; and that Newman identified himself with Froude in regard to them, speaking of " the *Transubstantiation* passages which have brought *us* into all sorts of trouble." To this we may add a letter (15 June 1834) in which he implies that the only difference between him and Froude was that the latter was more " un-guarded " in his *language :* " my tracts were abused as Popish . . especially for expressions about the Eucharist. Here, as you well know, it was you who were apt to be unguarded—not I." All this justifies us in concluding that Newman (logically, or illogically, is not the question) at this time accepted Transubstantiation, not " as held by Rome," but as held by himself, in some shape which we will call *quasi*-Transubstantiation, and which Froude did not distinguish from the full Roman doctrine.

This must be kept in mind. Whatever may have been Newman's fluctuations in his attitude towards a doctrine which centuries of theology have done their best to make abstruse, so much is certain—that Froude *believed* Newman, at this time to agree with him. " He led me gradually," said the *Apologia*, " to believe in the Real Presence." But what Froude believed in at this time, and what he believed that Newman, at this time accepted, was, not " the Real Presence," but

Transubstantiation. This we gather, not only from Froude's letter, but also from the explanation Newman himself appends to it.

"N.B.   Froude would not believe that I was in earnest, as I *was*, in shrinking from the views which he boldly followed out.   I *was* against Transubstantiation."

According to this, Froude is in the wrong. Newman is not " finessing." And the reader might suppose his meaning to be that he published Cosin as expressing his *own views* (at that time) *against* Transubstantiation. But that would be a total misapprehension. At all events, to Keble he had given, as his reason for publishing Cosin, *not* that Cosin would guard anyone *against* Transubstantiation, but that, while supposing they were reading a treatise *against* that doctrine ("as *if* against Transubstantiation") readers would have their minds drawn on to higher views of the Real Presence, and would no longer see anything strange in his "Transubstantiation passages" (as he himself called them) which had so offended Rickards in Newman's anonymous *Week-day Lecture*:

"They have no notion of a *real Presence*. I think Cosin will be useful in opening their minds, and preparing them for your tract. They will, as if against 'Transubstantiation,' often say, 'Who doubts this?' 'What repetition is this?' yet all the while will gain something, *e.g.*, I cannot conceive they will think my expressions in the Week-day Lecture *strange*, whatever they may think of their prudence, after reading Cosin."

The same letter treats "Cosin against Transubstantiation," *and* "a Tract against Hoadley," as being, *both*, preparations for a future Tract by Keble which was to advocate a *high Eucharistic doctrine* ; and, at

the conclusion, he apparently half-apologizes for
what he has done, because of the danger lest some
foolish readers might take Bishop Cosin as an
authority, and be led *away from*, and not *towards*
(though perhaps, not quite up to), Transubstantiation :
" I say all this to explain my publishing Cosin first,
and hope I have not overdone my view." What is
this " over-doing," but the very fault Froude had
complained of—"finessing too deep " ? Not content
with " finessing " himself, he desires his sister Jemima
to do the same. She was, at this time, on a visit to
the recalcitrant anti-transubstantiationist Rickards,
and he writes to her as follows :

"I talked to you about Hoadley because Rickards's great ground
against us is, that language about the Eucharist which was allowable
in the Fathers is dangerous since the Popish corruption.   To this
Keble answers, and I think well, that Hoadleyism has introduced a
new era, and that Protestantism, though allowable three centuries
since, is dangerous now.

"You will do a good work if you talk over Rickards, and make
him take in and recommend the Tracts, but I cannot retract one
single step from what I have said in them.   I cannot say with truth
that I repent of any one passage in them.   If it were all to come
over again (I do not think I should have the courage, for attacks
make one timid, but) I should wish to do just the same.   If he says
anything against the ' Week-day Lecture,' do not *argue*, merely speak
of Hoadleyism, and get him to read Bishop Cosin ; *not as if* Bishop
Cosin was a defence of us, but as containing a *true view*.   A book
like his gradually imbues the mind with the truth, so that, when it
comes back to what offended it at first, it is no longer startled."

The meaning of this is clear. Newman published
a tract against Transubstantiation, not to prepare
people *against* that doctrine, but to lead them to something *approximating to it* (though, possibly in his estimation, distinguishable from it). He was preparing

the way *for higher* views of the Eucharist by circu-
lating a treatise *against* a view that was *too "high."*
Whether this was right or wrong, different readers may
decide according to their tastes ; but there is no other
name for it (of a mild kind) than "finessing"—unless
it can be called an "economy."

§ 74. *Newman does not wish to become "a party
man"*

How far Newman was progressing in 1835 towards
some aspects of Romanism, may be inferred from a
series of papers called *Home Thoughts,* in the first of
which he stated the case so forcibly for Rome that
Rose urged him not to publish No. 2 without No. 3,
on the ground that the former, by itself, would certainly
seem to good Protestants to leave the Church of
England "in an awkward condition." But a still
more vehement impulse was now to come from Froude.

One important feature of Newman's conception of
his distinctive Anglican system had hitherto been "the
supremacy of Scripture." According to this, on "fundamentals," that is to say on matters necessary to
salvation, the Church is only authoritative when interpreting Scripture ; Tradition is subordinate to the
Bible. Froude's influence on his friend during the
last year of his life (he died in February, 1836), was
principally devoted to shaking his faith in this doctrine,
so as to prepare him to accept the tradition of the
Church as, in all respects, co-ordinate with Scripture.
The subject had been suggested by a remark of Newman's about the Anglican views not appearing to be
clearly and distinctly deducible from Scripture. He
was mooting the question (afterwards agitated in 1870)
of religious instruction for national schools :

"I should like your opinion whether there is any way in which, under colour of giving a pure Scripture education, we might yet inculcate our notions.   The difficulty is this—*are* our notions so on the surface of Scripture that a plain person ought to see them there, at least when suggested to him ?   Or again, *how far* is the unpopularity of our notions among readers of Scripture to be traced to Protestant blindness and prejudice ? "

In his answer Froude says :—

"I must say a word or two on your casual remark about the unpopularity of our notions among ' *Bible* Christians.'   Don't you think Newton's system would be unpopular with 'sky astronomers' just in the same way ?   The phenomena of the heavens are repugnant to Newton,* just in the same way as the letter of Scripture to the Church ; *i.e.* on the assumption that they contradict every notion which they do not make self-evident, which is the basis of ' Bible Christianity' and also of Protestantism ; and of which your trumpery principle about Scripture being the sole rule of faith in *fundamentals* (I nauseate the word) is but a mutilated edition, without the breadth and axiomatic character of the original."

This will suffice to bring before the reader, in its order of time, the rise of a question which will soon recur in larger dimensions.   But at this point there comes from Newman to Froude a remarkable avowal, the consideration of which will throw a good deal of light on his present position and future movements. Knowing, as we now do, Newman's peculiar views, we may be well astonished to find that he was *not* as yet thought to be *in any sense* " peculiar," and that he esteemed this a part of the strength of his position.   He was, in reality, a High Churchman of an extreme type, differing from that party in the direction of Evangelicalism in only this one point that he was not " dry " or lifeless, but carrying their Sacramentarian views to the highest pitch ; holding (perhaps with fluctuations), on the Eucharist, doctrines that could not popularly be

distinguished from Transubstantiation ; desiring a revival of the monastic system ; recommending a life of
celibacy for the clergy ; and looking forward to a re-
introduction of the discipline and supremacy of the
mediæval Church. And yet, so cautious and guarded
had he been that he thought himself to be generally
looked on as a man of no party : so he writes to
Froude :—

"I have at present some misgivings whether I have not been too
bold in the June Magazine on the subject of Monachism. You saw
it, and it is only my confidence in this unseen agitator which bears
me up. I doubt whether I am not burdening my well-wishers with
too heavy a load when I oblige them to take up and defend these
opinions too.

"You see the ground taken, as far as I am concerned, by our
fautores in many quarters, is that of my not being a party man or
peculiar in any sense. Now some one has told me that, in defending
Monachism, I have become peculiar. I can but throw myself in
answer upon the general Church, and avow (as I do) that if any one
will show me any opinion of mine which the Primitive Church condemned, I will renounce it ; any which it did not insist on, I will
not insist on it. Yet, after all, I am anxious about it, and shall draw
in my horns."

He received from Froude the reply that he must have
anticipated, and that he probably desired to provoke :

"I cannot see the harm of losing influence with people when you
can only retain it by sinking the points on which you differ from
them. Surely that would be *Propter vitam vivendi*, &c. What is
the good of influence, except to influence people?"

This would doubtless prevent Newman from "drawing
in his horns" and harden him against the dread of
being thought "peculiar." And in strict logic it is
hard to see how a man who holds the materialistic
views of Apostolical Succession and the Eucharist can

avoid professing the differences—fundamental and vital as they are—which divide him from other Christians, many of whom he must regard (one would suppose) as perishing for want of his distinctive truths. Still, if we want to realise how smoothly and affectionately Newman could write, at this time, on religious subjects to those who entirely differed from him, we shall derive much instruction from two letters of this period, written to his mother and to his aunt, the first, just before, the latter, probably after, the reply from Froude.

The former is a marvellous example of sympathetic skill. He wishes to minimize the differences of religious opinion between Mrs. Newman and himself, and accordingly he talks of the great interest of parochial work and how well content he could be to devote himself to it. But there are two drawbacks in a large parish—first the amount of secular business laid on a clergyman, attendance at vestries, &c. ; the other :—

—"that really, at the present day, we are all so ignorant of our duties, that I should be actually afraid myself, without a great deal more learning, to undertake an extensive charge. I find daily, from reading the Fathers, how ignorant we are in matters of practice, *e.g.* I mean the kind of mistakes, though not so flagrant, of the poor fellow who re-baptized a whole set of Dissenters. Hooker does a good deal for one, but even to master Hooker is no slight work. I do really fear that, for the want of knowing what is right and what is wrong, the best intentioned people are making the most serious and mischievous mistakes."

He adds that Rivington has written to say he means to give up the Tracts : " I cannot say quite that I am sorry, for what is done is done, and we shall make two volumes of them ; and I shall be saved the trouble in future." This, of itself, would be welcome news to his mother. She would be pleased to think that he attached so little importance to them. But, besides, what could be more calculated to shock an Evangelical Churchwoman, kindly disposed towards the more orthodox Nonconformists, than this " mistake " of the High Church parson who had " re-baptized a whole set of dissenters " ? How warmly would Mrs. Newman agree with her son in calling this mistake " flagrant "! And how natural to infer that if the reading of "the Fathers " led to the correction of such mistakes and came to much the same thing as "mastering Hooker," there was more to be said for " the Fathers " than the ordinary Protestant, or she herself, perhaps, supposed!

The letter to his aunt is a little later. In it he takes a higher flight. He is resisting the inroads of scepticism, doing battle for the faith, and defending the creeds. People say " what is the harm of Sabellianism ?" Let them learn from poor Blanco White ; who " has turned Socinian and written a book glorying in it. Now in the preface to this book he says : ' I have for some time been a *Sabellian*, but the veil is removed from my eyes, for I find *Sabellianism is but* Unitarianism in disguise.' " After that, who will speak slightingly of " the Constantinopolitan Fathers (who composed the Creed as we now use it) " ? This, then, is what he is working at. He deprecates any charge of presumptuous claims. We have seen that on the part of his eldest sister there had been a little feeling that her brother demanded an undue deference. If such an impression had reached his aunt, this letter would have gone far to dissipate it. He is reading to remedy a defect in himself "and (if so be) in some others." He is but one, he protests, of many instruments.

. . . "God has not (so I trust) abandoned this branch of His Church which He has set up in England, and though for our

many sins He has brought us into captivity to an evil world, and
sons of Belial are lords over us, yet from time to time He sends us
judges and deliverers as in the days of Gideon and Barak. I do
verily believe that some such movement is now going on, and that
the Philistines are to be smitten, and, believing it, I rejoice to join
myself to the army of rescue, as one of those who lapped with the
tongue when the rest bowed down to drink."

He then repeats that he takes nothing to himself
personally : Solomon's history is proof enough that
the builders of God's Church are not necessarily His
truest servants ; Barak is a token that the man who
makes most outward show may do little in comparison
with a woman into whose hand "the Lord delivered
Sisera ;" it is the prayers of those who have especial
leisure for prayer that do the Church most service ;
let his aunt give them the benefit of her continual
prayers, as she has his prayers morning and evening.

After reading these letters we can better understand
how it came to pass that Newman believed himself,
and was believed by others, to be a man of no particular party. Where he found, in any critic or adversary
the slightest token of complacency, self-will, independence of thought, or private judgment, he was as hard
as steel, and could "renounce" a brother and "not
permit" the thoughts of a sister : but in aged or middle-
aged Evangelicals of deep and genuine piety, who had
never departed from the old lines, he could overlook
almost every difference that did not extend to a phrase
of the Creed, and could tolerate, with a kindly con-
nivance, all the prejudices with which their faith was
ingrained.

§ 75. *Froude urges the authority of " Tradition "*

Semitic logic is said to have irresistibly deduced
from the text "thou shalt not seethe the kid in the

mother's milk," the conclusion that butter must not be eaten with meat ; mediæval logic, from other texts, has discovered the precise number of spirits that can poise themselves on the point of a needle. For such conclusions, little more is needed than the general recognition of some oracular text which authoritative interpreters are to be allowed to explain, sometimes in a literal, sometimes in a metaphorical, sense ; sometimes in both senses together ; without any regard to those laws of language, thought, and human nature, which would direct our interpretation of non-inspired utterances. It may be objected that this game may be played at by two antagonistic interpreters who may deduce from the same inspired original wholly opposite conclusions. But that objection has been anticipated in the phrase "*authoritative* interpreters." It is assumed that a particular set of conclusions deduced by this method of interpretation will drive all others out of the field by its superior " authority " ; that is to say, either because this particular set is encouraged by consent, favour, or reward, or because its competitors are discouraged by blame or punishment, the latter being sometimes direct, but in our days, mostly, indirect. Under these circumstances, if you have an oracle to fall back upon, you can prove anything from anything ; and the question arises, why was not Froude content to recognize, in name, Newman's " distinctive Anglican doctrine " of " the supremacy of Scripture," if, in reality, by giving Tradition the power of deducing whatever it likes from Scripture, he could make Tradition paramount ?

Perhaps he was uneasy in having to admit that such vitally important doctrines as those of sacerdotal absolution and penance could not be true unless they could be deduced from Scripture ; and yet could only be deduced from Scripture by hammering out the original metal into a very fine gold-leaf indeed. Newman might have urged, by way of comfort, that the doctrines *were* taught by Scripture, only in an " economy." But Froude did not in his heart like economies. He never talked of them without feeling sore ; and he mocked at himself even while he used them. With his high views of the function of the Church, it seemed to him absurdly illogical to assert that all the vital doctrines of the Christian religion must needs be included in that collection of books, composite documents, and letters, public and private, called the New Testament. Why not avow that they were taught by the voice of the living Church ? This once admitted, their battle was won against Private Judgment. For then, those who would hear God must listen to the Church. Newman, on the other hand, was most unwilling to give up the supremacy of Scripture. It was a "distinctive" part of his Anglican system and afforded a definite *locus standi* against Rome. Moreover, he was, at this very time, engaged in an anxious controversy on the Roman question with a French Abbé. Just at that moment, therefore, it was particularly disagreeable even to contemplate a change of front.

A correspondence on the subject between the two friends started in July, and was continued in the following month. Newman, in explaining his position, viz., that all Tradition (at least as regards Fundamentals) rests on Scripture—had urged that the Apostles' Creed is, in fact, "nothing but" the Baptismal Creed implied in Matthew xxviii. 19 (" In the name of the Father and the Son and the Holy Ghost"), adding that the subsequent clauses of the

Apostles' Creed about the Holy Catholic Church, the
Communion of Saints, &c., describe merely "the
medium through which God comes to us." Newman
said "nothing but;" but that was an exaggeration.
He *meant* that the Apostles' Creed was a *development*,
or *expansion*, of the words in St. Matthew's Gospel.
Froude, in his reply, brusquely pushes aside this
exaggeration, and attacks what he knew to be the
meaning :

> "You lug in the Apostles' Creed, and talk about expansions.
> What is the end of expansions? Will not the Romanists say that
> their whole system is an expansion of the Holy Catholic Church and
> the Communion of Saints?"

*What is to be the end of "expansions"? Where are
"developments" to end?* This indeed was a home-
thrust. It amounted to saying, "You can prove *anything* out of Scripture by 'expansions': is it not then
more creditable to your intellect, as well as more
reverent to the Church, to believe that truths of
religion are not to be squeezed out of Scripture in this
artificial way, but to be obediently received from our
inspired Mother?"

As if to sharpen the edge of Froude's criticism,
Rogers, at this very time, attacked Newman on the
subject of Scripture interpretation, though from a
different side. Newman seems never to have attempted a critical study of the Greek Testament. The
only reference that I have found to a possible interpo-
lation is in the *Essay on Miracles* written in 1826
when he was under Whately's influence, and this he
tacitly withdraws in his later works. With him, for
example, the Epistle to the Hebrews was always one
of St. Paul's Epistles, affording interesting proof how

far St. Paul's doctrine agreed with St. John's! Yet,
of course, if it was " distinctive " of Anglicanism to be
based on Scripture, a leading Anglican theologian
ought to know enough about Scripture to meet any
modern neological attacks on ancient interpretations
or criticisms.   And Rogers now warned him that if
the neologians were not met they would destroy his
very basis : " Unless prevented, I should have fancied
that intellectual people, and consequently, more or
less, the mass of candid people, would have got semi-
neological habits of viewing things, which, I suppose,
would leave you nothing to build a Church system on."
Here Newman was helpless and knew himself to be
so.   Only last vacation he had been aspiring to learn
German (presumably to grapple with the neologians)
and had been consulting his friend Bowden (who had
given him books for the purpose a dozen years before) ;
but nothing had come of it : and without German, the
enterprise was hopeless.   Thus simultaneously one
friend was making him ask himself, " Do I know anything of the Bible critically, and can I speak with any
security about the principles of Scriptural interpretation ? " while another was urging him to dispense
altogether with this tedious study : " Take the short
cut.   You may spend ages over Scripture interpretation, and then may only get from it what every one
but yourself will say cannot be got from it.   Tradition
is plain.   Take the Tradition of the Church."

In September 1835, Froude and Newman met at
the home of the former, both knowing that they met
for the last time.   The controversy had been recently
re-opened.   Froude had an intense dislike for Newman's word " Fundamentals," and a very plain and
common-sense view of " doctrines necessary to salva-

tion." *No doctrine*, he says, "is necessary to salvation to those who have not rejected it wilfully ;" and "to those who do reject wilfully," *every true doctrine* is "necessary to salvation." Therefore "doctrines necessary to salvation" (as they are called in one of the Articles) can only mean, he says, "terms of communion, *i.e.*, necessary to *covenanted* salvation." Four day afterwards, he had continued :—

"As to our controversies, you are now taking fresh ground, without owning, as you ought, that on our first basis I dished you. Of course if the Fathers maintain that 'nothing not deducible from Scripture ought to be insisted on as terms of communion,' I have nothing more to say. But again, if you allow Tradition an interpretative authority, I cannot see what is gained. For surely the doctrines of the Priesthood and the Eucharist may be proved from Scripture interpreted by tradition ; and if so, what is to hinder our insisting on them as terms of communion? I don't mean of course that this will bear out the Romanists, which is perhaps your only point, but it certainly would bear out our party in excommunicating Protestants."

During Newman's visit the question was of course resumed ; and toward the end of the year Froude is still harping on it to Rogers :—

.... " I have been thinking over and over again (*sic*) N.'s argument from the Fathers, that tradition, in order to be authoritative, must be in form interpretative, and can get no farther than that it is a convenient reason for† tolerating the (I forget which) Article. No reason why the Apostles should have confined their oral teaching to comments on Scripture seems apparent, and why their other oral teaching should have been more likely to be corrupted *semper, ubique, et ab omnibus.*"

There are no clear † indications of the immediate effect of this on Newman's position, but Froude has much the best of the argument from the common-sense point of view.   What is far more to the purpose, is, that his opinion would also ultimately commend itself to Newman as showing a deference for authority. "How do we know that it may *not* be true?" was always an argument that appealed forcibly to him : and when applied to the subject under consideration, it was still more forcible : "How do you know that the Apostles—who taught before the Scriptures were com- pleted—did not teach other truths beyond mere com- ments on Scripture ? And how do you know that these truths may not have been transmitted by Tradition in the Catholic Church from their days to ours ?"

§ 76. *Froude's Last Words*

A well-known passage in the *Apologia* lays great stress on one of Froude's last utterances, as having recurred to the memory of his surviving friend again and again in after years.   It is a protest against Newman's attacks on Rome :—

> " Before I finish I must enter another protest against your cursing and swearing at the end of the first *Via Media* as you do.   What good can it do?   I call it uncharitable to an excess.   How mistaken we may ourselves be on many points that are only gradually opening on us !   Surely we † should reserve 'blasphemous' † and 'impious' for denials of the articles of the faith."

Newman here interpolates a defence, as follows: "N.B. —Here I find one illustration among a thousand, of the meaning of my saying in the passage which Stanley, Faber, Whately, &c., have made so much of in my retractation in 1843, 'While I keep to our divines, I am safe,' &c.   *That* was the answer I should make to such protests as this of Froude's.—J. H. N." Newman's meaning appears to be this, that "our divines," *e.g.*, Bishop Bull and other orthodox divines

of the Church of England, systematically attacked the
Church of Rome ; and consequently that he, as a
member of the Church of England, was "safe" in
following their *consensus*. But how "safe"? Does
he mean morally "safe," *i.e.*, that he, the leader of a
new Movement was morally justified in thus attacking
the Church of Rome on grounds that he had not himself investigated ? or that he was intellectually "safe,"
i.e., sure to be right—as a man might feel if he adopted
a positive statement of fact on the authority of eminent
specialists?   In either case, the argument appears
discreditable.   But the curious fact is that Newman
himself appears to have admitted to Froude, at the
time, that it *was* discreditable, and that he had no
right to indulge in revilings.   The admission is made
in a reply to the last of all Froude's letters (27 January,
1836) in which he had accused Newman of "economy"
and "trickery" in one of the Tracts. Newman replies
immediately :—

> "As to my economies in my first Tracts I have much to say about
> them, were not writing a bore. First, I will willingly alter all
> revilings ; again, all serious charges about which I have changed my
> mind.   But, so far, I have not changed my mind, namely in thinking
> that Transubstantiation, as held by Rome*, involves, *in matter of fact*
> profane ideas.   If the union of the exalted nature of Christ with the
> qualities of bread be the doctrine of antiquity, I yield*; else, it does
> seem to me a substitution of something earthly for a heavenly
> mystery."

What the "revilings" were to which Froude definitely
objected we learn from Newman himself.   They were
in Tract 38, in which he had called certain Roman
doctrines—besides "unauthorized," "unscriptural," and
so on—"profane," "impious," "blasphemous," "gross,"
"monstrous," and "cruel."   Also in Tract 15, he had
asserted that Rome was "heretical," and that she

might have " forfeited her orders " by having " aposta-
tized " at the Council of Trent; at which it was " to
be feared the whole Roman Communion bound itself
by a perpetual bond and covenant, to the cause of
Antichrist."

In 1843 he retracted these expressions.   But what
did he feel about them now ?   When he retracted them,
he extenuated his past use of them on the ground that
he had felt " safe " in following the Anglican divines.
But here, in 1836, we find him willing not only to alter
all " revilings," but even to retract *all serious charges*
about which he had " changed his mind."   Thus,
apparently, he is throwing over " the Anglican divines "
and " safety," and straying into the use of private
judgment.   The explanation probably is that, at this
time, Froude, on his death-bed, seemed more than
ever to " exhort with authority " and to deliver a
message from heaven.   This special urgency impelled
the Romeward-flowing tide to a point from which it
afterwards receded, though soon to return and mount
yet higher.   Meantime we may note that, even on the
point of Transubstantiation, Newman was ready to
give way and to accept a doctrine that seemed to him,
in matter of fact, to involve profane ideas, if it could
be shown to be the doctrine of antiquity, that is to say,
of Tradition.   This was a long step towards the edge
of an inclined plane, which, once reached, might soon
take the traveller further than he anticipated.

§ 77. *Showing a fair front to the enemy*

Enough has been said to show that Newman was
not an ideal leader.   Yet the Movement spread.   So
rapid was its success that Newman himself said his

doctrines must be "in the air"; or sometimes he attributed it to "an unseen agitator." To some extent, he may have exaggerated its prosperity. The alarmist rumours of enemies, magnifying the Tractarian triumphs, were not to be taken literally. Too much weight was not to be attached to such evidence as the appearance of a Tract in the backwoods of America; or to reports that crowded congregations were hanging on the lips of a Tractarian preacher in some fashionable watering place. The masses of the middle and lower classes either knew nothing of the Movement, or knew it only to suspect it. Yet the Leader had a fair right, too, to be surprised at the rapidity of his progress. Partly, perhaps, he underrated his own intense energy and his power of transmitting it to others. The revival succeeded best, of course, with the young, who were first arrested, and then captivated by it. But older and more sceptical minds were, at least, interested, and forced to confess that—at all events as a reaction against the hollow and conventional religion of mere fashion—the Movement was worthy of success. Even the worldly or politically-minded might admit that these new Church Reformers were in earnest; that their scheme appeared likely to end in more than words; and that it might issue in results of which statesmen would have to take account.

That it should have fascinated some of the ablest of the young Oxford men is almost as intelligible as it is creditable to them. They must be judged by what the Tractarian project then promised, not by what its leader ultimately performed. If men must have something to believe, what else was there, in Oxford, with equal attractions? Certainly not Evangelicalism, a somewhat heavy yoke at all times for men of culture, but heavier than ever and without compensations, now that the fervid spirit of its prime had passed away. As for sound, orthodox, and lifeless Anglicanism, which was laxly enforced, rather than taught, by the Oxford authorities, the very fact that it was authoritative would supply a grateful stimulus to young and active minds to rebel against it; not, of course, through private judgment, but in the name of a still higher authority—the Catholic Church, to which the older dons and the Heads of Houses themselves could not refuse assent, if they would only take down their books and rub up their theology. The apparent nobility of a Gospel of self-denial attracted those who were religiously inclined. More logical minds were drawn towards a religion which did not claim from them the mere spasmodic raptures of isolated hours of ecstasy, but professed to cover and dominate their whole life from the cradle to the grave in a scientific way, recognizing their infirmities and sins; appointing definite remedies, prescribing habits, giving the penitent something to *do* at once so as not to let him waste regretful resolves in mere words; deprecating the gush of insincere, idle, or even too enthusiastic profession; despising hysterics and substituting a course of manly action, with due regard to cause and effect; and insisting upon obedience and attention to the Christian system as a whole and not to isolated texts. Men of learning, and students of history, gratefully acknowledged that, whatever might be the outcome of the Movement, it was doing good service in calling attention to the collective phenomena of Christianity, and in bringing to light the almost forgotten literature of the earliest teachers of the Church. In London,

the young lawyers were taken with the symmetry and
seeming consistency of the new system, and perhaps
still more with the measured language and self-control
apparent in many of its defenders. Some, too, of its
more spiritually - minded favourers were attracted
towards it by the simple fact that in an age of commercial morality and utilitarianism, when "public
opinion," instead of being a term of contempt, was
fast becoming a power to be flattered and propitiated,
and convictions were lightly sacrificed to the claims
of political partisanship, this Movement recognized
an Unseen Holiness which was altogether above human
morality, and to which it would fain force men to pay
homage, without any regard to what statesmen might call
expedient, or the trading classes might think sensible.

To be wise, now, about what happened sixty years
ago, is so easy, and so misleading, that we ought to
take some pains to put ourselves in the position of
those who were not wise, but sanguine, and consequently disappointed. For this purpose, we must fix
our thoughts on Tractarianism as it *seemed* to the
educated public in the year 1836, not on Tractarianism as it *was*, or was soon to be, in the mind of its
Leader. Those who were in the secret, knew that
the Leader was, step by step, committing himself to
an ecclesiasticism as rigid and despotic as that of
Rome. But the public were not in the secret, and
there was only a stray warning here and there that
came from men with exceptional powers of observation and prediction, such as Bunsen. Bunsen, as
Newman himself tells us, when the two first met,
"looked at him with interest," seeing in him a man
of ideas, a man who meant to go far, and would be
forced to go further. But this sagacious critic had

soon detected the weak inconsistency in the Tractarian scheme.   This little knot of Reformers was
exalting " Tradition " and " Antiquity "—while re-
serving for itself the task of determining—by a
process of picking and choosing—what " Tradition "
and " Antiquity " meant.   This, Bunsen called, " introducing Popery without Authority " : and he was
right, if such an oligarchy might be called an Anglican
Pope.   But few had Bunsen's forethought, and opportunities of judgment.   And there was much that we
know now, which Bunsen did not know.   He was not
aware that Froude, if not Newman, had discussed the
propriety of ultimately excommunicating the Evan·
gelical party ; that even Rose had been combining
with Newman to consider the establishment of " a
really working Court of Heresy " which might serve
as a "practical curb upon the exercise of the King's
power," and by which " the whole Church might be
kept in order " ; that the same pair of conspirators
had been asking whether "a clause might be slipped
into the Ecclesiastical Commission Bill for this
purpose " ; and that Froude, before his death, had
entirely severed himself, and practically severed
Newman also, from all connection with the Reformers
who had framed the Articles of the English Church.

Many, therefore, who were not behind the scenes,
might, without any discredit to their intellect or practical
judgment, have entertained hopes which we now—wise
after the event—see to have been baseless from the first.
There may well have been some laymen in those
days—there are probably some now—who believe
that the Christian religion, and no other, is fitted to
develop mankind and bring it to its goal, but that there
is something deeper in Christianity than has yet been

brought out, something wider than has hitherto entered into the minds of ecclesiastics or been firmly grasped by any church or sect. To such sanguine spirits the New Revival might naturally seem to promise great things. It might spiritualize the High Church, while systematizing the Low. The great stress laid by the Tractarians on rites, and on conformity to Antiquity, they might regard as a wholesome antidote against the prevalent excessive passion for Innovation, and as a means of re-connecting the national religion with the traditions of Christendom in its most vigorous and progressive days. The needs of human nature, they might say, however different in degree, are always the same in kind ; and such developments of Christianity as are proved by experience to have satisfied man's spiritual wants and to have tended towards righteousness, are not lightly to be laid aside, or, if for a time, at least only for such a period as may suffice to purify and reintroduce them in their purer shape. Some might reject both a Book and a Church as the highest Authority, and might assert that they could accept, in that capacity, nothing but a Spirit. Yet even these might admit that, for the masses of mankind, the Spirit must work through the Church as well as through the Book, and might hope that, in the New Anglicanism, they would find not a Dry Church, nor a Narrow Church, but a Church instinct with divine life and applying itself to all human needs. Such, at all events, appears to have been (early in 1836), the dream, alas, the vain dream, of a singularly able man, whose intimate conversation with Newman on this subject is detailed in one of the most interesting of the Letters.

It is addressed to Froude in the month before his death (January 1836), and describes a *tête à tête*

dinner with James, (afterwards Sir James) Stephen, the
Professor of Modern History at the University of
Cambridge, whose Ecclesiastical Biographies (to speak
of but one of his works) whoever begins, will finish, and
whoever finishes, will not forget.   Speaking his mind
with the most cordial frankness, Newman's host
did not hesitate to criticize very freely.   " He did not
like my *Arians*," says Newman.   It appeared to him to
"jump" about from one subject to another, and to be
" hastily written, though thought out carefully."   As to
Newman's two volumes of sermons he looked on them as
"a condescension," since every one wrote sermons ;
but important, as showing that the Tractarians had
something in them " which would be of essential service
in the present state of philosophy and religion."   Then
follow some words which show how, in his dread of the
pestilential Gospel of railways and commerce, this
thoughtful historian—skilled in history but quite un-
skilled in deciphering the subtle, many-sided, shifting,
imaginative nature which was to count for so very
much in making up the history of this particular
movement—was led to hope for an antidote in the
New Anglicanism :—

" He seemed to treat with utter scorn the notion that we were
favouring Popery.   This age of Mammon and this shrewd-minded
nation were in no danger of it.   The sermons had struck upon a
new vein ; it would be a great benefit done to the country if Quietism
could be shown to be consistent with good sense and activity.
Quietists and Mystics were commonly weak and eccentric ; if repose
and good sense could be married together, a service would be done
to the age.   Again, the philosophy of ' little things ' was a most
important ground.   Further, the most subtle enemy which Christianity
had ever had was Benthamism.   He had had a dream of attacking
it in his latter years himself.   He saw *every one* infected with it.
Now he thought our views had in them that which could grapple

with it ; and he wanted me to throw myself out of active business and think and write : that was my function : the more I wrote the better.

" He wanted from me a new philosophy. He wanted Christianity developed to meet the age—he thought that the Gospel had a kingly sway, and of right might appropriate all truth everywhere, new and old.

"There was much truth in Benthamism; that was its danger. Legislation and political economy were new sciences ; they involved *facts ;* Christianity might claim and rule them, but it could not annihilate them. What he feared was the religious men of the day opposing them *en masse.* There must be an eclectic process, &c."

It is somewhat painful to think what different notions —notions diametrically opposed—might be conveyed to the two interlocutors by the same phrases, "developed," "appropriate all truth," "ruling facts," &c. : so much might depend on their notions of "truth," and "facts," and on their greater or less reverence for them. However, this extract suffices to explain the impression under which even an able man of mature mind might at this time have looked hopefully on the Tractarian revival. Yet the last words, "eclectic process," show, in a flash, how fundamentally the two might differ. The theologian's "eclecticism," if it can be described as such, in borrowing from the Anglican divines and the Fathers, is hardly that which was contemplated by the historian.

They talked also of " the Church, sacraments, doctrines, &c. "; and Newman at first suspected that his host regarded these rather as "symbols of philosophy than as *truths*"; but he was undeceived on a further conversation. Mr. Stephen was perplexed, he says ; wished for an infallible guide ; made the most impressive remarks on life not being long enough for controversy ; and said "he would be a Papist if he could." Here again, perhaps, a great, though not clearly perceptible, gulf, divides two meanings of the same phrase. " I would be a Papist if I could," in Newman's mouth might mean, "if I could get over the notion that the Pope is connected with Antichrist"; or, "if the Roman Church did not insist on this or that as an essential part of faith or practice, &c." But, in other men, it might mean " If I could make up my mind to believe as to facts, that what is comfortable is also true," or "if I had strength of will sufficient to stifle the protests of conscience." We are perhaps on firmer ground when we read that Mr. Stephen did not "clearly take in" Newman's meaning, when the latter brought forward "the argument of Tradition." If it was the same argument that he brought forward against Froude, it is easy to understand that it might not be "clearly taken in" by so able, judicious, and learned a historian as the author of the *Lectures on the History of France*, and *Ecclesiastical Biographies*. In his concluding inference from this interesting conversation, Newman once more lets drop one of those ominous tokens of impending failure, which neither Bunsen nor Stephen could have anticipated. A prophet was needed; and the man in the prophet's place—though he knew spells by which he could fascinate the minds of many—did not feel himself to be a prophet, and sometimes felt himself to be less than even a mere teacher who had thought things out for himself:

" Go where I will, ' the fields are ready for harvest,' and none to reap them. If I might choose my place in the Church, I would (as far as I can see) be Master of the Temple. I am sure from what little I have seen of the young lawyers, I could do something with them. You and Keble are the philosophers, and I the rhetorician."

Newman is always a little in excess both when he excuses and when he condemns himself. In excusing, he takes far too small a share of the blame, and casts far too much on some enemy or other, who should bear little or none; in condemning, he denies himself almost every virtue except such inferior ones as he considers hardly worthy of the name, in order to attribute excellence to some friends who may perhaps deserve a fraction of what he assigns them. But, so far, he was right, in thinking that he had in himself too much of the rhetorical ecclesiastic, and too little of the prophet, to enable him to achieve that great and noble task suggested to him in this interview, of aiding Christianity to "claim and rule and appropriate all truth everywhere." His rhetorical qualities made him far too careless about *all* truth of *fact;* his ecclesiastical inclinations and studies made him specially indifferent to all but a very narrow class of facts, in a very narrow range. The task, therefore, was out of his star. But how much he could influence a circle extending beyond that of the "lawyers," and how much more he was than a mere rhetorician, will appear in the next chapter, which will attempt to set before the reader Newman in the pulpit.

APPENDIX

ON p. 168 above it has been shown that Froude protested against Keble's anti-transubstantiationist language in the *Christian Year*, and that Newman though he at first (anonymously) used Froude's language, afterwards appeared to recede publicly to a safer position.

Ultimately Froude gained the victory over Keble and Newman combined. For many years, it is true, the Author of the *Christian Year* resisted any alteration. But he resisted it on the extraordinary ground that the words " in the heart, *not* in the hands " might mean (in analogy with one or two passages in Scripture) " in the heart (*and*) not (*only*) in the hands," *i.e.*, " in the heart *as well as* in the hands;" and he declared that he himself *set this meaning on the words*. We may be still permitted to doubt whether he *originally* meant this ; and whether he did not by degrees persuade himself, first (though few English scholars would share the belief) that the words *might* naturally have this meaning, and afterwards, that he *had always interpreted* them in this and no other way.

Froude, at all events on 25 February, 1835, had never heard of this far-fetched interpretation of Keble's.

For on that date, eight years after the appearance of the *Christian Year*, he again expostulates with the author : " How can we possibly know that it is true to say, 'not in the hands' ? How can we say that it is not so ? " The argument deserved to prevail ; for it is characteristic of the whole of the Tractarian Movement. Indeed, it was used by Newman nearly thirty years afterwards, in the *Apologia*, about this same subject : " I say, Why should it not be ? Who's to hinder it ? What do I know of substance or matter ? " It was therefore in accordance with the fitness of things that Keble inclined by degrees to alter the censured passage ; and, in spite of the remonstrances of others, he not only altered it but connected the alteration with his " dear friend Hurrell Froude," whose *Remains*, he said, showed that " complaints were made of it thirty years ago." The passage now runs as follows :—

> " There present in the heart
>   *As in the hands*, th' eternal Priest
> Will his true self impart."

Thus does the spirit of Hurrell Froude still breathe in the pages of the *Christian Year*, influencing, and perhaps destined for many years to influence, the belief, and practice, of multitudes in the Anglican Church.

NOTES

NOTES TO THE FIRST VOLUME

THE following abbreviations are used :—A. = *Apologia* (Newman's) ;
C. = Church's *Oxford Movement;* E. T. M. = Mr. E. T. Mozley's
Reminiscences; Eluc. = Newman's *Elucidations of Hampden's Bampton Lectures;* Exp. = *Expositor* (Papers in, by Mr. A. W. Hutton) ;
F. = Mr. Fletcher's *Cardinal Newman;* F. W. N. = Professor F. W.
Newman's *Early Life of Cardinal Newman;* H. = Hare's (Julius Charles)
Charges; H. B. L. = Hampden's Bampton Lectures[1]; J. M. = James
Mozley's *Letters;* K. = *Keble, Life of,* by Right Hon. Sir J. T. Coleridge ;
L. = *Letters* (Newman's); O. = Mr. Oldcastle's *Cardinal Newman;*
P. = *Poems* (Newman's) ; Phil. = "*Philomythus*," by the author ; R. =
Remains of R. H. Froude, vol. i.; R. H. H. = Mr. R. H. Hutton's
Cardinal Newman; S. = *Sermons* (Newman's) *Plain and Parochial* (in
the first three vols. the earliest edition has been used) ; Subj. = *Sermons*
(Newman's) *on Subjects of the Day;* T. = Thirlwall's (Bishop) *Charges;*
U. = *University Sermons* (Newman's); V. = *Via Media* (Newman's) ;
W. = *Ward, Life of,* by Mr. Wilfrid Ward ; Wh. = *Whately, Life of,*
by Miss Whately ; W. M. = Mr. Wilfrid Meynell's *Cardinal Newman.*

Arabic numerals indicate the page; Roman, the volume. But in
reference to the *Plain and Parochial Sermons,* the first Arabic numeral
indicates the number of the sermon, and the second, the number of the
page. Passages from the *first three* volumes of these sermons are
quoted from the *first* edition ; but the *number* of the sermon will enable
the possessor of the later editions to verify without much difficulty.

Where the date of a letter is given in the text, the reference to the page
of Newman's Letters is sometimes omitted in the Notes, as the letters are
almost all in chronological order.

The letters a, b, c, &c. after the number of a page in the text, refer to
the first, second, third, &c. paragraphs in the text. Thus, " 124 (c),
S. ii. 12, 143," would mean that in the third paragraph of page 124, there
is a reference to the *Sermons* (*Plain and Parochial*), vol. ii., number 12,
page (1st ed.) 143.

[1] I. W. = Isaac Williams's *Autobiography* (1892), which has been used in re-
vising the Notes : he was, for some years, Newman's curate, and on affectionate
terms with him till his death in 1865.

v. (b)* " Roman Church." Since these words were printed, there has been published the *Autobiography of Isaac Williams*, once Newman's curate, which contains the following illustrative passage (I. W. 118-9) : " Nor has anything occasioned more defections to the Church of Rome than that many persons adopted opinions and principles which Newman latterly put forth, while he appeared to be with us, which necessarily led to the Roman Church ; and which he held as holding with the Church of Rome, without sufficiently considering what those principles were, and to what they led."

viii (a) F. W. N. Pref. v. ; ix. (a) U. 236 ; ix. (b) A. 147 ; ix. (b)* " In his (Newman's) *Essay on Ecclesiastical Miracles*," says Mr. Gore, in his Bampton Lectures (p. 56), "the *a priori* faculty, the 'illative sense,' is allowed almost to run riot, and destroy the distinction between a fact and an idea, between what is historical and what is supposed to be appropriate." Such a protest is all the more valuable because of its cool and dispassionate judgment on that state of mind which " destroys the distinction between a fact and an idea." In a note Mr. Gore adds, " My lecture was written, and perhaps preached, before the appearance of Dr. Abbott's *Philomythus*, with the tone and spirit of which one cannot but disclaim sympathy."

Yet is it not odd, too, how very hot we can become when a thief "destroys the distinction" between the "fact," i.e. *meum*, and the " idea," i.e. *suum* ? and how good-tempered we can be when a theologian merely "destroys the distinction" between the "fact," *i.e.* God's truth, and the " idea," *i.e.* man's lie, or, at the best, man's legend ? The theologian may be, of course, unconscious that he is largely influenced by the desire to defend a party, or make himself "comfortable" : still, surely, his unconsciousness does not entitle him to complete acquittal.

CHAPTER I (1801–16)

2 (a) "at the age of eleven," so L. i. 19, but F. W. N. 3, says "under the age of ten" ; 2 (a) A. 2 ; 4 (a) P. 201 ; 4 (b) P. 155 ; 5 (a) F. W. N. 6 ; 5 (c) F. W. N. 9 ; 6 (a) L. i. 55, A. 3 ; 7 (a) L. i. 14, quoting *Gr. of Assent*, 112 : 7 (d) L. i. 18, F. W. N. 3, L. i. 26 ; 8 (a) L. i. 320 ; 8 (b) F. W. N. 4 ; 9 (a) F. W. N. 3 ; 10 (a) "prayers," L. ii. 482, "souls " * : " I am sure," he writes in 1876 (O. 61, 62), concerning the death of Ambrose St. John, his companion for more than thirty years, "that the bereavement is one of those divine providences necessary for my attaining the Heavenly Rest, which he, through God's mercy, has already secured."

10 (b) L. i. 20 ; 10 (c) A. 4 ; 11 (b) L. i. 123, 22, 32 ; 12 (b) L. i. 25 ; 12 (d) L. i. 50 ; 13 (a) L. i. 22-3 ; 13 (c) L. i. 25, i. 416, ii. 441 ; 14 (b) A. 4 ; 15 (a) A. 5 ; 16 (a) A. 2 ; 16 (b) L. i. 10 ; 18 (a) A. 6 ; 19 (a) A. 7 ; 20 (a) L. ii. 472-3, A. 7.

CHAPTER II (1817-24)

22 (b)* L. i. 37. It must be remembered that, at this time, participation in the Holy Communion was compulsory upon the Oxford undergraduates ; 23 (b) L. i. 42, L. i. 62 ; 24 (c) "No ground for blaming any one." Newman was afterwards rather more sensitive than might have been expected about his failure, and enters into details. When he had to translate the Latin "proprium" in Virgil, he bethought himself (so he tells us) that Shakespeare uses the word "proper" to signify "his own"; and accordingly he so rendered the Latin. The Examiners treated it as ignorance, and Newman thus gently complains (L. i. 39) : "Though the examiners were conscientiously fair and considerate in their decisions they would understand a candidate better, and follow his lead and line of thought more sympathetically, if they understood his position of mind and intellectual habits than if these were new to them."

This is interesting, not only as a token of sensitiveness, but also because he does not appear to have recognized that "mixing of styles" in this way, even in a youth, denoted affectation, and deserved castigation from examiners. If the *whole passage* had been rendered in Shakespearian language, the examiners could not have misunderstood it ; but they ought hardly to be blamed (even so mildly) for failing to perceive that the error was not one of ignorance, but of bad taste.

Comp. L. i. 416, ii. 441, where it will be found that he recognized the danger of his own excessive versatility, which he calls "rhetorical or histrionic power"; and comp. L. i. 25, "I wrote in style as another might write in verse"; 25 (a) L. i. 46 ; 25 (b) L. i. 68 ; 26 (c) L. i. 68 ; 27 (c) L. ii. 196 ; 28 (a) L. ii. 197 ; 28 (b) L. i. 58 (he came of age 21 Feb. 1822), L. i. 69 ; 29 (a) L. i. 59 ; 32 (a) L. i. 104; 35 (b) L, i. 80; 39 (b) E. T. M. i. 13, 178 ; 37 (a) Exp. Sept. 1890, 224, 227-8 ; 38 (b) L. i. 116-7 ; 39 (a) L. i. 98 ; 41 (a) L. i. 83 ; 41 (b) L. i. 119, 89.

CHAPTER III (1800-24)

46 (b) C. 9 ; 53 (a)* a friend has kindly sent me the following communication from one who had experience of this custom : "I remember our going together to an early celebration at St. Mary's. The celebration was in the Chancel ; there has been no altar outside the screen since the Reformation. The Chancel is arranged like a College Chapel, and the clergy certainly came round and administered to us in our places. The gigantic almsdish with a large red stone in the middle I think was used —a dish about as large as an ordinary teatray. I know nothing about the custom, but it is most probable that Holy Communion was administered in the same way in the College Chapels before the Tractarian time, but I should think not in other churches. Probably it has been continued at St. Mary's at all extra-parochial services since the sixteenth century, and I expect Newman did not suspend it"; 60 (b) E. T. M. i.

13, the exact words are "some novelties, not to say surprises, for his oldest friends."

CHAPTER IV (1824-7)

67 (b) L. i. 156, L. i. 275 ; 69 (b) L. i. 122 ; 70 (b) A. 8-9, L. i. 120 ; 71 (a) A. 10 ; 72 (a) L. i. 120, (13 Jan. 1825) ; 73 (a) A. 25, F. W. N. 18, P. 34 ; 73 (b) F. W. N. 21 ; 74 (b) L. i. 126 ; 76 (a) Phil. 77 ; 78 (a) L. i. 98 ; 79 (a) L. i. 101 ; 80 (b) L. i. 102, 124 ; 81 (a) L. i. 130 ; 81 (b) L. i. 150 ; 82 (a) R. 59 ; 83 (b) L. i. 132 ; 84 (b) L. 134 ; 84 (c) F. W. N. 24 ; 85 (b) L. i. 140 ; 86 (a) P. 19 ; 86 (c) L. i. 140 ; 87 (b) F. W. N. 47 ; 89 (a) L. i. 142-3 ; 90 (b) L. i. 128 ; 91 (b) L. i. 144-5 ; 92 (a) L. i. 162 ; 93 (b) P. 23 ; 94 (c) L. i. 170.

CHAPTER V (1824-6)

98 (a) L. i. 89 ; 99 (a) S. vii. 1. 1 ; 100 (a) S. i. 2. 19 ; 101 (b) S. vii. 5. 71 ; 101 (c) vii. 5. 72, i. 25. 383 ; 102 (a) S. vii. 5. 73 ; 102 (c) ib. 72 ; 103 (b*) "notice." It is placed by N. in the year 1824 ; but he adds, "or, possibly, 1825." That it was 1825 is proved by the facts :—(1) that he was not ordained till June 1824 ; (2) that by August he had been visiting the sick man for "*some months past.*"

104 (a) S. i. 4. 55 ; 105 (a) ib. 61 ; 105 (a) † 1st ed. reads "to" for "before" 105 (b) U. 13 ; 106 (b) S. viii. 8. 113, 120 ; 108 (a) S. i. 1. 8 ; 108 (c) S. i. 1. 11 ; 109 (b)*. Sinners, for example, are warned by the insertion (p. 13) that "their doom may be fixed at any moment." And, whereas the first edition says, " I do not speak to you as aliens from God's mercies but as partakers of His gracious Covenant in Christ," the later adds, "and for this reason in especial peril." This last thought—of the "especial peril" for Christians as compared with the heathen, is very common in the later sermons.

CHAPTER VI (1828)

111 (a) L. ii. 197 ; 113 (a) * "initials": Comp. I. W. 70-1, " Pusey at this time was not one of us, and I have some recollection of a conversation which was the occasion of his joining us. He said, smiling, to Newman and wrapping his gown around him, as he used to do, ' I think you are too hard upon 'the Peculiars' as you call them (*i.e.* the Low Church party) ; you should conciliate them. I am thinking of writing a letter myself with that purpose,' or rather I think it was of printing a letter which had been the result of private correspondence. ' Well,' said Newman, ' suppose you let us have it for one of the Tracts.' ' Oh no,' said Pusey, ' I will not be one of you.' This was said in a playful manner ; and before we parted, Newman said, ' Suppose you let us have that letter of yours, which you intend writing, and attach your own name or signature

to it? You would not then be mixed up with us, or be in any way responsible for the Tracts.' 'Well,' Pusey said, at last, 'if you will let me do that, I will.'" This is interesting as showing that Pusey's goodness was not combined with insight : for, the passage continues, "that conciliating Tract on Baptism seemed to aggravate them, *i.e.* the Low Church party, more than the rest."

113 (b) L. ii. 211 ; 114 (a) L. ii. 298-9, 365, 381 ; 116 (b) A. 224 ; 117 (b) Dr. Martineau's *Essays*, i. 229, A. 224 ; 118 (b) J. M. 65, and comp. ib. 95 ; 119 (a) L. i. 229 ; 119 (b) L. ii. 344, A. 171, W. 353 ; 121 (a) L. i. 75, A. 17 ; 121 (b) A. 18 ; 125 (a) F. W. N. 81 ; 125 (b) A. 18, 19 ; 126 A. 18 ; 127 (a) L. ii. 43 ; 131 (c) K. 65 ; 133 (a) K. 282, 319 ; 134 (b) "well-nigh broken." Isaac Williams testifies to N.'s influence on Keble (I. W. 115-8) ; " In Keble's judgment and steadfastness I always had the greatest confidence ; but as every one has his weak side, so his is that, from his love and partiality to his friends, especially if they are at all persecuted, he has been apt to be so taken with their opinions, that from his humility he will often apparently adopt them for his own." Then, after mentioning Keble's statement of an intention to alter the *Christian Year*, so as to conform it to his new views, he adds, " It was only that, when Newman and others were in their transition state, and before they left, John Keble, for love's sake, held with them ; and I wished always to show that it was himself, his own former self, that was to be trusted, and that these notions did not belong to him. And as soon as they had left us it was otherwise. ' *Now that* '"—I italicize—"' *I have thrown off Newman's yoke*,'" said he (i.e. Keble) *one day to me*, "' *these things appear to me quite different*.' " 135 (a) K. 364, 403.

CHAPTER VII (1803-36)

136-8, A. 23-5 ; 138-40, R. 1-4 ; 142 (a) R. 99 ; 142 (c) R. 209 ; 143 (b) R. 433, 92 ; 146 (c) R. 396 ; 147 (b) L. ii. 242 ; 148 (c) R. 209 ; 149 (a) R. 322, 76 (written in 1826), 85 ; 149 (b) J. M. 103 ; 150 (b) R. 452, 450, 40, 41 ; 152 (b) R. 254, 321, 322 ; 153 (a) R. 364 ; 153 (b) * " the —— Tracts," *i.e.* "the Oxford Tracts" as Froude elsewhere calls them, *e.g.* L. ii. 159 : but, at that time, the Editors shrank from publishing the fact that, among themselves, the Tractarians habitually identified the *Tracts for the Times* with " Oxford."

That Newman calculated on the advantage to be derived from the connecting his views with " Oxford", is shown by L. i. 483 (to Bowden, 17 Nov.) : " Whenever you talk of the tracts, mind and persist they are not connected with the Association, but the production of ' Residents in Oxford.' I wish them called the 'Oxford Tracts,' but I cannot myself so call them for modesty's sake. So I think that soon I shall advertise them as ' Tracts for the Times by Residents in Oxford,' which '"—I italicize—" *of course, will soon be corrupted into Oxford Tracts.*"

On the preceding page (13 Nov.) he mentions the names of the most prominent supporters and authors of the Tracts : many of them, *e.g.* Keble, T. Keble, and Rickards, were *not* " Residents in Oxford."

154 (b) A. 123; 145 (a) † R. 425; 155 (b) † L. ii. 141.

CHAPTER VIII (1803-36)

158 (b) R. 236 ; 160, § 35, *" led Newman on,"* see I. W. 49 ; " Newman had a peculiar power of seizing intellectually the ἦθος and principles of another, and making them his own, as it were on trial. I was struck with this afterwards in a remarkable manner by the way in which he learned through me the γνῶμαι, as he called them, of Thomas Keble, of Bisley, his character and principles ; so that, at one time, when I walked daily with him, and we conversed on these subjects, I found the same views drawn out and expressed in his own way in his sermon at St. Mary's on the following Sunday."

160 (a) R. 308 ; 160 (c) R. 312 ; 160 (d) L. i. 458 ; 160 (f) R. 322 ; 161 (a).† This letter is printed in Newman's Letters, i. 444, with the bracketed words omitted, but with no marks denoting omission ; and " effectually " is substituted for " effectively." In the *Remains* it is dated 31 Aug.—a probable error, as another letter from Froude to Newman follows, and is also dated "August."

161 (c) R. 323 ; 162 (b) R. 335 ; 162 (c).* Here the Editors add a footnote ; " *i.e.* as necessary to salvation, Church communion, as fundamental, as the one standard of doctrine," etc. Parts of this letter occur in Letters, i. 484, with at least one omission (if the letter is correctly printed in the *Remains*) not indicated by any marks of omission.

163 (c) * R. 347. The Editors append the following footnote :—" (If they had had the *whole body* of the English Church in agreement with them. The sort and amount of alteration which the writer probably contemplated may be seen in *Tracts for the Times, Via Media*)."

163 (d) R. 413 ; 163 (f) U. 348 ; 164 (a) V. ii. 371 ; 164 (d) R. 363 ; 164 (f) R. 336 ; 165 (b) 389 ; 166 (b) R. 337, 372 ; 167 (a) R. 371 ; 168 (c) R. 326, L. ii. 31 ; 169 (a) L. ii. 174 ; 170 (a) P. 195-6 ; 171 (a) L. ii. 106 ; 172 (c) K. 241 ; 173 (a) R. 244 ; 174 (a) R. 400-1 ; 174 (c) R. 382 ; 174 (e)* " negroes." The Editors evidently regard this as an exceptional Christian condescension on the part of Froude. They seem to have forgotten what Froude told them, a few pages before (R. 335), that, at the Communion, " two hundred people were present," and " all classes were mixed indiscriminately."

177 (b) L. ii. 177.

CHAPTER IX (1828-9)

178 (a) A. 14 ; 179 (b) L. i. 181 ; 180 (a) L. i. 184 ; 181 (a) L. i. 182 ; 184 (a) R. 230 ; 185 (b) P. 33-7 ; 186 (c) L. i. 199 ; 187 (a) A. 7 ; 188 (a) L. i. 200 ; 189-190 (b) L. i. 204 ; 190 (b) A. 15, L. 205-6 ; 192 (a) * E. T. M. i. 178. Buckland was not a Cambridge man. But the story is told by

E. T. M. in connection with the general disgust felt by Keble and some of his friends at the attitude of men of science toward Revelation, and he mentions, in particular, the " disgust at Cambridge ' savans.'"

193 (a) R. 244.

CHAPTER X (1829-30)

195 (a) S. vii. 3. 29 ; 196 (a) P. 40, 42 ; 197 (b) E. T. M. i. 175, L. i. 220 †. N., in his revision of the Letter, substitutes "trust" for "faith," because, when in the Church of Rome, he preferred to reserve the latter word for what he believed to be its theological sense, *i.e.* "faith" in *dogma.*

197 (b) A. 174 ; 199 (a) L. i. 215 ; 200 (b) V. ii. 1, 9 ; 201 (b) L. i. 226 ; 201 (b)* " really mean." Quoted by F. W. N. (29) as uttered by Rickards to him : " He therefore took on himself to deny it right and left, ' because,' said he, ' to speak plainly, it was unworthy of him and really *mean ;* and now comes on me the mortification of having to go round and tell people that after all they were right, and it is your brother's."

203 (b) E. T. M. i. 176 ; 206 (c) L. i. 229 ; 207 (b) L. i. 234 ; 208 (a) L. i. 230 ; 209 (a) S. iii. 6. 86 ; 210 (a) S. vii. 7. 91 (28 March, 1830) and U. (13 April) 25-6 ; 211 (a) S. ii. 22, 298-9 ; 212 (b) * " Fatherhood " : there are indications, here and there, that Newman, especially in 1845, felt strong inclinations to scepticism, and that one great reason why he tried to constrain himself to believe *so much,* was that he felt that the alternative was to believe *nothing :* comp. I. W. 70 : " A little while before Henry [Wilberforce] joined the Church of Rome, Newman said to him, ' My temptation is to Scepticism,' a very remarkable confession, which the Bishop [of Oxford, Samuel Wilberforce] mentioned to me.'" Comp. A. 229.

CHAPTER XI (1831-2)

215 (a) * " mission." See A. 235, where stress is laid on the fact that the Father Dominic (who was to receive N. into the Roman Church) had had "thirty years' (almost) waiting." Such importance did N. attach to sacred numbers that, even when his convictions were clear that the Church of Rome was the true Church, he still wished to defer joining it for sixteen or seventeen months (A. 232) "which would be a full *seven years*" [the italics are mine] " from the time that my convictions first began to fall upon me."

216 (a) S. ii. 10. 127 ; 217 (a) U. 42 ; 218 (a) L. i. 237 ; 218 (b) L. i. 238 ; 219 (b) P. 61 ; 220 (a) S. i. 25. 383 ; 220 (b) L. ii. 83 ; 221 (a) L. i. 245 ; U. 350-1 ; 224 (a) L. i. 108, 249-50 ; 226 (b) L. i. 449 ; 228 (a) L. i. 250 (16 Oct. 1831) ; 229 (a) S. i. 10. 157 (9 Oct. 1831), S. i. 12. 183 (6 Nov.) ; 229 (b) U. 72 (11 Dec.) ; 230 (a) S. iii. 8. 111 (4 Dec.) ; 231 (a) * " immediate results," I. W. 54, " I can remember a strong feeling of difference I first felt in acting together with Newman, from what I had been accus-

tomed to ; that he was in the habit of looking for effect, which from the Bisley and Fairford School," *i.e.* the two Kebles, "I had been long habituated to avoid." At the same time, I. W. appears to have gone into the other extreme, and to have neglected the teaching of experience. Newman oscillated between the two extremes.

231 (a) S. ii. 32. 448-9 (30 Nov.); 233 (a) U. 83 (22 Jan. 1832), so in ed. of 1872, the text is somewhat different in ed. of 1843 ; 234-235 (a) U. 83-97 ; 235 (c) S. ii. 12. 147-8 (25 March, 1832) ; 236 (a) *ib.* 151.

CHAPTER XII (1832)

237 (a) L. i. 256 ; 239 (a) U. 111 (8 April, 1832) ; 240 (a) S. i. 21. 316-7 (22 April) ; 242 (b) i. 24. 363 (26 Aug. 1832) ; 243 (b) *ib.* 365 ; 245 (b) S. i. 7. 85 (16 Oct.) ; 245 (c) † S.' i. 7. 110. In later editions, the last words are "and can but timidly hope, not confidently determine, that we have true faith."

246 (a) *Coriolanus*, iii. 3. 73 ; 246 (b) U. 150 ; 247 (a) U. 151-2 ; 248-249 (a) U. 173, 174-5 (2 Dec. 1832) ; 250 (a) L. i. 282 ; 251 (b) * " mind." Isaac Williams, who was at this time N.'s curate, records the following impression of him (101) : " I had a secret uneasiness, not from anything said or implied, but from a want of repose about his character, that I thought he would start into some line different from Keble and Pusey though I knew not in what direction it would be. Often after walking together, when leaving him, have I heard a deep secret sigh which I could not interpret. It seemed to speak of weariness of the world and of aspirations for something he wished to do and had not yet done. . . . Repose and relaxation " [in social gatherings with a few intimate friends] " seemed to me to bring out the higher and better parts of Newman's character. I allow that something sarcastic and a freedom of remark would blend with such unbendings, but it was better out in playfulness than fermenting within."

CHAPTER XIII (DEC. 1832-JULY 1833)

253 (a) L. i. 302-3 ; 254 (a) L. i. 297 ; 255 (a) L. i. 318 ; 256 (a) P. 108 ; 257 (a) A. 15 ; 258 (a) L. 320-1 ; 259 (a) P. 62 ; 259 (b) P. 98 ; 261 (a) P. 123 ; 262 (a) P. 109 ; 263 (a) P. 129 ; 263 (c) L. i. 303 ; 264 (b) R. 293 ; 265 (a) L. i. 353 ; 265 (c) L. i. 354 ; 266 (b) L. i. 359 ; 267 (b) L. i. 361 ; 268 (a) L. i. 359 ; 268 (b) L. i. 355, 363 ; 270 (b) L. i. 338 (27 Jan.) ; 271 (a) L. i. 353 (28 Feb.), L. i. 375 ; 271 (c) L. i. 370 ; 272 (b) A. 33 ; 272 (b)—273 (a) R. 206 ; 275 (a) L. i. 385 ; 275 (c) L. i. 383 ; 276 (a) L. i. 384 ; 276 (c) L. i. 387 ; 279 (a) L. 383 ; 279 (b) L. i. 397 ; 280 (a)

A. 34 ; 280 (b) L. i. 412 ; 282 (a) L. i. 379, P. 132 ; 282 (c) L. 416 ;
284 (b) A. 53-4 ; 285 (b) P. 153-4 ; 286 (b) P. 192 ; 290 (a) P. 186 ; 292
(a) Wordsworth's *Prelude*, book ix.

CHAPTER XIV (1833)

293 (a) A. 35, 75, 93 ; 294 (a) L. i. 449 ; 294 (b) L. i. 433, 451 ; 294 (b)*
" shock people " : comp. I. W.'s account (p. 63) of his conversation with
Froude (1833) who said to him, " Isaac, we must make a row in the
world. Why should we not ? Only consider what the Peculiars have
done with a few half truths to work upon ! And, with our principles, if
we set resolutely to work, we can do the same " ; and he continued,
" Church principles, forced on people's notice, must do good. However,
we must try : and Newman and I are determined to set to work as soon
as he returns. We must have short tracts, and letters in the *British
Magazine* and verses . . . and get people to preach sermons on the
Apostolical Succession and the like." The reader will note that this
conversation took place before Newman's return to England from Sicily,
i.e. before 9 July, 1833.

296 (b) A. 47, Exp. (1890) p. 305, E. T. M. i. 315.* This passage must
not be interpreted to mean that Newman was " hopeful " about the good in
others, any more than he was hopeful about the good in himself. It
means that, in the aggressive period of 1833-6, Newman was " hopeful "
to excess, not only about the ultimate success of the Tractarian party,
but also about the aid that might be given by each ally who was fighting
for it. " At the time now under consideration " (*ib.*), " Newman seemed
to have *had hope of everybody*." And again (*ib.* i. 39), " It was scarcely
possible to be even a quarter of an hour in his company without a man
feeling himself to be invited to an onward step sufficient to tax his energy
or his faith." Then, it would seem, when his friends' " energy " or "faith "
disappointed him by failing, he did not readily forgive them.

297 (a) * " Keble." I wrote thus, because N. speaks sympathetically
of Pusey's attachment, and does not *censure* Keble's marriage : and I
feared to be thought hypercritical if I called attention to the dry tone of
the following (L. ii. 140, letter to Froude) : " Keble was married on the
10th and told no one. ' The College ' [the Provost] has but heard from
him that he *resigns his fellowship* on that day without a year of grace."
But I. W. (107) declares that N. was much annoyed at it. The whole
passage is worth quoting. He describes N.'s feelings when he met the
Bishop of Gloucester at a confirmation at Bisley (Thomas Keble's
parsonage) : " He expressed to me his disgust at so luxurious a dinner
prepared for a bishop. It would be better at such a time, he said, that
a bishop should only ask for a little dry bread and salt and water. These
things, and the great annoyance he always felt at John Keble's marriage,
indicated feelings not at all in unison with the established state of things
in the Church of England."

297 (a)* L. ii. 20. "Neander," a Greek name meaning "new-man," was playfully used by Wilberforce as a nick-name.

297 (b)—298 (a) F. W. N. 113 ; 298 (b) A. 47 ; 301 (b) J. M. 47 ; 302 (a) A. 47 ; 303 (b) A. 11, 380 ; 304 (b) L. i. 449 ; 304 (d) Wh. i. 482-3, ib. 24 ; 305 (b) L. i. 142 ; 306 (a)* . . . "the Editor had never read." The reasons for this conclusion are as follows :—(1) The Editor quotes only two of the four letters ; (2) they are the least interesting ; (3) the reference given is not to the *Apologia*, but to Whately's *Life;* (4) Newman's letter, as given in the Letters, differs (though not to any important extent) from the text in the *Apologia.*

306 (c) A. 381 ; 308 (a).* This bias of memory may explain a rather curious inaccuracy in the *Apologia* (236). "I left Oxford for good," he says, "on Monday, 23rd Feb., 1846. On the Saturday and Monday before, I was in my house at Littlemore, simply by myself, as I had been for the first day or two when I had originally taken possession of it." This brings before us a scene of picturesque and touching loneliness. A painter might well choose it for his subject. And on such a point it might have been supposed that Newman's memory could not possibly deceive him. But compare Meynell's *Cardinal Newman* (48) :—"In the *Apologia,* written nearly twenty years later, the Cardinal speaks of spending the last two days at Littlemore 'simply by myself'—a slip of memory. Father Bowles was there till the end ; and into his room Newman came each evening, and fell asleep in his chair, worn out with the day's packing."

308 (b) L. ii. 266 ; 309 (a)*. While acknowledging the receipt of a pamphlet of Hampden's which he had just received, N. (A, 57) calls its "appearance" "the *first step*" "towards interrupting" "peace" and "good understanding" in Oxford : which seems to imply that this was the *beginning* of the "provocation." There had been a previous edition of this pamphlet ; but it appears to have been its republication, at a critical time, which constituted the provocation.

CHAPTER XV (1833)

313 (a) E. T. M. i. 407 ; 314 (b) A. 40 ; 315 (b) A. 72, 166, 101 ; 316 (a) A. 70, 43 ; 316 (b) *S. on Various Occasions,* 127-8 ; 320 (b) V. i. Dedication, ib. 5 ; 321 (b) V. ii. 40, 22 ; 322 (a) V. ii. 16, 22 ; 322 (a)* "vague and general notion." Here a critic, to whose frank censorship of my proofs I am very greatly indebted, raises the following objection, "But surely, the date 1834 is the date given in the *Apologia* (quoted p. 329) as the year in which he *had* read 'Laud, Bramhall, Stillingfleet, and other Anglican divines.' So that he *had* done a good deal of sifting." To this I reply : (1) the words are, "In 1834 and the *following years*" ; (2) the

passage in the V. i. was written on or before 25 July, 1834; (3) he did not read (L. ii. 74) " Laud, Stillingfleet, &c." till the autumn of that year when he fell " into controversy with a Parisian Abbé "; if further evidence were needed, it might be shown that, in the Long Vacation, (3) he was editing Dionysius (L. ii. 49, 74) and (ib. 56-7) thinking about beginning German; after that, (4) he had been reading about the Anglican Convocation (ib. 61) and modern books (ib. 66) of an anti-Roman tendency. I therefore adhere to the statement that he committed himself to the Anglican Divines first, and read them afterwards.

322 (b) * V. i. 18, " understatement." He adds, " Now all this is very plausible, and is here in place, as far as this, that there certainly is a call upon us to exhibit our principles in action; and until, &c." Here " in place," seems to be N.'s way of saying " true "—if he applies his own sense to the words " doctrine," " principle," and " intellectual basis."

323 (a) V. i. 18, A. 69, 68; 324 (a) V. ii. 27; 324 (b) V. ii. 25, i. 19, " irrefragable."* The critic above mentioned urges that " Newman's prediction, "no party . . . Roman party," is proved true, every day, now; but the only proof N. could point to, as things had been so largely Evangelical and stagnant, was that the party he was trying to revive, had *had* an independent existence of Rome." But, because this was his " *only* proof," was he justified in calling it " *irrefragable*"? And did not the result show that, so far as *he* was concerned, he had no right to make so hasty a prediction? I leave it an open question whether the prediction will ultimately be found to be " true."

325 (b) V. ii. 30; 326 (a) V. ii. 31, † " this ought to be." It is not clear whether these remarks are intended to apply merely to *one* point in the Reformation, or to the whole. The mere letter of the context would indicate that they apply to *one*, viz., " An Article declaratory of the sanctity of places set apart to the worship of God." But this is so much *less* visionary, and more practicable, than other parts of the Reformation, that I incline to suppose the reference cannot be to this one part.

327 (b) L. i. 143; E. T. M. i. 180; 328 (a) A. 205; 329 (a) A. 43; 329 (b) A. 49.

CHAPTER XVI (1833)

332 (a) L. i. 440, " The Oxford Movement "*: see note on 153 (b) as to the private use, but public suppression, of the term " Oxford Tracts"; 332 (b) A. 76, 44, L. i. 439; 333 (b) L. i. 441; 334 (b) R. 319, L i. 439-40, R. 323. The *Letters*, under date 22 Aug. give (i. 444), " As to my preaching I have, on the whole, been successful. . . . . I have written a sermon on the duty of contemplating a time when the law of the land shall cease to be the law of the Church." But the same letter, *there*,

contains a passage about "colleges of unmarried priests" which in the *Remains* (almost verbatim) is assigned to *a different letter dated* 31 *Aug.* These circumstances throw uncertainty on the date of the letter quoted in the text ; in the *Remains* it is dated simply "Aug."

336-9, C. 99-103 ; 336 (a) †*. The version in *The Oxford Movement*, which I have followed, differs from the reprint in 1838 in one or two points : it inserts the address in capitals, "To . . . fellow-labourers," for which the ed. of 1838 substitutes the common-place "Thoughts on the Ministerial Commission respectfully addressed to the clergy" ; it also has the bold statement, "the bishop who ordained us gave us the Holy Ghost" ; for which, in 1838, is substituted, "through the Bishop who ordained us, we received the Holy Ghost."

340 (b) "some Prayer Books :" *e.g.* in two imprints of the Oxford University Press, dated 1849 and 1861 ; 341 (b) † "by prophecy," διὰ προφητείας.

342 (b)* "recognize it." To judge from *Froude's Remains* (339) Bishop Jewel took some such view as this, at least in some of his works ; but then, he was what Froude called " an irreverent Dissenter." It must not however be supposed that this view of Jewel was avowed by Newman or recognized by the Tracts.

343 (a) "heretical hands." Hence we find Froude, in 1834, regretting (R 385) that he did not receive his orders "from a Scotch Bishop" ; and one reason for this is that "the stream is purer." And hence, apparently, Newman's dread of the measures in 1841 which seemed to him to risk the "unchurching" of Anglicans by showing that the Bishops were heretical or were entering into communion with heretics.

343 (b) " Newman's."* I lay stress upon this, because his expressions in Tract 1 appear to materialize the theory to an extent not authorized (I should imagine) either by High Anglicanism or by Romanism.

CHAPTER XVII (1833-4)

355 (b) L. ii. 4 ; 357 (a) L. i. 478 ; 357 (b)—358 (a) C. 107-9 ; 339 (a) R. 337, L. ii. 66 (2 Oct. 1834) ; 360 (b) C. 105-6 ; 361 (a) R. 379 ; 361 (b) L. i. 485 ; 362-363, L. i. 490 (22 Nov. 1833) ; 364 (b) R. 336 (9 Jan. 1834), R. 339 (25 Jan.) ; 365 (a) S. v. 31. 307 ; 365 (b) L. ii. 47 (15 June, 1834) ; 366 (a)* "a notion of yours." Thomas Keble revived the Daily Service in Bisley (I. W. 75) in 1827, and Isaac Williams (ib. 76) describes it as one of the things he "imported from Bisley." Probably both he and Froude pressed it on N., but, for some time, ineffectually. The full sentence is (L. ii. 50), " It seems to me that the absurdity, as it appears to many, of Tom Keble's daily plan is, his praying to *empty benches*. Put yourself near the altar and you may be solitary. I see this agrees with a notion of yours" : so that " notion " refers not to the Daily Service

itself, but to the arrangement of it; 366 (b) "complains" (Aug. 1834), R. 363; 367 (a) R. 380, 385; "more and more." † This is from a letter in the *Remains* (388-90) dated 26 Dec. 1834. There is a letter from F. to N., of the same date, in the *Letters* (ii. 80-1). But not a word in the two is similar. Yet the letter is printed in the latter without anything to indicate that it is a mere (and very uninteresting) extract.

367 (a) R. 390-7.† There is nothing in common between the two versions dated "Jan." in the *Letters* (ii. 82) and in the *Remains* (390-7;) apparently each consists of different extracts from the same original. But, as the day of the month is not given, the two letters may be distinct.

R. 420 (25 Feb. 1835).

CHAPTER XVIII (1835)

370 (b) L. ii. 82, R. 390-7; 371 (a)* "doctrine." This view is confirmed by A. 192, where N., sketching (in 1841) the terms for union between the Anglican and Roman Churches, says that the former might "make some explanation of the doctrine of Transubstantiation." That is to say, the Church of England was to *accept* the doctrine of Transubstantiation, but *in a sense of its own.*

371 (b) A. 25; 372 (a) L. ii. 82; 372 (c). L. ii. 31 (24 March, 1834); 373 (a) L. ii. 41; 374 (b) L. ii. 107 (9 June, 1835); 375 (a) L. ii. 110 (22 June, 1835); 375 (c) R. 412 (2 July, 1835).* This is omitted in the extracts of the letter given in the *Letters* ii. 111. Marks of omission are, however, inserted. Yet the postscript is printed thus: " P.S. As to the laity having power in Synods, I don't know enough to have an opinion." This gives the reader the impression that there is no more. But the version in the *Remains* gives, " I don't know enough to have an opinion; but as far as I see," &c., and then follow ten lines about "Bishop Hicks," &c.

The omission of this passage in the *Letters* makes unintelligible a passage inserted by the Editor further on (p. 113), where Froude says, "As to your question about the laity in Convocation, I told you I had tried hard to think it admissible, but that Bishop Hicks . . . . has convinced me . . . ." &c.

375 (c)* "repugnant to Newton." To this the Editors append a footnote of a page and a half of small print. They do not seem to see that the Newtonian theory, though opposed to partial and superficial is confirmed by fuller, and more thorough, observation and experiment. And they quote with approval a statement of an imaginary disputant from the Romanist point of view, who says, " You tyrannically demand my unqualified assent to propositions entirely *opposed* to observation and experiment"! Froude, too, ignores the fact that, to make his analogy correct, he ought to show that the Church (like the Newtonian philosophy) can point to certain "observations and experiments" which

support her interpretations against those of superficial common sense. The Editors add, " It seems also to meet the *popular* argument against Transubstantiation, viz. on the ground, not of its being against the voice of antiquity, but of its contradicting sense."

376 (a) L. ii. 112 (July 1835) ; 376 (c) L. ii. 117 ; 377 (b) L. ii. 119 ; 378 (b) L. ii. 130 ; 381 (b) L. ii. 126–7 (23 Aug. 1835) ; 382 (a) L. ii. 127 ; 383 (a) L. ii. 128 (23 Aug. 1835), " last vacation," L. ii. 56 ; 384 (a) R. 419, *ib.* (3 Sept. 1835) ; 384 (c) R. 423, " for tolerating." This is quite in Froude's brusque style. The Editors spoil it by inserting " for [the Church's] tolerating."

384 (e) † " no clear indications." A passage in one of Newman's last letters (L. ii. 148) to Froude, speaks of the necessity of " drawing in his horns in the *Arians*" because he has already said that " *in fact* the Fathers did not deduce from Scripture, and the whole passage in the ' Disciplina ' is founded on the hypothesis of Apostolical tradition co-ordinate with Scripture." This is obscure, owing to the provoking omission of all reference to the subject (both in the *Remains* and in the *Letters*) in the scanty fragments given of that particular letter from Froude which elicited this reply from Newman.

385 (a) † L. ii. 141, R. 422 (1 Nov. 1835). The versions somewhat differ.

386 (a) L. ii. 164 (2 Feb.) ; 386 (b)* " as held by Rome " : see p. 371 above, where it is shown that Newman appears to have accepted the doctrine of Transubstantiation in *some* form, though not " as held by Rome." 386 (c) V. 415–8 ; 391 (a) ii. 86 ; 393–6 L. ii. 155–6 (17 Jan. 1836).

386 (b)* " I yield." I do not see how these words, and the whole of the letter, are compatible with any other interpretation than this, that Froude, at all events, held the doctrine of " Transubstantiation *as held by Rome*."

But, if so, how is this reconcilable with N.'s letter to Dr. Faussett in defence of Froude (V. ii. 225) published in 1838 : " There is nothing (as far as I am aware) in Mr. Froude's writings in countenance of the *local* presence on earth, as it is commonly understood," [this, of course, means absolutely nothing, and simply puts the unwary reader off the scent ; but the following should be noted]. ". . . Mr. Froude's strong language, then, had the sanction of our divines." Even this might perhaps be tolerated (though it would mislead everybody) on the plea that the " strong language " simply meant the language that had been criticized by Dr. Faussett.

But what are we to say to the next sentence (parts of which I italicize) : " How far, on the other hand, he was from agreeing with the Roman doctrine will be seen from a passage of his writings not yet published." And then he quotes from an unfinished Essay written *at an earlier date* than 1836, and (presumably) containing opinions subsequently discarded by Froude !

How can we justify Newman in writing of his friend, two years after his death, that he was "far from agreeing with the Roman doctrine," and forty or fifty years afterwards (L. ii. 82)   " N.B. Froude would not believe that I was in earnest, as I *was*, in shrinking from the VIEWS WHICH HE boldly followed out.   I *was* against TRANSUBSTANTIA-TION."   The italics are Newman's ; the capitals, mine.

APPENDIX

397 (b) K. 166 and foll. ; 398 (a) R. 104, A. 230, K. 166 and foll.

END OF VOL I

RICHARD CLAY AND SONS, LIMITED, LONDON AND BUNGAY.

www.ingramcontent.com/pod-product-compliance
Lightning Source LLC
Chambersburg PA
CBHW021324110726
47900CB00005B/1346